Praise for May McGoldrick's
breathtaking novels . . .

"Love triumphs in this richly romantic tale."
—Nora Roberts

"Wonderful! Just the right blend of historical
detail, romance, and intrigue." —Jill Marie Landis

"May McGoldrick brings history alive, painting
passion and intrigue across a broad, colorful
canvas." —Patricia Gaffney

"Fast-paced, emotionally charged . . . rich in
historical detail, sizzling with sensuality. A
new and very bright star." —*Romantic Times*

"Impressive. . . . A splendid Scottish tale, filled
with humor and suspense." —Arnette Lamb

"Brilliant. . . . A fast-paced, action-packed
historical romance brimming with insight into
the sixteenth-century Scottish-English conflict."
—*Affaire de Coeur*

"No one captures the magic and romance of the
British Isles like May McGoldrick."
—Miranda Jarrett

HIGHLAND TREASURE:
The Dreamer

May McGoldrick

AN ONYX BOOK

For Carla Patton—writer, doctor, and friend

May your dreams come true. . . .

ONYX
Published by New American Library, a division of
Penguin Putnam Inc., 375 Hudson Street,
New York, New York 10014, U.S.A.
Penguin Books Ltd, 27 Wrights Lane,
London W8 5TZ, England
Penguin Books Australia Ltd, Ringwood,
Victoria, Australia
Penguin Books Canada Ltd, 10 Alcorn Avenue,
Toronto, Ontario, Canada M4V 3B2
Penguin Books (N.Z.) Ltd, 182–190 Wairau Road,
Auckland 10, New Zealand

Penguin Books Ltd, Registered Offices:
Harmondsworth, Middlesex, England

First published by Onyx, an imprint of New American Library,
a division of Penguin Putnam Inc.

First Printing, May 2000
10 9 8 7 6 5 4 3 2 1

PUBLISHER'S NOTE
This is a work of fiction. Names, characters, places, and incidents either
are the product of the author's imagination or are used fictitiously,
and any resemblance to actual persons, living or dead, business
establishments, events or locales is entirely coincidental.

BOOKS ARE AVAILABLE AT QUANTITY DISCOUNTS WHEN USED TO PROMOTE
PRODUCTS OR SERVICES. FOR INFORMATION PLEASE WRITE TO PREMIUM
MARKETING DIVISION, PENGUIN PUTNAM INC., 375 HUDSON STREET, NEW
YORK, NEW YORK 10014.

Prologue

Jervaulx Abbey in Yorkshire, England
August 1535

"They've fled!"

Arthur Courtenay, the king's Deputy Lieutenant in Yorkshire, angrily spurred his steed past the flaring torches until the giant animal was snorting and tossing his head not a half pace away from the faces of the cowering servants and villagers.

"Where have they gone?" His voice rasped with barely controlled fury. "When?"

"These fools have all swallowed their tongues, m'lord."

Sir Arthur drew his sword, and the shoving throng fell away as he nudged the animal forward to the very steps of the abbey's chapter house.

"Drag the abbot out," he shouted. "And the monks, as well. Every fat, cowardly one of them. I'll stick their treasonous heads on pikes if they do not come forth with answers."

"M'lord!" The sound of one of the soldiers, calling as he ran from the small churchyard, drew the Deputy Lieutenant's head around. "M'lord, 'tis true. There is freshly packed earth behind the large crypt."

"What are you waiting for?" Courtenay wheeled the warhorse, forcing the fearful onlookers back even farther. "Start digging. And clear the yard of this rabble."

Riding into the graveyard, the Deputy Lieutenant dismounted in front of the crypt, a stone chapellike edifice, and threw the reins at a soldier standing nearby. Wordlessly, Sir Arthur stalked around the building, but stopped and whirled when a cloaked figure reached out of the shadows for him. He knew the man.

"You sent word too late, monk!" Courtenay rasped.

"Three prizes have escaped us, but the treasure has not."

" 'Tis here? Are you certain?"

"I saw the three sisters dragging the chest down here after the sun set. They must have dug that hole earlier, though, for all they did was place the chest in there and cover it."

Sir Arthur peered at the two men digging out the loose soil, as another stood over them with a torch. Their faces glistened with sweat and dirt.

"You told me that you've searched their belongings many times these past months. You told me that none of them could be hiding anything."

"We did search!" The man pulled the hood of his dark cloak farther forward on his face as one of the English soldiers walked past them. "But yesterday, two messengers arrived. The first brought news that their father, Edmund Percy, is dead in the Tower."

"Aye, and that treacherous Thomas More will be next," Sir Arthur spat. "His head will soon adorn London Bridge, as well. But what of it?"

"We expected *you* to bring the news of their father's death . . . and a warrant for their arrest at the same time."

"I had to wait for the Lord Chancellor to issue the warrant, and then"—he angrily scuffed at the dirt beneath his boots—"never mind all of that. You failed to send me the message in time, and that displeases me. But what of this second messenger?"

"The second one came from Nichola Percy, the mother."

"Do you believe she is nearby?"

The hooded man shook his head. "From what I've been able to glean from the abbot and the servants, she remains in hiding in the Borders, north of the Tweed. But as you thought, she has remained true to her daughters. In fact, she must have sent help, as well, for their escape."

"And you think the messenger brought the treasure?" Courtenay's question received only silence for an answer. "But it makes no sense for her to effect their escape, and yet still send them—"

A cry of discovery brought both men's heads around.

" 'Tis here! We've hit it, m'lord."

"Bring it out!"

The Deputy Lieutenant strode hurriedly to the side of the open grave, but the hooded man only moved as far as the shadows would allow.

The wooden chest was lifted out of the hole. Leaning over the dirt-covered box, Sir Arthur motioned to one of the soldiers to break the latch with the end of his halberd. With a single blow, the deed was done, and Courtenay pushed forward toward the unopened box. The anticipation was obvious in every face, and even the hooded man now stepped out of the shadows.

The Deputy Lieutenant crouched and pushed open the lid. Every man leaped back, scattering to a safe distance.

Every man, that is, but the hooded figure who, stepping past Sir Arthur, reached into the chest and picked up the squirming, hissing snake.

"What the devil?" Courtenay cried out angrily.

The cloaked man threw the snake back into the grave. "Catherine Percy, the eldest of the three, has an odd sense of humor . . . and no fear of adders."

"So this is it?" Sir Arthur barked. "This is to be our treasure?"

The man reached into the box again and picked out a rolled parchment. Opening it, he looked up and met the Deputy Lieutenant's gaze.

"Nay, m'lord! She also left us a map!"

Chapter 1

The dowager's gray eyes opened and slowly focused on the half armor before moving upward to the anxious face of the tall, red-haired man standing by her bed.

"Has Catherine Percy arrived?"

"Nay, Mother. Not yet."

"You will look after that young woman, John. You *will* honor our promise to protect her."

"Of course! You know the messenger brought word that she is safe and en route. There is nothing more that needs to be done."

The old woman coughed weakly and, lifting a frail hand, waved off the attentions of the young woman gliding around the bed. The invalid's eyes never left the warrior's face, and the attendant, her niece Susan, stepped back and picked up a piece of needlework, settling once again onto the stool beside the great curtained bed.

"Your bride, then! I assume she is here?"

He shook his head. "Nay, Mother. Ellen is still two days' ride away, at least."

"Then why are you here? To watch me die?"

A hint of a smile tugged at the corner of the warrior's mouth, but faded quickly. "If I recall correctly, you sent for me."

"Hmmph! I do not know why I should have!" the woman grumbled feebly. "But then, I've no more than a handful of breaths left in this wasted, old carcass. Maybe I simply thought you'd see fit to grant me my dying wish."

Quietly, he took her bony hands in his powerful grip. "You'll live, Mother. You'll live to see us wed. In fact—"

"I do not give a thistle puff to see a wedding." Lady Anne Stewart's eyes moved and rested on her niece's face as the young woman quietly stitched away at her work. If only Susan had been more like the other women—the court ladies or better yet, the bonny little fools who used any excuse to come to Balvenie Castle and fawn over her son, fighting for his attention.

Just then, Susan's eyes lifted and met hers. Whether the young woman glimpsed a hint of regret or perhaps disappointment in the dowager's face, Lady Anne didn't know, but her niece rose quickly to her feet, flushing crimson, and with a polite curtsy stepped out of the bedchamber. Mother and son were left alone.

The dowager let out a heavy breath. "I've forsaken all my other dreams, John. All I care about now is for you to bring me your wife—full in the belly with an heir."

"These things are not done overnight."

For the flash of a moment the sickly woman's eyes sharpened. "That's exactly when 'tis done. And I've seen enough mistresses of yours hanging about the gates to know you are an expert in the matter."

The warrior bit back his words as he released her hands.

"Do something useful. Prop me up a wee bit."

So John Stewart—earl of Athol, cousin to James V of Scotland, and laird of nearly all from Elgin to Huntly—pushed his great brand and his dirk behind him and gently lifted the tiny woman into a sitting position.

Lady Anne Stewart's expression was one of intense pain. As she settled against the pillows, her keen eyes studied her son's weary face. "They tell me you've been tearing up the countryside looking for cattle raiders."

"Aye. And when I get them, I'll hang them all from the nearest tree that'll hold the blackguards' weight."

"Clever lads, I take it." The dowager's brow furrowed as she gave another weak cough. "The same as before?"

"The same," Athol growled.

The dowager knew that for weeks her son had been scouring the glens and the rugged mountain terrain for the raiders. "There is an easier way to stop these men."

His patronizing glance was fleeting, but too open to go unnoticed.

"I do not know that anything but a noose or the edge of a sword that will convince these mongrel dogs."

"I know you think me a doddering old fool. But I have the answer. All you have to do . . . is . . . ask . . ."

Athol sat down on the edge of the bed as a spell of coughing shook the old woman's frame. A moment went by as she appeared to struggle for breath.

"Very well, I am asking," he said when she'd settled again. "Give me your advice."

She looked at him sternly, a glimmer of satisfaction in her gray eyes. "I tell you, John, it cannot be too soon for you to marry. You need a bairn to succeed you. That'll be the end to all your troubles."

"I've agreed, Mother. I know you've been impatient to see me settled. The plans are set and—"

"Plans . . . plans . . ." Her words gave way to another wrenching cough. "I had plans too. I brought

Susan up here with the plan of seeing you two wed. If you would have done as I—"

"Mother!"

There was warning in his tone, she knew. And they had been through this discussion months ago. "Well, what you say is not good enough. What good are plans when it comes to the troubles of your people? Nay! I tell you . . ."

Her words trailed off, and the laird turned to the window, where the sound of shouting rose from the rain-swept courtyard below. In an instant, the shouting could be heard below stairs. Striding across the floor, he yanked open the door of the chamber in time to see his thin, gloomy-faced old steward breathlessly mounting the top step down the corridor.

"M'lord!" the steward gasped, his face crimson from the exertion and the news. "M'lord, they've struck the farm at Muckle Long Brae."

The earl's face darkened ominously. "Were any of our people hurt?"

"Nay." The steward lowered his voice with a glance at the dowager, who was peering from the bed. "But the filthy dogs burned your new barn there."

"And the cattle?"

"They took a half dozen of the new blacks and turned out the rest, before setting the place afire."

"But what of Wat and his kin?"

"Trussed up like hogs, m'lord. But unhurt. His oldest lad's below, if you want to talk to him. The barn is ashes, he says, and Wat's set out after them."

"Saddle my horse, and gather the men." Outside the window, the rain had turned into a downpour. The steward disappeared down the corridor.

"John," the dowager called as he turned his grim visage toward her. "It'll be a dark and rainy night, and they've half a day's start on you, at least."

"Aye, but Wat's after them now, and they have to travel the same as we do."

"But you know these mountains hold a thousand hiding places for these brazen thieves."

He took a step restlessly toward the open door. "Aye, and I know most of them, Mother."

The woman began to cough again, holding up her hand for him to wait. "Let them have the cattle, John," she said finally. "Go and meet your bride."

Athol stared at her with scarcely concealed disbelief. "I've always respected you as the woman who brought me into this world. But you know that as earl of these lands, I take no direction from anyone—especially not from—"

"Not from your mother? From a woman?" The dowager let out a labored breath. "Well, 'tis pleasant to know that you at least have enough respect for me on my deathbed to grant me leave to remain your mother."

"I *have* to go, m'lady."

She raised a trembling hand in the air. "Wait, John. This may be the last . . . the last . . . we meet. You are my only son . . ."

The set of his firm jaw bespoke his will. She knew that no matter what affection he held for her, his people's needs would always drive his actions. "Please wait. Hear me. I know what lies behind the actions of this Adam of the Glen."

Athol's eyes narrowed, and the old woman knew she had bought another moment. He stepped toward the bed.

"How do you know anything about him? And how do you even know his name?"

"Even if my servants failed to keep me informed, I would know." She turned her pained gaze from Athol's face and stared at the dark ceiling above the window. "I know for a fact what he wants, for I have known him since he was a bairn."

Athol loomed over her in an instant. "No matter how hard I've tried, we've failed in every attempt to find the hiding place of the bastard. I've questioned every man and woman from here to Elgin. Not one of them has known a thing about this son of Satan. Not where he came from or why he suddenly has decided to make a hell of the lives of my people. And now my own mother tells me that she's known this man all along!" He took her hand firmly in his. "Very well, Mother. What is it that you know?"

Lady Anne Stewart's other hand reached over and gripped her son's arm. "Listen to me, John, and do what I say. On the grave of your father, I tell you he would be giving you the same advice if he were still alive . . . in spite of the wreckage that Adam has caused."

"Speak, Mother."

The dowager knew her son was a man feared by many, particularly when his people's welfare was at stake. Now, feeling his gray eyes boring into hers, feeling the bridled power of the fingers wrapped around hers, she knew why.

"No matter where you look for the man, he is certain to escape you. He knows these lands as well as you, John. And he knows your own people better than you would ever imagine."

"Aye, he knows what to steal from them."

"All the same. I'm telling you the truth." Her grip tightened on his wrist. "And no matter what you do, he'll continue with this destruction. Adam of the Glen will become bolder with every passing day. 'Tis no wonder that you feel him lurking around you. He won't give up . . . not until . . ."

A violent fit of coughing again left her gasping for breath for a few moments. Athol wrapped an arm around her shoulder and raised her higher in the bed. She shook her head at his offer of a cup.

"Nay. There . . . there will be no rest . . . no peace until you're wed. Not until the news of a bairn to succeed you spreads through your lands."

Athol stared down at her. "I do not understand this. I still—"

"Adam believes he has the right to live off your wealth." Her fingers trembled as they tightened on his arm. "The bastard son of a whore he might be, John Stewart, but what you do not know is that Adam of the Glen is your brother."

Chapter 2

Catherine Percy listened to the tinkling laughter of the woman riding behind her.

Ellen Crawford was young, clever, and certainly beautiful. And she was apparently to be the wife of John Stewart, earl of Athol. By chance, the two traveling parties had met just north of Stirling Castle, and Catherine had been delighted to be able to travel into the wilds of the Highlands in the company of another woman—especially one who had traveled this route before.

Glancing back in the direction of her traveling companion, Catherine wondered to what extent she could seek the assistance of the future countess of Athol. Or for that matter, how much she could reveal to her.

Certainly, Catherine thought, she was no longer in any immediate danger of being captured by the treacherous Deputy Lieutenant. And her sisters, too, were well on their way to safety. Any day now, Laura should be arriving at the Church of St. Duthac, on the eastern sea, and Adrianne, the youngest, was probably already settled in on an island called Bharra in the Western Isles.

But still, in order to start the school that Catherine had dreamed of for so long, she would need the assistance of people like the earl of Athol and this future bride of his. Indeed, she knew she would need their strong and open support before any of the locals would trust a half-English spinster enough to share in what she had to offer.

Looking about her, Catherine glanced at the unfamiliar faces of the travelers. Strangers, every one. Even after months of hiding, she still could not get accustomed to this constant dependence on others. She wondered if she could ever come to accept that she no longer had a home to call her own—no longer had a homeland to think about with pride.

Catherine sighed. She and her sisters were exiles. Since their father's death, they—like their mother—had been pursued and hunted across the windswept moors of Yorkshire, northward into the hills and river valleys of Northumberland, and finally into Scotland. And all because of the family's refusal to take King Henry's Oath of Supremacy. To accept the king as the head of the church.

Of course, she admitted silently, there was a lot more to it than that.

But so be it, Catherine thought stubbornly. Fate had taken them to this new land. To these rugged Highlands that their mother had long ago called home.

Shaking herself from her reverie, Catherine reminded herself that the time for grieving was long behind her. She had to look ahead and think of what must be done. Heaven had placed Ellen Crawford in her company, and it would be foolish to waste the opportunity of talking to her about the school and recruiting the future countess in her cause.

Determined on her course of action, she turned in her saddle and scanned the faces of the travelers who followed them on this long journey. She pulled her cloak around her as a breeze sprang up from the west. The sun had been fairly warm most of the day, but now had disappeared behind a bank of dark clouds moving in from the west.

Not seeing Ellen, her brow furrowed. As usual,

Catherine decided she must have been woolgathering and had missed Ellen somehow.

The warriors at the head of the long column of travelers were just starting down the craggy, heather-covered ridge they'd been crossing for the past hour. Beneath them, in a valley surrounded by steep rocky hills, Catherine could see a loch—its dark silver waters as smooth as a looking glass—reflecting the jumble of clouds that were quickly converging on the weary travelers.

Catherine searched the passing faces for any signs of the young woman. Having no luck there, she looked instead for David Hume, the leader of her own warriors. From what she remembered, the last time she'd seen Ellen Crawford, the young bride had been in deep discussion with him.

As the last of the packhorses carrying Ellen's trunks, and last of the travelers trailed by her, three of the kilted warriors who were accompanying Ellen stopped in response to her question about their lady's whereabouts.

With a sidelong smirk at his two companions, one of the three scratched his bearded chin before answering. "Sometimes Mistress Ellen simply needs to stretch her legs, mistress. If ye get my meaning."

"Of course. You mean she's walking her horse," Catherine replied. "And since I cannot find David Hume, my man must have stayed behind with her."

"Aye, m'lady." She watched him throw another knowing look at his fellows. "Though I should think Mistress Ellen's surely riding by now."

Frowning at the snickers coming from the two warriors, Catherine nodded curtly and pulled her mare's head around, coaxing her along the path after the other travelers.

"What odd manners these Highlanders have," she whispered into the mare's ear, a bit disconcerted at the conclusions the men had drawn over what was certainly an innocent stop.

They were nearly halfway down the steep, winding path before Catherine saw that Ellen Crawford and David Hume had once again joined the line of travelers. Looking up the hill at the young woman, she could see that Ellen's cheeks were flushed and her clothes somewhat disheveled.

" 'Tis no business of yours judging the affairs of others," she murmured, turning her gaze back to the trail. She herself had consciously chosen her studies over such behavior in her younger years, but how Ellen Crawford chose to live her life had nothing to do with her. Odd though, she thought, for a woman about to be married.

By the time the path widened enough to travel more than single file, the travelers had entered a thickly forested glen at the base of the ridge. Then the sky opened, and the rain, coming in on a gust of wind, prevented Catherine from discussing anything with Ellen Crawford. The rain was still falling hard when, an hour later, she spotted with weary relief the cone-topped towers of the hunting lodge at Corgarff. This, she knew, was one of the earl of Athol's hunting lodges. Less than a day's ride remained to Balvenie Castle.

As they rode under the pointed arch and into the small courtyard of the tower house, the servants of the lodge bustled about the arriving throng, leading them into a well-lit Great Hall, and laying before them a sumptuous dinner. Catherine, weary from the weeks of travel, did her best to play the role of agreeable foil to Ellen Crawford's youthful gaiety, but halfway through the dinner, she excused herself.

Up the winding stone steps, she was led to the Ladies' Chamber, a small and quaint combination of bedchamber and sitting room, and she eyed with longing the comfortable-looking bed.

She hung her heavy cloak on a hook by the little fire. Placing her leather satchel on a three-legged chair, she noted with curiosity the three doors to the chamber. Aside from the door she had entered from the main corridor—where she had seen the traveling gear of a number of their traveling escort—there was a door at each end of the room. Opening one, she peered into the Master's bedchamber. She knew that Ellen would be sleeping there tonight, and she stared for a moment at the huge damask-curtained bed that nearly filled one side of the lavishly furnished chamber.

Backing out and closing the door quietly, Catherine crossed her bedchamber to the other door. Moving through a small anteroom where she could see the wet gear of at least one of the warriors, she opened another door onto a landing and looked down a narrow coil of stairs. Cautiously, she descended halfway down the stone steps before the smell of the food and the noise of revelry assured her that she had little to fear regarding accommodations while under the earl's roof.

A few moments later, as she lay her head down on the bed, Catherine was only vaguely aware of the rain outside her window and the crackling hiss of the water dripping onto the fire.

And then, in the space of a moment, her dreams overtook her with the suddenness of a Yorkshire mist.

They had already arrested their father, and now they were coming after them! There were soldiers crowding the courtyard. The pound of horses' hooves, the shouts of men, the chaos of a castle under siege.

Catherine could hear the urgent cries of her mother, pleading with them to make haste into the fields, to hide themselves in a haycock. To remain unseen. To be silent!

She could feel the fear clutching at her throat. She

could not cry. She could not allow her sisters to sense her fear. Adrianne's hands were cold, tugging at her arm. Together, they pushed into the piled hay.

She stretched a hand out toward Laura, but her sister was not there. She'd been right behind her when they'd fled the house. Laura! Where was Laura?

A hand clamped onto her arm, holding her back. Nay, she could not let them take her. Laura!

"*Laura!*" Catherine sat upright in the bed and looked wildly at the figure retreating a step from the bed.

" 'Tis I, Catherine. 'Tis Ellen!"

It took her a long moment before she could pull herself from the shadows of the recurring nightmare. She felt her heart pounding ferociously at the walls of her chest, the sweat beading and dripping along the line of her jaw. "What . . . what is it?"

"Nothing! I just came up from the Great Hall, and I heard you crying out in your sleep."

Catherine turned and looked groggily at the open door leading to the Master's Chamber.

" 'Twas a dream." A nightmare! A horrible semblance of the long past mixed with her present. She ran a shaky hand over her brow, wiping away the sweat. Nay, Laura was safe! Safe . . . as was she, herself.

"Aye, but as long as you're awake, I was . . . well, I was wondering if you wouldn't mind sleeping in there for tonight."

Catherine stared blankly through the dim light at the young woman. "You . . . you want me to sleep with you?"

Ellen giggled and shook her head. "Nay, I was hoping you would change rooms with me. Every time I've been here before, I've slept in this chamber. So I thought . . . if you wouldn't mind . . . I'd be happier in here, you see."

"Well, I . . ." She frowned, trying to clear her mind, but before she could even think of an answer, Ellen was pulling the bedclothes back for her. "If you think . . ."

"You are a darling creature." Catherine felt the younger woman grasp her by the shoulders and direct her toward the open door. "I'll come and get you in the morning. You just go and crawl into that bed and go back to sleep."

Before she knew it, Catherine found herself standing in the middle of the Master's Chamber with a sound of the door closing behind her. Nearly asleep on her feet, she pushed the thick waves of hair back over her shoulder. As she climbed into the huge curtained bed, she could hear the far-off sound of voices and hushed laughing.

Ellen Crawford was up to some dangerous mischief, and such goings-on were incomprehensible to Catherine. True, she felt a pang of regret for being thought a fool by Ellen, but more important, she felt sorry for the good earl of Athol. Their upcoming marriage already had all the markings of a farce.

Once again, Catherine reminded herself, this was none of her business. Her plans were to tutor the young people of Athol's demesne, not to become the spiritual adviser to foundering brides.

Weariness soon overtook her, though, and the sound of the rain outside dulled her senses. She was so tired, she later remembered thinking. She needed sleep. Why, the great gates of York itself could fall on her, she decided, yawning. She was not going to wake up again until the sun was coming through that window.

In just a moment or two, slumber wrapped her in its velvet cloak, and outside the rain relented and eventually stopped.

This time, her dream was an old one. Even as she entered the mists of sleep, it occurred to Catherine that she had not had this dream in years. But there he was, her own knight of a thousand romances, tall and strong, coming to her after the great battle, claiming her for his own.

For he was now her husband. The dragon lay dead in its lair, the treasure of gold and rubies and emeralds returned to the castle's vault. Order and goodness reigned once again in the realm, and the night now offered its own promise.

But this time the dream was somehow different . . . changing . . . going into a world of fantasy she had never experienced before. She felt his body sink into the down mattress beside her, his arm slide across the planes of her belly, his large hand rest for a moment on her hip before drawing her against his warm, firm body.

It was all so real. Catherine's dreams often carried her to other worlds. Worlds she could see and smell and feel. Worlds that she, upon awakening, would be certain existed somewhere.

But this . . . this was like no dream she'd ever had, and she found herself shivering as her knight's hand moved over the thin linen of her shift to the hem. Her back arched reflexively as his long fingers gently caressed the skin of her belly and traced the curves at the base of her breasts. Her breath caught in her chest and she felt her body rise to his touch when his hand cupped the full roundness of her breast. And as his thumb drew tight circles around the hardening nipple, sparks of fire shot through her.

So new and yet so thrilling, Catherine sighed in her state of bliss. To have a mere touch make her insides quiver so exquisitely.

Something hot throbbed insistently against her thigh, and as her knight's hand again slid down over her belly, Catherine's lips opened and her breath began to shorten. A soft moan escaped her lips. Molten liquid was flowing within her, building in pulsing waves as his fingers slid through her downy mound. She felt him move, felt his body rising. There was a whisper, inaudible, almost a growl, and then her knight's lips were on her neck, moving, brushing against her earlobe, kissing the line of her jaw . . . her cheek. Catherine waited.

His kiss was gentle at first. A brush of lips, but so real. So unlike her long recurring dreams of the two of them drifting into each other's embrace, her body molding to his as the mist would softly steal around them. She could feel the pressure of his mouth. The groan of approval when she parted her lips. And then the knight's tongue swept deeply into her mouth, shocking her with a reality that left her gasping for breath. Catherine's eyes flew open.

This was no dream. This was not her knight. As she felt his knee press between her legs, she jerked her mouth away, breaking off the kiss. She tried to push at his chest.

"What the devil . . . ?" came the growl through the darkness.

This was no dream, she thought again with a flash of panic as the coarse skin of a man's chin rubbed hard against her cheek. She beat his naked shoulder with her one free hand. Grabbing at his long hair, she yanked with all her strength, but nothing could move the beast.

His hand came up quickly, catching hold of her wrist, but she reared up instinctively and bit down with all her strength on a powerful forearm.

The man gave an angry roar of pain and leaped back, snatching his hand away. But this was all the time she needed as she screamed at the top of her lungs.

"Hush, you cursed she-devil!" The man shouted, leaning over her again. But Catherine went wild beneath his shifting weight. Kicking him with all her strength in the groin, she twisted to the side, clawing her way to the edge of the bed. But the villain grabbed her by the waist.

"Wait! I'll not hurt you, though God knows, I—"

The door from the other chamber burst open and David Hume, holding a torch aloft, charged in, his sword flashing in the light.

Catherine's eyes darted from the warrior's naked skin to the gleaming flesh of Ellen Crawford in the open door behind him.

"Up, you villainous blackguard. Prepare to die!"

With a flick of his arm, her attacker tossed Catherine to the side and leaped toward David, snatching his own long sword from the floor beside the huge bed.

"Nay, you son of a whore! You're the dog who is about to choke in his own blood!"

Ellen's shocked gasp stopped the two men in their tracks.

"John!" she whispered, her panic evident in the single word. Raising her thin chemise over her breasts in a belated attempt to cover herself, the young woman started backing out the door.

Catherine's head snapped around as she saw her assailant move menacingly toward David Hume. Suddenly, there was no question in her mind whose blood would be shed on this floor. The red-haired giant Ellen had called John stood head and shoulders above David and from the powerful breadth of his shoulders, Catherine was certain that he could cut her would-be rescuer in half. And from the stunned look on his face, she doubted David would even think to lift his sword in defense.

"You—you're John Stewart!" her warrior stammered.

"Aye, you filthy dog. John Stewart, earl of Athol. And that wench you were keeping company with in the next chamber is none other than my . . . my intended."

It was sheer madness. There was no other explanation. But Catherine, in the next instant, found herself standing before the flaming-haired nobleman, blocking his approach.

"Stop!" she pleaded. "There has to be a better way to settle this than by drawing blood."

Athol hesitated, and as he stared down at her, the man's gray eyes flashed murderously. She stood her ground.

"You see, m'lord, I am Catherine Percy. David Hume here was entrusted with my safety, and . . . and I'm quite certain he must have had no prior knowledge that Ellen . . ."

The words dried up in her throat. She stared as the blade of his long sword gleamed in the torchlight.

"Out of my way, woman!"

Catherine's knees were ready to buckle, and her head suddenly felt light, but she raised her chin in defiance. "I cannot!"

Athol advanced a step, looking past her at the man standing by the door. Taking a deep breath, she raised a pleading hand and gazed with as much courage as she could muster into a face ablaze with fury.

"He was given the task of protecting my life until we reached our destination. And he has done an excellent job . . . er, up to now. But now that the task is *finished*." She paused, hoping that David would pick up her hint. "And now that his task is *finished*, I believe 'tis my duty to see him safely *away*."

There was no movement behind her. How could men be so thick-headed? she stormed inwardly. Away! Run! Flee!

"We are *here at the end of our journey*!" she pressed. "With the earl of Athol!"

"Out of my way, woman."

"At the *end* of our journey!"

That did it. David must have turned to flee with the speed of a falcon, dropping the torch by the doorway in his escape. Responding quickly, the earl reached out and tried to move around her. But Catherine was quicker, throwing herself against his chest.

It was like hitting a wall of moving rock at a gallop. Her breath was knocked from her lungs. She fell with the grace of a meal sack to the floor as Athol picked up the torch and strode from the chamber.

For a long while Catherine sat still in the dark, listening to the shouts and curses and then to the sounds of horses. She didn't know if it was the impact of hitting the man so hard or the cumulative effect of the entire episode that had left her unable to move. The lodge was in an uproar now, and she could hear the sound of people rushing about—while the steely voice of Athol could be heard above all of them, shouting commands and cursing violently.

What in heaven's name had she gotten herself into? she thought groggily, trying to push herself to her knees. Thank the Lord she had never developed a fondness for any man in particular—other than her dream-knight—nor for marriage in general. And in truth, what she had witnessed tonight was a clear reaffirmation of that view.

She was definitely not suited for matrimony. She could never make anyone a fit wife. She would never know how to deal with this open display of temper and this threat of violence. Nay. And what of this business of a man coming to his future wife's bed uninvited, then not even recognizing her as someone else. She brought her hands up to her flushed cheeks and again shook her head, pushing from her mind how wantonly she'd responded to him at first, when she'd thought it was just a dream.

She was still on her knees when the door to the Ladies' Chamber swung open. Closing her eyes, she felt him brush past her without pausing.

Pushing herself shakily to her feet, she stole a glance in the direction of the man who now stood by the bed. His back to her, he was muttering under his breath as he wrapped a kilt around him by the light of a wick lamp he had evidently carried in with him.

The earl of Athol, she thought with a pang of regret, was quite different from what she had hoped he would be.

The man was supposed to be an advocate of learning. She had expected him to be a serene, subdued-looking man. But his actions, his behavior, in bed and out . . . Catherine felt her heart start to race anew! Trying to force the memory of his mistaking her for Ellen Crawford from her mind, she stared at her host. He was certainly not at all what she had expected.

Ellen had told Catherine that the earl was past seven and thirty years of age. So even in her wildest of dreams, she hadn't been prepared for the handsome face and the solid wall of muscle that was just now trying to pull on long, muddy boots. With flowing, partially braided red hair tumbling over a pair of broad shoulders, he looked more like an outlaw than he did the cousin of a king.

Catherine couldn't help but guess what silly maneuvers she might have come up with as a young maiden to get the attention of a man like him. Not that with her unassuming appearance she'd ever have had even a chance of catching his eye. But all the same, she reminded herself, it was a blessing to know that her life had taken a different route. A far more sensible one.

She shook her head and started quietly for the door.

As long as she kept her distance, perhaps they could avoid meeting again for a while. In truth, right now, the incident that had occurred in that bed embarrassed her dreadfully, and she had no doubt he must—if he had a shred of respectability in him—be feeling as terrible as she.

Reaching the doorway, she started to breathe again. She had to put what happened behind her and, perhaps, they could pretend it had never taken place. He would not mention it, Catherine was quite certain, and she could quietly go about the task of opening her school.

"Mistress Catherine."

His hard voice raised the gooseflesh on the back of her neck. She turned slowly and faced him.

"I've sent for the damned priest. We'll be wed when the cursed old fool arrives."

Chapter 3

"Wed!" The man was obviously out of his mind. "To me?"

The Highlander turned his intense gray eyes on her. "Do you see someone else in this chamber whom I might be addressing?"

She looked about innocently. "Nay! But I'm no judge of the soundness of your mind!"

"Rest assured, mistress, I was speaking to you and not some apparition."

"You don't know me!" This was beyond bizarre. It was almost comical. "How could you marry someone whom you have only just met?"

"Are you not Catherine Percy?"

"I am, but—"

"And have you not been sent up here to be my ward?"

"Hardly, m'lord!" she responded. "I am five-and-twenty. Hardly of an age to be anyone's ward. Especially to one as unreasonable and brutish as yourself."

He stared at her, first in frigid silence, and then through slitted eyes as temper flashed across his face. "You certainly *talk* like some old crone! If I didn't have firsthand knowledge—of a rather intimate nature—I would almost be convinced from listening to you that you are some ancient creature. But I know, Catherine Percy, exactly what you are."

His words stung her, but she couldn't stop the deep

blush that crept into her face when his hard eyes began to study her from the tip of her head to her bare toes. Suddenly horrified that she was dressed in nothing more than a thin shift, she crossed her arms over her chest to hide whatever she could.

He raised one eyebrow at her actions. "A bit late for coyness, don't you think, considering all that you have willingly allowed me?"

"There was nothing 'willing' in my response to your ignoble behavior, and you know it. You were trying to force yourself upon me—like some heavy-handed brute."

"Did I, now?" His eyes flashed a challenge. "And is this the way you fight for your honor? By moaning at the most intimate of touches? By lifting yourself to a lover's caress . . . pardon me, an assailant's advances . . . and shivering at the touch of his lips against your skin?"

By the Virgin, she had done that, hadn't she? She brought her cold, trembling hands to her cheeks to cool the blazing skin. All she could do now was to whisper the truth. "I . . . I thought it all a dream."

She could have sworn a glint of humor softened the hardness of his glare. But it was only for an instant. "For a spinster, you certainly have interesting dreams. But tell me this . . . do you find fulfillment in them, as well? Or are you simply another frustrated—"

"Don't!" she snapped at him, though more severely than she'd intended. But he was mocking her. In his roguish way, he was trying to make her feel small, insignificant . . . a bit licentious, even. Looking up and meeting his challenging glare, Catherine suddenly felt the urge to strike back, to wash that arrogant hint of amusement off his face. "You are taking great pleasure in insulting me, I see. But I know what lies behind your boorish behavior."

"Do you?"

"Aye. Though your male pride spurns the truth, I believe you know who is responsible for everything that took place here tonight."

"I have no time for this foolishness."

"The truth is that *you* are the cause of all this—though your arrogance denies it."

"What do you mean by that?"

His eyes had once again turned murderous, but Catherine was too riled to back down.

"You are a man on the threshold of marriage—a man who obviously has had previous . . . previous knowledge of his intended's body. How is it possible that you did not know that the woman in your bed was not Ellen Crawford?"

" 'Twas dark. A mistake I intend to set right," he growled. "But what has that to do with the wench crawling into the bed of—"

"The connection is simple to see, m'lord," she interrupted. "To you, a woman clearly has no more value than a mattress or a prize cow!"

"No more than a m . . . ?" Athol stared at her in disbelief, his words trailing off.

"Aye. And one woman is as good as another, for all you care. So long as there is a willing body to bear your weight, what does it matter who 'tis?"

"You're daft, woman!"

"Am I? Look at Ellen. It seems to me she was quite aware of the man she was about to marry—a man indifferent to her!"

"Indifferent? Does madness run rampant in your family, mistress?"

"If it matters not a whit to you whom you lie with, then what should hold her?"

"Even if what you say were true—and I tell you 'tis not . . ." Athol faltered. "Well, I—I'm a man, for one thing, and she's—"

"Aye?"

Even in the dim light of the room, she could tell his face had turned pale. His brow appeared to be permanently creased with a frown, and his eyes locked on her.

"Did Ellen tell you this?"

"Nay, m'lord," she said quickly, suddenly touched by the pain in his gray eyes. How Ellen could possibly have preferred someone else's bed over this man's was certainly a mystery. "I . . . I concluded all of this from my own observation. Though courtship and marriage is not a subject I am well versed in, if you will recall from my mother's correspondence, my learning . . ."

"Here in Scotland, we say a wee bit of learning is a dangerous thing."

"I know that you don't believe that. Nonetheless, if you will allow me to continue. With regard to your faults when it comes to your relationship with Ellen . . ."

Catherine paused as he took a step toward her. He looked about ready to throttle her. As she watched him, his face gradually turned as deep a shade of red as his hair, and his voice was no more than a menacing growl.

"I will be your husband, Mistress Percy, and I command you never to speak again of this night . . . nor of Ellen either, for that matter! Is that understood?"

"I did not come to the Highlands for the purpose of marriage—to you or anyone else, m'lord. I should have thought my mother made that perfectly clear in her correspondence. I am here to open a school. To share my learning. To . . ."

She paused, distracted momentarily as he casually picked up his shirt and held it out in front of him. The shirt was still wet from his ride, and she was suddenly very aware of the sinewy musculature of the man's rugged upper body, the effortless power in the way he moved, in his very stance. Realizing that she was staring like some moonstruck maiden, she forced herself to take a breath, and then continued.

"M'lord, did you not correspond with my mother? Did she not explain the reason for my journey here?"

"She did! As I understand it, the only reason why you were sent up into the Highlands was to keep you from falling into the hands of the English king and his men."

"True, but . . ." She watched with a pang of disappointment as he tugged the wet shirt over his head.

"Well, your mother's bargain gave me complete control over you and your life."

"What do you mean, 'bargain'?"

He started pulling the tartan over one shoulder. "I am to protect you. I am to provide you with food and shelter. You are to teach my people some of your learning. But hearing you babble on tonight, I can't say I'm too thrilled by the prospect. Ah, and you are to obey my wishes."

For the first time she saw a dim ray of hope in his words. "You see? I am here to open a school."

"That was before. You are now here to wed me."

The earl of Athol might be the most stunningly handsome man she'd ever seen, but that did nothing to alter her opinion that his skull must be as thick as the walls of York. Still busy dressing himself, he seemed to have lost interest in her totally. But she wasn't about to be ignored.

"But why me? Up to a few moments ago, you were betrothed to another. You are *still* bound to her legally. I am certain if you and Ellen were to sit down—"

"That betrothal contract is finished. Besides, at the pace my former intended and her men rode out of here—with that bare-assed cur hot on her tail—I'd wager she's nearly halfway to Stirling by now. And knowing my temper and the compromising position she found herself in, that slut is undoubtedly thinking she's lucky still to have her head attached."

"Still, m'lord, I'm certain that with time will come healing and reconciliation—"

"This discussion is finished." He picked up his sword and slammed it into its scabbard.

"Nay, m'lord!" she protested, suddenly panicking as he headed toward the door. She rushed to block his exit. "I cannot become your wife."

"You *will*."

"But why me?"

"For two reasons. First, your honor and chastity have been compromised tonight. The whole household knows 'twas your bed that I climbed into, accident or no."

She had a chance, she thought. Perhaps she'd been too hard on him. She softened her tone and met his gaze.

"That's quite noble of you, m'lord, to consider my character and the possibility of vicious rumor. But what you don't know is that I care nothing about what others might think. I am far beyond a marriageable age, and I cannot be wounded by false innuendo, spread by—"

"You are wrong in what you say. But I have no time to try to convince a woman as foolish as you."

She opened her mouth to argue, but he quickly raised a hand and silenced her.

"And secondly. You will marry me because 'twas *your* doing that I am left without a bride this night."

"My doing?"

"Aye! Was that blackguard son of a whore not one of your men? Was it not your bedchamber that Ellen was occupying when he went to her?"

She was breathing fire as she shot back her response. "Are you implying that David Hume was coming to *my* bed?"

"Nay! That would have been no concern of mine. 'Tis just this. I lost the Crawford lass and you will take her place."

"I won't!" she snapped. He'd been deaf to everything she'd said before. "Here you go again. I'm not some stray mare wandering on the road for anyone's taking."

"Nay, you've wandered onto my land, so you're mine." He placed one hand on the hilt of his sword. "But I know you're no mare. You're a woman. And a virgin to boot. I can attest to that myself."

She clenched her fist. "My virginity is no business for you to speak of! I still—"

"I have no time for any more of this foolishness." Athol's gaze hardened into one of disdain. "I'll be having a wife *now*. I will have an heir to my holdings. You are here, you're of noble blood—in spite of it being half-English—and you're a virgin. That, at least, gives me the guarantee of knowing that I'll not be passing my wealth on to somebody else's bastard."

"You cannot force me to marry you! And I swear to you that you'll not be getting any heirs from me."

She could almost see the challenge in the glint of his gray eyes.

"You will marry me. And you will obey me. And you will be faithful to me . . . if I need to lock you in the dungeons of Balvenie Castle to be certain of it." An arrogant smile played over the edges of his mouth. "But as far as begetting a bairn, you'll take me into your bed."

She held her breath as his hand clamped on her chin and forced her gaze upward. It was so easy to close her mind to reason and fall prey to the man's stunning good looks. But Catherine knew that could only happen if he were to shut his mouth and never utter another arrogant word. An unlikely occurrence!

"But do not be fooled by dreamy notions of love.

I'll have none of that. A woman like you would normally be my least likely choice for a wife. But you are here, and you will *have* to do!"

She clenched her jaws shut to stifle the fury that threatened to spew out of her. John Stewart was mad. Clearly, her only chance lay in escape.

"It won't be long before the priest arrives. I'll have my men bring up your trunks. Dress properly for the wedding."

For the first time, the helplessness of her situation struck her. "I . . . I only have a small travel chest. I'm certain I have nothing more appropriate . . . than . . . than . . ."

She watched his gaze dip down and fix on her breasts as her heart hammered in response. "Then I shall ask the priest to join us in this chamber. It certainly will make for a quick consummation."

"I didn't mean my shift. What I was trying to say is that I have no dress fine enough—"

Catherine stopped, no longer able to continue as he stared silently down at her for another long moment. Finally, without another word, he stepped around her and left the room.

She waited until she heard the heavy door shut, listening for a moment more, and then she sprang into action. She had very little time and certainly no options—other than to escape this wild man and somehow find her way to the place where Laura had been sent to the north. Or was it the northeast? It was along the coast somewhere, of that she was certain. She knew this was not the time to worry about her route. Once she was away from here and free of Athol, then she could search out a way.

Forced marriage to a man like him would be her destruction. In the short moments they'd been in each other's company, he'd affected her senses. He'd made her mind a jumble, her body soft and willing. This

certainly would not do! She couldn't throw away a
lifetime of learning for one night's pleasure. And this
would be the extent of it, Catherine thought, remembering his words. He only wanted a willing body and
an heir. One night! That would be all!

Well! He would have to find someone else! Shaking
her head, she ran into the Ladies' Chamber. In fact,
her only chance of escape lay in leaving in the guise
of someone else.

Opening the door that led into the small anteroom,
Catherine looked for the traveling bags she had seen
before. Spying them in the corner, she quietly carried
one of the heavy leather bags back into her chamber.

Rummaging through the contents as quickly as she
could, Catherine guessed that the bag belonged to
David Hume. She pulled out a linen shirt, yanking it
over her head. It was a good thing he was a small
man, she thought. The heavens were clearly smiling on
her, Catherine decided, when she spotted the warrior's
discarded tartan and kilt beside the bed.

She knew exactly what she had to do. Dumping out
the rest of David's things, she hastily stuffed what she
could of her own belongings into the bag. Though
clumsy in her attempt to fasten the kilt around her
slender hips, with the use of a cord, she managed to
dress herself in the Highland gear in just a few moments. Realizing that his boots would never stay on
her feet, she quickly donned her own and then pulled
David's knee-length boots over them. The combination was unbelievably heavy, but it would have to do.
Making a quick knot of her hair, she shoved the black
mass into David's cap.

Then, taking a deep breath, Catherine hoisted the
bag onto her shoulder and slipped out through the
anteroom onto the landing beyond.

Peering through the darkness, she moved silently
down the narrow set of stairs. A few steps down,

though, she tripped in the oversized leather boots. Cursing silently as she caught herself, she pulled them up as well as she could, and continued on. Reaching an arched doorway at the bottom, she saw a door that she thought must lead outside. As she mustered her courage to run for it, though, she leaped back, flattening herself in the shadows. A portly servant, carrying a basket heaped with steaming bread, shouldered his way in through the door.

Catherine shot a glance through the door. In the gray light of dawn, she could see the courtyard, and a part of the outbuilding where the kitchens must be located.

And she could see a sprightly gelding standing with a little donkey beside a stone watering trough. They were both saddled, and—more important—they were unattended. The heavens were indeed smiling on her.

Putting her head down, Catherine moved swiftly through the open door and across the rain-softened ground of the courtyard. Looking neither right nor left, she strode quickly to the gelding and tossed the reins over its head. All she needed to do was to climb up onto this horse, and make the dash across the courtyard and through the arched passageway to freedom.

Taking one quick look around as she threw the leather bag across the steed's neck, she could see that the only people between her and that open arch were a half-dozen men and boys working on horses by the stables. She could make it, she thought joyfully. By the saints, she *would* make it!

Stepping onto a stone mounting block, Catherine had both hands on the saddle when she found herself being pulled backwards by two meaty pairs of hands.

"I do not think we'll be going, just yet," one growled.

"Get the bag," a voice commanded.

Trying to keep her feet under her as they hauled her across the courtyard, Catherine struggled against their hold, but she didn't dare make a sound. From their rough handling, she had a sudden thought that perhaps they hadn't discovered her identity. Perhaps they were simply taking her off to a dungeon. After all, she'd been caught trying to steal a horse. Her hopes continued to rise as she was dragged into the lodge through a door she hadn't seen before.

Her eyes were slow to adjust to the dark, but to calm her fears, she kept reminding herself that she was shrewd, she was fierce, she had a purpose. She would find a way to escape any prison John Stewart might build. At least, she was not being forced to marry the man against her will.

"Just as I expected."

Catherine's head snapped up at the sound of his voice, and she found Athol's fierce eyes staring down at her. It took all her strength to keep her knees from buckling beneath her weight as she felt the steely hands release her.

"Begin, priest."

Chapter 4

What the hell had he done?

Glancing at the backs of his two men as they trailed the obstinate woman out of the Great Hall, John Stewart's brow creased into a deep frown. By St. Andrew, what madness had overtaken him to force this poor lass to go through with such a wedding?

Rudely dressed in the borrowed tartan, Catherine Percy had been surly but silent throughout the ceremony—until the priest addressed her. But then, like a she-devil, she'd come to life, caterwauling like some eldritch creature over the infamy of such a wedding. At that point, however, Athol's patience had crumbled like dried parchment. His grip on her arm had been strong enough to break a bone, though she'd hardly acknowledged it at all. She'd simply glared fearlessly at him, her midnight-blue eyes blazing with reproach.

And they'd continued. She'd been left with no options. She'd been given no choice.

Ignoring the priest who was edging along the wall toward the door, Athol sank into his chair at the dais. So much for the trust that her family had placed in his hands! So much for the protection he'd promised to give. He ran a weary hand over his face. Well, she was safe, and she would continue to be—that was all he'd agreed to. What's done is done!

Staring into the fire crackling in the huge open hearth, John Stewart cursed his foolish temper. He'd been so riled after discovering Ellen with that thieving escort of his ward—his wife, he corrected himself—that he'd been about to burst with the need to strike out. But with the two vile creatures already gone, Catherine Percy had been the only one left. God knows, obstinate as she appeared to be, she probably didn't deserve marriage to him.

John Stewart had never been fool enough to think the imminent union between him and Ellen was a love match. She'd been his mistress in recent years, and as far as he could surmise, she'd had a healthy appetite for other men before they'd met. But what he'd never suspected was that she would be discontented with his generous offer of marriage. She was from a good family, true. But as far as her prospects for marriage, his name and his wealth were certainly superior to anything she would have ever hoped for elsewhere.

He stretched his long legs toward the fire and squeezed his eyes shut. But what had he been thinking tonight? This was all a mistake, that he was certain of! And wasn't it just his luck? Nay, he thought, cursing his temper. It wasn't just Fortune's wheel that had married him to Catherine Percy, a woman with the same scrupulous virtues as his cousin, Susan MacIntyre.

When the dowager brought Susan up to the Highlands more than six months ago with the intention of marrying the lass to him, he'd been appalled at his mother's choice. The fact that she was a dour-faced prude had not been Athol's only objection to the young woman. She had no life in her, no interest with anything beyond her damned needlework. By the devil, she didn't even like to hunt! He'd known old nuns with more blood in their veins. Nay, she was not the woman for him.

So he'd erred a bit in judgment. Asking for the hand of Ellen Crawford hadn't been the best of choices,

either. But if the time had come that he was to be
pressured into taking a wife, at least it could be someone that he would enjoy in bed.

Athol rose abruptly to his feet and strode to the
fire. But that was all, he thought, before he'd known
the truth about Adam of the Glen.

The devil take the man! A bastard brother! So
much for the ideal marriage he'd thought his parents
had been blessed with. But what was most amazing
was the fact that the dowager had somehow kept the
secret for all these years. That, in itself, gave Athol a
completely different view of his mother's power.

But why had she withheld the truth from him? He
knew of dozens of bastard children being raised in the
households of their noble fathers. So why was this
Adam treated as an exception? But more important,
what claim was this devil trying to establish by raiding
his lands?

There was a great deal that his mother had left to
explain. Using her frail health as an excuse, the dowager had refused to say any more, simply closing her
eyes. But Athol had drawn his own conclusions. As
little as it was that she had told him, at least he now
had a trail to follow.

The sound of his warrior's footsteps at the doorway
of the hall drew Athol's attention. Thomas, the captain of his warriors, wasn't trying to hide the pleased
expression as he crossed to the fireplace.

"Aye, Tosh." Athol growled. "Did you swallow the
yellow bird whole, or did you chew it a few times?"

"Well, m'lord, to be truthful, I think we've only just
got a glimpse of the bird, but the men are ready to
move anytime you are. Davie's just come back from
that wee spit of a village they call Knockandhu."

"And what word does he bring?"

"He says he found a few of the old folk there whose

memories might be jogged . . . if you yourself were to put the questions to them.''

Athol nodded his approval, but then stared at the blackened ceiling—where he knew, in a chamber above, a terrified woman sat waiting. Tosh stood and watched him, patiently awaiting his instructions.

"First,'' the earl said finally, "send one of the men to Balvenie with news of my marriage. My mother should know.''

"D'ye want him to spread the news as he goes, m'lord?''

"Nay! I want to make sure the Englishwoman is a wee bit more settled to her newly acquired station before we give her a chance to insult her people. Oh, and have someone speak to the priest. I want the marriage recorded properly, but he is to keep mum about the whole affair until I decide to make things known.''

Despite his hasty action, Athol wasn't about to announce his marriage. Until his new wife was safely and snugly ensconced behind the walls of Balvenie Castle, he wasn't going to risk her life unnecessarily. Nay, he decided, his mother's inference that the outlaw would end his mayhem as soon as Athol had a wife and an heir to succeed him made no sense.

But it didn't really matter. The truth was, Athol didn't want the man to back off. He wanted him out there, roaming the fields where he could be caught.

A bastard brother he might be, but as far as John Stewart was concerned, Adam of the Glen could grace a gallows as prettily as any lowborn thief.

Balvenie Castle, grim and forbidding, was a formidable-looking prison.

Catherine stared through the mist and the rain at the ominous, gray structure. Suddenly, her mount reared its head, jerking the reins in her hands, and the young woman felt a swift, hot bolt of anger shoot through her.

A forced marriage! A madman for a husband! Welcome to the far side of civilization. No wonder her mother had left these lands so long ago and never looked back!

Well! The earl of Athol was in for an unpleasant surprise. Catherine Percy had no intention of ever becoming a willing bride. She felt her spirits lighten a bit as they neared the arched opening into the castle's courtyard. The man didn't have a clue about her strength—about her perseverance. It would actually be pleasurable to dream of ways to torment the earl of Athol. She would get him for what he'd done and more. And she would get free of him. But first, she needed to focus on and assess the nature of her prison.

Near the front of the line of warriors Athol had assigned to escort her to the castle, a horse slipped on the muddy, narrow track. Knocking the legs from under the next horse, the beast started an avalanche of man and horseflesh down the slick incline. Catherine peered through the sheets of rain at the angry men and the terrified horses struggling to their feet at the base of the hill. It was the third time since leaving the hunting lodge this morning that such an incident had occurred. For the third time, no one appeared to have been hurt.

Amid the men's shouting and the slow efforts to bring the wild-eyed steeds and their surly riders up from the gully, Catherine sat quietly and stared at the crenellated walls and the corner towers. The great iron portcullis had been drawn up, and a handful of stable workers were trudging down through the rain and the mud toward the party.

The great stone castle stood on a hill at the junction of two long glens. The high curtain wall was surrounded by sloping stone walls and a deep ditch that

bristled with ancient pointed stakes. Catherine was
certain it must be a formidable-looking place on the
best of days. But today, with the gusts of wind and
rain stinging her face and the horses slipping and balk-
ing with every step, she thought it was easily the
bleakest, most forbidding place she'd ever seen.

The line of warriors began to move again up the
narrow path. As she crossed the plank bridge that
spanned the ditch, she passed the first of the stable
men. One lad peered up at her, dark red hair plastered
on a dirty, freckled forehead, but said nothing and
took hold of her mare's bridle, clucking and encouraging the animal up the last few yards of the incline.

The passage into the inner yard was dark, but in a
moment Catherine joined the crowd of jostling men
and horses in the stone-cobbled courtyard.

Across from the thatch-roofed stables that huddled
along one of the castle walls, servants stood peering
out of the smoking doorways of what were certainly
kitchens and a brew house. The well crouched in the
center of the cobbled yard, and at the far end, a three-
story stone building dominated the courtyard, looking
as ancient and as solid as any of the Highland's
craggy peaks.

Catherine drew in a deep breath and waved off the
proffered hand of the red-haired stable lad. Dismounting, she tried to wipe away some of the mud
and rain that she knew covered her face. Her travel
clothes were a mess, and she was soaked through to
the skin. She stood motionless as the horses were
taken off to the stables.

A thin, ancient servant, drenched as well just from
crossing the yard, approached her. The steward, no
doubt, she decided. She glanced only briefly at his
face, which was as gloomy and inhospitable as the
castle itself. With only a low, mumbled greeting, he
took her by the elbow, leading her across the yard

and up the wooden stairs into the Great Hall of the earl of Athol.

If Catherine had expected anything of a greeting, the absolute lack of interest in her arrival stunned her. While the servants at the hunting lodge at Corgarff had bustled about, making Ellen Crawford and the rest of the travelers comfortable, here at Balvenie Castle not a hand was raised in welcome. Left standing inside the door of the Great Hall, Catherine simply waited in vain for some sign—for any sign—of hospitality.

The Great Hall itself was a fine, old-fashioned chamber with some green-and-gold wall hangings and a number of tapestries of French design covering the various walls. At the far end of the hall, a huge hearth yawned behind a dais, and trestle tables and benches formed a large square around the open center. Rushes covered the floor and a few old dogs lay curled up in the corners and under benches. Aside from the tapestries, the walls were adorned with the heads and antlers of a huge assortment of animals, hanging alongside weapons she could not even identify.

But the oddest thing, Catherine thought, listening to the water drip off of her clothes into the rushes at her feet, was that there was not a soul in the hall. Though the fireplace was prepared with great logs for a fire, no one had even bothered to light it. There were no serving folk preparing for the night's meal, no crofters or warriors waiting to speak with the earl's steward or administrators, no clerks busy at the benches. The Great Hall of Balvenie Castle was cold and empty and silent.

For the first time today, Catherine felt like crying. Feeling the chill of the Hall settling into her bones, Catherine shuddered at the incredible sense of emptiness she was suddenly feeling.

But the time for such sentiments was short-lived,

for a grunt from the steward brought her head around. Behind the thin old man a short, heavyset servant wearing an unceasingly perplexed look on his face was carrying her travel chest and the rest of the meager possessions she'd brought along.

"Have you no serving woman coming along to wait on you?"

"Nay, but I can look after myself."

"We'll just see about that," the steward grumbled, starting toward the arched entry into a round stair tower, his porter on his heels. "This way."

Seeing no purpose in objecting—the Great Hall certainly offered no comforts—Catherine silently followed the two men up the stone steps. The dark, narrow corridor that greeted them on the next floor was hardly a surprise. It was as dismal as what she'd seen below.

Catherine followed them past a number of oak, ironbound doors that she assumed must lead to the quarters of the earl and his family. At the far end of the corridor, the two men turned into a seemingly endless gallery that she assumed must be above the kitchens and the brewhouse. Finally, they reached another narrower corridor, and the two men turned into an open door. Catherine stopped and backed up to allow an old woman carrying a basket half full of firewood to step out first. The serving woman's bleary eyes traveled up and down as she appraised Catherine's wet and disheveled condition. Finally, the old woman simply shook her head and, clucking like an old hen, disappeared along the semidarkness of the corridor.

Catherine looked down and ran a hand over her wet skirts. Soaked and covered with mud, she was a sorry sight indeed.

"Jean, one of the serving lasses, will be up to see to your needs."

Catherine looked up and met the steward's cool gaze. The other man had already wordlessly dumped her things inside the room and was heading back down the hall in the direction that they'd come.

"And Mistress Susan sends word she'll be coming to see you, as well, before supper."

Catherine simply nodded. She was cold, tired, and miserable. But clearly, that meant nothing to this dismal-looking man who was very plainly disappointed with his master's choice in a wife. His face still creased in a frown, the steward finally turned to go.

Catherine waited until the steward disappeared down the hall before stepping toward her chamber. Obviously, now that he had her inside the castle's curtain walls, the earl of Athol had little fear of her escaping. There were no guards posted in the corridor. No bar or lock on the door. Apparently, she was free to roam the keep.

As she looked up and down the corridor, the absolute stillness of the place only added to the chill that had settled into her bones. Resisting the urge to fight against anything and everything she was expected to do, Catherine forced herself across the threshold of the small chamber.

Her time would come, she reminded herself. Catherine pushed the door shut behind her and leaned heavily against it as she gazed about the room. Well, she thought with a sigh of relief, at least they hadn't put her in *his* chamber.

A tiny, new-lit fire flickered in a low, narrow hearth, and the room was still cold and damp. The wooden shutter on the window would surely do nothing to keep out the wet, whistling wind. The plastered walls of the small chamber were free of any hangings, and the simple, narrow bed lacked a canopy or any curtain that might add even the slightest refinement or comfort to the sparsely furnished room. Catherine let her eyes take an inventory of all that surrounded her. Other than the bed, a small chest and a single stool were the only pieces of furniture.

But she was used to this, she thought, pushing herself away from the door and walking toward her belongings by the fire. The years of happiness and comfort she'd been blessed with for nearly all of her childhood had abruptly ended when her father had been branded a traitor to his king. Living the life of a fugitive with her sisters and her mother, Catherine had learned long ago how to make do with what she had—and to seek happiness in her dreams. Dreams of a better future. And in dreams and plans of teaching all she'd learned in a school of her own.

The soft tap on the door was followed by the unceremonious entry of a young serving woman. Jean, no doubt. Catherine realized suddenly that she was still standing about in her wet traveling clothes. But watching the young woman cross the room carrying a large two-handled ewer gave Catherine a dim hope of warm water to wash away some of the grime of her travels.

"Mistress Susan said ye might be needing this."

"I'm obliged to you."

As the servant placed the ewer on the stool with an odd glance in her direction, Catherine considered the so far faceless Mistress Susan. This was the second time her name had come up since she had arrived at Balvenie Castle. Other than the earl's name, the only other information she'd been able to gather about the family had come from Ellen Crawford, and no mention had been made of a Susan.

Nonetheless, the earl's former intended had been quite outspoken in expressing her disappointment with Lady Anne Stewart, the dowager Countess Balvenie. From the way Ellen had described her, Catherine's impression was that the earl's mother was a sickly and yet personally overpowering woman who still very much controlled Balvenie Castle and, for that matter, her son as well.

"Also, mistress said to tell ye that Lady Anne takes an early supper—in her chambers, of course. So it'd be best for all if ye'd clean up as quick as ye can and be ready to pay the countess a visit before she calls for her food to be served."

"Very well," Catherine responded quietly. She was not about to return the servant's snappish tone. Then, as she undid the tie of her soaked traveling cloak, the serving woman reluctantly crossed the chamber to take the heavy garment off her shoulder.

"You are Jean, I take it."

"I am," she replied, eyeing with overt surprise the plain, unembroidered, dark wool dress that Catherine was wearing beneath her cloak. As the servant stood waiting, Catherine noticed the questioning look on her face. A frown quickly replaced the look. "If ye step out of the dress, I'll take that to the kitchens, as well, for washing."

"I am very grateful for your kindness." Catherine leaned down and opened her travel chest, taking out a clean shift, a blouse, and the only other dress she had in her possession—a modest, well-made woolen garment of deep blue. Walking quickly to the ewer of water on the stool, she looked hesitantly around for a cloth of some sort to wash herself. Realizing what Catherine needed, Jean promptly dropped the cloak in her hand on the rush-covered floor and opened the single chest in the room.

By the time she'd stepped out of her dress and removed her boots, Catherine's teeth were chattering. Standing in her chemise as Jean rummaged through the chest, she realized that even her undergarment was soaked and covered with mud to her knees.

"Most of the household still doesn't know yet, mistress, but I was told by Mistress Susan that ye are the master's new bride.''

Catherine accepted the cloth out of the younger woman's hand. Gritting her teeth and dipping the linen into the cold water in the ewer, she fought back the urge to deny it. Like it or not—for the time being, anyway—she was his wife.

''I do not know why the men are so slow to bring up your things, m'lady.''

Catherine hurriedly ran the cloth over her face and her skin, trying to get as much of the grime as she could. ''Everything I have is already here, Jean.''

A cloud of confusion again darkened the woman's eyes. ''But we were told—''

''I am Catherine Percy.''

The name evoked no glimmer of recognition in Jean's face.

''Before your master . . . took me as his wife, I was to work with the good fathers at Elgin Cathedral. To start a school here.''

Slowly the look of confusion was replaced by one of panic. The woman's hand suddenly flew to her mouth. ''By the saints, mistress, I do not think . . . why, Mistress Susan . . . and Lady Anne . . .''

The young maid's eyes suddenly cleared—perhaps at the vision of Catherine's blue lips—and she hurriedly moved to the fire, stacking more pieces of wood on the growing flames and racing back to her.

''Mistress, you'll catch your death in that wet shift. Here—out of that thing and let me get you dry!''

Catherine was too cold to argue. So, nodding obediently, she quickly pulled off the wet garment. A moment later, dry at last, she appreciatively accepted the soft blanket that Jean had yanked from the chest and was wrapping around her.

''Sit by the fire a wee bit, m'lady,'' Jean said, moving

the stool closer to the fire and placing the ewer on the floor. "Ye'll warm up in no time."

Settling before the hearth, Catherine watched the maid moving about the chamber, taking her few possessions out of her bag and airing them on the bed. There was an attentiveness that bordered on concern in Jean's manner now, and it was an attitude that had certainly been absent before.

Clearly, Catherine realized, her new husband had not even bothered to inform his household as to the identity of his new wife. But it was also interesting how greatly, and how openly these people were prepared to dislike her, thinking she was Ellen Crawford.

"I'll be back to dress ye in a wink, mistress. I need to be running along for just a moment . . . to tell Mistress Susan about . . . about . . . supper."

"Thank you, Jean. I can manage to dress myself, if you have other duties." The serving lass wanted to warn her mistress about the mix-up; Catherine could understand that perfectly. But then, as the young woman leaned down to pick up the soiled clothes, a question popped into Catherine's head, and she asked it before Jean could escape. "About your Mistress Susan. Is she . . . I mean, does she run the household?"

"Aye, mistress, that she does. Since Lady Anne has taken to her bed, Mistress Susan has taken charge of the castle." Jean lowered her voice to a whisper. "And I do not mind telling ye that she does a fine job of it, too. The serving folk are much happier taking directions from her. She's a great deal easier than Lady Anne and her tantrums. But then, she came up to Balvenie Castle to do just this sort of thing. My understanding is that she was trained for it from the time she was a wee lass."

"So Mistress Susan hasn't been living at Balvenie Castle all her life?"

"Nay, mistress. She only came here last summer, before the harvest. She was brought up here by the countess herself . . . to marry the master!"

The sun had only been winning its struggle with the rain clouds for about an hour when the burly, bristle-bearded miller led Athol and Tosh along the Kettles Brook. Behind them, where the broad creek tumbled into the Spey at the village of Rothes, the rest of the earl's men waited, happy for an hour's respite from a day of hard, wet riding.

"I know where my old man likes to fish, m'lord," the miller tossed over one broad shoulder. "We're not far, now."

Athol frowned and stared at the man's bald head, shining and beaded with sweat from the walk. Hopefully, the miller's father would have more information to share than the others he'd spoken with. They'd offered little enough.

The ancient, wizened little priest and his equally aged housekeeper at the village of Knockandhu had been more than happy to sit before a morning fire and share with Athol their memories of his father. With a gentleness and diplomacy that would have shocked those who knew him well, though, he'd finally gotten them down to business. Aye, the earl had spent a great deal of time, in the old days, at the little hunting lodge he'd kept there. They both recalled the hunting parties with Duncan, the laird of Ironcross Castle, and his family as well, joining in the festivities. Aye, the earl was a lusty, great-hearted man, that they agreed on wholeheartedly. But when it came to the rumors of the laird keeping a mistress there, they'd been vehement in their response. Nay, he'd kept no mistresses at Knockandhu. The earl was not that kind of man.

And then later, in the hovel nestled snugly against

the eastern slope of Corryhabbie Hill, Athol had spoken with a blind old woman who'd kept sheep there for longer than anyone remembered. It was she who'd supposedly cared for the earl after a boar had torn a hole in his side large enough to put your fist in. She'd smiled when Athol had delicately mentioned that there were still rumors abroad that she'd cared for more than just his wounds. Alas, nay, she'd said. He was a good and handsome man, and a generous laird, but he'd never been more than a friend to her . . . though she was as handsome a lass as any in those days, if she did say so herself.

The keeper of the Inn at Dalnoshaugh had no more to offer than the others, though he did recall the lass asked about, the one who'd drowned herself there in the river all those years back. That incident had nothing to do with the earl, though. In fact, the bridge keeper knew for a fact that the lass had been carrying the bairn of a godless, murdering outlaw whom the earl had subsequently searched out, caught, and hanged from the bridge there, bless his heart.

The mists rolling in around Cairn Uish were just beginning to blanket the descending sun when the miller turned to Athol and pointed ahead. There, beneath a great old oak overhanging the stream, an older, frailer version of the miller himself sat sleeping, fishing pole across his knee, a basket of trout beside him.

"Hullo, Wink," the miller shouted as they neared. "Wake up, old man."

The older miller raised his head and turned his head only slightly, picking up the end of his line and baiting the hook before tossing the line back in the water.

"Up, Wink, you've got folk here that want to be speaking with you."

"Quiet down, you fool," the old man spat out of

the side of his mouth. "D'ye want to be scaring off yer supper?"

"Never mind that," his son said as they came alongside of him. "The Laird of Balvenie himself has been traipsing all over the countryside looking for you, so get your carcass up."

Wink, who'd probably been the miller at Rothes when John Stewart's father was a bairn, turned his bristly face toward the visitors, and gave Athol an appraising look.

"Aye," he said without rising. "Ye've got the face of old King Jamie, rest his soul, but ye've got your father's height, too. Come and sit, m'lord, if ye'll not mind yer own soil for a place to be restin' yer arse."

Waving away Tosh and the miller, Athol took a seat on the grass, resting his back against one of the thick, gnarly roots that protruded from the ground.

"Ye've come to ask me about my daughter and yer father, have ye not?"

Stunned by the directness of the old man's question, Athol nodded. "Aye, Wink. I've heard some things—"

"Well, none of them are true, and ye can all go to the devil!"

Wink's son shouted from the distance. "Watch your tongue, old man."

"I'm not saying anything against your kin, miller."

"I told him, I'm telling you, and I'll tell anyone else who comes to call. My daughter was a good lass, a bit bold perhaps, but a good lass."

"Will you tell me what happened?"

"Aye, 'tis simple enough." The old man yanked in his line and dropped the fishing pole on the ground between them. "Yer good father came up to Rothes when Makyn was just a lass. They were building the church in the village, and the earl come up to see the doings. That's when Makyn asked him."

"Asked him what?"

"She wanted to be a nun, the brazen thing. So the laird gave her a bag of gold to get a good place at the cathedral at Elgin, and she went off without so much as a 'by yer leave' to her own father."

"That's it?"

"Aye, that's it."

"Then what of all the talk?"

" 'Twas all wickedness and lies, I tell ye." Wink glared at the earl. "They were all jealous that the laird would be so good to her and not to them."

"So there was no bairn."

"Nay, m'lord. There was no bairn."

"And your daughter went to Elgin."

"Aye, m'lord."

Athol's look of barely concealed skepticism was met with a look of anger from the old man.

"She's still there, for all I know. I told the other the same thing. Go and look for yerself!"

Athol stared at the man for a moment. "What other?" he asked quietly. "Has another been here before me?"

The aged miller looked away quickly. Clearly, his tongue had revealed more than he'd intended.

"Who has been here, miller?"

Wink hesitated a moment, mumbling to himself before turning and looking the earl directly in the eye.

"Adam, m'lord! Adam of the Glen! Why, the lad asked near the same questions that ye're asking now. I'm telling ye, the lad's keen to know the name of any mistress the laird might've had. But I sent him on his way, m'lord, that I did. Yer father kept no lasses here!"

Chapter 5

So why did he marry *her*? Catherine wondered. He could have had Susan and made everyone happy!

She frowned at the slender shoulders and tight braids curled beneath the starched cap of the young woman walking half a step before her. These were the same corridors that Catherine had traveled earlier, and the deepening of the gloom into night did nothing to improve their character. The only architectural relief was a narrow ledge that ran along the wall, beneath the occasional slit windows that looked down on the roof of the kitchens and the courtyard. Jean walked just ahead of the other two, carrying a flickering taper and occasionally glancing back inquisitively from one woman to the other.

Well, Catherine thought, it was no wonder that— even after knowing that she was not Ellen Crawford— Susan MacIntyre had had little to offer her but the most indifferent whisper of greeting.

Catherine furtively studied the other woman again. It was interesting to see how, in appearances anyway, she and Susan were so similar. Though Susan appeared to be a few years younger, they were both of medium height, with black hair and fair complexions. Susan had a sprinkling of freckles across her nose, but her tightly pursed mouth and downcast eyes allowed no hint of humor to break the somber look of her. Even her dress, black and plain, was modest to the point of primness, its neckline high with a collar of linen to hide any glimpse of skin. She appeared to have a taste for a fashion that made her look much older. Of course, Catherine knew she was somewhat partial to that style herself. She'd been taught early on that it was much better to have people remember you by your wit rather than the fanciness of your dress.

Lady Anne Stewart's chamber lay in the southwest corner of the castle. As they passed into the wider corridor, Catherine's eyes took in the fine tapestries hanging on the whitewashed, plastered walls. This section was clearly finer than the wing where Catherine had been placed, but even if it were her nature to complain, she was not about to. No doubt John Stewart's chambers were nearby, and she was grateful for the distance.

From the few words she'd been able to drag out of Susan, the earl's mother had become bedridden for the first time in her life, early in the summer, after a cough began to weaken her. But as the weeks had passed, the castle physician had shaken his head, speaking of the kink and then, the ague. And as the body of the aging woman grew thin and frail, Susan said, the dowager's spirit had grown weaker. Now, for more than a fortnight, the physician had been telling all that the end was not far away.

It occurred to Catherine that it was sad to meet someone under these conditions. No matter what mistakes Lady Anne might have made in raising such a stubborn son, she still commanded great respect in Catherine's mind, as one who had lived so long in such ruggedly wild country. She frowned as they neared the dowager's great oak door, thinking how, under different circumstances, they might even have developed a good and lasting relationship.

Putting such thoughts aside, Catherine followed

Susan quietly into the large, darkened chamber. The thickly perfumed air of the room struck Catherine like a slap in the face. Remaining by the entrance, she watched Susan whisper some orders to the two waiting women positioned by the dowager's bed. An ancient woman-in-waiting that Susan called Auld Mab sat silently listening by a wide hearth. From where she stood, Catherine couldn't see past the heavy, French damask bedcurtains, or make out anything of the figure stretched beneath the embroidered bedclothes. Instead, she let her gaze drift about the huge chamber. The fine furnishings were lavish and comfortable, and Catherine might have been impressed, were it not so grim. Darkness hung like a shroud in the room, and the heavily curtained windows seemed to be intentionally holding out all light, and all fresh air, as well.

Catherine heard the dowager cough weakly behind the curtains. The thought struck her that, between the smoke from the burning logs on the hearth and the closeness of the unaired sick chamber, it was a wonder that the older woman could possibly take in a full breath. Catherine could hardly breathe herself.

A low croak cut through the darkness. "Come close!"

When no one else moved, Catherine realized that the raspy words spoken from behind the curtains were directed at no one but her.

Wiping her wet palms on the skirt of her dress, Catherine threw a hesitant glance in Susan's direction and acknowledged her nod before approaching the canopied bed. As she came near, the two attendants and Susan all backed away to a respectful distance. Clenching her jaw, she prepared herself for the worst. Hadn't Jean told her that the dowager's wish had been for her son to wed Susan? Catherine could feel the mother's disapproval hanging in the air like the sword of Damocles above her head.

"Closer, I said! Come closer!"

Catherine stared at the gleaming amber stones of the rosary laced between the bony, wrinkled fingers of the older woman, and took another half step.

"Closer!"

So be it! she thought. Lifting her chin, she walked around the side of the bed, her gaze meeting and holding the piercing gray eyes of the aged woman. The sharpness of that look, the intensity that radiated from those eyes, bespoke intelligence and will. John Stewart had his mother's eyes. A long moment passed in silence as Lady Anne continued to examine her. And then she heard the noise.

Catherine first thought it was a cough. Then she feared that a spell might be coming on the ailing woman. But as the dowager continued to gasp for precious breaths, Catherine realized that the old woman was laughing at her.

Absolutely appalled, Catherine watched Lady Anne's shoulders begin to shake as a tear ran down the side of her pale, wrinkled face. Feeling her cheeks flush hot with embarrassment, Catherine had no doubt whatsoever that she was indeed an object of derision for the dowager.

" 'Tis a very great pleasure meeting you, too, m'lady," Catherine put in, trying to keep her tone civil. "And may I ask what I have done to be the source of such amusement for your ladyship?"

The dowager held up a bony hand as her laugh turned into a fairly credible sounding cough. She turned her face to the side, genuinely struggling to catch her breath. The thought of waiting for the others to come to the dowager's aid never entered her mind, and Catherine quickly slipped a steady hand behind the frail woman's back and moved her into a sitting position. It took only an instant to reach behind the

old woman and prop her up with a couple of the
down-filled pillows.

It still took a few more moments and a sip of some
greenish liquid that Susan brought in a cup before
Lady Anne's breathing became a bit less labored.
Backing up a half a step, Catherine stood and waited
until the dowager became calm again. Taking hold of
Susan's wrist with one hand, the frowning older
woman turned her gaze on Catherine, and raised an
accusing finger in the newcomer's direction.

"You might as well know now, Catherine Percy.
You will never do!"

She didn't have to ask. It was clear that dowager
was referring to her son, the earl. Catherine clasped
her hands tightly before her before looking up again
and meeting the other woman's gaze. She had been
talked to honestly and directly.

"And would you throw another fit if I were to tell
you that I find your words a blessing? That I have no
intention of becoming your daughter-in-law?"

"You lie."

"Let me burn in hell if I do."

The frown on the dowager's face slowly disappeared, replaced by the hint of an amusement around
her gray eyes.

"Leave us."

Catherine had already taken a step back before she
realized that the ailing woman's words were not directed at her. Without a word, Susan and the two
women in waiting slipped out of the chamber, closing
the door behind them.

"That worthless messenger my son sent failed to tell
me that the earl had not married the Crawford wench
as he had planned. The fool just said that the master
had married and that the new countess was coming."

Catherine could see that Ellen's and Lady Anne's
lack of affection was mutual.

"And Susan also tells me that you are the spinster daughter of that dear, restless Nichola Erskine."

"Nichola Percy," Catherine said. "She took my father's name when they wed."

"Aye, of course," she snapped. "I might be dying, young woman, but I'm not feebleminded."

When Catherine said nothing, Lady Anne continued.

"Although I haven't seen her for years, I still remember her quite well. She was a bonny lass, that Nichola Erskine, though far too spirited for her own good. Smart as a whip, too. But it doesn't appear you have inherited much from her." Catherine blushed in spite of herself as the dowager's gray eyes again scanned her hair, her face, her attire. "Och! A shame, really, that you are not at all like her."

Catherine's eyes flashed. "If I may be so bold as to correct you, m'lady. Contrary to what you just said, there are many who believe I've been blessed with my mother's talent for languages and her patience for learning, in general. And in spite of the world's overwrought regard for things as trifling as someone's looks, my mother's claim to fame in England has been her great learning. And the desire to teach what we have learned is a passion that we also share."

Catherine paused, trying to decide if she was being a bit snappish. Nay, she decided, just informative.

"Very well, my pert young mistress. I see you do have something of her in you. But I know nothing of this 'learning' business. Your conduct appears to me to be temper . . . and more than a wee bit of willfulness." She looked hard at Catherine's face. "Come closer."

Catherine stared, confused about the nature of the order.

"Pick up that wick lamp and come here beside me."

Silently, Catherine did as she was told.

"Sit."

Carefully, Catherine lowered herself onto the edge of the bed.

"Ah! I see it now," the dowager whispered, lifting her head with effort off the pillow and staring keenly into Catherine's face. "You have her eyes, lass. Those same eyes of midnight blue." She leaned back with a loud sigh. "Praise heaven for that, at least. There is hope, after all."

Catherine was now totally perplexed by the old woman. Putting the wick lamp down on the small table beside the bed, Catherine turned her attention back to the sickbed. Her voice sounded unsteady even to her own ears. "Hope for what?"

"For making you into a countess, Catherine Percy. For getting John to abide by his vows as well as beget an—" She abruptly stopped mid-sentence and looked into Catherine's face. "Was there a priest present when you two wed?"

"Aye, m'lady. But I was forced—"

"A priest, that's good! Now, I know there has been no four days of waiting . . . but did you two consummate the marriage?"

"Nay, m'lady. And if I have my way—"

"Och, the devil take him! That's no good at all!"

The dowager coughed for the first time since the two of them were left alone. Following Susan's practice, Catherine moved to the other side of the bed and brought a cup to the ailing woman's lips. The dowager took a sip and then pushed aside the foul-smelling brew. It occurred to Catherine that the old woman suddenly seemed to have no time for being ill . . . never mind dying.

"Knowing my condition, my son will not stay away for more than a few days at a time. So he'll be back. And soon. I'll have Susan move you into his chamber. And we must do something about the way you—"

"I'm quite happy about where I've been placed, m'lady."

"Are you, mistress?" the dowager said, one eyebrow shooting up in surprise.

"Aye," Catherine replied, looking intently at the woman. "I have no intention of moving."

"Is that so? Well, that room was intended as an insult when we thought you were that slattern, Ellen Crawford. 'Twas never meant to be a sanctuary for Nichola Erskine's daughter."

"Still, m'lady. I can assure you—"

"You can assure me of what?" Once again the gray eyes flashed with intelligence and challenge. "The only thing I want you to assure me of is a healthy bairn . . . a good, strong lad for the earl to raise as an heir."

"Really, Lady Anne . . ."

"D'ye really think you'd be happy living in that drafty little mouse hole, while your husband lives in the grandest of chambers, just across the keep? And will it make you happy to fast quietly in your chamber while he brings mistresses from court to sit in your place beside him in the Great Hall? To please him in his bed?" Lady Anne hitched an eyebrow at her. "Are you certain you're Nichola Erskine's daughter?"

Catherine's back stiffened at her words, but she chose not to respond to the final barb. "I have no intention of becoming either a laughingstock or a martyr, m'lady. But I do intend to send a letter to the Pope himself, requesting an annulment of this travesty of a marriage. And I have grounds for such a request, since that priest and the saints above were witnesses to the fact that I was forced to take my vows. There were no contracts of betrothal . . . no reading of the banns . . ." She felt the heat rise in her face. "And there was no consummation! That—"

"You are a silly lass, aren't you? And a dreamer, at that!"

"Lady Anne, I have no wish to stay wed to your son!"

" 'Tis not becoming to see Nichola's daughter play the fool!"

It was getting more difficult by the moment just to stand there and take the dowager's insults. But walking out on an ailing woman would serve no purpose. Lady Anne had some prior connection with her mother, and Catherine could use at least one ally here at Balvenie Castle. "Lady Anne, I understand you are concerned about your son, and the future of your family, but—"

"Are you so simple? So naive? Are you a fool, after all, lass?"

"Is there some purpose in calling me names?"

"Aye, there is! And if you'll give me a few more moments, I'll come up with more."

Catherine's hands were fisted at her sides, but she forced them open, laying them flat on the bedclothes as she tried to calm her temper. "M'lady, I still—"

" 'Tis you, child! Don't you understand? You are the one I'm thinking of, now!" Lady Anne untangled one hand from her rosary and reached over, placing it on Catherine's. "You! The one with no dowry. The one whose home now belongs to that baboon, Henry of England. You, lass, the one with a price on her head!"

Lady Anne motioned toward the cup, and Catherine brought it again to her lips. The old woman began to take a sip, then curled up her lip in distaste and pushed the cup away.

"I want you to tell me what cardinal, what bishop . . . what lowly curate even . . . will go for you to the pope? None that I know. I'm telling you, Catherine, you wouldn't be able to get even a poor-mouthed friar, his bony arse showing through a threadbare robe, to take such a frivolous document to Rome."

"Everything you say, about my family, my worth . . .

'tis true for one who is in search of a husband." Catherine heard the sound of her voice rising in the stuffy room, but she had no desire to restrain it. She would get her point across, if she had to shout it from the towers. "But the truth is that I have no need for one and never wanted one. I have always desired a life of study, and I would be quite prepared to retire to some convent if I cannot open a school, as my mother wrote to you and the earl. So even if what you say is true— about no one being willing to carry my request to Rome—I shall still defy your son's wishes. I shall *never* be a wife. If I have to lock myself in that chamber that you've assigned me until the Lord sees fit to take my spirit, I'll stay there until the earl of Athol forgets he even made that horrible mistake."

There was that rasping, airless sound again. That mortifying croak of a laugh no doubt intended to make Catherine feel a bit insecure in her position.

"Well, my dear. You are in for a lesson, and it won't be in Greek, I'm quite certain. But it will surely prove more useful to you than anything the Ancients have to teach you."

"And may I ask what this lesson might be?"

As Catherine stared at the dowager, the older woman's eyes glistened with a light that suddenly made her look much younger in age. "Nay, lass, you may not ask anything more. Now be on your way, and send those useless women back."

Lady Anne closed her eyes, dismissing Catherine, who turned away from the bed. As she crossed the chamber, she considered the dowager's last words. She was almost to the door when the raspy voice again cut through the darkness.

"Catherine!"

"Aye, m'lady?"

"I take back what I said before. You may do, after all!"

Chapter 6

He knew it. It was just a matter of perseverance.
John Stewart watched his bride slip quietly into the darkened Great Hall. She would not see him sitting in the shadows by the wall, he was quite certain of that. Only the flickering light of the dying fire behind the dais illuminated the Hall, and he smiled as she directed a quick and somewhat nervous glance toward the empty laird's seat. Two dozen men were sleeping on the benches, but none even stirred when one of the dogs lifted his head and growled at the intruder before yawning and laying his head down again.

She turned and hurried into the passage leading toward the kitchens.

Well, she would find little to sustain her there, Athol thought. He'd made certain of that earlier, directing the cook and the steward to lock away everything after the meal was cleared from the long trestle tables. And she was not to be fed. That had been his command. If she did not find his company—or for that matter, the company of his people—good enough to join them down in the Hall for meals, then she could damn well starve.

He'd arrived at Balvenie Castle before midday yesterday, and this was the first time she had stepped out of her bedchamber, ignoring all invitations.

Glancing in the direction that she'd disappeared, he

told himself that she'd be back. He was certain of that. But as the moments passed, the earl became a bit uneasy. Though the cook and the serving folk who slept in the kitchens were, for the most part, an amiable lot, Athol couldn't imagine they were, as a whole, very fond of this haughty, reclusive newcomer. Nay, he thought, sitting back and waiting. None would lay a hand on her.

John Stewart had, at first, been surprised that his ailing mother had placed his bride in the drafty old east section of the keep. This western section of the castle, where he had his own Great Chamber, had been rebuilt by his grandfather, and though a bit old-fashioned, it was far more comfortable than the crumbling buildings where Catherine had been deposited. In fact, he was even more surprised that the newcomer hadn't been chained to his bed, knowing his mother's obsession with him begetting an heir.

Well, it was time to do just that. By next summer, he could have a bairn bouncing on his knee.

The movement by the door drew his eyes. As he knew she would, Catherine entered the Hall again, bending to pat a dog's head before moving quietly from table to table, looking for food.

Catherine pressed the heel of her hand against her growling belly. She'd thought Balvenie Castle would hold much worse torment than an empty stomach, but this was bad enough.

Jean had been very apologetic when she'd come to Catherine's chamber with no supper last night, but she simply couldn't defy the earl's wishes. Catherine knew that he had come. How could she not? With all the ruckus he and his men had raised in the courtyard earlier, there was no ignoring him. And knowing he was here had stiffened her will to rebel. He wanted a wife? Well, let him get one elsewhere. He wouldn't have her. Just as she'd told Lady Anne, she would stay locked away as long as she must—until such time as he forgot that she even existed.

But she still needed to survive. So now, with the castle silent and sleeping, she had decided to venture out and collect water and food. And if there were an opportunity for escape, she would take it.

But nay, the woven iron bands of the portcullis cut off any chance of disappearing beyond the curtain wall into the Scottish night.

And her foray into the kitchen had been fruitless, as well. The expansive room, dominated by a huge double-arched hearth, had been crowded with sleeping bodies. Feeling her way back through the dark to the Great Hall, she had been very careful not to step on any sleeping dogs, nor on any tartan-wrapped warriors, either.

Catherine moved stealthily along the trestle tables. From the fading light of the fireplace, she could see only a half-dozen bowls and a ewer or two remaining out. Remnants of the night's drinking, she realized, picking up an empty bowl and sniffing it. And there was nothing of dinner itself, as far as she could tell.

Anxiety joining with the hunger already gnawing at her stomach, Catherine took a deep breath and tried to stop her knees from trembling. She wiped her wet palms on her dress beneath her cloak and reminded herself that she was no thief.

Even the dogs had a right to search for food.

John watched her reach for a ewer sitting beside the ear of the warrior lying on the next trestle table. The container was empty; he'd made sure of that himself. And her disappointment with that discovery showed up as she pushed back the cloak's hood from her head and brought a hand to her brow.

This was the closest she'd gotten to him, and the

fireplace nearby cast her face in a soft, amber glow. From where he sat in the shadow against the wall, his legs sprawled beneath the table before him, John knew she could not see his eyes watching her. She had a fine profile, he thought: the straight nose, the full lips, the high cheekbones that had flushed crimson at his inconsiderate words when he'd first met her in the hunting lodge at Corgarff.

And then she turned fully in his direction. Athol ceased to breathe. Those eyes. How could he have forgotten those eyes, so dark in this light, but so beautiful. She was staring at him—or rather, at the food on the bread trencher in front of him. Come a bit closer, he thought. Let me see the blue of those eyes.

Catherine took a hesitant step toward him and stopped again. She pushed her cloak back over her shoulders, and his eyes wandered over the ample curves of her shapely body. Suddenly, his mind became engulfed with memories of her in his bed. His hand on the silky skin of her hip. The way she'd moaned against his lips. The perfect fit of her breast in his palm. The way she had risen to the touch of his fingertips on her belly.

He should have known immediately that she wasn't the perpetually overeager Ellen Crawford. Nay, he admitted silently, from the first moment he'd climbed in that bed, he'd sensed something different there. Something infinitely better. But he'd been away from Ellen for so many months, and he'd never expected someone else to be in his bed. Certainly not this woman. And from the moment he'd stretched out beside her, he'd had only one thing on his mind.

He saw her take another step forward and her hand accidentally tipped a bowl sitting beside the ewer on the next table. She grabbed for it swiftly, and the thing made no noise. It must have had a few drops of ale in the bottom, for he watched her raise her hand to her lips. Athol felt a tingling surge in his loins as her delicate tongue licked the drops from her finger.

Perhaps he hadn't made such a bad choice, after all, he thought, his eyes fixed on her, his brain conjuring images of all that he would like to do with that mouth.

Finally, she thought. The drops of ale were bitter on her tongue, and Catherine moved carefully toward the next table. It was the closest to the wall, and she could see that there was indeed food on the trencher.

Her eyes flicked over to the motionless warrior slouched on the bench behind the table. He was leaning back against the dark, paneled wall. From what she could see, he must have fallen asleep with his supper still before him. She dared herself to take the last step that would put her within reach. All she needed to do was take the food and run.

She clenched her jaw, trying to build enough courage to act. His face was hidden in the shadows—his broad chest crossed by the same red-and-green tartan worn by nearly all of Athol's warriors.

Her stomach made a loud, complaining sound, and suddenly Catherine knew that her decision had been made for her. She reached out with both hands and grabbed for the trencher.

With incredible speed, the warrior's hands shot out and clamped on her wrists. A strangled gasp of panic escaped her lips, and Catherine found herself being tugged toward the table.

"Stop! I . . . I thought you were finished."

He stopped pulling her but did not release her, and Catherine found her throat clamp shut as the face moved out of the shadows and into the light.

"So you've decided at last to leave your self-imposed confinement and join me down here for some supper."

"I . . ." She couldn't think straight. His gray eyes

were dark in the firelight, but she could feel them piercing her soul.

"I know. You didn't want to bother with the folk who would be naturally inquisitive about their new mistress. You only wished for my attentions, is that right?"

She simply could not find her voice. The nearness of him—his hands holding her fast—was the most unsettling. Her face was burning, and yet there were chills running down her spine. It was like some raging fever, but not like any fever she'd ever endured before.

"You locked yourself away."

The odd hint of regret in his voice surprised her. She tore her gaze away, and stared at his mouth. His lips were full and sensuous. She had felt the press of those lips, and she forced back the memory as the heat flooded into her belly.

"I didn't . . . I thought . . . you . . ."

He let go of her wrists, and Catherine straightened immediately. Despite all her strong words to Lady Anne, just one moment in his presence was all it took for her to melt, to become soft and willing right before his eyes. What was wrong with her!

" 'Tis a relief to know that you had enough sense to decide against starvation." He leaned forward and pushed the trencher of food across the table. "Why not sit down and eat?"

She didn't stir. She couldn't. Not until she could control her own unexplainable response to him.

"No longer hungry? Or is it, perhaps, that you do not trust me!" As she continued to remain silent, he cocked an eyebrow and studied her. She felt the heat about to burst through the skin of her cheek. "You are blushing!"

"Nay," she managed to whisper. " 'Tis anger that you see."

She saw his eyes soften a bit. "This is better than I hoped. You are angry with me because I left you on our wedding night. Before we had a chance to consummate our union." He paused just long enough for Catherine to feel another rush of heat flood her cheeks. " 'Tis a Highland custom to wait half a week, but I promise to make up for any slight you may have felt. In fact, why not carry this food back to my bedchamber. We can start—"

"I'll eat here." She sat down quickly, pulling the trencher and the goblet toward her. She lifted the cup to her lips. The wine was heavenly compared to the bit of water she'd had over the past two days. She drank again.

"I would slow down on that, if I were you. I wouldn't want you blaming the wine when you end up in my bed this night."

As she placed the cup on the table, though, he produced a pitcher of wine from the bench beside him. Without hesitation, he filled the goblet to the top.

"On second thought, since this is your first time, perhaps it might help you to—"

"Could you please stop talking this way?" The wine must have gone to her head, she thought, since she no longer felt any fear of the man sitting before her. But, looking into those eyes, sparkling with amusement, she wondered if she'd ever truly feared him.

"Talking what way?"

"Talking nonsense. Talking matrimony and consummation! We both know that the vows we took meant nothing. So why pretend? Why carry on with this farce?"

She'd expected him to argue—or even lose his temper as she'd seen him do before. At least, she'd hoped for him to say something—anything. But he said nothing. Instead, he looked at her with a charming gleam emanating from the depths of his eyes. Catherine knew for certain then that she was in trouble.

And then her stomach growled. It was not even one of those small sounds that one can overlook. Nay, this was the kind of growl that can be heard above the din of a London fish market. The kind that would wake one's sisters from a sound sleep. The kind that allows one no opportunity for salvaging her dignity.

So she simply smiled sheepishly, shrugged her shoulders, dropped her gaze, and reached for the cheese on the trencher before her.

"The mutton is particularly good, I believe."

Catherine did not look up, certain that he would be leering at her suggestively, ready to remind her of what this food might cost her later, but he again proved her wrong in her assumptions about him. He was quiet for a while, and when she glanced up at him, Athol smiled and leaned back against the wall.

Moments later, she surveyed the empty trencher before her. The mutton *had* been particularly good. As was the bannock bread, and the capon, and the cheese. She sipped the wine and looked over the rim of the goblet at his handsome face. She wished he would say something, engage her in conversation. As if reading her mind, John Stewart began to speak, talking about Balvenie Castle, about its colorful past. He spoke of how his family came into possession of the castle after the Black Douglases fell from grace after losing to the king's forces at Arkinholm.

Listening to the resonant tones of his deep voice and sipping the wine, Catherine became swept up in the history. His knowledge was vast and his tales vividly detailed, and Catherine soon found herself in a world of chivalric knights and ignoble villains, of beautiful heroines and unending love affairs.

". . . So after the wedding of my great grandsire John Stewart, the first earl of Athol, to Margaret of the fallen Douglas clan, a condition was set that one red rose would be rendered each year on St. John the Baptist's Day . . ."

Catherine found herself drifting into the realm of her dreams. She could see her knight stepping into a large and empty hall. And her, waiting for him there in the middle, the rays of sun slanting in through the high windows, the golden light pooling around her. In his hand, he held a rose. A rose the color of blood, the color of life. Her knight, stepping closer, offering her the token. A token of love. She smiled, raising her hand to him. . . .

Catherine drifted out of her dreams as John Stewart's voice stopped. Her eyes took in the chiseled features of his face—the high forehead, the small web of wrinkles etched into the corners of his eyes, the thin line of a scar along his left cheekbone. She let her gaze wander along the strong line of his jaw, to the cleft in his chin, and finally to the full lips. There was a gentleness now in his face that warmed her, lulled her. She looked into his gray eyes and was suddenly lost in a world far more real and sensuous than any she'd found in her dreams. She lowered her gaze again to his mouth and found it as inviting as any forbidden fruit.

Catherine started as the cup slipped in her fingers, and she put it down. She must have had too much wine.

"I thank you . . . for sharing your . . ." She pushed herself shakily to her feet, and gestured vaguely at the table. "Your food . . . your company. I—"

He came to his feet, as well, and suddenly her head was spinning with thoughts of his earlier suggestions. She started to gather up the trencher and the cup on the table. "I'll . . . I'll just take these to the kitch—"

"No need." The weight of his large hand on hers checked the flurry of movement. His hand was so warm, so strong. "We have serving folk with little enough to do. But I believe Jean would be offended if she knew I let you wait on yourself."

Letting go of the cup and the trencher, Catherine pulled her hands out of his grip. "Then, I'll retire to my chamber."

"I hope I haven't bored you."

"Hardly, m'lord. 'Tis late."

"Very well. I'll walk you to your door."

She studied him for another moment, trying to calm her beating heart. What had she to complain about? He could be dragging her to his chamber—ravishing her. He was simply being courteous. She felt her face burn as a realization emerged from the turmoil in her brain. Disappointment. There, lurking in some shadowy recess, disappointment that he was not taking her burning body. Why shouldn't he want her?

By the saints, she argued silently, perhaps she *should* have wed when she was sixteen. This craziness, this eagerness she felt for the man was far, far too unsettling.

"Can I not walk my own wife to her chamber door?"

"Aye, you . . . I do not .. " She faltered and then gathered herself. "Aye, of course!"

John Stewart came around the table, lighting a taper at the remnants of the fire in the hearth. Wordlessly, the two worked their way out of the hall and up the dark, circular stairwell. Her mind was racing as they passed through the same dismal corridors she'd traveled earlier, and Catherine saw nothing of them. His presence beside her was terrifying and thrilling, and her heart was hammering so loudly that she was sure she could hear it echoing off the walls as they walked.

"And why is it, Catherine, that you were not wed when you were younger?"

His elbow brushed against her arm, and she felt the

fires spread from the point of contact up through her shoulder and into her chest.

"I—I've always been keen on learning."

"And your suitors objected to so much knowledge in a potential wife?"

"*You* did! I mean, *you* do." She paused an instant, hoping that he would correct her, but he ignored her answer. She glanced hesitantly at his direction and found his eyes roaming lazily over her face. His gaze fixed on her lips, and she forced herself to breathe. "As . . . as you already know, I am not the type of woman that one seeks as a wife. Even aside from my learning, which is for some reason enough to frighten off most men, I am also opinionated . . . and willful . . . and . . . well, I think you understand."

"Nay, I do not. Do you have more that is wrong with you?"

The passage narrowed at the turn, and Catherine brushed against his chest as they moved into the section of the castle where her chamber was located. She stumbled a bit and he reached out for her arm. His hand lingered a moment longer than it needed to, and her mind reeled at the effect of his touch.

"Nay! I . . . I have other qualities, as well!"

"Do you?"

She gave him a sidelong glance and found a smile softening the weathered features of his face.

"Well! I suppose I am not beautiful or desirable the way some other women are."

"Is that so?"

"Of course. A man might even look at me as something of a burden. As a woman suitable for some convent, where they do not have to look upon her face."

"And what blind fool planted that seed in your head?"

"You yourself called me an old crone."

"That's not true." They stopped at her door. "If I

remember correctly, I accused you of talking like one. I never . . . By the devil! So you are trying to rile me, are you?"

She leaned against the doorjamb and lifted her chin in challenge. "As I said before, being beneath the attentions of men, I have been able to hone other abilities, such as—"

"Other qualities, you mean, such as stubbornness, and willfulness . . . and the desire to teach?"

He actually did understand, so she rewarded him with a smile. But his response made her forget to breathe. He took a step toward her and gently ran the tips of his fingers across her lips.

"You have the most enchanting smile. A bewitching one." She waited, shivering with anticipation of what could come next. The memory of his lips against her own suddenly flooded her senses. She'd thought it was a dream, then, and there was something dreamlike in this moment, as well. "Take me inside your room."

Catherine thought she shook her head, but she wasn't completely certain.

"Then come to my chamber."

She smiled. "I told you before, I am not who you want me to be. I've a dream of being a teacher, of sharing what I know with—"

"One doesn't need to sacrifice one dream to pursue another." His hand reached out and touched her face, the backs of his fingers caressing the line of her jaw, the side of her neck. "Take your mother. From all I've heard elsewhere—in addition to being a learned lady, she was a fine wife and mother."

"Aye, but—"

"I know, lass, you do not have to say it—there are no men living who are as worthy as your father. But still, is it not a shame to lock away the passion that is a part of you? A part of us?"

"I express my passion through my teaching." She'd

always thought that was true. And it *was* true! She was certain of it—at least, until she'd met John Stewart. But she couldn't let him see through this weakness. Not when he was the cause. "The enthusiasm that I feel . . ."

He silenced her with the gentle touch of a finger on her lips. "Nay, Catherine. I'm talking of desire. Of the hunger that men and women feel for each other. Of the heat that you felt when I first came to your bed at the lodge."

Her mind searched for a logical reply, but her heart drummed in revolt, giving her away. "That was a—"

"I can see through you, lass. As hard as you might try, this outer skin—that the rest of the world might see—cannot hide from me who you really are. I see the real woman beneath, Catherine."

"You *do not* know me."

"Oh, but I do. Better than you think." He leaned toward her. All she could see were his full lips as they brushed against hers. "And I think 'tis time you started learning about yourself, as well."

"But I know all there is to . . ." The whisper died on her lips as his mouth took possession of hers. Her hands fisted and then fluttered open against his chest. As he pulled her tighter into his embrace, she felt herself melting, her lips parting, yielding to his, her body molding to him. She didn't know what boldness had taken control of her being, but she found herself rising on tiptoe as her arms encircled his neck. She felt, rather than heard, his groan of approval as her body pressed instinctively against his.

He drew back only slightly. "There can be no pretense between us." He nipped at her lower lip and gazed again into her eyes. "We have only passion."

She wanted to fight. This was madness. It was sweet and wild, and she had no idea what would come of it. Aye, it was madness, all right. Even during the most vivid encounters with her dream-knight, Catherine never had felt what she was feeling now. Her senses were so alive, so ready for his next touch. This time there was no sense of panic when his tongue swept into her mouth, and she moved in his arms to accommodate him.

Catherine was vaguely aware of her own surprise and exhilaration at the rising need within her. And somehow, somewhere, she must have given him a sign, for suddenly she felt his hand beginning to roam over her body. His fingers found their way inside her cloak, caressing the sides of her breasts. When he pinned her against the door with his hips, the feel of his hardening manhood elicited a gasp from her. No longer was there any fear. Only a sense of incredible wonder.

"I want you, Catherine," he murmured against her throat. "I want to bed my wife."

"But . . . but you care nothing for this wife. I'm nothing but a willing body, John Stewart, the same as the last one . . . or the next." Even to her own ears, her objection sounded weak, and her body betrayed her by arching against him. A muscular thigh pushed between hers, and she found herself gasping at the sweet pressure.

"Let me show you the ways of passion," he said and she closed her eyes as his hand boldly cupped her breast through her dress. "Let us put aside the words and do what both of us wants so much to do."

He didn't deny what she'd said. But for the life of her, she couldn't move away.

"I want you to know the sweet nectar of passion." His one hand pulled up the weight of her skirt, and she held her breath as it sought her waiting middle.

"Nectar or venom . . . it means my ruin. I—" She gasped as his fingers found her womanhood. His lips pressed against the skin of her neck, shocking her with their coolness.

"But to be ruined in such ecstasy." His voice was
a breath in her ear. "Let go of it, Catherine. Get ready
to take flight."

She didn't know what he meant, but the way his
palm was cupping her—the maddening pressure that
was building within her as he continued stroking her
with his fingers—her own breaths were now coming
in gasps.

"Aye, lass. If this is ruin, let it be a heavenly
wreck."

More! More! her mind screamed. Every bit of her
body cried to be touched. An insatiable need was rising, pulsing through her body, forcing her hands
around his neck, and drawing him tightly against her.
In the midst of this frenzy, she felt his hips press more
intimately against her middle. There was a shifting of
her weight in his arms.

"This would all be so much easier if you'd let me
take you inside."

She shook her head. That would mean surrender.
Not only in body, but in soul, as well. But still, she
didn't want him to stop. Placing her lips against the
side of his throat, she hoped that he'd understand.

"This is madness, Catherine. And you are not helping me in any way that you should."

"I know." She felt him pull back slightly and glance
down the corridor. They were standing in a dark and
empty hall. Only the flickering of the taper in the
sconce beside her door shed any light. The household
had been asleep long before she'd dared to leave her
room. But still, the inappropriateness of what she was
letting him do to her started creeping into her head.

But then, as if reading her mind, he lowered his
head and kissed her again. As if he could read her
desire, the magical touch of his fingers against her
flesh began anew.

She gasped and stifled a cry against his neck as she

suddenly found herself lifted effortlessly and carried across to the opposite wall. There he lowered her onto the ledge that ran beneath the windows.

"Not exactly a window seat, lass, but it'll have to do!"

She tightened her hold around his neck. "I'll fall!"

"Aye. Right into the courtyard." He pushed her skirts up, and she shuddered as he slid his hands along her thighs and over her hips. Stepping forward, he pressed himself between her knees. "But you won't fall. I won't let that happen, Cat."

She'd never done this. She'd never dreamed of really doing this. But still, as he pressed his hard body ever closer, she knew that she wanted this to happen. She knew that she trusted him.

"Wrap your legs around me, Cat."

She did what he asked as he reached between their bodies, pulling up his kilt.

There would be pain. She knew there would be pain. But when he touched her so gently with his fingertips—first probing and parting the folds of her womanhood—she lost the last shred of her control. Her release was sudden and explosive, and she buried her cries against his shoulder.

Her mind had not yet cleared when he entered her. Vaguely, she felt the tearing, but the pain was dulled by the waves of pleasure that continued to roll through her. He was deep within her, and she began to feel him. Slowly, at first, and then with gathering speed, he began to move. Catherine's mind began to take flight once again. To have him fit so perfectly inside her body. To feel his breaths so warm on her neck, in her ear. To hear his heart drumming so solidly in his chest. His thrusts were long and powerful, driving both of them to near madness. This was indeed rapture, she thought, as the bliss once again enveloped her.

Catherine held on. His shirt grew damp beneath her palm. She kissed his cheek, and tasted the sweat there.

Ever higher they rose, Catherine matching the driving beat of his body with her own, until once again, as ecstasy obliterated all thought within her, she felt his straining body go suddenly rigid, and she knew, somehow, that they soared in the same brilliant sky.

Moments later, as he placed his forehead against her cheek and softly kissed her own damp skin, Catherine felt the first flicker of hope brighten her spirit.

Perhaps marriage to John Stewart would not be so bad, after all.

Chapter 7

Standing motionless against the wall, Susan wished that she could cease breathing altogether. The two of them had no suspicion of her presence, and that was just the way she wanted to keep it. She was simply a lost soul, hidden and desperate amid the shadows of an ancient keep. And she would remain silent.

What she had come upon had shocked her; that was true enough. In fact, Susan's surprise had quickly turned to envy as her understanding of what she was witnessing became clear. Now, to see the two of them gathered so peacefully in each other's arms after the wild abandon of their lovemaking, made her all the more resentful of the two.

The mewing of a cat behind her, by the entrance to the circular stairwell at the end of the corridor, startled Susan. But it also attracted the attention of the Englishwoman. She watched as Catherine Percy lifted her head off John's shoulder and peered into the darkness. Susan stepped back farther into the shadows when she realized the other woman's eyes had detected her there.

Expecting a cry of alarm at the discovery, Susan was stunned when Catherine quickly pulled herself out of John's embrace. With only a murmur inaudible to Susan—and without so much as another glance in her direction—the Percy woman went around him, quickly disappearing inside her room.

Taking yet another step back toward the stairwell, Susan watched the look of disappointment steal over the earl's face as he stared at his wife's closed door.

Very well! she thought. Now perhaps you will know how I feel!

The bright sunlight poured in through the two windows of the earl's Great Chamber. Sitting behind a large work table, John Stewart dismissed his warrior before turning his attention to the three monks standing before him. Their gray robes were covered with the evidence of long, hard miles.

"And you claim to know my wife," he said abruptly.

The clerics glanced confusedly at each other before answering.

"Your wife? Perhaps there has been some misunderstanding, m'lord." The most heavyset of the three, Brother Bartholomew, appeared to speak for the other two. "We are here in search of Catherine Percy. And we were told that Balvenie Castle—"

"By whom?" Athol put in sharply. "Who told you the whereabouts of Catherine Percy?"

"She did herself, m'lord. Mistress Catherine told us she was coming here!" The man dabbed at his sweating upper lip with his filthy cuff. "As we told your men, m'lord, we are from Jervaulx Abbey, in Yorkshire. About the same time as Mistress Catherine and her sisters left the abbey, many of us fled, as well. We had word that the king's men were almost upon us. The king's Deputy Lieutenant had already looted an abbey to the south. We were next. We had no choice but to run, m'lord."

"So you left with Mistress Catherine and her sisters?"

"Aye, very nearly, m'lord. We have only our feet to carry us, though. We couldn't keep pace. But still she had insisted that we join her at Balvenie Castle.

With her hopes of opening a school—under your direction and close to Elgin Cathedral—she thought that the three of us could prove a great advantage."

Athol's expression clearly conveyed his doubt. "What do three English monks have that could possibly be of value to us here?"

Again, Bartholomew spoke for the others. "We have a long and traditional connection with the bishops at Elgin Cathedral. Why, I was myself a pupil of Sir Andrew Forman—bless his soul—when he was the Commendator of the Abbey of Cottingham in England. I also was privileged to have known Bishop Schaw and Sir Alexander Stewart, too. Aye, we were all greatly saddened to hear of his passing this summer."

"Is that so? And your connections to the Percys?"

"All three of us have served as tutors to Mistress Catherine and her sisters, m'lord. Of course, teaching those girls was something which we did out of respect to Lord Edmund Percy, their father . . . a great patron to our abbey. Naturally, the rest of our pupils at the abbey were the sons of our gentry."

Athol sat back in his chair. "No doubt a spoiled and undeserving throng of young jackals!"

"Ah . . . well . . ." The man obviously growing more nervous, again wiped his lip and then his brow with his sleeve.

"And what marvelous secrets do you three teach? That the Scots eat their young? That the heavens only smile on English soil?"

"Nay, m'lord!" Bartholomew gasped, as the others shook their heads in support.

"Nay, of course not. Well, out with it! I care naught that you can throw the names of the Elgin bishops at me! What are your special areas of expertise, and why should I allow you to stay here, living off of me and my people when I can use any priest from Elgin to do the same damned thing?"

The heavyset man began to nod at the man on his right. "Well, Brother Egbert here teaches elementary and advanced arithmetic, m'lord."

"This had better include map drawing if you wish to spend so much as a night on my land. By the devil, now that I think of it, there are two tutors at least that I know of at the cathedral quite proficient in arithmetic!"

Brother Bartholomew started to address his concern, but Athol raised a hand to silence and glanced fiercely at the pale, silent man half hiding behind his more corpulent companion.

"I was speaking to Brother Egbert," the earl snapped. "Can you not speak for yourself, monk?"

"Aye." The man nodded slowly. "I do teach map drawing also, m'lord. Though you'll have no need of me teaching that subject."

"Nay?"

"Nay, m'lord. Mistress Catherine is very proficient in the topic herself, and her hand's as steady as Vespucci's ever was."

"So you're telling me I won't be needing you?"

Brother Egbert nodded somberly.

"Probably none of you are worth my—"

Brother Bartholomew was quick to jump in again. "I, myself, teach geography, m'lord!"

"And I suppose you are one of those to mix fact and fiction, delving into astronomy and philosophy, while you're at it!"

The clergyman nodded cheerfully. "Aye! And Mistress Catherine complements my expertise, covering astrology and even navigation. She has always been an excellent student. At the abbey, she would often tutor those lads who would listen to a—"

"And is there any reason why Lady Catherine cannot teach anything you can teach?"

"Well, I . . . ah . . ." Brother Bartholomew's face turned a deep shade of red. "Nay, m'lord."

"I thought not." Athol turned to the tall, lanky man who had separated himself from the others, and now stood by one of the windows. "And what is it that you do? 'Twas Brother Paul, if my memory serves?"

The man nodded. "I teach Greek . . . and modern languages, as well."

Athol leaned on his elbows and stared blankly at the man. "Hardly important, wouldn't you say?"

"To a humanist's way of thinking, the languages are crucial, m'lord."

Brother Paul's gaze swung to the doorway, toward the woman who had just spoken the words.

John Stewart's eyes followed. He'd wanted to see her since long before sunrise, and now he let his eyes drink her in. She was so beautiful standing there, her furrowed brow clearly conveying the gravity with which she held this subject. But her deep blue dress, so prim and unassuming, could not hide from his mind's eye the perfection of her breasts or the silky skin of her long, firm thighs. As he gazed at her, his mind was flooded with other memories of last night.

Damn! She'd bewitched him! After returning to his chamber last night, all he'd been able to think about was Catherine Percy, and how her passion had—like the molten rock of the Vesuvian Mount—burst through that "old crone" façade the moment he'd touched her.

Scowling at the thought of the three interlopers in the chamber, Athol tore his eyes away from his wife and redirected his attention to the clerics. He wondered briefly how long she'd been there, listening to him question the monks. Again today, she'd refused to join him for the morning meal in the Great Hall, but at least now he knew she was aware of the events outside her chamber. And she had seen fit to leave her sanctuary to rescue her friends.

Her friends! She wasn't here to see him, but to protect these cowering English dogs. Feeling his anger begin to smolder at the thought, John Stewart turned his darkening gaze back on her. "I'm certain that our crofters' lads are all lying awake dreaming of a profession in the king's service abroad. But aside from them, would you explain to me what use something as difficult as Greek would be here in the Highlands?"

The monk named Paul opened his mouth to explain, but Athol's raised hand quickly silenced him.

"You had your chance. I directed this question to my wife."

"To read the Scriptures in their purer form!" She took a step into the room. "To enable us to clarify the corrupted Latin texts that have come down to us. To understand the ancient philosophers who have been lost to us for ages, and are now just beginning to be found in the Greek manuscripts. To help us study the ancient geography and the natural history and the mathematics as the ancients wrote it."

"But this is much more than one needs to learn at such an elementary level!"

She took another step, and he noticed the dark circles beneath her eyes. He wondered if she'd been crying, or had simply suffered through the same restless night he himself had.

"But my plans, if you are willing to hear them at last, are not only to open an elementary, but a grammar school for older ones, as well. Between the tutors from Elgin Cathedral and the four of us, we can prepare many students—from your lands and from those nearby—for higher education, perhaps even for the university, if you wish it."

"And are you so naive that you actually believe

many of my people or even those of the neighboring lairds will have such lofty goals? How many damned priests do you think the Highlands can hold?"

"Clearly, it could use a few more, m'lord, but that's beside the point. I might be lacking in knowledge of your people, but I'm not a simpleton. What we can offer here does not limit a student to a life as a cleric. Those days are passing, m'lord. A well-rounded education here would deepen one's understanding of life."

Athol stifled his urge to laugh, and forced himself to frown into her openly challenging expression. Her intelligence might be a wee bit deficient, but the weariness in her face had now evaporated, and he could not help but think how stunningly beautiful she was in daylight. The midnight-blue eyes that he'd considered engaging by candlelight, now had become irresistible. But for a court-educated Englishwoman, her ideas about fashion in both dress and coiffure were decidedly old-fashioned.

Athol shook off the thought and turned abruptly to the three clerics, who were staring hopefully at his wife. "Out, you three!"

Catherine was quick to come to their rescue. "Do they have your permission to remain here at Balvenie Castle?"

"That depends." He looked suggestively in her direction, which in turn brought immediate color to the flawless ivory of her cheek. "Aye, that depends on how well you and I can negotiate our differences over this potential school."

John Stewart knew he was being a villain, but he had every intention of using this school to conquer his new wife's resistance to him. Starving her out of her chamber had worked better than he'd expected, but he was far from through. And looking at the rebellion blazing now in the blue of her eyes, Athol could see that she was not yet ready to give up the battle.

However Catherine wanted to play this, he was willing to accommodate her and eager to begin. The quick tumble in the corridor last night—as momentous as it might have been to her—had only served to whet his appetite.

He was now ready for full engagement.

Chapter 8

With a startling speed, the black cat's claw tore at the flesh of the outstretched hand. The Deputy Lieutenant roared in anger as he brought the bleeding flesh to his mouth.

"The devil take them! Where did this fiend came from?"

The cloaked figure moved confidently to the hay pile and picked up the perched cat by the scuff of the neck. Lifting it up until they were face to face, he boldly stared into the animal's eyes. With a loud hiss, the cat twisted and tried to free itself of the man's grip.

" 'Tis a new mother!" He threw the animal on the dirt floor of the stable.

"I don't see it!" The Deputy Lieutenant, nursing his injured hand, used his other to pull at the bundles of straw against the wall. "I'm starting to think this was all a bloody lie . . . just a tactic by them to buy themselves some time. That blasted map was nothing more than a hoax. Here we've combed two counties and searched five abbeys, just to finally find ourselves in a crumbling old barn with a she-devil of a cat. We look like dolts, I tell you. They've played us for fools."

" 'Tis here!"

"Bloody hell, I say! Where is the cursed thing?"

The cloaked man waded farther into the straw, then knelt and reached into a hole in the floor. An instant later, he withdrew his hand with round balls of mewling black fur. "Kittens!"

"Damn you! Are you telling me that this is another one of these women's pranks? Kittens instead of the treasure we've been tearing up the countryside looking f—"

"Here. I knew it would be here."

Laying the kittens back in the straw, the cloaked man pulled a leather package out of the hole.

"We have another map!" he said, drawing out a rolled parchment.

Catherine hadn't expected to be totally left alone with him.

Glancing over her shoulder as the door of the outer chamber was closed behind the last departing monk, she tried to gather her courage before turning and facing her husband.

It had been a long and difficult night, lying there numb and isolated in her small bed. Her mind had continually drifted back to the image of Susan standing in the darkness of the corridor. Surprisingly, the shame of being caught had not been so much the tormenting factor as the knowledge that, by giving herself so freely to Athol, she had completely broken another woman's heart. It was obvious Susan MacIntyre was still in love with John Stewart. What else would drive a woman to take shelter in the darkness?

Later, when she'd been able to push past her guilt over Susan's future, the thoughts of her own weakness had driven her to tears. What she had felt in his embrace had been incredible, but how could it be that she had been so willing? How could she have allowed herself to be so easily seduced? Her life would never be the same now; she knew that.

A marriage was consummated. She was now his wife and beyond all hope of annulment. And as much as she had wanted to turn her back and flee Balvenie Castle, the possibility that she might already be carrying Athol's child made such an escape unthinkable.

By the break of dawn, Catherine had finally cried herself to sleep, convinced that she was ruined forever. But by midday, Jean had brought up the news of the three monks' arrival at the castle. Then Catherine's spirits had begun to rise. And as she had been getting herself ready to come down here, she found that she'd even given herself the permission to hope.

Catherine turned finally to the man sitting behind the desk. He was sitting back, his arms resting on the sides of his chair, his leather booted legs stretched out before him. And he was eyeing her with an expression she could not quite identify.

Perhaps, she thought, they could look past what had occurred. Quite possibly, now that the deed was done and they'd consummated their marriage, Athol would allow her to open the school and pursue her original plans. As for her own behavior, now that she'd, well, tasted the forbidden fruits of passion, she'd be able to put behind her the fanciful thoughts she'd entertained for so long. In fact, now that she was thinking of it, perhaps John Stewart was not as incredibly handsome as she remembered him to be. After all, the wine last night had certainly been the true cause of her weakness.

Catherine gazed at her husband and knew that her last thought was, of course, total nonsense. Dressed in a brilliant white shirt beneath his tartan, Athol still was the handsomest man she'd ever encountered in her life. But so be it, she thought. She was down here to discuss the school. Nothing would distract her.

"Shall I have some food brought up for you?"

She watched him push back his chair. "Nay, m'lord. I had enough last night to keep me for quite a while."

"It pains me to hear that."

"Nonetheless, m'lord, I'd just assume we begin talking about the school. Now that my old tutors have arrived, it might be an excellent time for me to continue on to Elgin Cathedral. Jean tells me 'tis only a day's ride, and—"

"Did I hurt you last night?"

"Nay." Her answer was quick, escaping her lips almost as a surprised whisper. But she couldn't stop the heat from spreading into her face. "M'lord, about the school—it will also be helpful if you would advise us on what building we could utilize for . . ."

"Why have you been crying?"

"I . . . I haven't been!" Nervously wrapping her arms around her waist, Catherine watched him slowly come to his feet. "Do you think it would be best if we were to find a place by the cathedral in Elgin, or do you think—"

"You do not lie well, Cat!"

Unconsciously, she backed up a step as he came around his desk. Her heart was now drumming loudly in her chest. "Perhaps, going back and forth to Elgin would make things too difficult. But still, if there is an abbey, perhaps, nearby, I . . ." Her words trailed off as he closed the distance between them.

"Why did you leave me so abruptly, last night?"

"I . . ." He stopped a half step away, and drew one of her hands from her waist. Her eyes darted in every direction, avoiding his face. "Perhaps . . . the neighboring lairds . . ."

"I was concerned about you, Cat."

"Were you?" she whispered, immediately angry with herself for even responding.

"Aye. I was."

Her breath caught in her chest as his hand lifted her chin and he looked into her eyes. Catherine found herself struggling weakly against what she knew would come next. His head bent slowly, and he sipped her lips.

She would die, Catherine thought, if she couldn't wrap her arms around his broad back and draw him closer. Clenching her hands into tight fists, though, she held back. He had too much control over her. Too much of John Stewart and, Catherine knew, she would be forfeiting all her dreams.

He pulled back slightly and looked into her face. "Where is my passionate Cat? What have you done with my fiery wife?"

She burned with heat as he traced her cheek softly with his thumb. "I . . . I thought that since we've already done what . . ."

"You thought, since we've made love once in a corridor . . ." He paused, waiting.

She nodded. "I thought your interest . . . in this . . . in me . . . I . . ."

"You thought wrong, Cat."

As his arms began to slide around her, panic quickly exploded in Catherine's brain. She pressed her hands against his chest, and separated herself from him. "I . . . I'm down here . . . to talk of the school."

"Fine! We'll talk of the school," he answered calmly. "But only after you kiss your husband." He reached for her again.

She pulled back and looked incredulously into his face. "A kiss? You'll let me present my case about the school after a *kiss*?"

He nodded innocently. She knew she would be a complete fool to believe him, so she didn't. Still, seeing no harm in the act, she quickly raised herself to her toes and placed a quick peck on his lips.

"Now about the school . . ."

"That was no kiss, lass," he growled.

"Now, why am I not surprised that you said that?"

"Just stating a fact. That was no kiss!"

He was making fun of her; she could see the amusement lurking in the corners of his eyes. "This has to be the oldest and most childish method anyone could use to lure a woman into his arms."

He placed his hands on her shoulders, bent his head, and looked directly into her eyes. "Aye! But do you have a better suggestion? Perhaps you'll be teaching improved methods in that school of yours. But before we can get to that, I still want you to kiss me."

Again, having him so close, Catherine felt herself melting inside. "But . . . why . . . why would you want a . . . a kiss?"

He smiled into her face, and she felt her heart beating louder than the thunder of any summer storm.

"Do you realize, you forget your words whenever I am near?"

" 'Tis . . . not true." Liar, she thought, taking a step back and coming to a halt against the door.

"Liar!" he whispered, closing the distance between them.

By the Virgin, what was she to do? Placing his palms against the door on either side of her head, he trapped her. Turning her eyes upward, she met his smoldering gaze.

"One kiss?"

He nodded. "One kiss to set the skies on fire . . . and then we talk about the school."

Suddenly, the humor of the situation struck her, lightening her mood. In all of her life, she had only twice kissed a man, and on both occasions, John Stewart had been the recipient. The thought that he was talking to her now as if she were some type of expert was truly amusing.

"Very well. If you are not willing to do what I ask"—his hands dropped onto her shoulders—"then I can find other uses of my time."

She held her breath as his fingers slid over the soft

wool of her dress and brushed lightly over her breasts. Without another thought, Catherine stood on tiptoe and closed her mouth tightly over his. As his tongue rubbed against hers, she knew that a simple kiss would never satiate their unquenchable desires.

His hands, moving as if drawn to each sensitive part of her, roamed her body—touching her, feeling her, caressing her through the dress that felt now like the finest gossamer. She moaned softly, running her fingers through his hair, drawing him closer.

"This time, Cat, I take you to my bed." He lowered his lips to her throat.

"Nay!" She shook her head, but she didn't fight him as he raised her hands above her head, holding her wrists with one hand and mouthing her breasts through the dress. "We . . . we can't. Not until you honor your word and first hear . . . about the school."

With his other hand, he brought her body hard against his hips. "If not the bed, then my desk . . . or the chair . . . will have to do. Some things cannot be put off, Cat."

Indeed, they can't, she thought, feeling the pulsing heat course through her. Catherine already felt herself shivering with the thought of having him inside her again.

"Aye," she whispered. "But—"

The sharp knocking on the door left her scurrying out of his arms. Slipping around him, she tried to pull out of his grasp, but Athol held her wrist firmly, keeping her within arm's reach.

"M'lord!"

The knocks became pounding of a fist on oak, and Catherine used her free hand to tuck the loose tendrils of her hair behind an ear. Athol's eyes, still riveted on her, scorched her with his desire.

"M'lord!" Catherine recognized the voice. It was the scar-faced warrior Jean called Tosh.

"What is it?" Athol released her and angrily yanked open the door.

"That wolf, Adam o' the Glen, is a-hunting again, m'lord. Some of the farmers have spotted some of his pack to the south, where the trail leads up out of Glen Rinnes o'er Corryhabbie Hill."

Without so much as a glance backward, John Stewart strode from the chamber. Catherine listened with great concern and confusion as her husband's shouts rang out to the men who had gathered in the Great Hall. Running to the window overlooking the bustling courtyard, she peered out as Athol and his men stormed out of the keep and onto the waiting horses.

Even from this distance, Catherine had a clear gauge of his anger. And it was frightening to know that what she saw was a perfect match of the earl's temperament that first night—when he'd discovered his future wife in the arms of another.

This Adam of the Glen must offer a real danger to her husband's people. Well, whoever this Adam was, Catherine thought, she wouldn't want to be the man when Athol got a hold of him.

Starting for the door, Catherine decided that there were too many unanswered questions about the affairs of her husband. Nay, the idea of reentering the seclusion of her small chamber was quickly losing its appeal.

Hurriedly climbing up the circular stairs, Catherine knew exactly what she wanted.

The truth about John Stewart. A glimpse of the man's soul. Some explanation why—for the life of her—she could not resist him. That was what she needed.

And what better source for all of this than the dowager herself.

Chapter 9

The open fire cast its glow against the line of rocks, stretching Adam of the Glen's shadow to monstrous proportions. Scowling into the darkness, the brigand chief was beginning to wear a path before the men cowering on the far side of the fire.

"And you tell me, two mounts this fine were simply turned loose and left to wander down the path into Glen Rinnes—with no one watching?" Adam's cold gray eyes focused on Robyn. "You do not suppose the beasts were carrying an invitation to a hanging at Balvenie Castle."

The burly outlaw shrugged. "It all fell out just as we told ye, master. The animals were just trotting about, as free as can be. Granted, the two were very thirsty and ye can see, they're both worn out with wherever they've come from. But there was no one tending them." The man turned to the rest of the group, and they all nodded in agreement. "We searched high and low, master, thinking there must be a good pocketful of coins to go with the animals, but there wasn't a soul that we could see."

Adam restlessly kicked a branch into the fire. "Is that when you were chased by Athol's men?"

A man, slouched against a boulder on the outskirts of the group, now spoke up. His pockmarked cheek carried the brand of a thief, and his eyes never looked straight at Adam.

"Nay, master. 'Twas Ren and me that drew 'em off. Some of the farmers were a wee bit shy about letting us take the sheep. But we had 'em off and away up into the hills before the laird's men appeared. They were mightily loath to leave their horses behind."

"Good thing for them, too, master," Robyn growled with a deep, mirthless chuckle. "For we'd have ta'en the whole lot of 'em if they'd followed Jock and Ren up into the hills."

Adam came to a stop before the fire. "Did he come after you himself—or is the vile creature still too smitten with the new bride to leave her side?"

"Nay, master. He was there quick enough. But we hid in our usual place and watched him and his men rush by, ne'er the wiser. No woman was holding *him* back, though, so far as we could see!"

Adam turned abruptly to Sykes, a red-haired, freckled lad crouching before the fire. "And about this new bride, lad! I want you to trick her out of that keep, d'ye understand? Whatever it takes to pull it off, Roy, bring her to us."

The boy's hands started to rub nervously across his knees. " 'Twill nae be a simple task, master. She doesn't even leave her own room long enough for a body to cast an eye on her. 'Twill take a bit of magic, I'm thinking, to trick her into the open."

Adam's movement was quick. The sound of the sword ripped from the sheath had not even penetrated the men's brains before the sight of the blade arcing through the night air flashed before them. Dropping to one knee as he turned, the brigand chief cleaved the fire in two, the explosion of sparks showering even the men sitting farthest from the center. Leaving his blade in the very center of the embers for a moment, Adam did not move until the outlaws quieted.

Then, raising the smoking steel high in the air, he turned and faced them.

"On this blade I swear to you all that I will deal with the devil if need be. My sole purpose in this miserable life is to make life hell for the villain who is laird of these lands." His fiery eyes swept over the faces of his men. "We've been attacking his farms—burning his barns—scaring his people half to death. But none of this will hurt him as much as the day we take his new wife."

Moving around the fire, Adam held his sword out over the heads of his followers. He stopped before the red-haired boy.

"Whatever ruse is needed, Roy Sykes, you use it. But bring the woman into the open. We'll be waiting, and then I'll truly teach John Stewart the meaning of vengeance."

Catherine accepted the blanket from Jean as she stepped out of the small wooden tub. Sitting on the small stool by the fire, she wrapped her shivering body inside the cocoonlike warmth and let Jean fuss over her dripping black ringlets.

"You have the most beautiful hair, mistress. If you'd allow me . . ."

Catherine just nodded vaguely, her mind intent on the activities of the afternoon and the time she'd spent in Lady Anne's sick chamber. The older woman had been nothing if not direct in her greeting.

When she'd entered the airless bedchamber, Catherine had exchanged a quick glance with Susan, who averted her eyes immediately, giving Catherine no hint of what the poor woman was going through. Since it was clear that Susan and the two waiting women were not going to leave the chamber until the dowager dismissed them, Catherine had approached the heavily curtained bed. Auld Mab was standing over the dowager and watching Catherine intently.

Without even a moment's pause, Lady Anne had

simply opened her gray eyes and asked if Catherine and the earl had consummated their vows yet.

Mortified, Catherine had stared for a moment. Though Susan and the two waiting women were absolutely silent, she could feel their eyes riveted to her back. Auld Mab's wrinkled face had threatened to crease into a smile, but the old woman fought it back.

What answer could she give? Catherine wondered. That the earl of Athol had indeed charmed her out of her virginity? That she'd been so eager for him that they'd never even made it to a marriage bed? That they'd made love in a corridor with Susan looking on?

Instead, Catherine had bowed her head in embarrassment, and the dowager had immediately sent Auld Mab, Susan, and the others out of the room.

Apparently, her open discomfort before had been answer enough for the older woman, though it occurred to Catherine that perhaps Susan had already told her, and Lady Anne was just seeking confirmation. Whatever the reason, the dowager had not repeated her question once they'd been left to themselves.

"I'll be back in a wink, mistress," Jean said, and Catherine absentmindedly watched the serving woman go out the door, only to return a moment later with something draped over her arm.

Drifting back to her thoughts of the afternoon's encounter, Catherine considered again what she'd learned about her husband from his mother.

First of all, she'd been surprised to learn that John Stewart was a university educated man. His accomplishments were many, and his mother had been more than happy to share what she knew of his exploits serving the Scottish kings at Flodden Field and later quelling unrest here in the Highlands. But for the most part, Lady Anne had dwelt on Athol's interest in his own people, and on his interest in education. He'd spent a number of years in his youth studying the classical writers in France.

The devil take the man, Catherine thought for the hundredth time, for giving her such a difficult time of it before the three monks, when he himself was apparently an advocate of the same things that they all believed in. Why, according to his mother, the man even read Greek! But then, Catherine decided as she thought of it, there had to be a reason for her own mother to pick Balvenie Castle as the destination for her travels.

Still lost in thought, Catherine was only vaguely aware of Jean unwrapping the blanket from around her and pulling the chemise over her head.

The information and the stories of John's childhood had been quite entertaining, and Catherine had been delighted to see the dowager become quite animated, brightening visibly as she spoke. Even now, though, as she recalled the talk, Catherine could feel the odd tug of jealousy in her breast at Lady Anne's references to a Joanna MacInnes of Ironcross Castle. The dowager had hinted that there had been some trouble regarding the two, but the older woman had been quick to add that the young woman was now Joanna Kerr, so all of that was now just "water down the brae."

Back in her own chamber, Jean had informed her that the reason why John Stewart had not wed years earlier was because of presumed arrangements which he'd had for the hand of Joanna MacInnes. Hard as it was for *her* to understand, Jean told her, Joanna had picked a Lowlander for a husband, and the earl had been left with no wife or bairns at all. Until now, of course!

She rose to her feet as Jean pushed a dress over her head.

Catherine could only guess at her husband's pain. For a man with his looks and position in life to wait this long to choose a wife, he must have clung for years to his love of this Joanna MacInnes.

Standing still as Jean continued to tighten the laces of the dress on her back, Catherine frowned into the fire as she recalled the end of her talk with the dowager.

Lady Anne's agreeable expression had quickly turned to a sneer when Catherine mentioned the name of Adam of the Glen. No matter what she'd asked, or how insistent she'd been to learn the reasons for her husband's actions at the news of the man, the dowager had simply refused to answer, demanding that Catherine not be meddling in business that was none of her concern.

That had been end of their discussion. As abrupt as the dowager had been in receiving her earlier, she'd been just as abrupt in dismissing her.

At Jean's soft command, Catherine sat down again on the stool and watched absentmindedly as the other woman slipped a pair of soft leather shoes onto her feet.

Tonight—she'd decided upon returning to her chamber—she was going down to the Great Hall to join in taking a meal with the rest of the household. Having learned that her husband had returned, Catherine knew that dinner might offer just the right opportunity to get answers to at least some of her questions.

If there was one thing that she was certain of now, Catherine knew that she had reached a point of no return in this marriage. Though she'd long ago given up her dreams of marriage, she had never thought that life would take her to this castle in the Highlands of Scotland. Her only salvation now lay in her ability to reform this roguish husband of hers. Some dreams she would not give up, and Athol would understand and agree to what she wanted to accomplish if it killed her.

But this meant she would have to first conquer her own weakness for the man. And to do this, she'd sought the help of Jean.

"Up you go, m'lady."

Catherine gazed with curiosity at the serving lass's pleased expression. "What's the matter?"

"I'd say the matter is, one look at you and the laird will be the one forgetting his words . . . and his head, too, for that matter."

Looking down at herself, Catherine immediately covered the exposed skin of her neck and chest with her hands. "Jean!"

"Nay, do not be doing that now, d'ye hear me?"

Catherine reluctantly let Jean pry her hands off the low, square neckline of the dress. "But . . . you can see so much . . . and the dress . . . is so white but for the golden threads . . ."

She stared down at the beautifully gold-embroidered dress that flared out below the waist, showing the even more elaborately embroidered underskirt.

"Aye. It looks wonderful with that bonny, raven hair of yours. And all that creamy skin spilling over like that . . . I'm telling ye, mistress, ye will have your school and everything else ye wish from the earl . . . all ye'll need do is be asking him."

"Still"—Catherine shook her head—"I know I said I wanted to look less severe, perhaps even . . . pleasing to the eye . . . but now I feel like a—a—"

"A wench?" The serving woman frowned deeply and straightened the bell-shaped sleeves of Catherine's dress. "Nay, mistress. I know of no wenches wearing white and gold such as this! Ye look like an angel, like an innocent dressed in her wedding dress. And from what I heard from some of the men, ye were a wee bit less than ladylike, wearing that Hume rascal's tartan and lashing priest and laird alike with that tongue of yours—not that anyone would be blaming ye!"

As Catherine opened her mouth to argue, Jean lifted a folded tartan from the bed and shook it open. Carefully, she draped Stewart of Athol's plaid over one shoulder.

"Well, I didn't really think ye'll be needing this on such a lovely evening. But then, we can't be standing around and arguing all night, as I know the master's already gone into the Great Hall to meet the guests."

"Oh?"

"Aye, and it would be best for all concerned if ye were to join him while the rest of the company's still sober."

Catherine nodded, happily running her fingers over the soft wool of the tartan. As she turned toward the door, she paused and pushed her thick, loose hair back over her shoulder.

"Now, are you certain I do not need to braid this?"

Jean shook her head firmly and lit a taper at the fire. "Be on your way, mistress. And hurry, before I change my mind and take that tartan away."

With a smile of appreciation, Catherine let herself be gently prodded into the corridor.

"Now, as ye requested," Jean said, closing the door behind them, "we've not told the laird ye are coming. Though some of the crofters and the master's council have been coming each day since word spread, ye must remember most of those down there will not make a move to accept ye until he has introduced ye as his own . . . as the new Countess Balvenie. So when ye get to the Hall, do not be shy. Ye must simply go and take your place beside him."

Nervously, Catherine pulled the tartan higher on her chest.

"Nay, mistress, do not be doing that." Jean stopped her and rearranged the tartan. There was far too much skin showing there, from Catherine's perspective, but she didn't fight the serving woman. "All will work out, mistress. Trust me! All will come about just as ye wish!"

Catherine nodded as they turned down the corridor again. But after taking a couple of steps, she came to a halt and stopped Jean with a hand on her arm.

"This dress! Where did this dress come from?"

The woman's mouth turned up mischievously. "We plundered Ellen Crawford's trunks. The master had paid for trunks of clothing to be made and sent up from Stirling."

"But—"

"Lady Anne directed that they be left in the stables." The woman shrugged her shoulders. "We thought, ye get the husband, 'tis only fitting ye get the clothes, as well."

"But, I can't—"

"Ye'd better hurry, mistress. At this pace, dinner will be over before ye get there, and I cannot swear that those blackguards down there will be fit company for ye for too much longer. And ye'll soon see, mistress, the laird is his most agreeable during his dinner."

Not the most, Catherine thought with a shy smile as they continued on. There were a few moments right in this corridor last night when John Stewart had been quite agreeable.

Athol laughed heartily as he picked up the pitcher and filled Susan's cup with more wine. Since returning to Balvenie, this was the first chance he'd had to hear about her trip to nearby Ironcross Castle a fortnight earlier.

"This is priceless news, Susan, to be sure. But tell me, what did Joanna do when her husband dropped like a stone to the floor?"

"M'lord, she started crying out to the midwife to forget about the birthing and see to him, instead. I had to see to him myself while she gave birth to the second bairn."

"Twin girls!" Athol shook his head in disbelief, enjoying the warm feeling the news had given him. Looking back at Susan, he placed an affectionate hand on her shoulder. "I am glad you were there, lass. With the two elder boys being the scamps that they are, Joanna must have been relieved to have you beside her . . . especially considering her own husband was of no use."

"Oh, he did come around soon enough, m'lord. And as soon as he had his hands on those bairns, there was no moving him from the mother's side." Susan glanced back at the trencher of food before her. "The good health of the twin newborns even had Joanna's grandmother, Lady MacInnes, showing better spirits than she's been in, of late. I only stayed until Mistress Joanna was up and about, for I wished to come back here to be by Lady Anne's side. Before I left, though, both the laird and his wife insisted on you coming to Ironcross to visit them as soon as you're able."

Smiling at the thought, Athol took a sip of his wine. Actually, that wouldn't be a bad idea, he thought. As agreeable as Catherine was turning out to be, it might actually be a pleasure to take her to Ironcross Castle and introduce her to Gavin and Joanna.

He smiled again at the thought of the meeting. After all, they would be expecting Ellen Crawford. It might be very interesting to see what those two would say, being introduced to his prim and proper-looking wife.

Och! Knowing them, they'd probably see it as a hopeful sign, that perhaps he was not beyond saving, after all! By the devil, that would take a bit of the fun out of it!

*   *   *

Nobody so much as turned a head in welcome!

Standing in the shadows beside the large doorway into the Great Hall, Catherine glanced somewhat wistfully at the merry groups of people crowding the long tables. The huge fire behind the dais was crackling, throwing a golden light over the room. Clumps of laughing men and women, all dependents of the laird apparently, gathered in the center of the room, as well, enjoying the evening. Dogs and children alike were roving about, stealing food where they could and running beneath the trestle tables. Unlike her first glimpse of the Hall on the day she'd arrived, the place was now alive with conversation and good-humored activity. Letting her eyes travel from one table to the next, Catherine was amazed by all the faces, still new to her.

In the far corner of the Hall, though, Catherine spotted the three monks from Jervaulx Abbey sitting among the castle folks of Balvenie. It warmed her heart to know that, though Athol had not given his final consent regarding the school, he'd still allowed them to stay. Perhaps, at least, she could interpret this as meaning that he was considering the request with favor.

A throng of warriors milled about in front of the dais, and Catherine stood on tiptoe to see her husband. Deep in her heart, she could feel that something was changing in her attitude toward the man. A feeling she had no desire to name was joining the physical attraction she had no inclination to admit.

The group of warriors moved off toward a table, and as Catherine's eyes caught sight of him seated in the great carved chair, she felt as though her throat were being squeezed shut.

John Stewart's hand lay on Susan's shoulder. A hearty laugh she'd never have thought him capable of rolled across the floor to her. Standing alone by the door, Catherine suddenly felt more alone and unwelcome than she'd ever felt in her life.

Unable to move, she stared at the two. Susan, dressed in an embroidered gown of deep green, appeared to be in total bliss. As she continued to speak to the earl, the young woman paused only to reach for her wine, turning and smiling coyly at the Highlander over the rim of her cup.

For the first time in her life, Catherine found herself entertaining the idea of tearing another woman's eyes out.

Forcibly quelling such a reaction, Catherine took a step farther into the shadows. It wasn't his actions that had her dashing away the odd tear, so much as her own response to what she'd witnessed. There was certainly nothing surprising in what he was doing. She was a fool to forget his warnings so soon. John Stewart had cautioned her not to be lulled into any dreamy notions of love. He'd said so quite clearly—in word *and* action. How openly he'd reminded her that a woman such as herself would never be his first choice for a wife. He was only looking for an heir and nothing more!

And after what had happened last night, perhaps that desire had been fulfilled already.

Catherine brought a hand to her mouth. Her lips were trembling. A few short moments of passion in a deserted corridor, and she'd thought his heart might have warmed to her? Whispering under her breath, she cursed herself for being so weak.

Though she threw one last look in his direction, she couldn't see him clearly because of the tears burning her eyes. Turning abruptly toward the door, Catherine quietly made her way out of the Hall. She'd been so much better off when she'd contained her fantasies to her dreams. For all those encounters she'd had with her knight, he'd never once hurt her the way she was hurting now. She'd never once felt the pain of white-hot metal piercing her chest as it was burning her insides now. She'd never before felt the agonizing venom that was now spreading through her veins.

Blinded by her tears, she started into the darkened stairwell. By now, Jean was no doubt finding something to eat in the kitchens, and Catherine would be glad for the solitude. She needed to get away from the crowd to sort out her feelings. Most important, she needed the time to rebuild the wall of dreams behind which she'd been able to hide for her entire life.

Her foot had not yet left the lowest step when the strong hands grabbed her from behind. Catherine never even had a chance to cry out before she felt herself being lifted by the waist and turned in the air before being lowered gently to earth—face to face with her husband.

Perhaps it was from fear, or perhaps from the shock of having found herself in his arms in the dark landing. Whatever it was, Catherine found herself staring into his piercing gray eyes, unable to breathe.

"So you've decided, Catherine Percy, to join me, at last. And are you prepared to let your people bend their knees to their countess?"

Chapter 10

Seeing her now, the embodiment of softness and emotion, of beauty and passion, John wondered how he had not before seen this in the woman. She was more like some ethereal creature, and he felt his loins stir with desire for her. He stared at her, waiting for an answer, but also trying to drink his fill of the sight before him. As if he ever could.

"Nay! I am prepared for no such thing!"

He laughed, eliciting a look of obvious shock from his bride. Taking her by the hand, he dragged her off the step into the landing and backed her against the stone wall.

"You must be out of your mind!" She tried to fight off his hold by using her fists and punching him in the chest. "I told you I won't do what you ask of me. I said—"

Ignoring her blows, he leaned down and placed a firm kiss on her stubborn mouth. She struggled for only a moment before melting into his arms. As he deepened the kiss, ravaging her willing mouth, he realized that he must be out of his mind. Certainly, Catherine Percy had a way of driving him mad. The way she fought him and then turned into a purring cat in his embrace, drove all reason from his brain, all sense of discipline from his will. In a way, his body's response to this stranger that he'd taken as a wife shook him a bit. But fear was not the sensation he was feeling now.

He pulled back slightly and looked down at her closed eyes, at her full, parted lips, at the dark, silken mass of hair that had run through his fingers when he'd planted her against the wall. By the Virgin, she was beautiful!

She slowly opened her eyes and met his gaze, her blue eyes misty with emotion. John Stewart was enslaved.

"I . . . I came . . . down here . . ."

"I know. To join me for supper!"

She nodded. Without stepping back, John started combing his fingers through her thick waves of ebony, enjoying the feel of them tumbling over his hand.

"You look beautiful like this."

A deep blush crept up from her neck into her cheeks, but then, before the color could fade, a flash of fire lit her eyes. "I was—I was in the Hall."

"I know! How could I have missed the daggers you hurled in my direction on your way out."

"If only . . . if only a few of them had found their mark!"

"Och, but they did, Countess! Can't you see what a bloody mess you've left me? I have more wounds than Süleyman has wives!"

She stared at him for a moment, and then smiled. When she did, John Stewart forgot how to breathe.

"Very well. I have changed my—my mind." She placed her open palm against his chest, and he took a half step back. Behind them, strains of music wafted out from the Hall. The traveling minstrel and his apprentice. "If you'll have me, I believe I *will* join you for supper . . . in the Hall."

He only nodded, for he didn't trust his voice to say the words. As he held out his hand to her, his eyes swept over the tartan she was wearing across the bodice of her dress. Seeing his own colors on her only intensified the feelings that were coursing through him. The plaid on her looked right to him. Very right.

"We had intended . . . well, to talk about the school earlier." She placed her hand in his as he led her toward the doors of the Hall. "On matters as important as this, I've found—"

As the two stepped into the Great Hall, they moved out of earshot of the red-haired stable lad, Roy Sykes, who descended from the upper landing and emerged from the darkness of the stairwell. He'd almost had her.

Cursing his luck, he stared after them.

The Great Hall became as silent as a tomb, voices and music stopping with an abruptness that filled Catherine with the sensation of being plunged underwater.

She almost wished she were deaf, so that she wouldn't know the awful absence of sound suddenly lost. She almost wished she were blind, so she wouldn't be so shaken by the sight of those in the crowd rising singly, and then in groups in response to their presence. She almost wished she were not a woman, so that she would not be so overwhelmed with feeling by the sudden outburst of their shouts and cheers.

She hadn't given much thought to the ramifications of walking inside that Hall on her husband's arm while wearing his tartan. But now, her folly would be sure to come back and haunt her, for there was no possible way of hiding the surprising array of emotions that were exploding within her. But that, in itself, appeared to please these men and women . . . and to please her husband even more.

Having been led to a space in front of the large dais, Catherine held tight to her husband's hand as he introduced her to the gathered clan as the new countess of Athol. But the raucous shouts of endorsement did nothing to prepare her for the roar of approval that followed when John Stewart, earl of Athol, swept her into his arms and kissed her passionately before the entire assembly.

Once back on her own feet, Catherine gave him a scowling glare, and as the minstrels struck up their music again, she leaned closer to him and whispered her complaint. "You are a rogue, John Stewart. That was particularly inappropriate."

"True, Cat. But I believe we crossed all boundaries of decorum the moment I climbed into your bed that first night at my hunting lodge."

"That was an innocent . . . well, understandable blunder on your part—and you know it." Catherine eyed the line of warriors forming down the middle of the Hall.

"But last night was not."

She turned just in time to catch sight of his wolfish grin.

"Now do not tell me you've already forgotten making love in the window seat in the gallery outside your chamber door?"

"Nay! Of course, I have not!" If only she could strike the arrogant boor. It certainly sounded as if he were gloating over what they'd done. "Last night was . . . well, a private thing. We weren't performing before a crowd . . . as you've just done!"

"You wouldn't say that if you knew the rumors floating about this keep. The last one I heard had to do with you—"

"Nay. Stop your wagging tongue!"

". . . With you, stripped down to bare skin, demanding that I make love to you atop the southwest tower."

She could feel the heat ready to set her cheeks aflame. Determined to give him no satisfaction, she stared out beyond the line of warriors at the friendly faces of the crofters and serving folk.

"And then there was the one, about the stable hands hearing your moans of—"

Whirling, Catherine kicked Athol on his booted shin, but gained nothing for her trouble beyond a devilish grin from him . . . and the loudest hoots of approval yet from those in the Great Hall.

After nodding graciously to her audience, Catherine turned her gaze on her husband and gave him her most innocent smile. "If you have finished this senseless blabbering," she whispered, "I believe your men are ready to take a turn."

"A turn?"

"Aye, are they not anxious to kiss the bride?" She loved the way his handsome face darkened immediately into a frown. "I see all of them have politely formed a line. I'm delighted to know that such a dear, English custom is also—"

"You are now in the Highlands." She tried to hide her pleased smile as Athol pulled her tightly to his side.

"Aye, as lovely and wild a place as ever God created. But still, John, considering all the raillery you are sure to take—"

"No man kisses you but me." She felt his fingers take hold of her chin. "No one but your husband. Understand?"

"Then you agree to stop your chattering when I tell you so?"

"Nay, I was only teasing you."

"Well, husband, so was I!"

For a moment his gray eyes locked on her own before she saw a smile break across his lips. He shook his head, and the firelight danced in his long, red hair.

"You turn into a fairy creature before a crowd, I see. Sharp-tongued and quick-witted as a pixie. I shall have to remember to keep you locked up inside my chamber, lass. At least there, left alone with me, you forget your words."

Left alone with him! She repeated the words in her head. Watching his eyes drop languidly to her lips and then even lower, Catherine felt the heat again rush into her face. The thought of being totally alone with him was absolutely enticing. Her eyes fixed involuntarily on his mouth.

She thought she heard a sound come from deep in his throat, but he quickly turned away from her and faced his people. At the nod of Athol's head, the music stopped and Catherine watched the first man—the warrior called Tosh—approach and drop to one knee. Once again faced with such an open display of acceptance and loyalty, she felt the tears starting to well up in her eyes.

As if this were their wedding day—as if they were all standing on the church steps—one by one, the Stewarts of Athol and those who lived under the earl's protection approached their laird and his lady. One by one, the Stewart knights and fighters knelt before Catherine and pledged their lives and their service to her.

The solemnity of their vows, added to the emotionally charged silence of the Hall, wrought unexpected feelings in Catherine. To think that for days, in the absence caused by her stubborn indifference to her husband's invitations, she had snubbed these good people! And yet here they were, welcoming her as their countess of their own free will, with no encouragement!

Running a quick hand across her damp cheeks, Catherine nodded to the last warrior delivering his oath and allowed her husband to lead her around the dais to her seat beside him.

"They approve of my choice."

Catherine glanced up hesitantly and, to her relief,

found the assembly returning to their tables. Once again strains of music filled the air.

"And would they have behaved any differently, if they had not?"

"Nay! I'd have drawn and quartered them where they stood."

She vainly waited for him to say more, but he turned and gestured to the gloomy-faced steward standing at the end of the dais. Something stung in Catherine's breast.

He could at least, she thought, make some sort of comment on the way she'd been received as opposed to the reception Ellen Crawford might have faced. But Athol appeared to have put the thought behind him, busying himself with the steward.

Silently chiding herself for being so fragile in her response to him, Catherine turned away from her husband, her eyes scanning the Hall for Susan. The young woman was nowhere to be found. Catherine turned her attention to the platter of food that was placed before her. She'd hoped she might find a friend in Susan. She realized now that she even hoped that the younger woman would help soothe some of the ache of being separated from her sisters.

But the way things were going, Catherine thought, they would be lucky if they didn't end up enemies. After all, as surprising as the whole situation was, John Stewart was now formally her husband, and he belonged to her.

Taking a small bite of her food, she glanced up and found Athol's gray eyes focused on her. Seeing the small furrow darkening his brow, she wondered if he had any idea that she was foolishly entertaining the notion of going to battle to preserve their farce of the marriage.

"I never imagined it would be this way." His face was serious, but she could see the smile in the corners of his eyes. "You're changing, Cat, and much faster than I would ever have hoped."

She almost choked on her food. Taking the cup, she sipped the wine and then looked into his face, which now clearly showed his amusement.

"I'm . . . ?" Catherine set down her cup. "What do you . . . ? Are you saying . . . ?"

"We're still very much in company, eldritch thing. There is no cause for you to forget your words."

"I was . . . not." She waved a hand at him. It was just too easy for him to fluster her. "I was just asking you to explain what you said, and then—"

"Catherine, I can read your mind."

She laughed at such absurdity. "Would you care to explain that, m'lord?"

"Laugh if you like. It matters naught if you believe me or not. But since I believe in fair play in single-handed combat, I thought you should be warned that I am armed with that formidable weapon."

The man spoke foolishness.

"To laugh off my words would be folly when you had not yet tested them!"

Catherine wrapped a hand around her goblet to gather her nerves. Had she spoken aloud her feelings?

"Nay, lass. You have not!" Athol sat back as she glanced sharply at him and smiled back at her. "There. I've warned you of the dangers you face. Now 'tis up to you to do whatever you think appropriate to arm yourself against me."

On impulse, she decided to humor him. "If what you say is the truth—if indeed you *can* read the jumbled skimble-skamble that runs through my mind—then when was it that you first noticed this . . . this gift? Or is it that you can read the minds of all around you? And is it just humans, or can you read the thoughts of animals, as well?"

The devil take the man. And that heart melting

smile, too, she thought, angry at the heat she felt racing into her face. And those eyes!

"Ah, lass, not a charitable thought, that! But to answer your questions . . . nay, I've never had a gift of reading other people's minds. Once or twice, though, I've been fairly certain what one of my dogs was thinking. And horses? Why, one time I recall a hunter letting me know he was feeling a wee bit fagged . . . just before he threw me, jumping over a bog. But you're the first of your kind that has opened up to me in such a manner."

She stared into his eyes with as much doubt as she could muster. "And what do you think all of this might mean? Am I still no more than that stray mare that has wandered onto Stewart lands? Am I just another of your possessions? Perhaps, m'lord, if you really put your mind to it, you might even receive messages from a bedpost . . . or a chamber pot!"

"Aye, true enough, Cat! But none of those would provide half the fun of being able to rile you."

She leaned toward him, lowering her voice so that her words would only be heard by him. "Then I guess 'tis time that I warned *you,* m'lord. Rile me too many times in this fashion and you'll feel the lash of my tongue and the battering of my wit. And do not be fooled by any frailty you see in this woman's body, for I've conquered men tougher than you."

"I'm certain you have, sweetness." The earl's booming laugh drew every eye to the dais. "By the devil, we'll have a fine time of it, Catherine. This is sure to be far better than anything I could have hoped for."

"I do not think—"

"Have you finished eating, lass?"

"Nay, but—" Before she could finish her thought, his mouth descended and Athol kissed her again, fully and thoroughly.

She pushed him away and, after glancing out at the

throng, stared at the table before her. "All eyes are upon us."

"Aye, as you say, m'lady. Then I believe 'tis time we left these discourteous villains to find their amusements where they will." She felt his strong hand wrap around hers beneath the dais. She followed the path of his scorching gaze as it dropped suggestively to her breasts. "And we can find our own elsewhere, as well!"

Catherine tried to ignore the warmth spreading through her middle. "Before coming down here, I promised myself not to allow you to seduce me again until we had a chance to speak of the school."

"Is that so?"

The heat of his hand on her thigh began to scatter her thoughts, and Catherine forced herself to concentrate.

"Name your conditions, Cat."

"An elementary and a grammar school—both at Elgin."

"They have a fine grammar school there already," he replied, shaking his head. "You can have the elementary school right here at Balvenie."

"But it would be so much easier to start both schools at the same time."

His growl, followed by the tug of his hand as he shoved his chair back and came to his feet, told her she was running out of time.

"I'll concede to having them both here as long as you agree to provide for maintenance of the tutors we bring back from Elgin!"

"You'll start with one school."

Catherine quickly considered her options. She already had more than she'd dared hoped to get from the man. Still, though, she sensed that she could get more.

"Two schools. And I'll teach—"

"Nay. One school for now!"

"Perhaps if I could show you the benefits of having the two . . ."

Catherine had no choice but to let herself be led across the Great Hall, returning the smiles and nods, the bows and curtsies as he propelled her toward the great arched doorway. She didn't have to glance around to know that every eye was upon them, that every tongue would be clucking about her husband's intent as soon as the two of them had pushed their way out of the chamber.

In the dim light of the corridor outside the Hall, she planted her feet, preparing to berate him for his behavior. And she would have, but before she could speak, the master of Balvenie Castle lifted her into his arms with a devilish grin, and sped down the dark corridor.

"Ah, lass, I'll have to feed you more. You weigh no more than a sparrow!"

Dizzy at the sensation of being carried like this, she couldn't find her voice or summon any kind of protest. Instead, she found herself wrapping her arms around his neck for support. To save herself from falling, she told herself. But what a lie! The giddiness she felt, the excitement of what was surely to follow, left her shivering with anticipation.

He tightened his hold on her, and she found her face pressed to the skin of his throat.

He lengthened his strides. "You keep that up, Cat, and we won't make it to my bedchamber."

She liked the huskiness that she could hear in his voice. There was something thrilling in the tightness of his iron-hard arms holding her. She puzzled at the thought that she actually affected him like this.

She considered his threat. "Ah! But I thought . . . I thought you so much stronger . . . than—"

"Strength has nothing to do with it, lass."

He quirked a half-smile at her and then kicked open a door before passing through it. Catherine's eyes hardly had a chance to focus as they swept through Athol's outer chamber. The door to his bedchamber lay directly ahead. She held her breath.

With a suddenness that shocked her, he halted at the door, staring at it as if it were some insurmountable obstacle. Glancing at the door and then into his handsome face, Catherine found herself burning with expectation.

His voice was no more than a growl, and he did not look at her. "Once I've taken you inside this chamber, you're mine, Catherine Percy!"

Slowly, his gaze dropped to her, and she met his gray, piercing eyes in the dim light of the room. "But I have been yours, John Stewart . . . from the moment you wed me."

"Aye, in body you've been mine! But in spirit . . ." He shook his head slowly. "I want your trust. I want you to accept me as your husband. I want all of you, Cat."

She never took her eyes from his face. Even in this light, she could see the muscles in his cheek flickering beneath the skin.

"I gave you my body. I'll give you all the passion within me. But as to the rest—" Catherine tightened her hold on his powerful neck and raised her face closer to his—"you'll have to earn my trust."

She never gave him a chance to voice his response, instead threading her fingers into his hair, she kissed his mouth the way he himself had taught her to kiss. When she broke off the kiss and drew back, she could not be certain which one of them was more affected.

"Catherine, I—"

"Nay, John. I need you! But do you plan to stand here all night and waste this . . ."

Athol pushed his way through the door into the

bedchamber, and Catherine found herself being gently placed on her feet. Still holding her close to his chest, he dropped the door latch in place.

Catherine placed a kiss in the hollow of his throat, resisting the thought of letting go of her grip on his neck. Having his strength surround her like this was an enjoyment totally unexpected.

"Does this mean you intend to allow me to walk the rest of the way of my free will?"

"It would be quite easy to toss you onto my bed and have my way with you. You are far too tempting, lass, even for the celibate saint I know you aspire to be."

"Well, m'lord, saintliness is—we both know very well—not an end you have any possibility of achieving."

"Aye, and 'tis a blessing for both of us."

She arched her back as he lowered his mouth to her neck. His lips brushed over the skin beneath her ear, stirring the banked fires of desire deep within her. She felt the roaming of his hands as they slid from her back downward over to her buttocks. She thrilled at the pressure of his strong fingers, drawing her hips against his hardening manhood.

Catherine opened her lips, forcing air into her lungs. More than anything right now, she wanted her husband to take her. She needed him. Deep in her belly, she ached to have him, to feel him inside of her, to know again the sensation of having her body wrapped around his, drawing his essence in. The very thought of him driving into her . . .

"Not so fast," he murmured in her ear, his breath hot as he ran his tongue over the sensitive ridges of her ear. "Having such thoughts will only be my undoing . . . and put an untimely end to such pleasures."

Her mind whirling with the myriad of sensations that were colliding within her, Catherine leaned back in his arms and looked confusedly into his face. "What did you say?"

His fingers worked themselves beneath her tartan and cupped her breasts. Lights were pulsing through vaporous mists in her brain, and she leaned against the door to support her own weight.

"I simply said, not so fast. We'll get there soon. But not yet, my sweet!"

She mentally pushed away at the bright mists. This couldn't be. He couldn't be reading her mind. It was just that she was too inexperienced and eager in this game of passion. He was guessing at her thoughts.

"Think what you will." He leaned down and kissed her again so deeply that, when he pulled back, she remained where she was for a long moment, dazed by the power of his passion. "But be prepared, lass. This night will be filled with all the pleasures our passionate natures can devise."

"Tell me what to do, John. Teach me." Her own voice sounded like that of a stranger. Her needs, it occurred to her, seemed to belong to someone else. To someone outside of her, and yet living at the very center of her womanhood.

"Undress for me."

She looked up and met his burning eyes.

"Take off the tartan, Cat."

Holding his gaze, her hand moved up to the brooch at her shoulder. As the plaid fell from her shoulders, she watched his eyes follow, pausing to gaze appreciatively on the exposed tops of her breasts before sweeping downward.

Meeting her gaze, Athol reached out and took hold of her hand, drawing her to the center of the bed-chamber. There he left her and crossed to the fire.

This was the first time since leaving the Great Hall that Catherine had been even a step away from her husband, and she let her eyes survey the chamber. A crackling fire in the hearth spread a comfortable warmth through the chamber as well as bathing it in a golden glow. Before the hearth, a table and chairs stood beside a huge settle, and across from the fire, a giant canopied bed stood against a paneled wall. Her eyes lingered on the bed with its damask curtains and intricately carved wood.

"Nay. Not yet!"

She looked back and found her husband standing beside the hearth with his hand outstretched to her.

"We'll save that for the last, Cat."

Catherine never hesitated as she took the few short steps into his arms. The way he wrapped her in his embrace—the heat she felt at the immediate and possessive caress of his hands over her body—all made her head whirl with excitement.

John Stewart backed into the settle beside the fire and drew her onto his lap. She placed her arm around his neck and found herself looking into his magical eyes. "Why here?"

" 'Tis the farthest place from the bed." She could feel his hands undoing the laces on the back of her dress. " 'Tis also the brightest spot in the chamber." She gasped and looked down as one of his hands pulled down at the neckline of her dress causing both of her breasts to spill wantonly into the open. "And 'tis also the warmest spot—short of being beneath the comforter on the bed—which we are saving for later."

She held her breath as his head descended, his tongue starting to make circles around one of her nipples. In a flash, she felt the tightening in her breast and watched with widening eyes as her flesh extended, beckoning toward his lips. He took her fully into his mouth, and she found herself melting with pleasure.

A moment later, as he pulled back and stood her up between his legs, Catherine watched him with a wondering eye as he pushed her dress and the thin

chemise downward over her hips. She was now burning with need, every part of her on fire, every bit of
her tingling with desire, and he, too, seemed lost in
the moment. The way his eyes roamed every inch of
her naked body, the way his hands gently traveled
over her curves, cupping, caressing, shaping her hips,
her buttocks, her belly, her breasts—each tender touch
sending her spiraling higher. When his mouth suckled
her again, she wanted to cry out with joy.

He wanted her. He was as much affected by her
woman's body as she was by this passion that he was
so keen to raise in her. They were in this together.
The two of them as one.

Gradually, a boldness crept into her veins, and
Catherine moved closer, sliding her hands over his
powerful shoulders.

"Teach me. Show me what to do."

"You are more than . . ." He paused, drawing back
and gazing at her. "You are so beautiful."

To have *him* forget his words brought a smile to
her face. Taking one of his hands, she raised it to her
lips and placed a kiss on each finger. "Show me,
John."

The handsome planes of his face became tense. She
thought she could see something akin to pain around
his eyes.

"One touch by you, Cat . . . and I'll be undone
for certain."

"One touch is all?" she murmured, remembering
the way she'd felt last night when his fingers had
wrought magic within her. Lowering herself slowly to
her knees, she held his gaze. "Promise me? One
touch?"

Pulling at his shirt, she placed her lips against the
skin of his chest, tasting him as he had tasted her. Her
hands, resting only for a moment on his knees, slid
beneath the soft wool of his kilt.

"Catherine . . . you'll be the death of me."

"Aye, but you're no coward, I know." Feeling bolder with each passing moment, she continued to place chaste kisses on his chest, his throat, his chin, as her fingers continued their slow journey upward over his taut, muscular thighs. "And how could a poor scholar, such as I am, be the undoing of the great and powerful earl of Athol?"

"Cat!"

He drew a sharp breath as she found her mark. Wrapping her fingers around him, she was awestruck at the size of him. Hesitantly, she looked up and found his eyes concentrating on her face.

"You could not have been so large last night." She used her thumb to feel the softness of the head while her hand moved curiously the length of his manhood. Real concern began to edge into her voice. "Do you get larger, John? For even like this, we no longer can possibly fit."

His fingers were rough when they dug into her hair and brought her mouth roughly against his. His kiss was raw, his tongue delving deeply. When he pulled back, Catherine suddenly found herself being lifted into the air and carried swiftly to the bed.

"So much for saving the bed for last."

"Aye, and 'tis your fault completely." His voice was a mere growl as he threw back the covering and dropped her none too gently onto the bed. He quickly kicked off his boots.

"I asked you to teach me . . . but you refused." She moved to the middle of the great bed. "I had to learn for mysel—"

The shirt was not coming off quickly enough, and Catherine's words caught in her throat when he ripped it open in the front. The sight of his golden skin and the sinewy musculature of his chest caused her heart to pound more feverishly than before.

"I still . . . I think . . . John . . . the size . . ."

His kilt dropped to the floor. Catherine's eyes moved downward, fixing on his huge arousal before flitting again to his face.

"It can't possibly . . . !"

"Just leave it to me, lass."

All she could do was gasp as Athol leaned over, took hold of her ankles and dragged her back to the edge of the bed. She had no time even to guess at his next move before he bent over her and clasped her nipple between his lips.

Any thought of resistance quickly gave way to pleasure, but it was a moment or two before Catherine could take in her next breath. And then, when he moved down her body, caressing her belly with his lips and tongue, moving even lower until he settled at the aching juncture of her thighs, she felt the molten fluids erupt in her body in a fiery sensation of pulsing energy. Catherine cried out in the ecstasy of release as her whole body came undone.

Too blind with waves of bliss sweeping her along on passion's currents, Catherine was mindless of her earlier concerns. She wanted him inside of her, and she reached out wildly, taking hold of his hair and raising him up. She felt him sink his shaft into her, and she raised her hips with a cry of wonder as he embedded himself fully within her.

And then, as he began his long, slow thrusts, Catherine was again lost to the world as he carried her to yet another shattering level of rapturous bliss. But this time, they came together in a joyous, dizzying union of body and spirit.

Moments later, John's streaming body still draped across hers, Catherine sent a quiet blessing heavenward. She had so much to be thankful for. Most of all, she wanted to thank the Lord for giving her the strength to tame this man. Running a gentle hand over his strong shoulders, she placed a kiss on his chest.

John Stewart, the earl of Athol, was certainly no longer the dangerous lion she'd once feared.

Chapter 11

As the first rays of the morning sun stretched across the chamber, John Stewart sleepily reached for his wife. But where the soft, inviting curves of her perfect body had lain—enticing him, welcoming him over and over during the night—now only the cool emptiness of the bedclothes awaited his touch. Abruptly lifting his head and staring across at her side of the empty bed, John smiled, cursing her out loud for her stubbornness in leaving him like this.

Swinging his long legs over the side of the bed, the earl sat brooding for a moment. Here she was, placed in the most decrepit of all rooms in the oldest quarter of the keep, and she readily gives up the comforts of his chamber to return to that hole. How many women could he think of that would be so steadfast in refusing such luxury? None, he thought decisively. Of course, it figures he would have to marry the one and only one.

Nay, he thought, quickly correcting himself. There was another. Joanna MacInnes had spent months roaming like a ghost in the caverns beneath Ironcross Castle until Gavin Kerr came north to take ownership of that keep. Aye! There was one other woman unaffected by life's creature comforts.

Pushing himself to his feet and moving into the warmth of the sun, John couldn't help but smile at the hand of fate. He might have lost the hand of Joanna

MacInnes, but here he had blindly walked into a marriage with a woman with such similar principles.

And he had a lot to be thankful for, considering all that had been said and done. Catherine Percy was turning out to be a jewel of a wife. Even aside from her vast learning, which was—in his opinion—an unexpected treasure in a woman, she had a lot of spirit and a fiery passion beneath her prim and proper appearance. She was indeed turning out to be a perfect wife.

And he had her just where he wanted her.

Feeling the stirring in his loins at a mere thought of what they'd shared, Athol could not recollect any night of carnal pleasures in the past that could match up to the one he'd just spent with Catherine.

There was something more, though. Something he'd have to be very careful of. She'd never spoken the words, but just having her naked limbs entwined with his own—her midnight-blue eyes gazing into his— John knew. He'd seen the look of devotion and trust in her face. She belonged to him in body and soul.

Hell, he thought, shrugging off his misgivings. She'd chosen to fall in love. By St. Andrew, he'd even warned her! She could never say he didn't.

But winning over his wife had been an easy chore. All he'd had to do was peel away one thin layer of resistance. Who could have known what cooperative riches he'd find beneath?

Aye, taming Catherine Percy had indeed been a very easy task.

Once again the angry hawk dived past the men at the top, this time striking hard at the shoulder of the man clinging to the face of the cliff below them. The sound of his curses rang out.

"Have you got it?" The Deputy Lieutenant's roar reverberated off the rocks. "Was it there, man?"

"Aye, m'lord," came the gruff reply.

"Bring him up."

As the soldiers hauled their pale and bloodied mate up over the edge, Sir Arthur Courtenay stepped toward the man. It took only a glimpse of the rolled parchment to tell him that, once again, there was no treasure to be had. Not here, anyway.

"Snakes! Black cats! Jagged cliffs. We should have burned those three as witches when we had a chance. I *hate* these Percy women! Where did you find it this time?" He snatched the parchment from the soldier's hand. "Was there a dragon protecting the vault?"

"Might as well have been, m'lord." He showed his bloody forearm and shoulder to his commander. "The cursed thing was hidden under the hawk's nest. Why, if I hadn't been able to get my hands up, that filthy devil would have torn my face off, sure as we're standing!"

The cloaked man stepped forward and took the parchment from the Deputy Lieutenant's hand.

"One should never molest the mother when she has her babies in the nest."

"Aye," the soldier sneered. "But I made damn sure to toss the little buggers down the cliff after her first dive at me."

The cloaked man turned away, unrolling the parchment with a look at the Deputy Lieutenant. "To be sure, Sir Arthur, you have only the finest of men to serve you!"

"But they *do* serve me, and I suggest you keep your prating tongue still." The two men stared angrily at one another for a long moment before Sir Arthur continued, breaking the silence. "So what is it this time, as if I didn't know. It wouldn't be another map from the three bitches, now, would it?"

The cloaked man gazed stonily at the map for a long moment. Then, without warning, the man tossed the parchment into Sir Arthur's hands. Fury blazed in the eyes of the king's Deputy Lieutenant.

"Aye. 'Tis exactly that. Another map for us . . . courtesy of the Mistresses Percy."

"This is the end!" Sir Arthur exploded hurling the map to the ground. "I'll not play the fool for these traitorous sluts anymore. 'Tis time we did something more than waste our valuable days traipsing all over the damned countryside. I told you a fortnight ago nothing would come of this! I'm telling you that they've taken the treasure with them! The wenches are in Scotland laughing at us this moment. They've taken it and left us with noth—"

"I know for a fact that they did not."

The Deputy Lieutenant eyed the other man suspiciously. "You know?"

"The treasure is here . . . somewhere." The cloaked man picked up the map from the dirt. "And there is a map—"

"Then one of them must have it! I wager 'tis the eldest! Bloody hell, I should have gone after her—as I wanted to from the first—rather than waste my time following this futile trail."

"As I've told you before, 'tis not just one of them that has the answer, 'tis the three together. That's why we must follow the maps. They left these here for a reason, and I'm telling you we cannot ignore them. The mother has corresponded with them, and these maps could very well lead to the prize we seek."

The Deputy Lieutenant began pacing back and forth along the ledge. Finally, he stopped and faced the man. "Nay! I'll not be put off again. We'll go after the eldest first. Didn't you tell me that she went to Elgin? We have some of the maps . . . perhaps she has the final key. And if she cannot lead us to it on her own, I'll stretch her on the rack until she tells us where the other two sisters are."

The cloaked man's brow deepened into a frown. " 'Tis not so easy. My men have sent me word that she has been wedded to the earl of Athol—the cousin to the Scottish king."

"Your men?!" Sir Arthur exploded. "You have people close to her, and yet you say nothing to me? Are you telling me that all along you have been in a position to bring her back, and you have not acted?"

The cloaked man raised himself to his full height. "If I were you, I should not be too hasty in passing judgment over what I have done. If it weren't for me, you would still know nothing at all of the connection between the Percys and the Treasure of—"

"Enough!" the Deputy Lieutenant interrupted, eyeing the gawking soldiers standing nearby. "You've told me this until I'm sick to death of it!"

Moving closer, Sir Andrew grasped the man's cloak in his fist and drew him down until their faces were eye to eye.

"When are you bringing her back?" he rasped, the threat evident in his voice.

"When the time is right." The cloaked man whispered, his gaze never wavering as he extricated himself from the king's servant.

"Bah!" the Deputy Lieutenant turned on his heel and strode again to the cliff's edge.

"But in the meantime, Sir Arthur, we have another map that may lead us closer to our goal. So if you're finished chastising me for the good that I've done in keeping at least one of Nichola Percy's daughters within our reach, then I believe we should continue our endeavors."

"Aye, for now," Courtenay replied, keeping his back turned.

The commander's eye was caught by the falcon circling in the sun above them, and his voice dropped to a murmur. "Though I wonder, Nichola Percy, how you would respond if I were to drag your hatchlings from the nest."

*   *   *

The late summer sun beat down relentlessly on the two riders and their balky, old mules.

Catherine glanced over her shoulder at the flushed face of the exhausted monk. Brother Bartholomew was wiping the sweat off his brow with the sleeve of his robe, and she slowed down to let him catch up to her.

The monk looked up and met her gaze. "I still can't understand, mistress, why we couldn't take the trail through the Glen of Rothes as the young stable hand directed us. The boy insisted that going that way would be the safest and the easiest route to Elgin."

"This was the same lad that gave us these fine mounts, too, Brother." Catherine smiled, patting her ancient mule. She let her eyes wander over the craggy hills and thick green forests of pine and of oak, and then downward into the glen with its smattering of open meadows beneath them. "But you know my fondness for the hills, Bartholomew. Do you know, since my arrival here, a day hasn't passed without my serving woman Jean talking of how 'bonny' Ben Aigan looks from these Mannoch Hills—near the place where she was raised. That's it . . . there across the glen. 'Tis breathtaking, don't you think so?"

The monk glanced at the peak noncommittally and gave a low grunt as he pushed his mule past her along the path through the hills. Satisfied for the moment, Catherine turned her own attention to the rocky trail.

Actually, the truth of the matter behind taking this road was quite different. That stable lad, Roy Sykes, had simply been too agreeable in believing that her husband had allowed the two of them to journey to Elgin without an escort. Indeed, considering that the red-haired young man had given them two of the frailest old mules in the stables, Catherine was convinced that the young man had probably beaten a track to her husband's chamber door the moment she and the monk had ridden out through Balvenie's arched gate.

Catherine scanned the open areas of the glen as far as her eyes could see. At least, she thought, if she wanted to wield her own authority, it would be better to avoid having Athol stop her before she reached Elgin. By riding into the hills and following the glen, they had a chance, anyway, of finishing the journey without being overtaken. The more arduous route would take them longer, but from what she gathered from Jean, they could easily make it by sunset.

And Jean's information about these hills had proved accurate thus far. Based on what she'd learned from the serving woman, Catherine was completely confident that they'd find their way to the ancient walled city and its revered cathedral. She'd always had a good sense of direction. And with these hills as unfrequented as they appeared to be, Catherine believed they may have found the safest route for their passage, as well.

Urging her own mule forward, she tried to think ahead to all that needed to be done. In the past, when the three sisters had been together, it had been so much easier to work through their designs. Among the three, Catherine had always been the dreamer—the one with the vision of what they could and should do. Laura, on the other hand, had been their voice of reason. She and her logical mind had saved them many a time when they could have brought themselves serious trouble. But Adrianne, the youngest, was a true trouble-maker—borne to torment any who preached tranquility. Though in public Catherine and Laura had to restrain their sister's behavior, in private they were her greatest admirers. Her unbridled energy and daring served as an inspiration to them.

The path broadened out a bit and she rode up next

to the portly monk. The sun was no longer directly overhead, and she gazed ahead at the next series of hills. Catherine knew that if she wanted to open this school, she would need to perform the tasks her two sisters would normally have done. She frowned and then sighed, missing them more than ever.

One thing she had not dared to mention to her husband yet was that once she had the school open and functioning smoothly, she hoped to bring her sisters to Balvenie to stay. Laura and Adrianne were as accomplished in their studies as she was, herself. There was no reason why Catherine couldn't put them to work as tutors in the school. John Stewart surely could not have any objection to that . . . she hoped.

First things first, though. She had to open the school. Catherine had received her husband's approval to do it. Now, the most crucial step lay in getting the bishop's aid, as well. This, she knew, was something she had to achieve in all haste. Something told her that if she were to leave it to her husband, it would be many months and the birth of an heir before he might feel inclined to speak on her behalf.

"To the bishop . . ." she murmured, more to herself than to her companion.

Brother Bartholomew turned and peered at her a moment before speaking. "Now, mistress, I hope that you understand that I've never met Patrick Hepburn, the new bishop here."

Catherine nodded. "I know that, Bartholomew. But do not worry. Without divulging my intentions to a certain young woman whom I accompanied north, I did learn a few things on my own about him. I believe he will be agreeable to our cause."

"I know that he was the son of the first earl of Bothwell, mistress. You don't know him through your mother?"

She smiled at him. It amused her once again that

every English monk she'd ever met had been so capti-
vated with the scope of her mother's connections. As
far as they were concerned, Nichola Percy must be
known to every nobleman in Europe.

"I don't know if my mother has met him or not.
Lady Nichola is an Erskine and not a Bothwell, Bartholomew. But from what I've been able to gather, a
distant cousin of mine was at St. Andrew's at the same
time as Bishop Hepburn was the Prior there. So anyway, using that connection, my mother has notified
him of our desire to open the school . . . and our need
for assistance."

"We would have been much better off bringing
Brother Egbert and Brother Paul with us, mistress,"
the monk admonished. " 'Tis one thing for a man in
his position to react affably to a letter, but faced with
a woman of your tender years, he might simply hesitate. It would not be unreasonable for him to question
your ability to undertake such a large task."

"Unreasonable?" Catherine could hear the sharpness in her tone. "If that is the case, Bartholomew,
the presence of two more English monks will do little
to put his mind at ease. Nay, you and the good brothers came to the Highlands at my request. I believe it
must be my qualifications and beliefs that convince
him in the end."

Brother Bartholomew gazed at her reflectively and
then nodded. If he was going to cast his lot in with
her, she thought, then he and the other two monks
would have to recognize that she would be treated as
an equal in teaching their prospective students.

"Aye, mistress. You're right, of course. And this dream
of yours will become a reality, I've no doubt of it."

Thank the Lord, she thought. At least someone was
reading her mind at the proper moment. And she was
certain that this monk, at least, believed in her.

". . . And having the earl of Athol, not simply as

your patron but as your husband, adds so much to your support and your qualifications. Why, to have a husband as wealthy and powerful . . ."

Catherine sighed and urged her mule on ahead. It was her own fault. If she'd not been quite so hasty in departing this morning, asking the early riser, Brother Bartholomew, to escort her, she might have had Brother Egbert or even Brother Paul to accompany her, and then she wouldn't be listening to the portly monk's old-fashioned ideas. Although the man had been true to his promise to their father when it came to teaching Catherine and her sisters so many years back, the monk still held onto a bag full of ancient notions about the place of women in a man's world.

Well, so be it, Catherine thought, again nudging her mount faster along the path. He was here, and she was going to put him to work in the school as much as she possibly could. She'd known from the start that she couldn't manage a school single-handedly.

This train of thought ended abruptly, and she reined her mare to a halt. Ahead in the distance, a stand of trees edged over the ridge of the hill. There, along the line of undergrowth that spilled downward into the glen, something had flashed in the midday sun.

As the vulnerability of their position struck home, Catherine yanked the head of her mule around and spurred the beast back in the direction they had come. Seeing a wooded hollow down the hill, away from the glen, she gestured for Brother Bartholomew to follow in silence. In a moment they were hidden in the shadows of the trees.

She didn't know what danger—if any—lay ahead, but she was no fool. She was not about to walk blindly into any trap.

John Stewart had been understanding when his wife had missed the morning meal. More than likely she was still abed, he'd decided with a satisfied smile, trying to catch up on the sleep that he'd deprived her of for most of the night. But when she failed to join him for the noon meal as well, he found himself becoming a bit worried about her health.

Hell, he thought, ignoring the surprised looks on his men's faces as he abruptly left the Great Hall. Waving off Tosh, the earl stalked toward the stairwell.

As he moved up the dark stairs, he scowled at his own foolishness. Nay, it wasn't foolishness. He could at least be honest enough to admit that he'd missed her this morning, he told himself. So what if—during the entire time he'd spent listening to the troubles and resolving the disputes of his crofters—his mind had continued to wander to thoughts of Catherine. So what if—even later, when he'd been training with his men—her face, her eyes, her smile had continued to flash before his mind's eye.

Hell, there was nothing wrong with a man being infatuated with his own wife! Of course not! By the devil, the newness of marriage alone was better entertainment than any he'd ever had.

A moment later, Athol paused upon reaching her chamber door. Lifting his hand to knock, he frowned, suddenly feeling like a fool to be knocking at a door in his own keep. He should just go right in, he thought, still hesitating. But then, what if she were still sleeping? A smile tugged at the edges of his mouth. Wouldn't it be much more pleasant just to slip quietly in and awaken her using some alternative method? The thought of making love to her now sent his hand immediately to the door handle.

"She's not in there, m'lord."

Athol immediately turned and faced the approaching serving woman. "Nay? Then where is she? Is she with my mother?"

Jean shook her head. "I just came from the dowager's bedchamber. She hasn't been seen there all morning!"

"With Susan, then?"

The serving woman ran her fingers over the bolts of wool cloth she was carrying. "The last I saw of her, m'lord, was last night. When I helped her dress to join ye in the Great Hall." The woman stared at the cloth. "She . . . she didn't appear to be needing me later. But this morning, when I came to see if Lady Catherine wanted help in dressing, all I could find were the clothes she wore last night."

Athol felt the knot of worry forming in his gut. "Have you checked everywhere? The courtyard . . . the garden . . . the chapel?"

"Aye, m'lord."

"And you never thought to let me know?"

Jean flashed a defiant look at him. "When she wasn't anywhere else, I thought she'd simply chosen to return to your chamber, m'lord."

"Of all the—" Athol pushed into the chamber and scanned the room. By the bed, he stood still. Her presence hung in the air like a sweet mist. His concern suddenly grew tenfold.

Jean stood in the doorway. "If she's not in your chamber, m'lord, then I do not think she's still in the castle."

He shot her a killing look. "What do you mean by that?" he snapped.

"Her traveling clothes . . . her cloak . . . they're missing, m'lord."

Athol fought to keep his anger from boiling over. "Do you have *any* idea where she might have gone?"

The serving woman gave a small nod but did not lift her eyes.

"Where?"

"She's been talking about the opening of the school . . . and asking . . . many questions about

Elgin . . . about the best route to travel to the cathedral. She said she had to get there . . . sometime, m'lord . . . to see the bishop. I never thought, m'lord, she would even consider doing it alone!"

Stifling an urge to bang either his head or Jean's against the wall, Athol strode from the room, glaring at the serving woman as she scurried out of his path. Turning his steps toward the Great Hall, the earl considered the stubbornness of the woman . . . of his wife. His mind flooded with all the dangers she might already have encountered on such a foolhardy jaunt. His shouts were fierce as he broke into the Hall. And of all things, it had been only yesterday that another crofter had spotted the bastard Adam of the Glen roaming the hills around the Balvenie Castle.

He would kill him. With his own bare hands, he would tear his throat out. If Adam ever dared harm his wife—even touched a hair on her rock-hard head—the villain would suffer a death that even Torquemada, the Grand Inquisitor, would blush at.

Charging out of the hall and into the bright sunlight, John Stewart cursed himself for allowing this weakness for a woman to creep into his heart. Why couldn't he just keep her at a safe distance from him? Why did he have to become so damned attached to her? The last thing in this world that he needed was entanglement with a headstrong woman, particularly the woman he was married to!

The feelings that were bordering on panic as he crossed the courtyard to the stables told him that it was too late to question what was past. The fact was that he was indeed bewitched by his wife, and he would get her back if he had to chase Adam of the Glen to the very gates of Hell.

Chapter 12

The last vestiges of the sun's light were being beaten back from the forest path, and darkness was pressing its claim on the two weary travelers. Catherine, placing a hand under the heavyset monk's elbow, helped him to climb over a fallen tree. With a resolute sigh, he halted.

"I cannot go any farther than this, mistress. You'll rob me of even my last breath if you force me to walk so much as another stone's throw."

"We are almost there, Brother Bartholomew. At the top of the last hill, we could see the smoke from Elgin. In fact, I'm certain I could see the very walls of the town."

The man shook his head and planted his wide arse on the tree trunk. "Nay, Catherine. I saw nothing. Let me rest here." The monk puffed out his rosy cheeks. "I say we are lost, and we are never going to get there. In fact, since midday I have been asking myself how I could let you talk me into leaving our mules behind in the hills. At least, with those animals carrying us, we might have had a chance."

"I told you before, Brother Bartholomew. They would have made far too much noise."

"Ah! And bring down the wrath of your imaginary thieves on our heads. I still think 'twas nothing more than your imagination that we were in danger. The things you have forced me to do! Climbing those steep hills! I think Lucifer's legions could not have devised a more devilish punishment. And all the time, the gentle paths of the glen below . . . beckoning . . ." He shook his head. "Nay, mistress. I have been all the way to Rome, and an experienced pilgrim like myself should never have—"

"Hush!" Catherine's sudden gesture silenced the complaining monk. Taking the man quickly by the hand and dragging him from the path, she pulled him behind a large tree trunk. "They are coming! I heard a horse. Do you hear them?"

"Nay, but I'll believe you. And when they come by, we can ask for help. Beg for a ride, perhaps. As good Christian men, they'll be certain to pity us and—"

"Nay!" She adamantly shook her head, and then peered through the trees in the direction they had come. "As an experienced traveler, you surely know what robbers and cutthroats do to wayfarers who fall into their bloody clutches! Good Christians, no doubt! These must be the same good Christians who were waiting to pounce on us in the hills. They are searching for us, Brother Pilgrim."

"For us?" For the first time, Catherine's earlier warning appeared to have sunk in. Clutching on to Catherine's cloak, Brother Bartholomew looked anxiously into her face. "But what should we do? Where can we hide?"

She took only a moment to study their surroundings. "There is no place to hide here! Surely, we cannot climb these trees, for even if we did, they are certain to discover us."

"Then what shall we do? Tell me, Catherine. What shall we do?"

"I say we run! Push for the walls of the city! And I believe we have not a moment to waste! Come, Brother! Run for your life."

The words had not completely left Catherine's

mouth when the monk started up the path with more energy than she'd seen him exert all day. Finding this much better than his earlier whining, she fought down a grin and started after him.

Falling in behind him, Catherine considered their situation. Elgin had to be fairly close now. She hadn't really seen or heard any indication that those waiting in the hills were pursuing them, but going at this pace, she and the portly monk were certain to arrive at Elgin Cathedral before nightfall.

And the first thing she had to do when they arrived was to send a messenger to her husband at Balvenie Castle. The last thing she wanted was to have him worrying about her after all the pleasantness that had passed between them last night!

Nay! Worrying him was not something she ever intended to do!

Entering his own ornately decorated Great Hall, Patrick Hepburn, the young bishop of Moray, came to an abrupt stop at the sight of the irate earl of Athol.

"I assume, my good earl, that you are not here to congratulate us on the finish of the cathedral's thirty-year restoration. You did see the middle tower, did you not? Aren't the figures of Bishop Innes and—"

"Aye, I saw the blasted thing. And you assume correctly, Patrick. I'm not here for any such thing. I am here to retrieve my wife."

"So!" A slow smile broke out on the youthful face of the bishop. "So the rumors we've heard are true. You have taken an English *cleric* as a wife. Really, such an act is so unusual . . . so progressive . . ."

"I'm happy to be able to amuse you, Your Excellency," Athol growled, speaking through clenched teeth in his effort not to unleash his fury on the jolly bishop. "But Catherine Percy, my wife, left Balvenie Castle this morning to—"

"Oh, a woman?" the bishop said with mock disappointment.

"Aye, of course, a woman!"

"Without you? She left the castle without you?'

"Aye, without me!" Athol barked. "And she was accompanied by a damned English monk."

"You are very kind, Athol, to be providing shelter to every English refugee fleeing—"

"I am *not* providing shelter to the bloody English monks. I was just trying to—"

"I, too, believe 'tis a worthy cause." The bishop nodded approvingly. "With those henchmen of Henry Tudor's tearing through the abbeys in the south of England, 'tis only a matter of time—"

"Right now, Patrick, I do not give a tinker's damn about Henry Tudor, Suleyman the Magnificent, or the devil himself!" Seeing the bishop draw breath to reply—no doubt about the merits of helping clerics—Athol barreled on. "What I want to know from you is whether my wife has arrived here yet!"

"You believe that she was headed here?" Still thoroughly amused, the cleric looked down at his soft, white hands. "I hope she's beautiful, my good earl. A beautiful woman is the rarest of God's creatu—"

"She was . . . she is!" John sputtered. "She *was* headed here. As I tried to say earlier, she left Balvenie Castle this morning with a blasted monk named Bartholomew, and they were definitely heading for Elgin Cathedral!"

"How delightful! But why would she want to come here without you?"

" 'Tis not so much that she wanted to come here *without me* as to the fact that she's eager to solicit your help in starting a school at Balvenie Castle and—"

"How fascinating! And your feelings on such a project?"

"Catherine has my consent. But still . . ."

"Is she not the eldest daughter of Nichola Erskine?"

"She is, Patrick." Athol felt his temper about to explode. "Before nightfall totally descends, I need to know if she has arrived here at the cathedral!"

The bishop waved a hand vaguely in the air. "I remember receiving a letter from the mother. Based on what I recall of the letter, your wife is a very educated woman, quite capable of accomplishing the task she has chosen for herself."

"I have no argument with anything you say. Is she HERE?!"

"No need to shout, John. I can hear quite well."

Athol tried to calm himself, though his fingers itched to throttle the rosy-cheeked cleric. Suddenly, thoughts of Catherine's threatened annulment raced through his mind. Nay, he thought, trying to dismiss the idea. They had already consummated their marriage. She had even seemed fairly . . . well, pleased with the arrangement now. Nay, their passionate moments did not speak of a woman unfulfilled. Still, he had to assure himself that she was not here. That this all too worldly priest was not providing her with a refuge against him.

He would use Patrick Hepburn's hide for a saddlebag if the wee bishop was keeping her.

" 'Tis dangerous out there in those hills, Patrick! My men and I took the direct route to Elgin and did not catch up with them. So if you tell me that my wife and her companion have not yet arrived, then I need to go out in search of them *now*! Adam of the Glen is out there, and the blackguard would love to have my wife in his clutches . . . of that I have no doubt. The wolf has been at my door for months now, raiding my lands and terrorizing my people."

The bishop nodded with concern. "Aye, so I have heard. You really should catch the villain. I think the gates of Balvenie Castle would look quite lovely adorned with Adam's head on a pike."

Athol clenched his jaw tightly. "So would I. But is my—"

"If Adam's thievery were to spill over into the lands of my bishopric, we would really need to talk about—"

"Not now!" John Stewart interrupted, taking a half step toward the man. "My wife, Patrick! Is she here?"

The bishop looked up, evidently startled by the apprehension in the earl's tone. Patrick Hepburn looked carefully at Athol's troubled and exasperated expression.

" 'Tis pleasing for me to know that your extended wait before choosing a wife was not in vain. It sounds to me as if you are really concerned about the woman, though I must say that I am surprised, after hearing how Catherine Percy was literally dragged before you to take her vows."

The reason for the bishop's reluctance to answer now became clear. The priest who married them at the hunting lodge must have reported the incident to the bishop. Well, there was no point in denying the truth.

"A great deal has changed since then, Patrick."

"So I see." The bishop turned and crossed to one of the large windows overlooking the courtyard. "Now, concerning the whereabouts of your wife. 'Tis nearly dark."

"I know that! Has she arrived?"

"I should say that she has."

As a sudden relief washed over him, John watched the bishop raise his pudgy hand and point out through the glass. Moving rapidly to the window and looking out, John saw the two ragged-looking travelers making their way past the old porter at the gate of the walled enclosure. Pushing the hood of her cloak back, Cath-

erine was explaining their presence to the porter and
looking purposefully toward the bishop's palace. The
heavyset monk accompanying her was chirping continuously in her ear. Even in the growing gloom, Athol
could tell that she was annoyed with whatever it was
Brother Bartholomew was saying.

In an instant, the sense of relief caused by the
knowledge of her safety was replaced with a growing
fury at her recklessness, and John Stewart started for
the door.

With unexpected quickness, the bishop grabbed the
sleeve of Athol's shirt, detaining him. "You will not be
too harsh with her, my friend, for what she has done?"

The earl stared at the man. "The hell I won't. She
is my wife now, and she must understand that there
are dangers that surround us in these hills. As the
countess of Athol, she is more valuable to renegades
like Adam of the Glen—and more vulnerable—than
she was while escaping England. Nay, Patrick, she will
learn that she cannot foolishly endanger her own life
and someone else's so impulsively."

The bishop nodded. "Aye, she has to understand
all of those things. But I believe 'tis more important
that she learn to trust *your* judgment and take you
into her confidence in matters such as this."

Athol cocked an eyebrow at him. "A curious position for a churchman to take, but I intend to see to
that as well. Now, if you'll pardon me, Patrick . . ."

"I'm looking forward to meeting her, John. Bring
her in and—"

"We'll not be availing ourselves of your hospitality tonight."

The bishop raised a soft hand in the air. "But—"

"Nay, she's going home immediately, if I have to
tie her to the back of my horse." With a curt nod, he
started for the door.

"Well"—the bishop called after—"then please pass

on my encouragement regarding the school. At least, leave her jovial-looking friend, and I'll tell him what we can do to help. Oh, and John!"

Exasperated, the earl of Athol whirled at the door. "Be gentle!"

He came out the door into the courtyard with all the delicacy of a charging bull.

Slowing her steps as she moved across the yard, Catherine's initial excitement at seeing her husband here quickly turned to caution. His long strides and the scowl darkening his looks made it clear that he did not share her enthusiasm about this meeting. Realizing that this was probably not the best place for Brother Bartholomew, she stopped, turned, and quietly advised the monk to continue on to the chapter house, where she could meet him later. But her traveling companion gave her only the most perfunctory of bows before practically running the few remaining steps to the oncoming earl of Athol.

"I cannot tell you, m'lord, how happy I am to find you here. Considering the fact that we quite nearly lost our lives during our journey here, the idea of having to return to Balvenie Castle on our own, unprotected, has been most dreadful! Most dreadful, indeed!"

Catherine watched her husband ignore the cleric, passing him without so much as a glance and closing the distance between them. His eyes bore into hers and he stopped an arm's length from her. The monk, continuing to chatter away, was instantly at the earl's elbow, gesturing and whining.

"The dangers we faced in these hills were terrifying, m'lord—far more frightening than anything I've encountered in my entire life."

Catherine rolled her eyes. Certainly, her husband

would recognize the ridiculousness of the monk's over-
statement.

"One moment, we're faced with cutthroats and
thieves in the hills, and the next we're forced to leave
our mules and walk over the most mountainous
ground God ever created. Why, Hannibal and his ele-
phants couldn't have crossed the terrain we covered
today. You do not know, m'lord—"

"That is enough, Brother Bartholomew," Catherine
interrupted, turning her gaze from her husband to the
monk. The cleric continued to puff and throw his
hands in the air. "I am certain the earl has a very
good idea of how our trip went."

"Nay, Lady Catherine. I haven't even begun to tell
of the assassins who nearly caught us not two leagues
from here."

Her gaze darted back to Athol's face. His eyes
shone with fury.

"Oh, aye," she scoffed, though not very convinc-
ingly, she thought. She tried to make her words drip
with sarcasm. "If it were not for our superior speed
afoot, they'd have certainly caught us at the very gates
of Elgin itself."

"True!" the monk agreed. "And I think they were
the same band of murderers that chased us most of
the day. They followed us from the hills, m'lord, ready
to cut our throats, if they were to catch us."

The darkness of Athol's scowl was starting to make
her nervous. She turned sternly to the monk. "We
arrived safely. There is no reason now to exaggerate
the details of our journey, Brother Bartholomew."

"Exaggerate?" the monk huffed. "You were the
one who pointed out the flash of their blades in the
sunlight, mistress."

"I was just looking for an excuse to travel into the
hills," she lied. "You, of all people, should know my
fondness for this high country."

"Nay, you are being too modest, mistress. Certainly, your husband should know the courage you showed." The monk turned toward the earl, and Catherine had to control her urge to stuff the man's hood in his mouth.

"I would say . . . there were fifty . . . maybe a hundred of them closing in on us . . ."

Catherine looked pleadingly at her husband. But he simply stood there directing his murderous gaze at her, taking in all the decoratively embellished gibberish the monk was so eloquently delivering into his ear. Well, darkness had all but descended upon them, and she turned as a torch flared up by the pen between the stables and the gatekeeper's cell. Suddenly, she became very aware of her aching feet, and her interest in listening to much more of this dissipated. She turned toward her husband.

"If you'll forgive me, I have not yet accomplished the task that brought me to Elgin and the cathedral. So while you catch up on Brother Bartholomew's tales of the murderers haunting these hills, I think I'll just continue on to the chapter house to inquire about the possibility of seeing the bishop tonight regarding the matter of the school."

With an authoritative sweep of his arm, the earl of Athol brushed the monk back and stepped in, cutting off Catherine's line of retreat. "You'll not be moving from this spot until such time as *I* move you."

Realizing that weariness was probably contributing to her urge to snap at him in response, Catherine bit her tongue and tried to retain her composure. His words sounded threatening, but she knew that it would be pointless to bait him. Staring into her husband's face, she did not flinch as she met his dark scowl.

"Husband, you appear to be overly agitated by some of these overstated accounts of the day's happenings. I can assure you, once I've had a chance to speak with the bishop, I will put your mind to rest on all that we encountered on the journey from Balvenie Castle."

She tried to take a step around him, but his powerful hand took hold of her arm, and she felt the viselike strength of his grip. Knowing that Brother Bartholomew would be a witness to everything they said and did, she decided against chastising him for this rough handling of her. Instead, in her mind's eye she tried to recall the gentle and passionate man she'd spent last night with, and gave him her sweetest smile.

His scowl wavered for a moment, and Catherine decided to take advantage of the change.

"If you will allow me, husband, I do not know if His Excellency's evening meal is—"

"Leave us, monk!"

Athol's curt order sent the man scurrying toward the chapter house in an instant. Catherine watched as anger once again clouded her husband's face. Feeling a bit vulnerable at being left alone with him like this, she raised herself on tiptoe and glanced around the courtyard as the vespers bell began to ring. The workers in the stables and the smithy beside it were crossing the courtyard toward the cathedral, casting curious looks in their direction, but steering a wide path around them. They were alone, except for the old gatekeeper, who sat dozing on a block of wood by the courtyard entrance.

"No one can save you from my wrath, my sweet." He tugged on her arm, pulling her across the courtyard toward the stables.

"Saving?! I can't see why I should need saving. Considering the fact that I have done nothing wrong, I find your attitude completely uncalled for. Do you hear me? Uncalled for!"

In the deep shadow by the stable wall, he swung her around none too gently until she faced him fully.

"For a woman who considers herself blessed with a fair amount of intelligence, you act with less sense than those old mules you stole from me."

"Stole?"

"Aye, stole. But the mules, at least, knew enough to make their way down into the glen where they could be found."

"I'm delighted you were able to find your valuable *property* undamaged, m'lord." Catherine could see the muscles in his jaw flicker dangerously. His face flushed crimson, and his eyes blazed with anger. Well, she thought, she might as well let him vent his anger. Crossing her arms, she nodded encouragingly. "Very well, husband. Let me hear your complaint!"

"Catherine Percy, do not try to pacify me. I can read your mind."

She nodded again, this time giving him a weak smile. "Come, I am waiting! You want to rant and rave and tear me in two? Well! I am ready!"

"I—I . . . cannot understand how a woman like you, a stranger in country as rough as . . ." He sputtered on, assailing her with reasons why her journey from Balvenie Castle had been so ill-judged, but she was not listening. At the height of his anger, his eyes had turned as dark as the night, and Catherine gazed up, admiring their intensity as well as their tendency to change color along with his mood. And for the thousandth time, she again noticed his long dark eyelashes. She couldn't help but wonder what beautiful children he would father. Children! She smiled inwardly. Not so many days ago, she had been appalled by the very thought of marriage to this man, and here she was daydreaming about bairns.

"Stop that!" He snapped the words out. "You are not even listening to me!"

His hands were on her shoulders. She shook herself

out of her reverie and nodded. But she couldn't stop her gaze from fixing on his full lips.

"Catherine! You haven't heard a word of what I've been saying! How could you be so . . ."

She wished he would kiss her. Until this moment, she hadn't fully realized how much she'd missed him today. In fact, seeing him charging toward her out of the bishop's residence tonight, she had nearly cast aside her dignity and run into his arms. She wondered vaguely if he would still be so angry if she'd done that.

"Catherine! Stop distracting me!"

She looked up and let her eyes roam his face. His long red hair looked almost black in the darkness. She could just make out the tight braids, pulled back with the rest of his long, thick hair and tied with a thong at the nape of his neck. She wondered what he would do if she were to raise herself on tiptoe and kiss his chin, his jaw, his neck.

"That does it!"

As Athol took her roughly by the hand, Catherine found herself being hauled through the stable door. The smell of fresh straw and horses warmed her. Such a comforting smell, she thought.

"What are you doing?"

"Finding a place that's a wee bit more private! Where every window facing on the courtyard won't have a view of the earl of Athol and his obstinate wife. We need to have a . . . a *private* talk." His voice dropped to a growl. "And do not think for a moment that I do not know what was just going through your mind."

He was dragging her toward the low-hanging hayloft. "I'm sorry! I didn't mean to be so . . . so obvious!"

Turning, he placed his hands on her waist and literally threw her into the loft, scaling the short ladder after her.

Catherine was still trying to catch her breath when she heard the low rumble escape his lips. Stunned, she stared at him as he stretched out beside her. It was a laugh—she was certain of it. He had actually laughed!

"Obvious? To no one but me, Cat. But I'm telling you this, my sweet, we are far from finished discussing your rashness in coming here alone."

She started to reply, but then stopped.

Well, first things first, she decided. After all, there was no reason she could think of for continuing the argument. Why, he might just forget all about it by the time they were done with this private . . . er, talk.

Catherine turned to him and smiled.

Chapter 13

The frightened stable hand took two steps back at the approach of his leader.

"I tried, master! I told them both that the only route to Elgin was through the Glen of Rothes! I even gave them the oldest mules in the stables. The ones I knew would be easy to—"

"Tried!" Adam of the Glen spat out with disdain as he brushed past the trembling man. He stalked to the fire.

Roy Sykes raised a nervous hand to the side of his head as if checking to make certain it was still connected to his shoulders.

"Master, they'd barely left the gates of Balvenie before I came running with the news."

Adam stared into the fire. "By now he must have learned of your treachery."

Roy stared at the broad back of the giant Highlander. The leader's broadsword was still strapped to his back. "Aye, I'm sure some of the stable hands saw me talk to Lady Catherine before she left. They're certain to tell the laird who 'twas that gave her the mules. He'll hang me for not telling him about her leaving. Please, master, do not send me back to face him."

The Highlander turned and stared darkly into the terrified man's face. "But you'd face my wrath before his? I should have Ren tie you to that tree and let the kites peck out your eyes!"

Roy Sykes dropped to his knees and clasped his hands. "Do not send me back, master. But please spare my life! I did what I thought you'd be wanting. I never thought that the Englishwoman and the monk would take it on themselves to travel across the hills!"

Adam of the Glen turned to the scarfaced man who crouched before the fire, listening. "He says you must be blind, Ren. For you tell me they never passed by you, either."

"Aye, if the lad says so, then I must be blind." Ren turned a murderous look at the stable hand. "For we had the shepherd's trail across the Mannoch Hills blocked. There was no way some lowland bitch, traveling with a fat monk, could have gone past us. We'd have smelled them coming a league off."

"You were watching the shepherd's trail?"

"Aye, and there was not a soul—"

"And you didn't spread your men back to the river?"

"Aye . . . well, we did as the day wore on." Ren looked away uneasily. "But there was no sign of them, master."

"By the devil!" Adam snapped. "Then they *could* have gone around you!"

"Nay!" Ren squirmed visibly. "Well, aye. But master . . . you said so yourself. These are just two English lapdogs—a monk and a lass. How would they—"

The huge Highlander exploded, kicking dirt at his warrior. "By 'is Bones, I am tired of having to do every bit of thinking around here! For the first time in months, I have a real chance to avenge myself on that blackguard, Athol, and all of you suddenly decide to play the fools . . . at the same time!"

The gathering of warriors shifted uneasily and began

to murmur among themselves. Adam turned his wrath on them fully. "She was out there! A flower to be picked. But none of you had enough courage, enough wit—"

Adam stopped mid-sentence at the sound of a soft whistle from the darkness beyond the light of the fire.

With a parting glare at Roy Sykes and Ren, the leader strode past the ruined stone hut at the edge of the clearing and toward the spot where he knew his visitor waited.

The only light seeping into the stable came from the torch out by the pen, but Catherine Percy was beautiful in any light.

Reluctantly rolling away from her, Athol slid to the edge of the loft and dropped to the dirt floor. With a sigh, Catherine followed him, and John Stewart gently lowered her to the ground, placing a soft kiss on her still parted lips. Gathering her tightly to him, he warmed at the feel of her body against his, the pressure of her hands on his back. He tucked a loose tendril of black hair behind her ear.

"I have become a wanton and wicked woman."

John gazed soberly at her. "Aye, no doubt about it. In fact, I'm certain the bishop would have grave things to say about a woman who is so corrupt that she *wants* her husband to make love to her. But now that I think of it, I do not care *what* the bishop's views might be on the subject."

Her quiet laugh brought a smile to his face, and he kissed her hair.

"So you are telling me you think there is nothing odd about a husband making love to his wife in the very shadow of the cathedral?"

"Nothing odd, at all!" He grinned at her. "Certainly not odd when one remembers that this is the same husband who took his wife's virginity in the window of a darkened corridor, cheerfully forsaking the blissful comforts of a wedding bed."

She nestled closer against his chest and sighed contentedly. "I very much like the way this husband views some things."

John Stewart chuckled to himself. He'd married an enchantress. There was a power she wielded over him. It flared up and blazed—controlling his body, his sense of discipline, even his heart, it seemed. She had the power to transform him from an angry man to a panting school lad in the space of a moment. And now, here she stood, satisfied and seemingly unconcerned about the potent force that dwelt within her . . . or about the reprimand he had planned to lay about her pretty ears.

"You are no longer angry with me!"

But not completely oblivious, he thought.

"Catherine"—he started, pulling back slightly and framing her pretty face in his large hands—"I suppose I cannot blame you completely for what happened today. You cannot be even half aware of the danger dogging your steps here in the Highlands, or you wouldn't be traipsing so recklessly through these hills."

"I am much hardier than you think, John."

"By St. Andrew, I know you are hardy enough! But our enemies here are much more cunning than the ones you've escaped from in England."

"I have done no wrong for any of these people to hate me!" Her midnight-blue eyes widened. "Or is it because I am half English that you think me in danger among your people?"

" 'Tis neither of those things," he whispered quietly. "Just by marrying me, Catherine, you've become a target for those who wish to destroy me."

"And why would one want to destroy you?" Her voice gentled, and he felt her words caress his spirit.

"You are a good leader to your people. From everything I can see, they honor and respect you as their earl and laird."

Her confidence in him was precious. Looking into her face, he traced her lower lip with his thumb. With a sudden rush of anger, he drew her fiercely to his chest. The helplessness he'd felt after learning she'd gone had been maddening. "Never do that to me again, Cat! Never put yourself in danger as you did today."

She pushed herself away from his chest and met his gaze. "For me to recognize friend from foe, John, I need to learn the truth about you. I need to know who is your enemy and why he is so determined to do us harm, though I think there is danger inside the heavy curtain walls of Balvenie Castle as well as outside."

"You mean the stable hand, Roy Sykes."

She nodded. " 'Twas not until we were away into the hills, and I caught a glimpse of an ambush ahead of us, that I realized there was a reason for him being so easy to persuade."

"When we return, I want you to point out the spot where they were waiting for you." Athol clenched his jaw. Thus far, they'd successfully eluded him every time he'd chased them, but he'd run the rascals right into the ground this time, if it took him a year. He glanced up, realizing she was looking intently at him. "But how was it that you didn't think I was the one waiting for you to pass by?"

"You? Waiting?" She shook her head. "Nay, you're not one to wait and ambush! In fact, to be truthful I expected to see you and your men racing through the glen. That's why we took to the hills."

"I see," he muttered. She knew him better than he'd have imagined. "And how were you able to find your way to Elgin without a guide?"

" 'Twas not difficult." She shrugged. "I have a fairly
good sense of direction. But more importantly, how
did you learn of Roy Sykes's betrayal? When I put
the pieces together, I wondered if that was the reason
why it took you so long to come after us. To tell the
truth, it wasn't so much the fear of any brigands ahead
as 'twas the thought of my husband's fury behind that
had me scurrying."

"Wait a moment," he growled. Realizing that they
had left her cloak in the loft, Athol turned and moved
back through the darkness of the stable. A fine hunter
tossed his head as the earl passed. The bishop's, no
doubt, he thought. When he reached Catherine, she
was standing by the open door, gazing out past the
flickering torch toward the cathedral. A number of
canons and cowled clerics were moving across the
courtyard from the chapter house. He shook out the
cloak before wrapping it around her shoulders.

" 'Twas past midday when I learned that you were
missing. And from what I could gather, immediately
after you and the monk left, Roy Sykes disappeared,
as well. Hearing that the stable hand had gone rather
than coming after me, I had a fairly clear indication
that the lad was up to no good."

"Has he been at Balvenie for all of his life?"

"Nay." He shook his head. "And I suppose I should
have been more suspicious of him from the beginning.
He came begging for a meal and some work just about
the same time as Adam of the Glen began raiding the
outlying farms. We'd just lost a stable hand to a fever,
and the lad knew horses. But I should have suspected
a connection."

"Who is this Adam of the Glen, John?"

He tried to step back into darkness of the stable,
but her gentle touch on his arm held him.

"Please tell me about him. How am I supposed to
protect myself when I know nothing about this shad-

owy phantom who is lurking and lying in wait for me?"

"Well, I know only a wee bit more about him, myself."

"You're not being honest with me, husband! You must know more, and your mother . . . well, the dowager certainly didn't react to the mention of his name as if 'twere nothing. She—"

"What did she tell you about him?" His words came out harsher than he'd intended.

"Very little! But her withdrawal was sharp and swift, and said much more than any words might have. She was deeply affected by the mention of Adam of the Glen. He's more than just some local thief, isn't he?"

Athol turned and walked back to the hunter's stall. If he himself could only get his own mother to say more, he thought, stroking the horse's fetlock. His search for the old earl's likely mistresses had all come to naught. No one had been able to point him in the direction of Adam's mother. And then, to learn that the cagey devil himself was conducting the same search made no sense to Athol.

"John! Tell me what you know!"

She had moved right behind him. He felt the soft touch of her hands on his back—trying to ease the tension that had crept into his body. He turned around and faced her.

"He is my half-brother. The bastard son of my father. Until a few weeks ago, I had no knowledge that such a person even existed. I certainly had no idea that the rogue raiding my lands was my own blood kin."

Even in the darkness, Athol couldn't miss the shadow of sorrow that momentarily enveloped her. "And you assume that he knows this, as well?"

A sudden anger swept through him. Turning on her,

he started pacing between the stalls. "Aye, I believe he does, or he wouldn't be so damned intent on ruining my holdings. But other than that, I do not know a thing about him. I sure as hell do not know why he waited so many years before wreaking havoc on my people's lives."

"How long has it been? Since he started, I mean."

"Six months . . . more or less." He turned his angry glare on her. "But where was he before that? From the descriptions of my own folk, he's no lad . . . and a giant at that. Why, all of the sudden, has he come?" Frustrated, he smashed the palm of his hand against a post. The entire stable shuddered, sending a couple of birds that had been roosting in the eaves fluttering off and causing the horses in the stalls to neigh and stamp their feet nervously.

"Perhaps he, too, found out the truth just recently." Her troubled eyes met his. "Who revealed the truth about him to you?"

"My mother—and do not bother asking her, for she appears to have taken an oath of silence on the subject. No matter how I've approached her, she remains steadfast in her refusal to speak. And her fading health serves as an excuse to end any discussion she finds unpleasant."

She took a hesitant step toward him. "And I am certain you have been a most understanding son. It cannot be too pleasant knowing her husband fathered a bastard son."

"Nay, that isn't it," he retorted gruffly. "I do not know where you've been kept, but a man taking a maid is no more uncommon in the Highlands than 'tis anywhere else—England included. The strange part of it all is that Adam's existence should have been kept a secret from me!"

Noticing her dash a tear from her cheek brought him up short. Extending a hand, he lifted her chin when she tried to turn her face away. "What is wrong now, lass? What is all this?"

She pushed his hand away. "And you think that is acceptable behavior, too? Are you planning to populate your land with bastard sons and daughters, as well?"

Her concern—her obvious struggle to stop the quivering in her lower lip—touched something within him. Athol knew that Catherine had fallen in love with him, and her behavior now only reinforced that knowledge. But clearly no romantic notions on her part were capable of deterring her from disobeying his wishes and leaving the safety of Balvenie Castle. Neither would he allow any romantic inclinations to cloud his thinking. His face tightened.

"You are asking more of me than I ever promised you that first night."

Her voice was quiet but clear. "I've already given you more of myself than I ever thought imaginable that first night."

"I warned you, did I not?"

"Aye, you did."

"And you regret it already?"

She shook her head. "Nay, I do not as yet! And I will not so long as you continue to prove yourself a worthy husband!"

Her attempt at arrogance brought a smile to his lips. "Then to answer your question. I will not attempt to populate Balvenie Castle with bastards so long as you continue to prove yourself a worthy wife."

"I have been the perfect wife, and I certainly plan to remain so!"

He took a step forward and, after checking her appearance, pulled the hood of her cloak over her head and started her toward the door.

"We clearly have to make some changes in your perception of what makes a perfect wife."

"I do not know what you mean!"

"The perfect wife does not leave her husband's bed and ride out into the dangers of an unknown countryside." As they stepped out into the light of the torch, he paused and looked at Catherine's face. Already, she was paying no attention to him whatsoever.

So be it, he decided. Hell. What good would it be to scold her, anyway? And he was actually beginning to enjoy her daydreaming, especially when he was at the center of it. After the lovemaking they'd just enjoyed, how could he be disappointed with this trait in his wife?

In his perfect wife, he corrected himself silently.

Chapter 14

The raids continued.

Outside of Balvenie Castle, Adam of the Glen continued with his destruction of Athol's lands with a frustrated John Stewart dogging his heels. Meanwhile, anytime he reappeared inside the walls, an increasingly frustrated Catherine relentlessly—and unsuccessfully—pursued her husband to secure an escort back to Elgin Cathedral.

More than a fortnight had passed since John Stewart had dragged her back to Balvenie Castle. As a "punishment" he had not allowed her to speak to the bishop before their departure, and though Brother Bartholomew had been left behind, Catherine still had no clue as to her requests regarding the school. Understanding the power of the church hierarchy, Catherine knew that having permission of the earl, her husband, was only half the battle for her project. Little would be done without the support of the bishop. And to think, she had been within a few steps of the bishop's palace!

As the days passed, Catherine was becoming more and more anxious to go back to Elgin. During one stretch of good weather, she had found herself sorely tempted to take one of the other monks and make the journey once again. But Athol's men had received clear instructions on that score. They were very, very sorry, but the countess was not allowed outside the gates with a horse, mule, or nanny goat. And if she wanted to walk into the village in the glen below the castle walls, then they would be more than happy to escort her. Had she thought of taking a turn about the gardens for air?

One night, as she paced her chamber restlessly, the sound of horses and the shouts of men could be heard from the courtyard. Jean's knock sounded at the door before Catherine could even reach it. Together, they crossed the chilly corridor to the long, thin windows overlooking the courtyard. Athol had been gone for several days—a lifetime, it seemed—but there he was, dismounting in front of the Great Hall. Catherine's spirits lifted immediately. Finally, he had returned.

Within moments, there were calls for hot water and food to be sent to the earl's chamber, and Jean went scurrying with the rest of the serving folk.

Well, no matter how tired the man must be, she decided, she would go to him and make him help her as he'd promised. But there was no telling who might be with him, so Catherine quickly dressed, practicing her argument a number of times as she did.

Opening the door, Catherine shivered as a brisk cross breeze whistled in from the corridor, blowing out the taper in her hand. Turning back into the room, she crossed to her bed and picked up the Stewart tartan, wrapping it around her shoulders for warmth.

Deciding that a lit taper was unnecessary, she closed her door behind her and started down the corridor. Before she had gone two steps, though, the scuff of a shoe on the floor in front of her froze her in her tracks. Someone was coming, and she knew it couldn't be Jean. Without a second thought, she stepped silently into an alcove by a window, and an instant later a shadow sailed past her. During the daylight, she would have assumed it was one of the servants, but now . . .

Her curiosity piqued, Catherine moved out from her hiding place and peered into the darkness where the shadow had disappeared. Silently, she followed.

It was a woman—she was certain of it. Even in the dim light of the moon filtering in through the narrow windows of the passage, Catherine could tell that it was a woman.

When the shadowy figure disappeared into the pitch blackness of the circular stairwell, Catherine paused. If it were Susan, why was she again haunting this part of the keep? If it were someone else, did she dare follow her into the darkness?

Taking a deep breath, she edged into the stairwell. The sound of a light step drifted up from below. Catherine followed, hugging the wall as she descended. Step by step she followed, listening for any sign ahead.

Suddenly she stopped. The low, heavy scrape of wood sounded and then the breath of a woman, released as if struggling with a great weight. It *was* Susan—Catherine no longer had any doubt.

She waited, suddenly panicking at the thought that the young woman might return the way she'd come. Beneath this corner of the keep were storage rooms and guard's quarters, but so far as she knew, no one ever used this stairwell to reach the upper floors. There was no sound at all from below now, and finally Catherine mustered her courage and continued down. At the bottom landing, her fingers found a great wooden door, banded and studded with iron. Cobwebs around the door clung to her fingers and hair. Susan had not gone out through there. Another door, equally filthy with disuse, met her a few steps farther.

Continuing around, her head suddenly brushed the lowering stairwell. Feeling with her hand in the darkness, she realized she had reached a dead end. The walls were stone, and she frowned, puzzled by Susan's disappearance.

If she had only a lit taper, she swore. Staying a moment longer and trying to listen for any sounds, Catherine finally gave up on the chase and started back up the stairs the same way she'd descended.

Approaching her own doorway along the same corridor, Catherine paused, remembering Susan standing in the same spot the night when John had made love to her for the first time. Too embarrassed at having been caught, and also concerned about the state of the other woman's feelings, Catherine had not given much thought to why, at that late hour of the night, Susan had been roaming through this older section of the keep. But now, as she turned around and glanced again at the entrance to the stairwell, Catherine began to understand things a bit better.

But wherever it was that Susan was going, and whatever it was that she was doing, remained a mystery to Catherine. And this was a side to Susan that was completely unexpected.

Passing by her door, though, and heading toward the newer section of the keep, Catherine knew that she had more pressing matters to consider. Matters like settling once and for all her request to return to Elgin to speak to the bishop.

All was quiet in the household by the time Catherine reached her husband's chamber door. Thinking for a moment of how exhausted he must be after nearly a week chasing the raiders through the hills, she suddenly had second thoughts. She paused, her hand lifted to knock.

But then she thought, what other choice did she have but to awaken him? Athol could as well be gone tomorrow for another endless hunt, and she would never even get an opportunity to speak with him. An unexpected pang of sadness cut into her chest at the thought that he could go off again without even taking time to send for her.

Well, she decided, she would not wait to be sent for.

Her knuckles only met with thin air as the door opened abruptly. Startled, she looked up and found her husband's dark and weary face gazing down at her. The trace of a smile tugged at the corner of his mouth.

He stood in the doorway, as silent as a statue, and his eyes raked over her body. Her face flushed hot in an instant, and she was suddenly conscious of the pulse pounding in her temple. Athol cocked his head slightly to the side, his gaze pausing at the Stewart tartan she wore around her shoulders. Then, without a word of greeting, he leaned down and placed a firm kiss on her lips.

"I'm glad you're here, lass," he growled finally. "I was coming after you."

"After me?" she croaked. His one large hand wrapped around her wrist and dragged her into his outer chamber, closing the door behind them.

"You can keep that hole in the wall you call a bedchamber, if you like, but when I am here at Balvenie Castle, I expect you to share my bed with me."

Vaguely, it occurred to Catherine that she should object to such a command, but instead, the words spread a warmth through her. Wordlessly, and with somewhat unsteady legs, she followed her husband as he guided her through the doorway leading into his bedchamber.

Stepping into the room, she immediately spotted the huge half-barrel that sat by the fire. Feeling the release of his hold on her wrist, Catherine turned and watched him as he latched his door. The intimacy of his action shot a bolt of fire through her, and her head suddenly whirled with dizziness. Crossing to the hearth, Athol lifted a huge kettle of water from the hook over the fire and added the steaming liquid to the water already in the tub.

"I . . . heard . . . I've heard that . . ."

"I can see I've stayed away too long." He turned toward her and yanked his shirt over his head. "You are again forgetting your words when we are alone."

She took a step back and tried to gather her wits. She had to voice her request before he came close enough to touch her. "I want to return to Elgin."

He unfastened his kilt and the dark wool pooled at his feet. She couldn't stop her eyes from scanning the long, sinewy muscles of his chest, the taut skin of his stomach, the wispy trail of reddish hair leading to his—

Catherine jerked her eyes away. "I need to see the bishop!" she exclaimed.

"A strong reaction to your husband's body, Cat. But I need to take a bath!"

He wasn't taking her seriously. "Well! You can't take a bath until you at least agree to stop your people from harassing me when I tell them I wish to go to Elgin."

He moved toward the tub and stepped into the water. "You are in no position to bargain."

She saw him sit back into the tub and give her a devilish smile. But at the same time she didn't miss the softening of his gaze as she unwrapped the tartan from her shoulders and placed it on the bed.

Dressed in a simple linen dress that Jean had sewn for her this past week, Catherine felt like anything but a seductress. But still, knowing that her husband was the most agreeable whenever they were involved in a passionate encounter, she prepared herself to put all her power to good use. After all, it was for a good cause, and certainly worth a try.

"As I mentioned before," she said, "I need to get back to Elgin."

"I heard you, Cat, and you won't be going. So put it out of your mind."

"I won't put it out of my mind!" She reached up, slowly pulling at the laces that tied the front of her dress. She could not help but shiver with excitement at the way he froze in the tub, his eyes following the movement of her hands. "I have already traveled that route. I can take the other two monks as companions, if it makes you feel—"

"You are not going," he said vaguely.

She pulled at the neckline of the dress and started pushing the garment over one shoulder. She could see that he'd ceased breathing. "Getting your approval for the school was only half the battle. I need to see the bishop to secure tutors and—"

"Tutors?" His gaze flickered for a moment to her face. "My answer has not changed."

Catherine pushed the dress over her other shoulder. In an instant, it had slipped over her hips and fallen to the floor. His scorching gaze told her that although he had a thorough knowledge of what lay beneath her thin chemise, that knowledge did nothing to diminish the desire he was feeling now.

"Suddenly, I am wondering if you would be interested in a bargain."

"You are a wanton thing, Cat." He smiled faintly and nodded. "Perhaps I would, at that."

Gathering her courage, Catherine took a small step toward the tub. "If you were to stop imprisoning me here and allow me to gather what I need for the school, I in return will—"

"Aye?"

"Wash your back for you?"

His laugh was hearty and brought a smile to her lips.

"Why is it that I have an idea you'd be willing to do a great deal more than that . . . for this school of yours?"

"Very well! I'll wash your back and arms and . . .

and dry you, as well. But, in return you must hold to your promise."

"Come here."

His command was lazy, its seductive note clear above the crackle of the fire. She shook her head. "Nay, not until—"

"You'll come here . . . or I'll come out after you."

She again shook her head, taking a step back and putting a chair in between them. "Not until I have your word on—"

"You already have my approval for the school."

"Aye, but without the assistance of the bishop—assistance I wanted to get from him at Elgin last time—I don't know how . . ." Catherine's words caught in her throat as Athol rose suddenly from the tub. Her eyes widened at the sight of his wet and fully aroused manhood before lifting her eyes to meet his meaningful gaze. She forced out her words. "You—you never even gave me the chance to see Patrick Hepburn!"

"Are you going to come over here of your own accord or would you like me to come after you?"

"You . . . Stop, John. You still haven't given me an answer that suits me."

"You come and wash my back, Cat, and I promise I'll give you an answer that suits you."

She still looked at him doubtfully. "And I have your word of honor?"

"You have," he nodded with a sly smile, slowly lowering himself again into the water. "You come here, and I'll give you what you are after."

There was no denying him. And there was no denying her own desires. Walking slowly toward him, she watched his eyes as they roamed her body. When she reached his side, he held up a wet cloth.

"There you are, lass," he said. But as she reached for it, his hand darted out, taking hold of her wrist and looping his other arm around her waist. She was on his lap in the water before she could even cry out.

"Ah! Now this is much better," he whispered devilishly, nestling her comfortably until she was half immersed into the water. Catherine could feel his arousal pressing intimately against her. "Perhaps, first I'll wash you, my sweet."

With her feet still dangling on the outside of the tub and her arm around his shoulder, she looked up and met his intent gaze. "Before we get any further into this . . . this . . ."

"Bathing? Lovemaking?"

"Whatever!" She tried to not be too aware of the warm water he was pouring with his huge hand over her breasts, soaking the thin chemise until it was transparent. "Your—your promise. I can leave for Elgin tomorrow."

"Nay, you won't!"

She stiffened in his arms and started fighting his hold. "You blackguard! I should have known that I could never—"

"Sit still. You are splashing half the water out of the tub."

She turned into a hellcat. "When I am done with you, you will be mourning a lot more than just some water!"

"You cannot go to Elgin."

She tried to pull herself from his lap, but his steely grip on her waist held her in place.

"You promised me, and now you are reneging—"

"Nay, I'm not," he growled, pressing his lips to the bare skin of her neck. She couldn't stop her excitement at the feel of his lips, but still she wouldn't give up her struggle. "You wanted the bishop's blessing and assistance in opening your school . . ."

She slapped him soundly on the chest and tried to pull away.

"The bishop has given all of that, my wild thing. I'm sure there is no reason for waging war in a warm bath over such things."

Catherine went limp for a moment in his arms. Then, turning and placing both hands on his shoulders, she looked into his face. "What did you say?"

"I said you do not have to go to Elgin. The bishop has already promised you all the support that you'll be needing."

This time she willingly allowed him to pull her tightly against him. Her breasts pressed hard against his chest. "And how long have you known this? Was it Brother Bartholomew who talked him over to our side?"

He already appeared to have lost all interest in the discussion. She shivered when his hand caressed the side of her breast—his mouth descending and placing lazy kisses on her face. She lay her head over on his muscular arm. She too suddenly found it hard concentrating. "Is . . . is he back already, and no one told me?"

"I've met my end of the bargain," he said hoarsely, his hand dropping into the water. She could feel his fingers move up under the hem of her wet chemise and slide along the skin of her thigh. All Catherine could do was to hold her breath and sink against him in anticipation of what was to come. "Now 'tis your turn, I believe."

Chapter 15

Arthur Courtenay quaffed the last of the wine in his cup and wiped his velvet sleeve across his mouth. Staring into the fire, he sat back in the only chair in the small chamber and sent the cup clanging into a darkened corner.

"Sluts, bitches, and buggering priests," he muttered, his words slurring together. "Well, you'll not make a fool of me. I'll have that treasure."

The muffled sounds of men's voices in the Great Hall beyond the thick oaken door could be heard. The king's Deputy Lieutenant stood up, steadied himself, and moved toward the door. As he pulled it open, the faces of his soldiers and a fierce-looking stranger turned to him.

"M'lord!" The newcomer approached and bowed. "I come from the Lord Chancellor."

"Aye, sir knight, enter," Courtenay growled, turning his back and moving across the chamber to the fire. "And be quick."

With his face in shadow, the Deputy Lieutenant stood with his back to the fire as the hard-faced courtier entered. Courtenay made no effort to make the man comfortable. Leather and mail gleamed beneath the man's cloak, and wild shadows and light licked the walls around him.

"What is it, then?"

"The Lord Chancellor sends his—"

"Get on with it, man," Courtenay spat out. "What have you to say? I haven't all night."

The knight stared at him for a moment. "Aye, m'lord. 'Tis this. The king wants to know what progress has been made to capture the traitor Percy's wife and daughters."

Sir Arthur stood silently for a long moment, considering his answer carefully.

"Tell the Lord Chancellor that we know the whereabouts of the eldest sister. She has fled to the north. She has taken refuge near Elgin, but we know where she is. She will not escape us. The other two sisters and the mother are also in Scotland, but we will find them as well, as soon as the eldest is caught. Tell your master that, sir knight."

"Is there anything else, m'lord?"

Courtenay stared steadily into the steely eyes of the knight. "That is all, knight. Now, get out."

As the door closed behind the courtier, Sir Arthur turned and stared into the flames. He would burn in hell before he would tell them anything more. He would find those damned Percys, and the treasure would be his. Only his.

Catherine breathed deeply the soft tang of the autumn air and tried to clear her mind of the thoughts that had been tormenting her these past few days.

Although she'd heard tales of the terrible damp and cold that can afflict the Highlands, the autumn still felt much like late summer, and the days continued to be mostly sunny and pleasant. Moving ahead of her large group of accomplices into the protected alcove of the garden, she nodded to the women, who hurriedly spread the blanket and placed the cushioned chair beside the low wall. The smell of roses still blooming in the trim hedge along the grassy path hung in the air.

Looking back, Catherine motioned toward Tosh, who had carried the frail, but loudly complaining woman down from the castle to the gardens. Carefully, with more gentleness than one might have thought possible from the scarred and rugged warrior, he placed her in the chair. The accompanying servants were quick to tuck a blanket and offer a cup of medicinal tea to the ailing woman.

The dowager pushed the cup away disdainfully. She glared fiercely at her daughter-in-law. "Catherine Percy, the time has finally arrived when I can truly say I regret the day I first laid eyes on your homely face."

Ignoring the insult, Catherine smiled pleasantly at the group and dismissed all of them for the time being. With a wry smile, Tosh took up a position beneath a gnarled pear tree at the far end of the garden. Catherine could see that from there he could keep an eye out for any potential danger.

As for the rest, the parting looks were mixed. Some were obviously amazed, though pleased, to have someone in the castle brave enough to induce the dowager to leave her chamber. Others were obviously worried for Catherine and the possible outcome of leaving her alone with the demanding invalid. Nonetheless, the women turned back up the hill toward the castle gates, leaving only Auld Mab—the dowager's oldest companion—and Jean, who together wandered off to talk of the herbs and autumn flowers that remained in the garden beds.

Catherine smiled at her husband's mother. Her little plan was working out nicely. The color in the old woman's cheek was already better than Catherine had seen it in weeks. But the ease of bringing the dowager out for some air lay simply in the fact that Susan had not been at Lady Anne's bedside when Catherine had announced the little outing. The younger woman seemed perfectly content to take care of her aunt in the confines of the airless chamber, and Catherine had a good idea that she would be certain to object to such a rash change of pace. It didn't hurt, though, that Auld Mab had quickly sided with Catherine.

And by the time they returned to the keep, the dowager's chamber would be cleaned and well-aired.

"You'll be the death of me," the dowager started again before the last serving woman had hastily fled the garden. "I am certain to get a chill. Mark me, I'll be dead by nightfall."

Again ignoring the old woman's comments, Catherine removed her cloak and, spreading it on the blanket, took the volume of poetry she'd chosen from her husband's library out of the great inside pocket of the cloak.

"I never expected you to be so villainous, young woman. You want my position, my chambers, no doubt. Why, I . . ."

Catherine sat on the ground next to the dowager's feet, receiving a mild nudge from the older woman's foot for her efforts. She smiled, opened the book to a marked passage, and began to read aloud.

"Where, in a lusty plain, I made my way,
I found a river, pleasant to behold,
Embroidered all with flowers gay.
There, through glittering stones of gold,
The crystal water ran clear and cold,
And in my ear, a melody.
The sounds of joy and harmony . . ."

Lady Anne Stewart continued with her complaints. "Do not think this is any way to treat me, young woman."

Catherine continued to read.

". . . At the last, beholding all these things,
I saw a garden, with walls around.
Amid the flowers I suddenly spied
Fortune, the goddess, and on the ground
Before her feet, a wheel . . ."

Catherine paused for a moment, and then read on.

Accepting her fate of remaining John Stewart's wife
and staying at Balvenie Castle, she was now determined to find peace with the others who lived there.
Resolved on her mission, Catherine knew her most
important challenge lay in the earl's mother. Though
the dowager acted infirm, the young woman was convinced Lady Anne Stewart had plenty of life left in
her. She just needed some provocation and a purpose
to live. If all worked out as Catherine planned, the
aging woman would have plenty of both today.

But that was not all. Catherine herself desperately
needed knowledge and support that she knew the
dowager could provide. Selfish as it was, she had to
admit inwardly that this outing was as much for herself
as for the ailing mother of her husband.

Finishing the page, Catherine looked up and found
Lady Anne leaning forward in the chair. The older
woman's eyes were fixed longingly on the book in
Catherine's lap. She waited until the older woman's
gaze lifted and met hers.

"You've been prying into my past."

"I've been seeking out your interests," Catherine
corrected. "Your love for verse, both in reading and
composing, is well known among the folk of Balvenie Castle."

The dowager glanced back down at the page. " 'Tis
the work of the first James Stewart to reign as king
of Scotland."

"Aye." Catherine nodded. "The *King's Quair.*"

"Why are you doing this?" Lady Anne sank back

heavily in the chair. "Why must you bother? You could let me be! I do not need all these daily visits, you know! The constant bickering with me at my bedside! Don't you understand that I just want to be left to die!"

Although the sharpness of her tongue was clearly intended to rile Catherine, the vulnerability in the older woman's expression and voice touched Catherine inwardly. They were each tormented in some way. And whether they admitted it or not, they each longed for love.

Looking up and meeting the piercing gray eyes, Catherine wrapped a hand around the thin fingers, trying to put some warmth into them.

"Do you remember the first day that we met? The day that you called me a fool for asking the unreasonable . . . for wishing the impossible . . . for not recognizing and appreciating my good fortune and all I had to be thankful for?'

"Do not compare yourself to me! And if you start calling me names in the same fashion I did to you, I'll have Tosh whip you across the glen and up the side of Ben Aigan!" The dowager paused and when she spoke again, her voice shook a bit. "I am old and spent. I've had a full life and am now ready to relieve you and my son of the troubles of caring for an invalid. But you, on the other hand . . . you are young, strong, full of life. And despite my mocking you on that first day, I believe you are just the perfect wife for John. You do not need an old fool like me—"

"But I *do* need you," Catherine broke in. "Despite any show of strength, I am frightened, Lady Anne. And I need your help desperately."

The dowager stared at her in surprise.

"What have you to be frightened of? Has my son hurt you in some—?"

"Nay, Countess. 'Tisn't that at all."

"Then what? You have people around you who will help you with your school. Everything may seem to be taking too long in getting started, but—"

"That's not the problem, either." Catherine shook her head. "Though I didn't know I already had the bishop's approval, I know that planning and arranging the rest is something that I can easily handle."

"Then what else, child? You and your sisters and your mother are all safely out of England. What could be bothering you?"

Catherine couldn't stop the heat from spreading into her cheeks. The feelings that were coursing through her were so new that she didn't know how to restrain them.

"'Tis . . . 'tis a suspicion that I have." Catherine closed the book and placed it on the blanket. She tried to pull her hand from the dowager's lap, but the old woman grasped it tight. Her grip was surprisingly strong.

"What is it, Catherine?"

"I . . . do not know for certain. But . . . I think . . . I . . . have these signs . . . of what I know goes along with . . ." She took a deep breath. " . . . In one who is with child."

"Bless the Lord! By the Holy Mother, 'tis a wondrous day!" The dowager's face brightened immediately and her loud laugh drew the looks of Tosh and the two other women in the garden. "Have you told Athol the news?"

Catherine shook her head. "I wasn't certain. I still am not. But I do not have anyone here at Balvenie Castle that I felt confident enough to . . . well, no one who I could be sure was knowledgeable . . . of whom I could ask such things."

Lady Anne beamed a moment, then squeezed Catherine's hand before charging on with her questions. Catherine answered her, giving a detailed description of her periodic lightheadedness, of her queasiness at the smell of the cooking wafting up from the kitchens, and of not experiencing her monthly.

"Aye, it must be," the dowager whispered, almost to herself. "I knew I could count on Nichola Erskine's daughter making me a happy woman before I die."

"But that is what I mean," Catherine argued. "I am frightened. I don't know what to do!"

" 'Tis easy, child! Many a woman before you has gone through this. With the help of a midwife, some herbal teas Auld Mab there can fix up, and a few prayers—"

"Not the birthing, dowager. That is not even real to me yet. What has me frightened right now is the thought of how my husband will treat me once he discovers the truth."

"He'll be delighted, lass. He wants a bairn. That was why he chose a wife."

Lady Anne's words confirmed her fears. She couldn't stop the tears from gathering in her eyes.

"And then what?" she asked miserably. "Now that I am bearing his child, don't you think that he'll lose interest in me? He has told me more than once that I should not harbor any dreamy notions about our marriage. He's told me often enough that there is no love that will ever grow between us!"

"He's a fool, Catherine—like all men. And you are foolish to believe him."

"Please don't try to tell me things I know are not true." Catherine slipped her hand from the old woman's and sat back on the blanket. A patch of clouds covered the sun for a moment before passing by. "I remember the conditions under which we married."

"You remember and yet you allowed yourself to fall in love with him. Knowing the danger, still you could not protect your heart."

Catherine's vision became a blur as she stared at

her hands clasped in her lap. She hadn't been able to voice the truth to her husband. She hadn't even permitted herself to admit it inwardly. But here it was, plainly and clearly said by the dowager—she had fallen helplessly in love with John Stewart.

"It warms my heart to know you care about him so much. 'Tis a blessing to learn that, despite all of his foolish delays, John has ended up marrying someone as worthy as you."

These were the kindest words Lady Anne had ever spoken to Catherine, and yet they only served to choke her more with emotion.

"But I . . . I don't know what to do!"

"Tell him the truth, child. All of it! About your love. About the bairn! Only a dolt of a man wouldn't be affected by such a revelation."

"But 'tis not so easy." Catherine looked up and met Lady Anne's intense eyes. "Do you consider John like yourself or like his father?"

The older woman cocked an eyebrow at her. "Why, he is very much like his father! In appearance, he is the spitting image. The same height. The same build. The same handsome Stewart face that made me fall in love with his father the first moment I laid eyes on him. Why do you ask that, lass?'

"Because . . . well, what of his temperament, Lady Anne?"

"You know yourself our temperaments are not the same. Nay, in that Athol is very much like his father— easy to rile and passionate. And my husband was a man who was fearless in his determination to win— especially when setting a wrong to right. If there were ever any two people who had so much in common—" Lady Anne's words came to an abrupt stop.

Catherine had to bite her lips to stop their trembling. Whatever she did, she couldn't hold back the ache that was breaking her heart in two.

"My answer was not what you'd hoped to hear, was it, Catherine?"

"I asked for the truth. You simply told me what I expected."

The dowager's frail hand reached over and wiped a tear from Catherine's cheek. "I can see that you know the truth. You know about Adam, don't you?"

Catherine gave a small nod, unable to find her voice.

"I now understand why you are distressed. You believe that now that you are with child, he'll lose interest in you. That he, like his father, will wander. Is that it?"

Again, all Catherine could do was to give a simple nod.

"But such an assumption is erroneous, my dear." The dowager's frail fingers rested on Catherine's shoulders. "Though it has only been a short while that you two have known one another, I assure you that I've never seen my son more enchanted with a woman than he is with you. I know you think me indifferent to what goes on in this castle. Well, there is not a bit of news that my serving women do not bring back to me. I know everything." The dowager gave Catherine a knowing smile. "Everything. From what I understand, if you are not waiting for him in his chamber when he returns to Balvenie, then he comes after you. This is a very good start, child."

"But isn't this the same as 'twas between you and your husband, Lady Anne?" Catherine's question appeared to catch the dowager off guard, and the older woman looked sharply away. "From what I've been able to gather from some of the older servants, the old earl was a devoted husband, a man committed to his wife and to his son."

Catherine waited for an answer, hoping against hope that Lady Anne would tell her that their marriage had all been false—a loveless arrangement that had simply connected two great families. That there had never been anything between them. But the dowager chose silence instead.

A brisk breeze riffled the leaves of the rosebushes, and the late buds bowed their heads before it. Running her hands over her arms to ward off the sudden chill, Catherine looked up at the dowager, suddenly concerned about the woman's frail condition. She appeared lost in her thoughts.

"Perhaps, Lady Anne, I should call Tosh! I think 'tis time that we—"

"We *did* have a wonderful marriage." Her voice sounded hoarse. "I thought myself blessed that I had a husband who had eyes for no other woman but me."

Seeing the pain reflected so plainly in the older woman's face made Catherine feel guilty for even asking the question. She wrapped a hand around Lady Anne's bony fingers. "I should not have brought up such things. I am sorry for being so unfeeling."

The dowager shook her head and gave a slight smile. "Don't be! We had a good life, Athol and I. And though I was hurt because of what he did, I still cannot imagine my life without him."

"You forgave him for what he did and stayed beside him. I am not sure I could ever have been silent!"

"Nay, my dear! I was anything but silent. I made life miserable for the rutting goat until he took away his bastard son where I no longer had to lay eyes on him. I—"

"He brought Adam to you?" Though Catherine knew she should end this discussion, the old woman's revelation shocked her.

"Aye! He brought him to me as an infant. To take care of the little creature. I would have just as soon left him out on the hillside for the fairies to steal, and I told him so."

"But how could he expect you to . . . to . . ."

" 'Twas a different time, then."

"Lady Anne, did you—were you aware that he had taken a mistress?"

The dowager closed her eyes, but not before Catherine saw the tears that had gathered in their gray depths.

"Why didn't he leave the child with its mother? What purpose was there in bringing him to you?"

"The mother could not keep the bairn, he told me." The dowager shook her head and then looked into her daughter-in-law's eyes. "Catherine, Athol was a man—and men do such things—but I believe he regretted his unfaithfulness. I believe he did not want the bairn to suffer for his own lust."

"But when you would not keep the child, the earl took him away."

"Aye."

"And you believe this is why he has returned? To avenge himself on his father's family?"

" 'Tis difficult to say. Very difficult."

Catherine watched as the dowager leaned back heavily in the chair. The old woman's expression grew hard. She asked nothing more about Adam of the Glen. Indeed, she had not set out to learn about her husband's bastard brother as much as to seek advice about her own fears in dealing with John Stewart. But here she was, no more secure in her own weakness, and yet perplexed about the events that could have shaped another man. Her husband's enemy. Her husband's brother.

Glancing at Lady Anne, Catherine noticed the old woman shiver slightly, and with a wave at Tosh and the two women, she quickly rose to her feet.

"You must do what you think is right." The dowager's quiet voice drew Catherine's attention back to her. The woman was again looking at her with eyes shining with affection. "Though perhaps 'tis best to have him wait a bit on the good news. He might be more willing to reveal some of what he carries in his heart if all good things are not so easily bestowed on him."

"Then you'll keep my secret!"

"Aye. I will, for the time being." The dowager's face grew stern. "But only with the condition that you'll not judge him based on his father's weakness. 'Tis bad enough that I carry the regret of not raising Adam as my own. I could not stand to see my son also suffer for his father's mistakes."

Catherine stared for a moment at the aging woman. This was exactly what she had been doing. Expecting, fearing that her husband would behave like his father, like other men.

A few days ago, when John had mentioned that he'd like to take her to Ironcross Castle to meet his friends, Joanna and Gavin Kerr, Catherine had recalled the talk of Joanna MacInnes. The woman had been John's intended prior to marrying Gavin Kerr. It had been then that Catherine had started tormenting herself with fears that he was already tired of her and wanted to visit his "true" love. Indeed, she had wondered how he would react if he were to find out that she was already carrying his child. Perhaps then, she thought, there would be no reason at all for taking her along.

The old woman waved away the approaching warrior and the women and took hold of Catherine's hand.

"Listen to an old woman, child. Don't allow these things to distress you so. I can see the misery etched in your face." The dowager's voice was strong and yet gentle. "You've already allowed yourself to love him. Dwell on the good, and push aside the rest. I told you before, and I tell you again—never has he been so enchanted by a woman. Go ahead and work your wiles, lass . . . and have some faith in him, too."

Catherine tried to smile.

"Do what your heart tells you to do about the bairn. But trust me, Catherine, 'twill not be long before you know for certain that he has already entrusted his heart to you."

Placing her other hand over the dowager's affectionately, Catherine smiled. Perhaps her path was not as fraught with trouble as she had been imagining. Perhaps there was hope after all that her marriage might be as she'd dreamed it could be.

Chapter 16

The glow of fading embers in the hearth was the only source of light in the large bedchamber. Catherine, quietly sliding out of the bed, gazed wistfully at the handsome curve of her husband's muscular torso stretched so comfortably across the bed. The features of his chiseled face were relaxed in sleep, and she had to fight the urge to crawl back into the bed and forget about what she had planned to do with the rest of this night.

Determined to go through with it, though, she padded softly across the floor and hastily dressed herself. It had been a magical night, making love in the golden glow of the fire, thrilling at the sensations he wrought in her, losing herself as his tender touch and powerful body brought her time and time again to a point of ecstasy—to a wild and pulsing place surely not far from heaven itself. And unlike the other nights when they would playfully argue, barter, and bargain over everything and anything—before losing themselves in their frenzied passion—this night had been the most peaceful they'd ever shared.

She'd needed assurance; he'd given her tenderness.

She'd wanted commitment; he'd given her passion.

She'd sighed out his name; he had made her tremble.

Catherine was happy that this night had been so

different. The pure, simply joy of drowning in the moment, in the night, in each other, had been a blessing.

Finished dressing, Catherine gave him a final look and smiled. Perhaps she didn't have to challenge him, rile him, and please him at every turn. Perhaps he had already accepted her and her many moods. Perhaps it was time for her to trust her heart—and for that matter, her husband—and reveal to him that bit of news that was certain to make him a happy man.

She sent a kiss across the chamber and promised herself that she'd do just that—as soon as she was done solving the riddle that she was determined to unravel before this night was over.

Blowing out the taper at the sound of approaching steps, the monk hurriedly closed the top of the chest and pushed the open travel bag beneath the bed. Moving quickly toward the doorway, he silently peeked through the slightly open door.

The hurrying figure of the passing woman was a familiar sight to the cleric, but he held his breath a moment later at the sight of Catherine Percy's shadow following close after the first one. She did not turn into her chamber, and he breathed a sigh of relief.

Letting a moment pass after the two had disappeared down the corridor, the monk cast a thoughtful glance back at the bedchamber before making up his mind and taking off after the two. Whatever the younger woman, Mistress Susan, was up to, he cared very little about, but having Catherine Percy's life possibly in jeopardy was something that he could not allow.

Slipping out of the bedchamber, the monk followed quietly in the wake of the two women. Regardless of his orders, regardless of the greater interest which lay behind his mission, the monk knew that he could not let Catherine come to harm. How could he just shrug off feelings of loyalty for a woman he had known for so many years? Nay, he could not.

There was a great deal of mystery surrounding this Susan MacIntyre. But it was up to him to make certain Catherine Percy would not fall a victim to her own obstinacy. Catherine was fearless when it came to pursuing her dreams. And she was far, far too trusting in her own abilities.

And all of this made her a prime target for foul play.

After spending many nights hiding in the dark alcoves of this passageway, Catherine was now well-accustomed to Susan's ritual. In fact, searching the bottom of the stairwell in the light of the day, she had also discovered the trap door where Susan made her periodic escapes. It was very curious that she only seemed to steal away on nights when Athol and his men were in the castle.

Discovering where the younger woman went those nights had become an obsession with Catherine. But for some reason, telling her husband or asking Jean or the other serving women about Susan's habits was something that she could not bring herself to do.

Of all the inhabitants of Balvenie Castle, Susan MacIntyre was the one person that Catherine had not been able to befriend. And as far as Catherine was concerned, this failure had not been for a lack of trying.

There was an aloofness in the younger woman that Catherine had at first attributed to her displacement as acting mistress of Balvenie Castle, to being told that she was not to be the chosen wife of the earl, to seeing someone else move in and take her place. But Catherine's opinion had since changed.

There was something else. A mystery that she could not quite piece together. Susan was distant, true. But she also lived in a dream world that Catherine knew she herself sometimes inhabited. Susan was silent but not hostile toward Catherine—the woman who had robbed her of her rightful place.

In return, Catherine did not carry a grudge at having all her attempts of companionship rejected by the younger woman. But at the same time, she couldn't stop herself from wondering what it was that drove Susan down through a trap door in the middle of the night.

Recognizing the sound of the same door rising on its hinges, Catherine waited in the shadows for her turn. But this time, rather than giving up the chase and turning back to her own chamber, she moved on in pursuit. Touching her husband's dagger at her belt for comfort, she waited a few moments before easing open the trap door. Taking Athol's weapon had been a parting thought, one that she had hoped would give her some feeling of security against the unknown that lay ahead.

There was a rude ladder beneath the trap door, and as she stepped down into the musty passage, Catherine slowly lowered the door behind her. It was pitch black in the tunnel, and at the bottom of the ladder, she found by feeling with her hands that the narrow passage went in one direction only. A footfall ahead drew her attention, and she moved carefully through the darkness.

A feeling of excitement sent a chill down her back, and Catherine wrapped her cloak more tightly around her. This was so much like the days of her past when she and her sisters would set off to do mischief in the middle of the night. What a fearless bunch they had been as a group! How much easier this all would be if they had not had to separate.

That helped nothing, she thought. Focusing her

mind's eye on her goal, Catherine pushed such melancholy thoughts from her mind.

Using her hands to guide her, she pushed on, not daring to slow down for fear of getting lost should the tunnel branch off and she should lose contact with the woman before her. She could still hear Susan's occasional footstep, or her kicking of a stray pebble on the passage floor. The passage, though, had done nothing but go straight ahead, and she prayed for continued good luck.

For what seemed like a millennium, she followed. How long it had taken to carve this tunnel through the rocky terrain on which Balvenie Castle sat, Catherine could not even guess. The thought only flickered through her mind though, for she had other, more pressing matters at hand. As she groped along, she couldn't help but wonder if this chase would lead to anything.

Suddenly, the passage dipped sharply downward, and a few moments later, she heard sounds of Susan—directly in front of her—obviously struggling through some opening. From the distance they had traveled, she guessed that they must be far beyond the curtain wall of the castle. But on the other hand, she thought, trying to recall which direction the tunnel had gone once she'd climbed down from the secret door, they might have gone only as far as the orchards or the gardens in the opposite direction. Either way, Catherine was fairly certain that they must be outside of the castle.

Waiting until all sounds of Susan had receded into the darkness, Catherine again moved forward in pursuit, only to have her progress immediately arrested by a wall of stone.

From the time she'd stepped past the trap door, the feel of the walls had made her think that these passages were older than Balvenie itself. But this barrier appeared to have been intended to block the tunnel.

Knowing that the other woman had passed through the barrier made Catherine even more determined to find the way out. Feeling with her hands along the rough stone blocks, she could find no opening. The ceiling of the tunnel seemed to be high, though, for as high as she reached, she could not reach the top. Finding a narrow foothold on one wall of the tunnel, Catherine hoisted herself up and grabbed for the barrier.

Her fingers caught on the edge of an opening. A toehold on the barrier itself allowed her to pull herself up to the level of the opening. It was small, barely wide enough for her shoulders to pass through. In an instant, however, Catherine had wriggled her way into the tiny passageway, and after several yards, the opening widened, and she found that she was able to get to her hands and knees.

She halted when she heard a noise behind her. Ceasing to breathe, she tried to look back, but could see only darkness. Catherine looked forward again, certain that whatever lay ahead, Susan was there. And then she heard the noise again. A small scrape—the sound of metal against stone somewhere behind her. A man's grunt. Catherine's hand slowly reached down, wrapping around the handle of the dirk at her belt.

Could someone have followed her in the same way she had followed Susan? she wondered.

All of a sudden, the vulnerability of her situation hit her hard, and hastily Catherine scrambled forward in the tunnel. How could she protect herself in such a confined space? As far as she knew, she had no enemy. But it wasn't very long ago that Roy Sykes had disappeared from Balvenie Castle. Some had said that he'd feared the earl's wrath and had left before he could be punished for helping Catherine and Brother Bartholomew depart for Elgin. Others said that he'd always been a suspicious fellow and most likely had left to join the ranks of outlaws who had banded together under Adam of the Glen.

Either way, as far as Catherine was concerned, facing an opponent in this narrow tunnel presented real danger, and she pressed forward with little concern about the sounds of her own progress.

Catherine could feel a breath of cool air on her face, and soon realized that the passage was again becoming smaller. She paused for a moment, listening. She could hear nothing behind her, but that did little to make her feel safe. Again crawling forward on her belly, she pushed on until her hands suddenly met with solid rock. Panic seized her for a moment, but her hands—searching for some opening—found a small hole by her shoulder, and she crawled through.

In a moment, the tight sides of the passage opened up and she knew she was in a larger space. Standing up carefully, she had the sense of being in a cave of some sort, and listened for any sign of Susan. There was nothing.

It was not difficult deciding which way to go. Turning her face in the direction of the fresh air, Catherine started forward carefully through the darkness.

She didn't see what was coming until she was already entangled in the tough thorny briars covering the entrance to the cave. Swallowing her scream of surprise and then her cry of pain, she struggled wildly for a moment before realizing the futility of such an act.

The long thorns were already embedded in her cloak and her dress, and she could feel the sharp barbs digging into her face. Taking a calming breath, Catherine tried to minimize the damage and extricate herself from the tangle.

The briars were thick and treacherous, but she soon freed herself from the sharp barbs. Stepping back, she tried to feel for some opening, but the passage again appeared blocked. She listened again for some sound, either ahead or behind her, but she could hear nothing.

When they were children, Catherine and her sisters had once had a secret place where they had played. It too was a place surrounded by briars, the long thorns protecting them. There, within the confines of the intricate web of branches, they had built an imaginary home where Laura could constantly engage in plans of improvement while Adrianne had swung a stick sword about, chafing for the opportunity to conquer distant lands. Catherine still recalled the way they had needed to crawl along the ground beneath the thorns . . .

She dropped to her knees. Sure enough, there was an opening, and the cool night air swept back her hair as she crawled through.

Emerging on the other side, Catherine stood and looked about her. There was a damp chill in the air, and she pulled the cloak tightly around her. She was standing in a wide, rocky ditch, and the briars behind her formed a kind of hedge. There was no sign of Susan. Cautiously, Catherine crossed to the far side of the trench and climbed the steep wall until her face was even with the top.

Not far down the hillside from the ditch, a cluster of small cottages huddled against the slope. The few windows were dark, though wisps of smoke could be seen coming from the smoke holes in the sod roofs. The glen lay below, and she turned to look back up the hill. The castle loomed black and ominous in the distance, and she was surprised at how far the tunnel had taken her from the curtain walls. Not far from the trench, clumps of scraggly young trees pointed toward the dark forest groves that covered the top of the east ridge of the glen, and Catherine decided that Susan must have gone that way.

As she crossed the ground toward the trees, the sounds of restless sheep and the sporadic lowing of a cow drifted up the hill. She was not far from the first strand of trees when the clouds covered the half moon and the going became nearly impossible.

"I can't believe I've done this," she muttered under her breath, looking up at where the moon had been. "You can't see a thi—"

The hand clamped roughly over her mouth, and Catherine never had even a chance to cry out. The attacker was big, and she grabbed for the dagger at her belt as he threw her violently onto the heather-covered hillside. He shoved her face into the earth, and she could feel his weight on her and her dirk pinned beneath her. A second assailant yanked at her hair, and as she opened her mouth to scream, the villain stuffed a filthy rag in her mouth. They were strong, and Catherine panicked as she felt a leather thong bind her hands behind her.

"Well, Jock," one growled as he jerked her to her feet, "won't the master be pleased to have this bonny bird."

At the sounds of some distant commotion, John Stewart was out of bed and at the door of his chamber in an instant. Pulling his shirt over his head and yanking open the door into his outer chamber, he was immediately confronted by Tosh.

"There was a fire in the keep, m'lord. But 'tis already under control. With the exception of a singed blanket or two, and some smoke, it appears that everything was spared."

Athol quickly wrapped his kilt around his waist. "Do you know how it started?"

"Nay, m'lord. There's no telling. But my guess is that one of the servants dropped a taper going through the old section of the keep. The whole thing was under control before I even got there."

"Wait for me, I want to see it." Having so many of his crofters' buildings burned by Adam of the Glen was making Athol very suspicious when it came to fire. Turning back to his bedchamber, though, he wanted first to put Catherine's mind at ease regarding the incident.

Pushing the door shut in his warrior's face, Athol came to an abrupt stop at the sight of his empty bed.

"By the devil," he muttered, throwing his hands in the air in frustration. "Why am I not surprised?"

No matter what he said—no matter how passionate their lovemaking had been—he always found her gone in the morning, having stolen off at some time during the night to her own drafty little chamber. This seemed to be a last shred of the independence that she appeared so stubborn about relinquishing. Well, he thought, considering how agreeable she'd become, perhaps it was foolishness to allow something so little to rile him so much.

Turning around and stalking past Tosh in the outer chamber, Athol grumbled over his shoulder. "So where exactly was the fire?"

" 'Twas in the upstairs corridor of the old section, m'lord. Just outside of the chamber given to Lady Catherine when she arrived."

Athol turned sharply to his man. "The fire was near her chamber? Are you certain no one was hurt?"

"No one, m'lord! In fact, the English monk who got there first managed to put out most of the flames while shouting for help."

Breaking into a run, John Stewart raced up the stairwell and along the corridors into the old section of the keep, cursing himself for being such a fool. How could he let her remain there, when she could have been sleeping safely in his arms? And because of the recklessness of some sleepy servant, she could have been hurt!

There was a pall of smoke hanging as low as his head in the corridor outside Catherine's door, and Athol pushed through the crowd of warriors and serving folk. They had already begun to clean up the mess, and burned rushes lay in a pile beside a badly scorched blanket. Nodding to his old steward and the servants who were carefully sweeping the blackened cinders from the oak floor, the earl pushed open the door and walked in. But the room lay vacant. The bed untouched. Her belongings hung on pegs in the same orderly fashion as always. The smell of smoke was comparatively faint in here.

Stepping immediately out, Athol turned to Jean, who stood eyeing the rushes with a perplexed look on her face.

"Where is Lady Catherine, Jean?"

"Not here, m'lord." The serving woman looked suddenly concerned. "We thought—beg your pardon—we thought she was with you."

"Was she here when the fire broke out?"

Jean bit her lip and then shook her head. "In fact, after the monk, I was the first to arrive here. Though I didn't need to be told, he made sure I knocked at the mistress's door. By then the fire was out, but he wanted to be sure that Lady Catherine knew everything was fine and she was in no danger. But she wasn't there, m'lord. Are ye telling me . . . ?"

Athol couldn't keep the worry from his voice as he turned to Auld Mab, who had just pushed through the throng. "Is Lady Catherine with the dowager, Mab?"

The ancient woman shook her head. "Nay, m'lord. Your mother sent me to check on the commotion. I've not seen hide nor hair of your wife."

The crowd opened a path for him as the earl of Athol moved quickly down the corridor. Tosh was at his heels. His commands were sharp, though he himself could hear the note of concern in his voice.

"Gather every one of the men. I want this place turned upside down until you find Lady Catherine. Make sure no one opened the gates for her. And if anyone gave her a mule and sent her on her merry way, I want his tongue nailed to the stable wall." He whirled and glared at his man. "I do not care what it takes, I want her found. And I want you to send the English monks to me in the Great Hall. I want to make sure there is nothing else that I should know."

With a curt nod, Tosh ran ahead as Athol moved to the long thin window. With a sharp curse, he smashed a fist against the wall. He was so worried about her that he couldn't even think. His mind . . . and his heart . . . were no more than a jumble of fears. Never in his whole life had he ever felt so vulnerable to the outside world.

By St. Andrew, he vowed, after he'd found her, he would chain her to his bed if that was the only way he could keep her safe. Whatever it took, he would convince her. He would even pour out his heart to make her understand what worrying about her did to him.

When he'd taken Catherine Percy as a wife, Athol had never imagined he could be plagued with such thoughts. How could he ever have known that loving her could become an obsession—that keeping her safe would become the greatest challenge of his life!

Chapter 17

Although the auburn-haired Adam of the Glen was broader in build than her husband, he was not as tall as Athol, and he was not even close to being as handsome. Still, though, the resemblance was stunning. To Catherine's thinking, there could be no doubt that they were indeed brothers.

After being captured by the two brutes, she'd been blindfolded and walked a long way. Not long after beginning the trek, she had been able to work the gag out of her mouth, but whether her captors noticed it or not, she had no idea. Either way, she made no attempt to cry out, and thankfully they made no effort to replace it.

They'd climbed into the hills that she guessed lay to the east of the castle, and then the smell of pine and the feel of needles beneath her feet told her that they were traveling through a thick wood. Up hills and down they'd walked, until suddenly the ground became jagged with rock, and they'd started down a tortuously steep path filled with loose gravel. As they'd passed again into some woods, the air took on a smell that created in Catherine's mind a vision of the abandoned, water-filled stone quarry where she and her sisters had played and learned to swim as children. The sound of falling water reached her ear from somewhere nearby.

In a few moments she was startled at the sensation

of being lifted up as the three of them splashed across a small brook. Woods again, and then the smell of a campfire, and then the voices of more rough men, surprised and questioning as she was led past a crackling fire and shoved without ceremony onto the ground.

It wasn't long until the leader had returned to the encampment, and when he'd yanked the blindfold from her eyes, Catherine had stared into the face of a man clearly weighing his options. She even sensed a hint of puzzlement in his eyes as he frowned at her. Two men, obviously the ones who brought her, stood nearby, gloating until one ventured to speak.

" 'Twas a good night's work, master, wouldn't ye say?"

"Aye, Ren," the leader replied vaguely, rubbing his chin with a huge hand. He waved Ren off when the outlaw began to speak again. "Let me think a moment."

Without another word, Adam of the Glen began to pace back and forth between Catherine and the fire. But Catherine, soon tiring of the man's brooding silence and his dizzying march, turned her attention to the sorry-looking group gathered about. Despite their Highland dress and their rough handling of her, most of them looked no different than the many farmers she'd known in her life. Clearly, from their curious stares, they saw her as a great prize, and all of them were expectantly awaiting their leader's next move.

Perhaps, she thought—returning their stares—she had already become prejudiced in her affection toward those farmers of her husband's that she'd met. But she was certain none of Athol's people would have treated her so roughly. None, of course, but Roy Sykes, she quickly corrected. Her scowl came to rest once again on the red-headed young man crouched against the decrepit ruin of a stone hut. As he had done before, the stable hand averted his eyes and focused on the stick of knotted wood he was whittling away at with his dirk.

Turning her attention back to Adam of the Glen, Catherine realized that he had finally come to a stop and was again appraising her closely. Looking up into his dark gaze, she was tempted to meet his brooding fierceness with the same method that she had found so successful with her husband . . . ignoring him. But this was different, she knew, and she did not want to miss anything that she could learn about the man.

"This is fine work for grown men to be doing," she said brightly, casting a meaningful look at Ren and the other man. Surprisingly, Ren shuffled his weight from one foot to the other and stared at Adam's back. The other looked down in what might have been judged as embarrassment. Catherine almost laughed at the two of them.

Adam did laugh—a sharp, curt, mirthless bark. "Aye. Fine work," he snapped. "I finally have him where I want. He'll be crawling to me in search of the prize."

Catherine was not happy having him towering over her as they conversed. So, her hands still tied behind her back, she struggled a bit to get her balance and then came to her feet.

"I assume you are speaking of my husband, since I have no brothers. And as far as my father goes—though he did indeed consider each of his daughters a prize, unfortunately he was killed in the Tower of London this past summer."

"What's all that to us?'

"Well, I just don't know who exactly you think will come crawling, for unless my father's spirit is haunting these hills, I can't imagine who might be rising to your bait." She took a half step toward Adam, her voice taking on a confidential tone. "I assure you, my husband will *not* come crawling for anyone."

"You do not seem to be mindful of your position, Countess."

Before answering, Catherine cocked a meaningful eyebrow in the direction of his gathered men and then said quietly, "I do not think we should be discussing this in front of your men. I understand your need to retain your position of authority, and since I can speak nothing except the absolute truth, I honestly believe it would be best if you sent them off a distance."

His jaw dropped open for a moment, but he quickly recovered. His expression, however, remained that of a man looking at a madwoman.

Catherine leaned toward him and lowered her voice even more. "Of course, you shouldn't do that if you are afraid of me. Though I'm bound up like a sheaf of barley, you can see that I am still armed!" Using her head, she motioned toward the dirk tucked into her belt. The same one that, with her hands tied behind her back, was no good to her now. "I can, of course, understand your concern. I'm a very dangerous opponent. The possibility that I might bring you some harm—"

Adam of the Glen turned abruptly and shouted out an order, and his men immediately moved off to other fires, out of earshot. There was no question who commanded here. Catherine watched in silence as some began to settle in for the night, covering themselves in cloaks or tartans, while others huddled together, talking and laughing. Finally, the outlaw leader turned his attention back to her. Taking her by the arm, he led her around the corner of the ruined cottage. Turning, he faced her directly.

"Countess—"

"Now"—she broke in with a toss of her head—"regarding your words that I am not being mindful of what you consider a vulnerable position . . ." She paused for effect, raising her voice a bit as she continued. "To tell you the truth, I cannot see any reason why I should be *fearful* of you. Considering the fact that we are kin, now. We are as good as brother and sister, are we not?'

He took a menacing step toward her. "Don't mix foolishness with the truth, Countess. I'm not a man to be trifled with." Reaching out, he snatched the dagger from her belt with one swift motion. Hefting the weapon in his hand, he eyed the keen-edged blade. It flashed in the firelight as he turned it. "The first thing that you have to remember is that I am your enemy. The second thing is that I have sworn to destroy everything that belongs to your husband."

"I don't believe—"

"It doesn't matter what you believe, Countess," he rumbled on. "For the past few weeks, I have tended my traps, waiting to capture you . . . as I have. You are nothing more than a pawn, a trifle, in the larger scheme of things. So you might consider shivering and weeping, for that—and begging—might be the only thing that will spare your pretty throat from the edge of this dagger."

Perhaps she should have been afraid, but a rising anger was the only thing Catherine could feel. This Adam of this Glen was beginning to irritate her. She gave up any attempt to hold her tongue.

"I do have to thank you for such a thoughtful recommendation regarding what I should and shouldn't do! But considering the source of this great wisdom, I'm afraid I'll just have to decline your offer. In fact, let me illuminate for you how *wrong* you are on all accounts."

"There is nothing—"

"Aye, nothing you can learn, I suppose," she scoffed. "Well, first of all, I have done you no wrong, brother-in-law. Nothing for you to hate me or wish me harm."

"I told you, you are just—"

"I know. I know."

"You are his wife, and—"

"As far as this grand scheme of destroying your own brother, I believe your troubles must come from some twisted understanding, since you've given him no chance—"

"You do not know the betrayal—"

"I am not done," she said sharply, silencing him as his eyebrows shot up in surprise. "John Stewart is the one betrayed here, from what I can see. But moving on to the rest of your errors, I do not belong to my husband like the rest of his possessions of lands and wealth. I am his wife. A thinking human being! Aye, a rational creature. And he is a man far superior to you, in my thinking, because he recognizes me as such."

"If you think—"

"I am still speaking." She spoke her words through clenched teeth. "And as far as your . . . trap! You must be an absolute simpleton with hired fools to run your errands if you think my presence here is the result of some wondrous plan invented by you and carried out by those baboons who brought me here."

Adam looked at her suspiciously. "What's that?"

"I came out of Balvenie Castle of my own free will. Like the last time, when I eluded your men in the hills, if I'd had any desire not to be caught, you would not have touched me, no matter how clever you think you are."

Catherine let out a breath and stared unblinkingly into his murderous glare. Her only chance of success here lay in the hope that he did not have the ability to read her mind—as his brother did. Her stretching of the truth about coming here on her own free will sounded quite convincing, though, she thought, even to her own ears.

"If you are finished—"

"I am not!" she added sharply. "Now as far as your recommendation of shivering and weeping and begging, I will gladly choose to have that blade cut my throat rather than grovel before such arrogant disregard for what is right. 'Tis the way my father went before me, Adam, and I'll take death over the life of a coward anytime."

He stared at her for a long moment, and then a glint of amusement appeared in the corners of his eyes.

"Well, now at least I know why my blackguard of a brother chose a wife like you! You have the courage that Athol himself lacks."

"I will disregard that comment, since it was spoken out of ignorance by someone who does not know John Stewart."

A bitter laugh erupted from the giant Highlander. "Now 'tis you who is in error, mistress! I know him much better than you think."

"The same way that he knows *you*, I suppose? Tell me how well two grown men can know one another when, in their entire lives, they have never met? When one of them didn't even know the other existed until half a year ago? When any blood connection between them was a well-hidden secret until just a few weeks ago!"

Adam's face expressed very clearly his confusion at her words, but it quickly darkened with mistrust. " 'Tis easy to lie about such matters! If he told you this, then I *know* him now to be a liar as well as a coward. I believe he has *always* known about me. And nothing you can do or say will change my opinion on that little fact."

Catherine opened her mouth to speak and then closed it again. It was true that she and Athol had been married only a short time, but when it came to trusting him—though she would not openly admit it—

she had absolute faith in him. If John Stewart said that he had only just learned that he had a half-brother, then she believed him. But what was more important, Adam believed that Athol had been aware all along of their kinship. No wonder Adam's hatred of his brother ran so deep.

"Now, as to your show of courage," he started again. "Do not be so witless as to think I can be swayed. No matter what you say to defend him, my fight remains with your husband." He lifted her chin with the blade of the dirk. "And I'll do anything . . . I'll use every means at my disposal to bring him down!"

The blade was cold on her skin, but her eyes never wavered for an instant. "And I'll do whatever I must to stop you from doing just that."

He laughed and lowered the blade. "I'm certain you will, lass. But that's a weak threat, considering you are my hostage now and helpless, at best."

"But once again, you are wrong there, as well!" She didn't know how it came to her, but suddenly she knew the answer. Susan! It was more than possible.

She looked up and appraised Adam of the Glen with renewed interest. He was indeed a handsome man. And a well-spoken one. And in his dealings with her, he had not once acted in an overly rough or abusive way as she would have expected a villain to behave. Catherine's gaze drifted away from Adam and scanned the darkness around the clearing. She tried to imagine how the two could have met!

"I respect you for wanting to do the heroic thing, but you've been married to a blackguard, and I—"

"He's no more a blackguard than you." She lifted her chin and stared straight into his face. "The earl of Athol has always worked hard to do what is best for his people. No less. Why, as I understand it, you've been living off the fruits of his labor for this past half-year. What have you seen? People starving, abused, or overworked? Nay, I think not. And I imagine, deep inside, you know that what I say is true."

He turned away, but she stepped around him until she could look into his face.

" 'Tis not he, Adam, who is stealing and burning and terrifying the innocent folk who simply want to live out their lives in peace."

He gave a low, dangerous laugh. "Nay? Not stealing? What has he stolen from me? You are not only a doting fool, but even for a woman you are very naive about men. Innocence? Peace? What do you know about it? Or about me? You barely know me, and yet you think you can pass judgment—"

"I know you enough to trust you, Adam of the Glen."

"Then you are truly a fool."

"Am I? Why do you think I've had no fear for my life since we met?" She turned and glanced at the small window in the wall of the stone cottage. She hoped that she was right. "But my confidence was not generated by firsthand experience, rather by having faith in the worthiness that another woman has obviously seen in you."

It was slight, but her probing eyes didn't miss his reaction to her words.

"I believe in you," she continued, not wanting to give him time to recover. "Since I know that Susan has found you worthy enough to bestow her trust in you . . . worthy enough to give you her heart."

"Susan? Who the devil is this woman you speak of?" His voice was harsh, but his expression too guarded to be effective.

"But perhaps I was too hasty in thinking you worthy," Catherine scolded. "When one thinks of all the danger she puts herself in, coming here to you in the middle of the night, and you speak of her as if she were some . . . some . . ."

"By the devil!" He turned abruptly from her and flung the dagger violently onto the ground by the cottage. "I knew she'd be found out, and I've told her not to do it! She's been as stubborn as a—"

"Adam," Catherine said softly. "Don't you see that, as women, we do what we must? That we'll walk across fire, defy demons, risk the very wrath of God for what . . . and for whom . . . we love?"

The outlaw leader said nothing. His eyes fixed on something behind Catherine, and she turned to see Susan standing by the corner of the ruined cottage.

"I told you to stay put!" he growled.

Susan's dark eyes remained locked on Adam before her gaze flickered and came to rest on the captive. Catherine felt the gentle understanding pass between them. The sense of kinship that only women can know.

"How could I?" Susan shook her head, walking to him. "She is right, you know. She knows about women and love."

Catherine silently watched as gazes locked. There was so much that hung in the air. And though she was only an observer, she could almost hear their unspoken words.

I love you!

I, too, love you. But I am an outlaw! A criminal!

I love you, all the same!

But there is nothing that I can give you. Nothing!

Catherine watched as Susan silently drew her hand out of the cloak and laid it gently against his cheek. Cursing under his breath, he drew her fiercely to him, and Catherine looked away. She turned her back on them and crossed the clearing to the fire. She crouched and looked into the flames. They paid the price every

day for these few moments; she would not deprive
them of a single one.

In the light of how much these two must suffer for
this illicit love, Catherine's own problems seemed so
trivial. She was in love. She was carrying her husband's heir. She had the power to make him happy.
And yet, she thought with a tinge of bitterness, she
selfishly continued to withhold this knowledge of the
bairn from him.

Feeling wretched, she tried to push aside her own
weakness in wanting him to love her back, tried to
push aside the ridiculous desire of somehow extracting
from him a promise of fidelity in their marriage, tried
instead to focus on what she could do for *him* if she
were ever to escape from this encampment.

John Stewart had enough problems already. He certainly didn't need the added worry of a stubborn
spouse.

Some time passed; Catherine had no idea how
much. The night grew colder, but she paid no heed to
it. The fire was warm, and before long she'd lost herself in her dreams.

She was back in a land she knew so well. The mists
hung on the craggy hills and the sky was a rainbow
of crystalline colors. It was the calm after the storm.
In her arms she held a child at the threshold of a
garden. A cooing, gray-eyed son. The son of her
knight. Placing a soft kiss on the infant's brow, she
stepped out into the meadow at the sound of her
knight's approach.

Looking up into his misty eyes, she felt her body
sing when he gathered both her and their son in his
embrace.

And then she knew it was time. At last, the time
had come to take her vow. Looking up again into his
handsome face, she whispered the words that she had
so long been keeping locked within her heart.

The knight drew her lips to his. His kiss was tender. Then John Stewart simply held her.

" 'Tis time we returned to Balvenie Castle."

Catherine turned and looked up confusedly at Susan. "Here, let me cut your bonds!"

While Susan reached behind her and sliced through the thongs tying her wrists, Catherine twisted around and looked in the direction where Adam of Glen had last been. He was gone, and so were the others.

Like a band of ghosts, they had all vanished. Visible signs of their encampment were still in evidence, but there wasn't an outlaw to be seen. A cough came from behind her. Turning, she saw the two men who had captured her standing by the edge of the clearing.

"Where did he go?"

"Where he can think, he said."

Her hands finally free, Catherine slowly came to her feet and started rubbing the soreness out of her wrists.

"Here is your dirk!"

Catherine, still confused, looked at the proffered dagger in Susan's hand. "He is letting me go?"

Susan nodded. "But we'd better hurry back to Balvenie. 'Tis only an hour or so before dawn, and we have a long way to go."

"Wait." Catherine tried to sort out what was happening. For Susan—and Adam—just to set her free with no promise of silence was beyond her understanding. They'd not even asked her to remain silent. Extracted no oath to keep their secret. Surely, the younger woman would be in terrible trouble if Athol ever discovered any of this. And yet, Susan was willing to trust her, to allow her to return with her to the castle. "I don't—"

"Your face is a mess!" Susan whispered, frowning at the sight of Catherine's face. "The scratches from the briars at the cave entrance . . ."

"I'll tell them that I fell onto the rose bushes in the

garden," Catherine said breezily. "and my cloak and my clothes are ragged from . . . falling in the dirt . . . while chasing Jean's nieces in the stable yard. And the marks on my wrists . . . Well, no one has to see or know anything about my wrists. Your secret is safe with me, Susan. But—"

The younger woman placed an affectionate hand on her arm. "Adam is angry with me . . . and with himself. He is moving his camp farther from the castle, where I cannot come to him at night. But thank you, Catherine."

Catherine placed her hand on top of Susan's and smiled into her face. "I am doing this as much for myself as for you. As much for my husband as for Adam of the Glen. We have to try to help them overcome their differences."

"But there is nothing that can be done! I tried to make Adam understand that Athol is not the devil that he thinks him to be. As you did tonight, I tried to tell him that the earl did not know of their kinship. But without any way of bringing out the truth of their past . . . it was just impossible."

"Based on the little information that we each have," Catherine said, "perhaps there are questions that can be answered now."

Susan's eyes bore her conviction when she spoke the words. "Adam is not evil. His anger comes from suffering. From pain that he truly believes was caused by John Stewart."

"But how could he intentionally cause harm to someone that he didn't even know existed?"

"Aye!" Susan whispered. " 'Tis impossible. But how can we change anything?"

"We can . . . and we will . . . because now 'tis the two of us," Catherine said with conviction. "I know we cannot change the past, Susan, but we have the power to fashion the future. That is our only chance. The future must belong to us."

Together, they moved past their escorts and into the darkness.

Chapter 18

Once he'd questioned the English monks—and gained nothing by it—John Stewart became a raving terror.

The stables and its inhabitants were his next targets and, with every stable hand trailing in his wake, Athol personally counted every stallion, mare, gelding, and mule. None were missing. The warriors and the porter's lads who tended the gates were questioned individually. A little past sundown, the portcullis had been lowered, the great oak and iron gates shut, and no one had gone either in or out since then.

Torches flared, lighting the courtyards as warriors and serving folk moved to and fro, and every kitchen, cellar, and storeroom was searched. Athol was everywhere, but to no avail. Catherine was nowhere to be found.

By the time he met Auld Mab at the entrance to the Great Hall, he was feeling the tug of panic on his nerves, but he set his jaw and forced down the steely taste in his mouth. The old woman, too, had disappointing news. The serving folk had gone through every room in the castle—except the dowager's chambers and his own. There was no trace of her.

As he turned away, he felt a pressure building within him. He wanted to shout, lash out, pound something into powder. And he would, too. The next person who brought him bad news.

He whirled, facing a dozen men and women.

"Search everything again!" he shouted. "Find her."

Storming up the stairwell to the second floor, he felt the sharp edges of fear clawing at his insides. Where she had disappeared to he couldn't even guess. If she'd run off to Elgin again, he'd personally flay her alive. But his worst fear lay in the possibility that she had actually been the victim of foul play. What if there were more like Roy Sykes living under his roof? What if they had seized upon Catherine's adventurous nature and lured her some way out of the keep?

But how?

Knowing that he would leave no stone unturned, Athol shouted for Tosh, ordering him to send four parties of warriors out into the night to search the village and the glen and the surrounding hills for some trace of her. Moments later, the sound of horses and men could be heard moving out of the courtyard through the low, arched gate.

If this were any castle but Balvenie, Athol knew he would be concerned about secret passages and subterranean tunnels. He knew well enough that nearby Ironcross Castle was riddled with them. He'd nearly lost his life in one. But it was not the case here.

His family had taken possession of the castle years ago, when the Black Douglases had been whipped so badly at Arkinholm. The fear of the rebellious Douglases trying to take the castle back had haunted the minds of that first Stewart earl of Athol, and the man had not hesitated to torture and bribe the former inhabitants' serving folk until he knew every possible weakness in the castle. It had not taken long to block up the three tunnels that led under the curtain walls.

But there was no way Catherine would even think of searching out such things. There was no way she would even know of the three old trap doors that lay hidden around the keep. What woman in her right mind would follow a tunnel to nowhere?

Nay! He thought, shaking his head. Even if she had found a trap door, what good would it do her? She wouldn't be foolish enough to step into a moldering dark passage. It would serve no purpose. There could be no way out for her there.

She was a stubborn woman, true. But she was hardly one to waste her time.

But still, he thought, climbing the stairwell for the hundredth time, he could not simply stand and wait. The sky in the east had already taken on a grayish hue, and soon the sun would push up past the wooded hills to the east.

There was one other thing he still had to do. He'd considered going up and questioning his mother before. He knew from Auld Mab that the dowager was awake and concerned.

He should go see her, he decided with a frown. Tosh had told him of Catherine taking the ailing woman out into the gardens. And he'd also heard that Lady Anne appeared to be no worse after the afternoon of fresh air in his wife's company. In fact, Auld Mab had confided, the dowager had seemed, as a result, to be in as good a mood as she'd seen her in months.

He would go and talk to his mother. He could at least ask her if she was privy to anything that might be brewing in Catherine Percy's pretty head.

It was curious how the dowager seemed to be taking a liking to Catherine. His mother had never been very cordial with any of the women he'd known. But though he found the growing affection between them refreshing, he still found himself at odds with his mother. She knew more than she was telling about Adam of the Glen, and her silence was beginning to wear on him.

Nay. He hadn't the patience for Lady Anne right

now, certainly not with the reproaches she was sure
to heap upon his head. He'd deserve them all, of
course, but he didn't have time for them now. More
than likely, Lady Anne would have no answer that
would be of any use to him, but she would be ruthless
in her censure of everything that he'd done to prove
himself unworthy of his wife's affection.

Deciding that he was fretting about the wrong thing
at the wrong time, Athol reversed his direction and
started back down toward the storerooms. Unlikely as
it seemed that Catherine could be in one of the tunnels, he wasn't about to let any possibility slip past
him. Calling for torches as he passed the Great Hall,
he continued his decent. He would do a personal inspection of all three trap doors and the tunnels leading
from them.

And God help her if he found her there.

Sir Arthur Courtenay eyed the two renegade Scots
standing before him in their outlandish Highland gear.
He knew that these cutthroats could be trusted to
carry out his instructions, but he would as soon hang
them as look at them.

Standing before the hearth of the ramshackle manor
house he'd taken possession of, the king's Deputy
Lieutenant continued to bark out his instructions in
terms so specific that they could not fail to understand
him. Before he was finished, though, the approach of
one of his own officers from outside drew his attention.

"He is arrived, m'lord, as you said he would." The
soldier cast a look of disdain in the direction of the
Highlanders.

"Did you stop him?"

"Aye, m'lord. He's in the stable yard, and a mite
upset over us handling him as we have."

"I don't care how you handle him. Just keep him
out. What did he say?"

"He said nothing until we closed ranks on him. Then he started spouting off that your lordship can't be searching out the maps without him. He 'insists,' m'lord, to know what's been found."

"Did you tell him 'tis no longer his business to be involving himself in the king's concerns?"

"Aye, that I did, m'lord, and the lads are enjoying the ruckus he's making. He's demanding to see you right away."

The king's deputy rose slowly to his feet and glared at the man. "Well, tell the monk to go to hell, for the king no longer has any use for his useless carcass."

"I tried to be insulting, m'lord, but he—"

"You have other means, Captain!"

"Aye, m'lord, but he's a priest, and the men—"

"If the filthy swine curses you, then kick his teeth out, but *keep him out of here*!"

The officer nodded as he turned and strode out of the hall. The Deputy Lieutenant turned to the two waiting men.

"Use whatever deceit you must. Hire as many hands as you need, if you must take her by force. But bring her back to me. Do you understand?"

The two soldiers nodded confidently in response.

"With good horses, we'll have the lass here inside of a fortnight," one said as they turned to go.

Once he was alone, Sir Arthur moved away from the fire and gazed with disgust at the roughly sketched map that lay beside a small open box on the table. Finding this had been the last straw. The haughty bitches had buried the box in the midden heap of this very house.

He stared at it, his face growing paler as his fury grew. The new map clearly pointed out the next stop on this endless chase. There, a bright red X sat in the burying ground of his own ancestors at his manor house in the south of Yorkshire.

Indeed, this was the last straw. Well, he wasn't going to travel to the south of Yorkshire. He wasn't going to the south of anywhere. By the devil, he was through letting those three wenches lead him around by the cock.

Sir Arthur Courtenay turned and stared into the fire. It was time for those Percy bitches to pay.

John Stewart's inspection of the first two trap doors and the tunnels beneath them turned up nothing. Now, moving across the courtyard, he paused as Tosh and his men rode in through the low, arched gate. Dawn was just breaking gray and cold, and a steady rain was beginning to fall. Athol did not even notice.

"Nothing, m'lord!" The veteran warrior leaped from his horse. "The hills are as quiet as can be. There are no fresh tracks of anyone around the castle that we could see. But I do not know how she—"

"How about the village? Any new faces? Anything?"

"We searched, m'lord. And we checked every crofter's hut and hovel for leagues in every direction! 'Tis as if she just disappeared from the face of the earth!"

John Stewart stared at his man, suddenly conscious of the blood pulsing in his temples. It was as if his heart were crying out in pain, and he didn't know which way to turn next. Unlike his wife, he was not a religious man. But, by the saints, just about then, even *he* could see the value of reaching out in his need. Silently, he sent a plea up to the heavens.

"I will question my mother." He spoke the words almost to himself. What other options remained? he wondered. He climbed the steps and entered the Great Hall.

"Perhaps I should alert Mistress Susan to prepare the dowager first."

Tosh's words had merit. The last thing he needed

to do now was to frighten his mother with the news that Catherine simply could not be found.

"Aye. Go on. I still have one more thing that I need to check on. Tell Susan I'll be with the dowager in her chamber presently."

As Tosh moved off, Athol turned to the now empty Great Hall, and his mind was immediately flooded with images of the recent past. Of the first time he'd seen her here, searching for food. Of the first time he'd escorted his wife into this Hall. Of her beautiful face, accepting the proffered oaths of fealty from his people. It was almost too much for him, and he strode quickly to the stairwell.

In a few moments, he was standing by her door. In his mind's eye he could see them both, making love by the window, and he found himself engulfed by the vision of her bewitching smile. Of those midnight-blue eyes that had cast a spell over his heart. Of her goddess-like body that drove him to madness.

He paused and took a breath by her closed door. What could ever replace the way her soul had opened up to him from the day they'd met, giving him glimpses of her innermost thoughts?

But even in her absence, he still could sense her around him. He could feel her and that tortured him even more, because he could not find her. This, he thought sadly, is what it is to be haunted.

Resting a hand on her door, he gazed at the ledge across the corridor, wishing her here. The sky was gray beyond it, and he called with his heart and his soul for her to come back to him. Once again, to be a part of him. To stay forever and ever by his side.

"Catherine!" Involuntarily, he pushed at her door and it swung open easily on its hinges.

He didn't have to look into the darkness, nor even step in, to know that she was back.

"Catherine!"

"I am here, John."

Her voice came quietly out of the darkness of her chamber. At that moment, he was quite certain he had never heard a sound so magical.

Suddenly, he was at her side, enveloping her in his arms, drawing her so tightly to him that they were molded as one.

"Catherine."

Her body was shaking. Her mouth was as greedy as his, and as their lips met, all his prayers were answered in an instant. And while his mouth tried to punish and yet find relief, his hands searched, caressing her body, making sure that she was not harmed. Making sure that she was real.

He clutched her fiercely to him and whispered in her ear. "Catherine! Where were you?"

"Hush! Just hold me."

Her mind was troubled. He could feel her concerns pounding inside his own head.

Seating himself on the bed and gathering her on his lap, Athol just held her as she'd asked. She was not the only one who wanted to be held. He, too, needed her embrace. He still could not believe that she was real. That, indeed, his wife had returned.

Only a moment of silence passed, but in that moment the realization struck him that he knew would change him forever—without her, he was not complete. He was only whole with her beside him. She was his wife as he was her husband. Catherine possessed him, possessed his love, possessed his very soul.

"Catherine!" he said at last. He could still hear the concern in his voice, but he was much calmer now. "Where were you, lass?"

"I . . . I had to come back to my room."

Athol's spine stiffened. He could feel a shadow darken the space between them. The incompleteness of her statement, her unspoken words, made the an-

swer a lie. He pushed her away from his chest and
tried to look into her eyes in the darkness of the room.
He had been through too much tonight to be able to
stomach any more games. She shivered slightly and
held on to his arm.

"You left my bed, but you didn't return here. Catherine, what is this all about? Where did you go?"

The sound of steps coming to a sudden stop by the
open door of her chamber startled them both, and
Athol leaped up, turning his anger on the intruder.
Tosh stood with a lighted taper in the doorway. The
initial look of shock on the warrior's face quickly
turned to concern as he stared at his laird's wife. Athol
whirled and looked at Catherine.

"By St. Andrew!" he exploded. "What is this?"

She was a mess. A scratched and bloody mess.
Shouting at his man to bring in the light, he placed
her on the edge of the bed and ordered Tosh to
fetch Jean.

Kneeling before her and turning her face toward
the light, he tried to get a better look at the source
of the blood.

" 'Tis nothing!" she said softly. "Just a bit of
carelessness . . . a briar bush . . ."

They were scratch marks, indeed. Running his hand
through her soft mane of hair, he found thorns from
briar bushes still tangled in her tresses.

"Where did you disappear to? I searched every
inch—"

The sudden appearance of her serving woman with
more light stopped Athol's questions. Stepping back
from the bed, he watched observantly as Jean began
fussing over her mistress. A moment later, another
serving woman appeared with an ewer of water.

Going to the window, Athol pulled open the shutter
and glanced around the chamber. These walls were

solid stone. The iron-barred window offered no escape, either.

One of the kitchen workers arrived and quickly began to build up the fire. Her gaze, too, flitted about the room, collecting information to report to the castle's inhabitants.

"Leave the rest of the wood. Out you go," he ordered, shooing her out the door. Catherine was watching him as Jean dabbed gently at her face. He moved around the chamber. Spotting her cloak on a small settle beside the hearth, John walked toward it and studied it closely. The garment was caked with dirt, and the thick wool cloth had thorns and pulls in the material, attesting to her confessed encounter with a briar bush. But there were no briars inside the castle, that much he knew.

As he picked up the cloak, his gaze fell on his own dirk lying beneath the garment. Picking up the weapon, he turned it in his hand. He looked up and found Catherine's eyes on him.

However hard he tried to be angry—knowing that she was holding back, that she was not trusting him with something of the gravest importance—still, all he could see in her eyes were tenderness and affection for him. And that was enough to undo him, for his own emotions were raw and far too close to the surface.

Going to the door, he stepped out. Tosh was there with a number of others.

"Go and tell Susan to put my mother and the household at ease. Find Auld Mab, as well."

Without another word, Athol strode back into the chamber and crossed to the window. Jean had finished doctoring Catherine's face and was taking clean clothing out of the wooden chest. As she prepared to dress his wife, Athol moved to the hearth and crouched before it, building up the fire himself.

More than anything else right now, he wanted to

gather Catherine in his arms and carry her to his own
chamber where he would assail her first with questions
before making love to her. Somehow, he needed to
release some of this madness that roared in his veins,
and he was uncertain which one of those two things
would work best. But he would wait, knowing that
first of all, she must be tended to.

But there was no way that he could bring himself
to leave her—not for any reason. The fear of losing
her again—fear based on his lack of knowledge regarding where she had disappeared to and how she'd
gotten back—put him quite on the edge.

Catherine's soft-spoken dismissal of her serving
woman gave him the sign to turn around. He kept his
mouth shut and his temper in check until Jean had
shut the chamber door on her way out. Then there
was no holding him back.

"Catherine Percy Stewart! From now on, I will have
a guard accompany you between the rooms of this
keep. After what you did tonight, under no condition
will I trust you to be left alone for even an instant.
After the pain you caused me in finding you
missing . . . after what my people had to go
through . . ." He went on, pacing back and forth,
venting his anger, scolding her energetically—at first.
But soon, the words began to lose their vigor, fading
gradually. Trying to regain his glare, he found his
throat tightening with emotion. He couldn't stop himself from admiring his tough, little angel.

Now dressed in a white, long-sleeved nightshirt,
with her hair uncoiled and spread like a silky blanket
around her shoulders, her misty eyes shining in her
scratched face, John Stewart lost all desire to scold.
He stopped and took a step toward her. Immediately,
she rose from the bed and threw herself into his arms.

He gathered her tightly against him, pressing his lips
against her hair, her brow, lingering on the long, deep

scratches on her face. "Catherine! I thought I would go mad. Where did you disappear to?"

She didn't immediately answer, and he once again felt a stab of pain in his heart. He took a fistful of her hair and pulled it back gently so he could look into her face.

"Do not, Catherine! Do not think of a lie."

"I thought I would be able to," she said softly. "But I cannot."

"Then tell me where you went! And why is it that no matter how hard we searched, we could not find you?"

She used the tip of her fingers to trace the line of his jaw. "I discovered a secret tunnel."

"The one at the bottom of the stairwell in this section of the keep?" It was the only one he had not yet checked.

"Aye." She nodded. "I went through it to the end."

"That tunnel is blocked. You couldn't have gone out that way!"

"But I did! There is a small opening high in the wall blocking the passage. I was able to slide through it. But when I reached the end, there were briar bushes blocking the opening into the cave. I didn't see them, and before I knew it, I was tangled in them."

He knew she was speaking the truth. This much of it, anyway.

"That's how I got the scratches on my face. And the dirt on my dress."

"But why, lass?" he said exasperatedly. "Why did you decide to do something so absurd in the middle of the night? And how did you learn of the tunnels beneath the castle?"

She averted her eyes and pressed her cheek tightly against his chest. "Please, John. Please do not ask me questions that I cannot answer. I *did* have a reason for this madness, and I *will* tell you the truth . . . as soon as I can."

"And this is the trust of husband and wife?" John pulled her back so that he could look into her face. "Do you expect me simply to forget about this and be happy with such a cryptic answer?"

"I simply ask you to trust me."

"As you trust me?" His hands tightened on her shoulders. "Catherine, from the first moment we met, you have never once done as I've told you. You have never obeyed any direction I've given. When have you, even once, trusted my judgment? And now you just expect me to remain silent and trust you regarding something that may jeopardize the safety of people who depend on me?"

She reached up and took hold of his hand, pressing it to her shoulder. "I know I've been a difficult wife. I admit I've been persistent and stubborn. And I accept the fact that I am nothing like what you would desire in a woman."

She leaned her face against his arm. The simple gesture, added to her softly spoken words, had an effect on him. Athol's anger melted away, and in its place he could feel the rippling tide of affection and love.

"But despite all of my flaws," she continued, "I want you to trust me when I tell you that I'll never do anything to bring harm to you or your people. Though you believe I have no regard for the value of your judgment, I have opened up my heart to you, husband. I have given you a place with the things I value most. I . . ."

He was too affected by her words to be able to say anything himself. Lifting his hands and framing her delicate face, he stared into the depths of her misty blue eyes.

"I love you, John Stewart," she whispered as sparkling tears escaped, running down and scorching his fingers with their heat. "As much as you may think me unworthy of your trust, I—"

He kissed her with all the passion that was burning in his heart. He sipped her lips, trying to quench the insatiable thirst of his soul.

"What am I going to do with you?" he said a moment later, pulling back slightly and combing his fingers through her hair. He pressed soft kisses against the injured skin of her face.

"Keep me! Trust me! Swear to me that you will remain my husband!"

She hadn't said love me. And he understood. Considering the base knave he'd been, ordering her never to confuse the purpose for their marriage with *love,* he understood perfectly her words. She did not want that rejection again.

He was indeed undeserving of her affection.

I love you, Catherine! I do! He could think the words—scream them in his thoughts—but she would never be able to read his mind.

But to say the words now would serve no purpose. She would not believe him. She would think them simply meaningless sounds. Nay, he would wait for the right moment. The perfect moment. The moment when he would sweep her off her feet with his declaration . . . as she had done to him.

His voice was husky and raw with emotion when he spoke again. "I am your husband and, though I did not know you then as I know you now, I have always had every intention of honoring my vows to you."

"You are and always will be the only man in my life."

His thumb gently wiped away the tracks of tears on her cheeks. "I will cherish you, Catherine, and protect you . . . if you will allow me. And I promise I will be worthy of your trust."

Catherine's chin lifted, her eyes moving until they entrapped him in their misty depths. "And you! Will you keep me as the *only* woman in your life?"

"My sweet Catherine." He smiled as the warmth spread through him. "I do not think another woman exists who could take me from anger to desire in the span of a heartbeat. You are my weakness. You are a habit that I can no longer do without. You will be the only woman in my life."

She looked down and then smiled shyly. The same enchanting smile that always seduced him.

"John, will you take me? Make love to me?"

Athol cocked an eyebrow at her, and when she looked up, she had mischief in her eyes.

"I have a bit more to reveal to you, but 'tis something I could only divulge when I am certain that you are feeling completely agreeable."

John couldn't hold back his laughter as he drew her roughly into his embrace. He devoured her smiling lips and let her push him down on the narrow bed. He lay still as she started undressing him.

"Considering what you did to me this past night, it might take a very long time before I'll ever again be completely agreeable."

"We have time," she whispered, placing kisses on his bare chest. Unfastening his kilt, she lifted the nightshirt to her waist and nestled against his rising manhood. She nipped at his jaw, encouraging him to start. "I'll do whatever you say, husband . . . follow your lead . . . do what must be done to prepare you for the news."

"I like the sound of this. Your learned methods of persuasion. Your argument from a position of strength!"

"And trust me," she gasped as he entered her body. "You'll appreciate the rest, as well!"

Chapter 19

Lady Anne Stewart dismissed all but Auld Mab. Motioning for the door to be barred, the dowager pulled herself to a sitting position as the ancient servant placed the lighted taper in a carved wooden holder on the bedside table.

"Did she tell him where she went?"

"Not while the others were there. But from the looks of her, she must have done battle with a dragon."

"I'll wager the dragon lost." The dowager pointed to the large chest sitting against the opposite wall. "Bring it to me!"

The serving woman moved briskly to the chest and, after opening it, started taking out and putting on the floor pieces of folded linens and clothing one layer at a time.

While watching her, the dowager sat straighter in the bed. "Is my son still with her?"

"Aye, Jean said he is, m'lady. And from the looks of things he might stay there for some time."

A pleased smile broke out on the dowager's face. "That Catherine Percy has more control over her husband than she knows herself! That's good! Very good! This is exactly what John needs. A woman as smart as he is, himself."

Smoothing the quilted bedclothes across her lap, Lady Anne nodded approvingly when her maid removed a small, ornate box from the bottom of the large chest and brought it to her.

"Was everything on top of it left untouched as you arranged it before?"

"Aye, 'twas, m'lady. The same as ye directed."

The dowager reached inside of the neckline of her bed gown and started pulling out a long chain. Auld Mab helped her to pull it over her head and produce the key.

"When the sun is up, I want you to go and bring Catherine to me."

"What happens if the earl is still abed? I know he is customarily an early riser, but—"

The two women exchanged a knowing look. "In that case, I want you to wait." The dowager smiled. "If she is woman enough to keep him in bed when the sun is in the sky, then we can be patient enough to wait before giving this token of her mother's to her."

The dowager put the key into the lock of the chest and turned it. Once the lid was lifted, she patted the sealed parchment that Nichola Erskine had sent her to give to Catherine.

"After having it so long, why have ye decided to give it to her now? Ye might have given it to her earlier."

The dowager looked up and met the sharp blue eyes of Auld Mab. Of all of the servants she'd had for years, this woman was the only true confidante she'd ever had.

"Nichola asked me to hold on to this until I was certain that the lass was safe. That she was set to stay for good."

"A very wise woman, to know beforehand, about the earl and her daughter."

The dowager met the older woman's knowing smile with one of her own before closing the lid. "You might say we both . . . guessed. We both hoped. And we both planned for them as far as we could. The rest one can only leave to the hand of fate."

"Has Nichola been told of the marriage?"

"Aye, she has." The dowager placed the small chest next to her hip on the bedclothes and lifted a bony finger to her lips. "Her daughters think there is no way for them to get hold of their mother. But have no fear, Mab. Nichola Erskine has an eye on all of them."

The noise of the household stirring in the corridors. The shouts and smells of bread wafting up from the kitchens. The clang of swords as the men trained in the courtyard.

Nay, none of the everyday routines of the Highland castle were going to move John Stewart.

He gazed down at the woman tucked in his embrace. He didn't want to tear his eyes from her angelic face as she slept. He sure as hell wasn't going to disturb her. Whatever her ordeal had been last night, it had exhausted her so much that she'd fallen asleep the moment they'd finished their lovemaking.

Now it appeared that the rain had stopped, for the sky outside the window was brightening. Casting his gaze about the small bedchamber, his eyes lit on the cloak, and he looked back at the thin scratches on her face. There was no reason for him to doubt what she'd told him regarding where she'd been. But still, her motive for going puzzled him. He still intended to ask her the questions he'd meant to ask this morning . . . before they both had been overcome by the moment's desires.

Tracing with the tip of his fingers a long scratch that crossed her brow, Athol leaned down and placed a soft kiss on the wound. There were no words to describe the ache he'd felt in his heart, imagining her hurt or in pain. Before meeting her, he'd known many women. He'd experienced passion, the physical power of desire. But Catherine had managed to awaken so much more in him. His continuous hunger for her, his need to be with her, his desire to have her by him in all things, all of this was new to him. All of this—he was certain—meant that the love that he had for her was like no other.

And somehow he had to make her hear this. He had to make her believe it. He wanted her to believe it the same way that he had believed her own profession of love.

He watched her eyelids flutter and open. The midnight-blue orbs gradually focused on his face. She immediately lifted her head off his arm.

" 'Tis morning! I forgot to leave your bed."

He smiled and rolled onto his back, pulling her body on top of him and reveling in the feel of her skin against his. He brushed her lips with his own.

"Your secrets are spilling out, lass." He ran his hands over the smooth curves of her back as she nestled her body against him. "As you can see, this is your bed and your chamber. But you might as well get used to the idea that if you leave my bed in the middle of the night, from now on I'll follow you . . . wherever you go."

She feigned an angry frown and then glanced around the room, inspecting the burned-out embers in the hearth, the cast-off clothing on the floor. Her eyes narrowed though at seeing the pile.

"I fell asleep, I take it."

"Not so very quickly." He slowly pushed the blanket off her shoulders and gazed appreciatively at her shoulders, at her full breasts pressed seductively against his chest. "But aye, you fell asleep. In fact, our bodies were still as one when you drifted off to the fairylands."

"And—bold thing that you are—you removed my shift?"

"I did." He loved the way she wrapped her arms around his neck, pressing her body closer to his. "I thought having you in my arms, in the condition God made you, would give me the advantage I sought."

"Advantage?" she smiled, nipping at his chin.

"Aye! I thought, considering the draftiness of this wee hole you call a bedchamber, you'd stay with me at least for the warmth of my body."

Catherine now gave him one of her magical smiles. When she did that, he thought contentedly, she made him feel like a lovestruck abbey school lad.

"Shouldn't you be up and about?" She slowly slid against his body, placing kisses on his throat, his chin, his chest.

"Can you not feel it, woman? I am up."

"That I can, husband. But don't you have warriors that need you to oversee their work? Crofters with disputes that have to be heard? Pheasant and deer that need to be hunted?"

"Aye! There are all those things and more. But first, there is a wife that needs to be made love to." He rolled both of them around until she lay pinned beneath him. He lowered his head and flicked at her breasts with his tongue. The nipples hardened under his attentions, and he took a moment to suckle them both.

Catherine arched her back, moaning softly into his ear, writhing under his weight.

Athol raised his head. "I'd say this is the most important part of my day. To pleasure my wife." He ran a hand down over a quivering belly and slipped a finger into her wet folds. She gasped, moving against his hand as he stroked the source of pleasure.

"You mustn't forget that as a peer to the realm, I am expected to make every effort to supply my people . . . and my king . . . with the fifth earl of Athol. Making an heir is a difficult task, but a noble one that, as a loyal subject, I must attempt. 'Tis a duty we mustn't shirk, lass. In fact, 'tis a duty that we must spend more time working at."

A moment passed before his teasing words sank in, and then she suddenly became very still. Lifting his head, he looked down at her misty eyes, her flushed face.

"What's wrong, Catherine?" Concerned that he might have hurt her somehow, he quickly rolled a little and took her face in one hand. "Are you well?"

She paused and gnawed for a moment at her lip.

"There was something I meant to tell you last night."

"Is that all," he said, relieved. "Well, 'tis not too late, my sweet. You can tell me now."

Catherine drew a deep breath and gazed into his eyes.

"Your king would be proud, m'lord, for I already carry your bairn!"

Torture is not an occupation for the squeamish, but neither the king's Deputy Lieutenant nor those he employed for that purpose could ever be accused of having weak stomachs.

In fact, the sounds coming from a nearby chamber brought a satisfied smirk to Arthur Courtenay's face. That sounds like progress, he thought. Progress, indeed.

As he paused to allow the Abbot of Jervaulx to pass before him into the small cell, a monk who was being questioned in the room next door suddenly appeared. Bloody, naked, and crawling on his hands and knees, the cleric dragged himself out of the cell and collapsed on the stone floor of the narrow corridor as a sweating brute stepped out, a whip shiny with blood in his hand.

"Yer not thinkin' o' leaving us already." The torturer spat before seeing the small group behind him. Upon seeing them, he bowed apologetically. "Beggin' yer pardon, m'lord."

The abbot took a step toward the injured man, but the Deputy Lieutenant blocked his way. The priest stared at him uncomprehendingly, for a moment, then lowered his head, murmuring in Latin as he made the sign of the cross in the direction of his fallen charge.

"I would save your blessings, Abbot, for you may need them for yourself before this day is finished."

The white-haired priest made no response to the threat, but took his time finishing his prayer. He gave one last look at the fallen monk before stepping past Sir Arthur, through the cell door before them.

The Deputy Lieutenant, entering behind him, walked over to a small wiry man who was stripped to the waist and standing over the lacerated body of another monk. The cleric appeared unconscious, his wrists tied above his head to an iron ring that had been driven into the wall.

"Do you see what awaits you, Abbot?"

The monk by the wall stirred. A hand twitching, a foot moving slightly across the dirt, the man's head lifted in an attempt to see the newcomers. His eyes were nearly swollen shut.

"The fate of all men is the same, Sir Arthur," the abbot replied, bending over the badly beaten body. "But what we have to answer for, thereafter, will be quite different."

"Do not try to frighten me with schoolboys' tales, priest." He kicked at the naked leg of the monk. "This arrogant fool has baited me and tested my patience for far too long."

The abbot said nothing, but the wounded monk opened his mouth, mumbling unintelligible words through puffed, split lips.

"Not so eloquent today, it seems." Sir Arthur

sneered at the man. He turned to the abbot. "I'll tell
you this, old man. As the king's deputy, I answer to
one man in this world. And my solemn oath to
Henry—God's own anointed king—requires that I
obey his wishes." Courtenay took the abbot's cowl in
his fist and dragged the older man up until he could
look directly into his face. His rasping voice was cold
and harsh. "And he *wishes* to have the Treasure of
Tiberius turned over to him."

"Not . . . the . . . king . . ." the monk gasped. He
coughed, blood spattering the floor and the hem of
the abbot's gown. He gathered his strength and peered
up accusingly at the Deputy Lieutenant. " 'Tis . . . you!
Not . . . the king . . ."

The abbot turned his gaze from the monk's broken
face to the cold, haughty features of Sir Arthur. He
shook his head. "I have no knowledge of any treasure.
This . . . this Treasure of Tiberius. I don't know what
you are talking about."

"You lie!" Courtenay spat, shoving the abbot onto
the ground beside the other man. "Those Percy
bitches did not start digging the same day that they
left. They *knew* someone would be looking . . . and
they took steps to hide the treasure."

"I tell you I don't know what—"

"I only came to know of the treasure through this
monk, when he came asking . . . nay, begging me to
tell him what their father knew!" Sir Arthur yanked
the older man up again by the cowl and stared menacingly at him. "If 'twas not for me that they were devising this merry 'robin chase the worm,' then who was
to be the robin?"

The abbot gaped blankly.

"From what I have just learned this morning, for
weeks they were traveling to a number of the northern
shires' abbeys and monasteries. Don't try to tell me
that you don't know where they went—or when they

were away from your abbey. Don't try to tell me you
didn't send someone after them!"

With a vicious butt to the abbot's head, the deputy
turned and flung the aging monk against the rough
stone wall. Stunned and gasping for breath, the old
man sagged and slipped down beside the bloodied
monk. Blood began to trickle from his forehead.

"From the first moment I learned of this treasure,
you have all been lying to me. But now my patience
is spent. That time is finished. I've already sent men
to bring the Percy sluts to me. Between you two and
them, I'll get what I am after."

Through the blood and the pain, the monk bound
to the wall still managed a hideous grimace that might
have been a smile. "You admit . . . 'tis you . . . only
you . . . and you don't . . . know . . . don't know . . ."

The deputy loomed over him. "You think you can
bring on death just by baiting me? Nay, my arrogant
friend. You've got more pain coming than you ever
thought possible."

"I know . . . you . . . won't kill me. You . . . don't
know . . . what the treas . . . treasure . . . is."

The mouth of the king's deputy curled at one corner. " 'Pride cometh before the fall.' We will make
you cry out just for the sport of it. For now that I
have the great abbot here with us, he can—"

"I don't know what you two speak of, Sir Arthur."
The abbot was panting for breath, his face showing
his confusion. "True, the Percy girls were my charges
for a time. But this . . . this treasure? By the Virgin,
I know of no treasure."

The monk let his head roll against the stone wall
and gave a choked laugh. "You don't . . . know . . .
he won't know. 'Tis a secret!"

The Deputy Lieutenant gave the monk a vicious
backhand, causing fresh blood to spurt from his mis-
shapen face.

"I know all I need to know. You have told me so yourself. The Treasure of Tiberius is the greatest treasure in Christendom! Many have killed to possess it, you said." His voice lowered to a rasping whisper. " 'Twas the real—though secret—reason for an entire Crusade, you said. But the whereabouts of it . . . now, that's the mystery, you said. Until 'twas learned that the Percy's—"

"You . . . know . . . nothing! Its worth . . . its hiding . . . place . . . fool."

Arthur Courtenay drove a fist into the monk's face, causing the man's head to snap around and spraying blood halfway across the cell.

"Well, my two buggering whoresons. Between the two of you, I'll learn what I need to know before the first of those sluts is brought to my lair." The deputy nodded to his jailer to approach the abbot. "And make no mistake about it. Before I am through, you'll tell me what you know about the Treasure of Tiberius—and those sluts will beg me on their knees to let them lead me to it!"

As the heavy damask curtains were pulled open, the late morning sun spilled in, chasing the gloom from the large bedchamber.

Nodding her approval to the serving woman who stood with an uncertain look by one of the shutters, Catherine gently placed a hand on Susan's sleeve as she passed and whispered something into her ear. The younger woman nodded and hurried from the room without a word.

"Catherine Stewart!" the dowager scolded from where she sat propped up with pillows in her bed. "It does not please me to have ultimatums delivered to me in advance of your arrival."

Catherine smiled at the departing Auld Mab. The older woman paused only long enough to shoo another young serving woman from her place on a small stool by the hearth. The dowager and Catherine were left alone.

"Mother-in-law, I was not so much issuing an ultimatum as offering alternatives for such a pleasant day."

The dowager groused a bit and then patted the bed beside her. Catherine obediently moved closer and sat on the edge.

"And I suppose you call going blind with all the coverings to the windows removed a pleasant alternative to being dragged outside in the gardens where I can catch my death?"

Catherine smiled cheerfully and placed a hand on top of Lady Anne's. "Do you know this is the first time you have called me by my husband's name?"

"You're trying to change the subject."

"Nay, mother-in-law. I am glowing at your acceptance."

The dowager's gray eyes gentled as they met Catherine's. "You are carrying a bairn. A bairn of my own blood lineage. Despite all your stubbornness and willful disregard for my health, I've decided to put up with you."

Catherine smiled more openly. Pushing off her soft shoes, she climbed onto the bed and tucked her feet under her. "I told him."

"Which part did you tell him?"

"All of it." She beamed and whispered, "I told him how much I love him, and I revealed the truth that I am with child."

The older woman's eyes narrowed. "And?"

Catherine's eyes rounded as they met dowager's. "That was all! I thought 'twas enough."

"Aye, for any man! But I want to know how he took it!"

"I *think* he was pleased." Catherine could hear the note of uncertainty in her voice.

"I knew I did wrong not having him beaten more as a lad. The spoiled, ill-humored knave! Is that all he said? That he was pleased?"

Catherine bit on her lower lip and watched the tempest brewing in the dowager's face. She'd seen this in Athol's face, as well. In some ways, he was definitely his mother's son.

"I think you are being too harsh on him," Catherine said at last.

"Am I?"

"When I told him that I am in love with him . . . well . . . he was tender . . . affectionate. But at the news that he was to be a father! Well! I think he was too stunned to explain himself. He was . . . quiet, subdued. So I have decided to accept his reaction as being pleased!"

In fact, the more Catherine thought about her husband's immediate response, the better she felt about it. He had certainly been polite, nodding and forcing a smile—even hugging her and mumbling something about how wonderful it all was. And then he had simply retreated into his thoughts, obviously considering what it all meant.

"So you are not angry, child? You are not going to run way to Elgin or flee on foot to the borders in search of your mother for my son's treatment of you?"

Catherine wrapped her hand around Lady Anne's. "Nay, m'lady. I believe my mother has enough troubles on her mind. She has no need to be bothered with the day-to-day tribulations of a newly married daughter. So I'm sorry to disappoint you, mother-in-law, but I am here to stay."

"Very well!" she said, pushing Catherine's hand away and trying unsuccessfully to hide her pleasure at hearing Catherine's revelations. The dowager pointed at the small chest sitting on top of a table beside the bed. "Move that here, between us."

With a questioning glance at the older woman, Catherine did as she was told. Seating herself again on the bed, she watched as the dowager removed a chain from around her neck. As Lady Anne fingered the key at the end of the chain, Catherine considered another conversation that they had not quite finished.

"Do you know where your husband took Adam after you asked to have the bairn taken away?"

Lady Anne looked angrily at Catherine. "Young woman, you are not here to discuss Adam of the Glen! And I do not wish to hear that name mentioned again in my presence. Is that understood?"

Catherine stubbornly shook her head. "I'm afraid I cannot agree to that, m'lady! As long as my husband is tormented by the man and—"

"I have something of your mother's for you."

The dowager's words immediately silenced Catherine. Her gaze moved from the old woman's face to the key dangling at the end of the chain to the chest that sat between them.

"She had a messenger bring this to me right after I sent her the news that my son had forced you to become his wife."

"You have a way of corresponding with my mother? You know where she is?"

The dowager waved a dismissive hand in the air before turning the key in the lock. "Disregard what I just told you, since even under pain of death, I will not again admit it."

"But she is my mother, Lady Anne! I—"

" 'Tis her wish, Catherine! Do not rebel against your own mother's wishes. 'Tis for your safety and the safety of your sisters that she doesn't want her place of refuge known." The dowager opened the small chest, took a small package from the inside, and handed it to her. "Be content with the knowledge that she is guiding your lives from a distance and—"

"What do you mean, she is 'guiding' our lives? She found each of us a safe home in her native land. Are you telling me now that she is taking an active hand in—"

"Aye, aye, lass. Have it your way. If you want to believe the moon . . . or some mushroom . . . controls your destiny, think it so!" A secretive look flashed across Lady Anne's wrinkled brow. "But open the packet and release me from your mother's damnable curse."

"Curse?" Catherine looked down confusedly at the package in her hand.

"She sent this thing, swearing me to greater secrecy than Moses knew in sending the Jews out of Egypt. And then she has the impertinence to write me that I cannot even die until such time that I decide you are secure enough here to receive this package."

Catherine's fingers touched the softness of the parchment, and a knot formed in her throat. Her mother had held this in her own fingers.

The dowager leaned back wearily against the pillows. "So, there you have it, daughter-in-law. Open it! I am done with it."

Quickly, Catherine turned and dropped the packet in the dowager's lap.

"If you think that you can die now, simply because you have fulfilled a promise to my mother, then you are wrong." She shook her head resolutely. "I'm not accepting this."

"Stop your babbling, you blue-eyed harridan, and open the package."

"Only if you stop talking as if the angel of death were perched at your bedside."

"Have no fear about that, lass. There is no angel in this room—that I can see! Only an eldritch creature with a sharp tongue and wit enough to worry me to death."

Catherine frowned. "I do not find that humorous, Lady Anne. I've become quite fond of you, and here you are accusing me of—"

"Just open it, Catherine, before I have Auld Mab come in here and toss it into the fire!"

Reluctantly taking the package again from the dowager's hand, Catherine broke open the seal and unfolded the parchment on her lap. Inside of it she found a section of an ancient map, and opened it, as well.

"She must think I am very secure here to have forwarded this to me."

The older woman peered down at the marks and symbols on the vellum sheet. "What is this, Catherine," she said caustically, "the map to Jerusalem?"

"Nay, Lady Anne!" Catherine whispered. " 'Tis a portion of the map to the hiding place of the Treasure of Tiberius."

"Treasure?" The dowager leaned forward, her face lit with interest. "Now this has the ring of something that could stir an old woman's blood."

" 'Tis very valuable. It has been in the safekeeping of my family since the time of Crusades to the Holy Land."

Catherine's fingers traced the fine lines of the map as she read over her mother's message. When she was finished, she looked up at the dowager.

"Though I've never seen it, I know this is only one of three portions that make up a greater map. When the time is right, Laura and Adrianne shall also receive their own portions of the map. And if the need arrives—should my mother not survive this terrible time—then the three of us shall act together and move the treasure to a safer place."

The dowager's face was dark with concern. "It

sounds a wee bit complicated, Catherine . . . and dangerous, too."

"It must be complicated—to make finding the treasure impossible for those who are after it."

"Are there many who know of it?"

"Aye, Lady Anne. A number of groups of men know of it and seek it!" Catherine lowered her voice. "We were told stories as children that those who seek the Treasure of Tiberius were everywhere—searching the four corners of the world. I believe they could even be here in the Highlands, and some of these people are ruthless, greedy men who misunderstand the value of the treasure. For them, no crime is too horrible. No action is too hateful. In their quest, no life is so sacred that it will not be snuffed out if that will help them claim their prize!"

The dowager frowned, worry deepening the lines of her face.

"There is another group, though," Catherine continued, "who have a truer understanding of Tiberius and want it for a specific purpose. Because of who they are, my mother never believed them to be vicious or violent men. But what their true motives are is unknown to my sisters and me."

The older woman reached out and squeezed her daughter-in-law's hand with her bony fingers.

"Catherine, however valuable this treasure is, 'tis not so valuable that you need to risk your life for it. I tell you that you won't be needing anything here. Your husband took you with no dowry, and he will provide you with all the riches of the world, should you ask for it. I want you safe and away from this madness. Whatever you need will be provided, Catherine, and everything I have is yours. Perhaps, if your sisters require it . . ."

Catherine placed a hand affectionately on top of the

dowager's. The old woman's generosity warmed her heart, but her concern meant even more.

"I've never considered this as wealth, and I know my sisters do not see it that way, either. We all have been told, though, that 'tis our responsibility to keep it safe." Catherine's gaze dropped to the lines and symbols. "Why, when my father was imprisoned by the king, and our mother told us of the treasure, my sisters and I spent a great deal of time establishing a false trail, though 'tis possible no one will ever follow it. But the Treasure of Tiberius is nothing I would desire for myself. 'Tis too much for any one person to possess."

"Well, I'm too old and too wise to ask any more questions. The last thing I want is to find myself any deeper in your mother's accursed schemes." The dowager pushed the chest toward Catherine and handed her the chain and the key. "So as long as you promise not to run off without your husband to some mysterious treasure trove, then I'll try to be civil and even assist you with whatever you need regarding the school . . . my grandchild—"

"And answer some of my questions regarding Athol and even Adam?"

"You are a bold and obstinate hussy!"

"I am only a concerned wife. One who is trying as well to become a devoted daughter."

The dowager leaned heavily against the pillows, shooting an exasperated glance at Catherine. "You'll never give up, will you, child!"

She gently squeezed one of Lady Anne's thin hands. "There is too much that is not known, mother-in-law. Somehow, we must end this war between them, and I believe you—as much as anyone—will be grateful to have it all behind us."

The dowager stared down at their joined hands. "I do not know, Catherine! 'Tis all so . . . so frightening!"

Catherine waited until the older woman's gaze lifted to her face, and when she spoke, her voice was steady.

"Lady Anne, the only chance we have of shaping a better world is by knowing the past. This is what I believe and what I teach. Adam and John must know their past, as well, before they can fashion their future."

Chapter 20

"She's left the dowager countess's chambers, m'lord."

"Aye?" Athol said, glancing up quickly from the letter that had just arrived from court. Once again, a small company of English forces had moved north, taking a position in the disputed Scottish borderlands. There was other news, as well. "Where is she now?"

A moment later, dismissing the clan councillors who were hovering nearby and waving off Tosh, the laird moved out of the Great Hall and through the courtyard toward the gardens. The sun was warm on his face, but the clouds to the west foretold of stormy weather ahead. A wave from the warrior by the gate indicated that Catherine had just passed through the archway.

Without her being aware of it, he'd had his men bringing him news of every move she'd made this morning. He'd wanted to steal a moment alone with her before leaving again, and now he hurried after her. The gardens would give him the perfect opportunity.

He wanted to see her before leaving, but there was something else, as well. He'd seen the bruise marks on her wrists this morning, and he wanted to ask her about it. With her news of the bairn, she'd knocked the thought from his head, but he still wanted to know why the marks on her wrists looked as though her hands had been tied.

Already well accustomed to the stubborn nature of his wife, John Stewart knew that his only hope of finding an answer to this question lay in asking her directly. He'd never be able to force it out of her.

A number of kitchen workers were gathering herbs at the far end of the garden, and beyond them Athol could see two lads from the village driving a half-dozen cows up from the glen. Catherine was nowhere in sight, however.

Moving toward a small stand of pines beyond the gardens, Athol caught a glimpse of her, and stopped as Susan stepped from beneath a pear tree and greeted Catherine with a hug. The warm embrace that the two women gave each other pleased John at first, but his smile quickly turned to a frown as suspicion cut sharply into his brain.

Since when had the two women become friends? he wondered. And why should they be? Frowning at them, he suddenly wondered what he should do with Susan now that he'd taken Catherine as his wife. With Catherine as the Countess Balvenie, Susan would certainly not be needed as mistress of the castle.

Since he was the earl and also Susan's cousin, he mused, his appropriate action would probably be to arrange a good marriage for her. And that he would do, he decided, but not until he and his high-spirited wife were a wee bit more settled. And he would certainly not be able to give the plan the time it deserved until his business with Adam of the Glen was finished—for good.

Unseen, Athol watched as the two women—who appeared to be talking very seriously about a small wooden box Catherine was carrying—moved down the slope into the far end of the gardens. A breeze was blowing and Catherine's hair, loosely braided down her back, shone in the bright sunlight. How different these two women were, he thought, wondering how he'd ever thought them in any way similar. Perhaps it was a good thing that Catherine would have Susan as a companion.

But then, as he began to think on this new friendship, he suddenly remembered his own impending departure and his desire to see and talk to Catherine before he left.

As he stepped into the garden, Susan was the first to spot him and announced his arrival to Catherine. The look of sheer pleasure that shone in his wife's face as she turned toward him was a reward well worth waiting for.

Joining the two women, Athol took one of Catherine's hands tightly in his own and gathered her into a tight embrace with an affectionate growl.

"Well, Susan. I—" he stopped, realizing as he released Catherine that Susan was already well on her way to Balvenie's gates. "Did I interrupt some master planning session?"

He did not wait for an answer, though, and trapped her full lips beneath his own. It was still incredible to him how sweet she tasted . . . and how easily he found himself distracted at her nearness and by her loving response to him.

Stepping over to a low, turf-covered bench, Athol took the small wooden chest out of Catherine's hand and put it down. Sitting down, he drew her onto his lap and laid a hand protectively on her stomach.

"Tell me, Countess. Have I told you today how happy I am about the news of your bairn?"

Her cheeks turned red with the prettiest blush. She looked up and he felt the magic of her midnight-blue eyes slide like velvet over his soul.

"Nay, m'lord earl, you said very little this morning. But 'twas not very difficult to read your mind."

"Read my mind?" He frowned playfully. "I wonder if 'tis a good thing for a lass as unruly as you to be running about with that kind of power in your possession."

"You claim to read my mind, so what is wrong with me reading yours?"

He ran his thumb over her soft cheek. "Well, for one thing, most everything that you think or feel eventually finds its way to your lips, anyway. But with me—"

"I know."

She placed her hand firmly on his heart in the same protective way that he had laid his hand on her belly. He wondered if she could feel the pounding of that heart.

"You, John, like to keep your feelings hidden deep in your heart. You think 'tis a weakness to say the things that you feel—a mistake to let others glimpse the truth of who you are." She smiled at him. "Unless 'tis your temper that takes charge."

"But then," he replied quietly, "you have your own way of dealing with that."

She sighed softly and leaned against his chest. "A woman has to find a way to survive."

He found himself pulling her even more tightly against his chest. The peace he felt at this moment, the perfection of the fit between them—together like this—he could not imagine a greater, more glorious moment in life.

He shook off the feeling. "I have to leave Balvenie for a short time, lass. But when I—"

"Where?" Catherine pulled back and looked with concern into his face.

He grinned at her. "I've been coming and going from the first day we wed, and this is the first time you've asked."

A pretty frown darkened her brow. " 'Tis more than just for me than I ask. Our bairn would like to know."

"Liar!" He laughed and kissed her on the bridge of

the nose. He knew that she had given him her heart, but still she withheld her trust. That was why she had not told him the complete truth of what occurred last night. But who had he to blame but himself for that, he thought. Nay, when it came to trust, he would have to set the precedent. Well, from now on, he would tell her everything.

"I am taking a few men to the earl of Huntly's castle. 'Tis less than a half day's ride to the east. I received word this morning that the earl has arrived there."

"So you're not going to hunt Adam?"

"Nay, Catherine. Not exactly." Athol gazed out across the glen thoughtfully. "Though we have not ridden into Huntly's lands in search of Adam. All his trails have seemed to lead us in other directions."

He considered the possibility for a moment. It was possible that his bastard brother had been hiding in the hills between here and Huntly Castle all this time. It was one place they had not looked. And if that were true, what his mother had told him—about knowing Adam and about Adam knowing these lands—would make perfect sense.

"John, if you are not going in search of Adam, why must you go?"

"Huntly has sent me news from Stirling, but I have another reason for going now. I think the earl may have some answers for me."

"Answers?"

"Aye! Answers to everything. From the identity of the woman who was my father's mistress, to where Adam has been up to now. He may even know the reason for Adam's decision to wreak havoc on my lands. But I won't learn anything sitting here, my dove. So—"

Catherine was not ready to let him up.

"Perhaps, once you learn his motives—learn what

it was that set him off on such a dangerous path—
perhaps then you can negotiate a peace with him."

"There will be no negotiating with this devil. The
only peace either of us will know will be when his
head is sitting atop a pike above Balvenie's gates."

Catherine's sudden shudder made him regret his
harsh words. Despite all her courage, she was still an
expectant mother. She deserved a wee bit more
gentleness.

"I worry about you," she whispered softly. "About
this whole business of two brothers who can hate without knowing one another."

"I do not hate him, but he's brought the fight to
my door, and he must pay for the harm he's done."

"Aye, John, but just think of it! If things were different, if you two were not at odds, think how pleasurable it could be to have a brother. You and he share
your father's blood!"

He turned his gaze from Catherine's face to hide
his own emotions. It was difficult to admit that she
spoke the truth. In reality, he knew that if he truly
set his mind to it, he could catch Adam of the Glen.
Instead though, since learning of their kinship through
his mother, he'd chosen to chase after answers—to try
to discover the reasons behind his bastard brother's
actions.

Catherine's soft touch on his chin brought his gaze
back to her face. Her eyes swam with unshed tears.
"I want you to come back safely to me. And while
you are away—if you find the answers that you are
seeking—then I only ask that you not act in haste."

"If I did not know my wife better, I'd say you were
worried about Adam of the Glen."

"My loyalty lies where my heart is . . . and that is
with you." She placed both hands on his shoulders
and gazed into his eyes. "And I want you to have no

regret—years from now—over something you might do in haste this day."

"Adam deserves the punishment that awaits him."

"Perhaps that is so, John. But 'twas because of your father's wrongdoing that Adam was born in the first place. You should know that his faithlessness hurt your mother deeply. And yet, so many years later, 'tis your mother who feels guilty for not accepting and raising Adam as her own. She is convinced that 'tis because of *her* actions that you two are now at each other's throat."

"That's nonsense. 'Tis—"

"You are her son as much as your father's." Catherine's feathery touch caressed his face. "I love you so much. I do not want to see you suffer for the rash act of an angry moment."

She brushed her lips on his chin, across his lips and then looked into his face.

"I believe in you, John Stewart, and I know you will do the right thing. Just hurry and come back to us, since your bairn and I both will be needing you."

Trying to calm herself, Catherine shifted the small chest from beneath one arm to the other and stepped into the Great Hall. Susan was not there, either.

John would be just fine, she kept reminding herself. After all, this was his land. These were his people. He was traveling with his own men—men armed and sworn to serve and protect him.

But by the Virgin, she worried, gnawing her lip, why couldn't he have taken more of his warriors with him . . . as he *had* been doing? Why had he left Tosh behind?

Trying to recall how many of Adam's men she had seen in the encampment, Catherine couldn't help but worry about what would ever happen if Adam were to set a trap for Athol. She would remember to her dying day the look of hatred she'd seen in Adam's eyes.

She should have gone with him! Perhaps with her there, the other man . . .

Catherine shook her head. She was losing her mind. The earl of Athol had managed to survive many battles without her. He would come back. He had to.

"Mistress Catherine."

She jumped at the sound of the monk's voice in her ear. Turning sharply to Brother Bartholomew, she gave him her darkest scowl. "Now I know you're pleased with yourself, Brother, over your time with the bishop at Elgin, but I see no reason for you to be scaring me half to death."

"I do beg your forgiveness, mistress, but . . . aye, what a lovely man Bishop Patrick is!"

"Humph!" Catherine said, keeping an eye open for Susan. "I wouldn't know."

"M'lady, I know I haven't had a chance to speak to you privately since my return, but you've been scurrying here, and scurrying there."

"Humph!" she said again with a frown.

"But we're so happy to find you here."

Catherine looked at him as he gestured to the other two monks sitting at a table on the far side of the Great Hall.

"Very well, Brother," she responded thoughtfully, starting across the Hall. "Perhaps now would be a good time to talk."

Sitting at the table with the three clerics, Catherine clutched the wooden chest in her lap and listened to Bartholomew tell what the bishop had agreed to supply. When he was finished, she in turn informed them of the earl's position on the school and of all the other details that she had finalized so far with him.

When she was finished, Catherine turned to the

monks and waited for any questions they might have. All three appeared quite content with her news.

"Very well!" she said, standing up and glancing down at the wooden chest in her hands. "I may just recommend to my husband that we hold discussions in the Great Hall. It certainly makes for productive use of time."

"You have something else on your mind, I take it?" Brother Bartholomew asked. "Something we can be of assistance with?"

Catherine purposely hesitated, then nodded to Brother Bartholomew's question.

"Aye, you can. I was looking for Mistress Susan." She scanned the faces of some folk just entering the Great Hall. "But now that you ask, I wonder if one of you sweet men might take this chest to my chamber. I'm getting a bit tired of carrying it to and fro."

She turned to the monks and found three sets of eyes staring at the ornate box which she held before her.

"Remembering your pranks of years past, mistress." Brother Paul grinned. "I have learned never to take anything from your hand that might contain some species of vermin or a viper."

Catherine feigned a look of shock and turned to Brother Egbert. "You have certainly never been afraid of my tricks, good brother. So if *you* would be kind enough to take it." She lowered her voice to a whisper. " 'Tis a keepsake newly arrived from my mother—"

"I'll be more than happy to take it, mistress." Brother Bartholomew broke in.

Catherine turned and looked attentively at the portly monk. "That is quite thoughtful of you. You realize that the safekeeping of this chest is something I would not entrust to just anyone."

The monk nodded solemnly and took the chest out of Catherine's hands.

"The safekeeping of all you hold dear is a task I take to heart, mistress."

Safely ensconced in Susan's bedchamber, Catherine gazed at her companion's ashen face and almost regretted revealing the truth of where Athol had gone.

Moving to where Susan sat somberly on the side of the bed, Catherine took her hands. "But why are you so upset about this news? What is it that you know? Tell me, Susan."

The younger woman's misty gaze lifted and caught Catherine's. "That's where Adam has gone, as well. Before we left last night, he told me that, after moving his camp, he was going to ride east—to await the arrival of the earl of Huntly."

Catherine felt the knot form in her belly, and suddenly a wave of nausea washed over her. Even as she fought down the bile rising in her throat, she knew the sickness had nothing to do with the child that she was carrying, but rather the possible danger awaiting the father. Standing and crossing to the window, she pulled open the shutters and breathed in a chest full of air.

This was exactly what she feared. She would never forgive herself if John were hurt.

A moment later, she felt Susan's gentle touch on her shoulder. "We are more helpless in this than we thought."

Catherine turned around and faced her. The trembling lips told her of her new friend's fear. She herself would need to be strong, Catherine reminded herself. The same way that she'd been strong with her sisters through the ordeal of her father's death and the absence of their mother.

"Nay, Susan," Catherine announced at last. "We do

not have to be helpless. We're assuming the worst will happen . . . and without cause. They may not even encounter one another between here and Huntly Castle. And if all goes well and both of them return unharmed from this trip, then we will have a second chance to set things right. But we must be prepared."

The younger woman twisted her hands together in a nervous gesture and nodded her agreement. "I suppose you're right."

"Aye. That's the spirit. First, we must consider what we know."

"About their pasts, you mean?"

"Aye." Feeling a bit better and more in control, Catherine walked back to the middle of the room. "We know they were sired by the same father. Lady Anne said as much to Athol."

"True. Adam has said so many times."

Catherine turned to Susan. "Do you know how Adam came to learn the truth? Did he ever say that? Did he always know it?"

"From what he told me, he knew nothing about being a Stewart until the age of fifteen, when he was sent to London and held prisoner when the Treaty of Bruges was signed."

Catherine couldn't keep the note of surprise out of her voice. "But that treaty ended the war with France—the war between England and France! Why should he be sent to prison?"

Susan's face was grim. "Because he was . . . he is . . . of Stewart blood."

"I do not understand why—"

"Because Scotland and France have always been allied against the English. Thirteen years ago, when the treaty was signed, a number of men—all kin to the king—were gathered and shipped to England to be kept in prisons as surety against the articles of the peace. So they came after him. 'Twas only then that he was told he was the son of the earl of Athol and half-brother to the earl's heir."

"How could neither brother have known?"

Susan shook her head. "Since he was a bairn, Adam was raised as a member of the earl of Huntly's household. He was never told who his true parents were, but was treated well and given the same education as any noble-blooded lad. The earl of Huntly treated him like his own kin, and Adam told me that for many years, he simply assumed he was the bastard son of the earl, himself."

"And he was taken at the age of fifteen!" Catherine began pacing the room. "What happened to him then?"

"He was held in the Tower of London for twelve years—treated with less dignity than the river rats that swarmed in each night. He told me that during all those years the only thing that kept him alive was the thought of returning to Scotland and taking revenge on the man who had put him there. The legitimate son of John Stewart! The brother that he'd learned to hate."

Catherine shook her head. "But that cannot be. Athol never knew about Adam's existence until only days before we wed. There was no way he could be held responsible for sending him there. And I am certain he knows none of this even now. Nothing of where Adam has been or the reason for his hatred!"

Susan sat heavily on the side of the bed. "I know. But I have had no way of telling Adam's side of things. And what could I have said to Adam about the earl? What could I have said in his defense that Adam would have believed?"

"But about this treaty?" Catherine pressed. "Adam believes that John had some influence in it? But how could he? He was a young man himself then!"

"Adam told me that one of those he was imprisoned

with had told him that John Stewart had given him up." She looked grimly at Catherine. "John Stewart."

"Aye, but thirteen years ago . . . wasn't the father still alive then? He was John Stewart, as well."

"Your husband was the one who stood to gain by such a decision—"

"Aye, but 'twas a decision he knew nothing about," Catherine cut in. "Think on it. What choice did the old earl have? Someone had to go! He had to send a son. As other Stewarts did. How many of them would send their firstborn?"

Susan's words were so soft, but so full of pain, that Catherine could feel her own heart ache for the woman. "So he picked his elder son to stay."

"And his second son to go." Seeing the tears beginning to trickle down Susan's face, Catherine crouched before the younger woman. " 'Tis very sad, Susan."

"Adam will hurt all the more to learn of this! To think that his mother rejected him, deserted him. That his father, too . . . that his own father chose to send him off—" The tears choked off Susan's words. "Who has not rejected him? Betrayed him?"

Catherine sat beside her, holding her as the young woman sobbed out her sadness for the man she loved. When the shuddering subsided, Catherine wiped the tears from Susan's face.

"Maybe 'tis better this way. Those who are gone are to be blamed. He must make peace with the kin he has left."

Susan shook her head. "He will not believe what we say. He is so full of hatred for Athol that—"

"Perhaps we can prove to him what we know to be true. Through the earl of Huntly . . . perhaps even through the documents that signed him over. I am certain there must be a way to make him understand."

" 'Tis just that he has spent all of his life without love."

"But no longer, Susan. He has you now. And if we can help him through to the truth, he might have a brother in John, as well. And a sister in me."

The young woman nodded, but Catherine knew that she was not still convinced. And who could blame her? To make Adam simply forget the past seemed to be as great a challenge as having Athol ignore the destruction the other man had brought to his people and his lands.

A tremendous undertaking for all of them.

In an attempt to shake off the gloom that was settling on them, Catherine placed a gentle hand on Susan's shoulder and looked into her face. "Tell me how you two met."

Susan blushed and stared down at her hands. "My journey to Balvenie happened to coincide with Adam's arrival in Scotland. My party was attacked and some of the warriors escorting me fled in the melee." A faint smile broke out on the young woman's lips. "I was left nearly alone to ward off Adam and his men."

"It must have been terrifying for you!"

"Aye. 'Twas a wild scene! I'd never seen such a thing. I am the youngest of eight in my family, Catherine. This trip was my first venture into the world. I put up a great show of courage, though, I think. I believe . . . my actions . . . well, amused Adam. They talked of cutting throats, since we carried very little of value. And I didn't care for the way some of the men looked at me. But then Adam cursed at his men and told them to take the horses and point my escort toward Balvenie." Susan's voice took on a dreamy tone. "He reached down and caught me up with one hand. He sat me on his horse in front of him, and we were away like the wind."

"He took you prisoner?"

"Aye," Susan whispered. "He carried me to a grove of trees not far from the village down the hill from the castle. We just . . . we talked for a long while. Something happened to us that day, Catherine. When we parted, we both knew it would not be for long."

"But you were coming here to become Athol's wife, were you not?"

"Aye, to Lady Anne's thinking—and wishing." Susan smiled as she looked up. "Though after meeting Adam of the Glen, I knew I could never have gone through with it. So after arriving here, I became as sour and severe a young hag as anyone could imagine. There was no way that John Stewart could ever take a liking to someone like me."

"And here, a few short months later, he did exactly that." Catherine laughed. "He married a sour and severe *old* hag!"

"Perhaps." Susan's eyes shone with mischief as they turned on Catherine. "Though seeing what went on that night in the corridor outside of your chamber, I'd say he soon developed a very different way of seeing women like us."

Catherine blushed at the recollection of Susan witnessing their lovemaking. Unconsciously laying a hand over the treasure she was carrying within her, she met Susan's eyes again. "Enough of that, you imp. Tell me how you found a way to go and see Adam again?"

"Roy Sykes came to the castle soon after I arrived. He was our messenger for a while. I know you must think me a traitor, knowing the whereabouts of Adam of the Glen and still keeping quiet to Athol—"

"I have no ill will toward anything you've done. Now, if you had brought him inside the walls of this keep, and delivered up these folk to him . . ."

"Adam would never hurt an innocent. From the first time I learned of the secret passages—through Auld Mab—and found a way to steal out of the castle and return unheeded, he never asked that I betray Athol or Lady Anne. I know he has been raiding and acting the part of an outlaw, but in truth I know he is an honorable man. In all his raids, he has never yet shed any blood without cause. He wants his brother to feel his vengeance, but in the same way that he let you go last night, he will not bring his wrath down on an innocent. Athol, he believes, is the one who needs to be punished. He alone."

Catherine again had to fight back the worry from choking her. "And this is why we must set him right. We must find a way for them both to see the truth."

"Aye." Susan nodded. "There is no other choice."

Catherine rose to her feet and began to pace the room again. Between the two of them, she was certain they had explained most of Adam's and John's past. But there were still some things that made no sense.

"Susan, why do you think the old earl took Adam to Huntly instead of just leaving him with the child's mother? You mentioned he was educated and treated well before being sent to England. And how can you explain the fact that no one knows of any mistress that the old earl kept? Everyone says that the dowager and her husband had a close marriage—that he had no other women."

"Adam has tried to find out who his mother is . . . or was. He has searched this entire area, but has found nothing."

"And John has done the same, and he too has found nothing. He told me that much himself."

Susan paused, her eyes focusing on Catherine's face. "I tried to tell Adam that perhaps she was dead. That many women die in childbirth. But he said that she is alive."

"How does he know that?"

"He does not know for certain, but when he was freed from the Tower, there was a special envoy sent to ransom him. 'Twas not an envoy from the Scottish king, that much they told him. But something they

said, some vague reference, made Adam believe the
envoy came on behalf of his mother."

Catherine considered that for a moment and then
shook her head. "To send an envoy to ransom a politi-
cal prisoner would have taken a great deal of gold.
What woman would have command of such wealth?"

Susan nodded. "Not some peasant woman, that is
for certain."

"If 'twas not the king, and not Athol or Lady
Anne . . ."

"I believe that Adam has decided that if 'twas not
his mother who ransomed him, then the gold must
have come from the one person who knows his past,
the only one with enough wealth to pay the kind of
ransom the English king would demand."

"Huntly."

"Aye. Adam believes that his mother may have
begged Huntly on his behalf. That is why he has gone
to wait for the earl of Huntly now."

A damp wet breeze swept into the chamber. Catherine hugged her middle and looked in the direction of
the window. The blue sky had disappeared, replaced
by a low, fast-moving mass of wind-driven gray. As
she watched, a gust of rain drenched in an instant the
narrow stone sill. The rain began to fall in sheets then.

She could not allow herself to think of what might
happen at Huntly now. She had to focus on what else
they could learn right here at Balvenie Castle.

She had to prepare. She had to be ready.

Chapter 21

John Stewart, earl of Athol, stood before the fire in the Great Hall of Huntly Castle, steam from his clothes like a mist about him.

" 'Twas his wish, John," the earl of Huntly told him. " 'Twas your father's wish that you never be told."

"But why?" Athol asked, glaring at the wizened man sitting in his carved chair. Huntly was a legend in Scotland. Warrior, statesman, counselor to kings, and loyal friend to John Stewart and his father before him. "Why should my father bring a bastard child to my mother—and yet choose to keep it from me? Why, m'lord?"

"As close as we were, your father always kept his own counsel on some things. But I believe I can answer that." Huntly's sharp gray eyes softened slightly, and his gaze fixed on the fire behind Athol. "I know you remember your father as a strong man—as one who would never bend to anyone or anything in his life."

"Aye." Athol folded his arms across his chest. "That's how I remember him."

"I remember him as an honorable man," Huntly continued. "And one who loved your mother very much. Not always the case, you know, among those in our position."

"So I understand, m'lord," the tall Highlander responded grimly. "But he made a mistake."

"Aye. Not a terrible mistake, by many men's standards, but a mistake that he felt besmirched his

honor . . . and brought unhappiness to your mother. But
as an honorable man, he would not turn his back on his
responsibility. So when your mother refused to accept
the bairn as her own, he brought the lad to me."

"He trusted you."

"Aye. He wanted Adam raised with all the privi-
leges of an earl's son. At that time you were too young
to understand such things, so you were told nothing.
But later . . . well, later I believe he thought it would
serve no purpose in you knowing."

"Why?" Athol asked, impatience in his tone.

Huntly did not look into John's face as he told him
of the terms of the Treaty of Bruges—and of a father's
choice. Athol listened with growing dismay to the
aging earl.

He'd never known.

". . . 'Twas a matter of hiding you or having you
both flee Scotland, but his honor and his loyalty would
not allow such an arrangement. He was forced to
abide by the terms of the treaty. He had to choose."

Athol crossed to the table and took a seat beside
the earl of Huntly. That had taken place more than
twelve years ago. To this day, he still remembered the
long spells of melancholy that afflicted his father at
the end of his life.

"The choice killed him."

Huntly paused before answering. "Aye. Your father
died within a year after that. You recall that he sent
for me before he died."

John nodded at the memory.

"He wanted to make certain that you would hear nothing of the truth. He did not believe that Adam would survive that imprisonment. If Scotland broke the treaty, the
hostages would certainly die, and your father had no faith
in the earl of Angus and the Douglases, who were in
power at the time." Huntly laid a hand on Athol's arm.

"Knowing *your* sense of honor, he was fearful that you would go to England and take Adam's place."

John Stewart ran a weary hand over his face. Of course he would have. He was the legitimate son. It was his place to be there.

"You were educated and brought up to be laird of your people. As much as he loved both his sons, he felt a responsibility to your mother, to you, and to the people of the glens around Balvenie Castle."

"And what of Adam?" He stood, crossed to the hearth, and stared into the flames. *What of him? What his brother must have suffered!*

Huntly broke into his thoughts. "I knew it then, and I see now that your father was right. Not telling you the truth was the right thing to do. Without you succeeding your father, your people would never be living as they do now."

"Aye, but Adam rightfully holds me responsible for what is past. And here, I have been so ignorant of the truth that instead of seeking him out and trying to make him understand, instead of trying to make reparations, I have been hunting him like an animal across the land."

"I'm more at fault in that than anyone else." The earl of Huntly rose to his feet and stepped up beside Athol. "When I heard of Adam's freedom six months ago, I should have guessed at the confusion that would cloud his thinking. But with England again at war with France, I have been under great pressure. In fact 'twas not until just a few hours ago—"

"Is he here?"

The earl of Huntly paused, his eyes steadily measuring John. "Yesterday, I would not have answered you. Today, I know you see him in a very different light."

"Is he here, and does he know what I know?"

Huntly shook his head. "He is no longer here, John. But what I have told you, I have also told him."

John let out a breath and waited for the earl to continue. So, they both knew the truth now.

"He was as shocked as you, my friend, and even more affected by it all, I think."

For a moment, he wondered—if their fates had been reversed—how he himself would have taken such news. It is much easier to turn your anger on someone you hold responsible for your misery, than to think that Fortune has simply chosen to frown on you.

"Do you know where he is now?"

The earl of Huntly hesitated, and then shook his head, but somehow John was not convinced of the other man's total ignorance.

" 'Tis time that Adam shared in the land and fortune our father left to me. 'Tis time that we made our peace."

"You can do what you like with your own lands, John, but you do not need to worry about Adam going hungry. As you know, I have no direct heir, and I'm not getting any younger. I've already spoken to the king and the council, and they have agreed. One of the reasons for my journey north was to give Adam title to this castle and the lands I have here. But I do not believe all the wealth in the world matters much to him right now. He needs some time to reconsider his life and what he wants for the future."

But this wasn't enough, Athol thought. Not for him. He had to find Adam. They both had to come to terms with the past . . . and the future.

Catherine's words came back to him. Of her trust in his sense of what was right. Of her insistence of having him open his heart and letting his words express his feelings.

John Stewart knew that he was blessed with an incredibly intelligent and beautiful wife. He was blessed with a child growing in her womb. And now he knew that he was blessed with a brother.

It was up to him to make things work.

*   *   *

The storm had continued unabated through the night, and the morning's cold, wet air lay in patches in the corridors of the Balvenie Castle like a company of marsh ghosts.

Catherine placed a hand on Susan's arm at the top of the stairwell.

"Wait for me while I go back and get a wrap."

Turning, she ran back along the corridor toward her chamber.

In truth, for the hundredth time since yesterday, Catherine wanted to check on the wooden chest sitting prominently on the stool beside the hearth in her chamber. Brother Bartholomew had done as he had been charged the day before, delivering it to Jean upstairs. But as she hurried toward her chamber, she wondered whether the portly monk had shaken the box or perhaps even examined the lock. In fact, Catherine couldn't help but wonder how long it would be before the ornate box would be taken or at least broken open.

She was no fool. She had spent most of her life knowing that she must be watchful of those seeking the Tiberian treasure. She did not fear them—well, not those she suspected to be near. She knew that most of these people would not harm her, but she must be on her guard. And she would lure them out, if any were indeed here at Balvenie Castle, as she suspected.

The elaborate diversions she and her sisters had gone to the trouble to devise—to confuse those who might be searching—had kept their minds active during a time of great distress. But now, alone in the Highlands, she simply hadn't the time for any such nonsense. Her simple trap would just have to do.

Opening the door to her chamber and spotting the chest where she'd left it brought an immediate frown to Catherine's face. Moving closer she cast a cursory glance at the lock. It appeared untouched.

Picking up the Stewart tartan that lay across the foot of her bed, Catherine draped it about her shoulders. Catherine turned and looked around the chamber. Perhaps she was being too obvious, she thought suddenly. After all, she'd simply left the wooden casket in the open.

Moving briskly to the head of the bed, she tucked the small chest beneath pillows and bedding, piling everything back on top of it. Standing back with an approving nod, she turned and headed out the door.

As she returned to her friend at the stairwell, Catherine again considered what she and Susan had learned that morning.

Having cornered Auld Mab on her way to the kitchens, the two had tried to glean a bit more information about the past than Catherine had learned from the dowager.

More than anything, they now wanted to know who Adam's mother was. But Auld Mab's lips were sealed on that point. Glaring alternately at Susan and Catherine, the old woman had pointedly told them that she would never reveal anything that might still be hurtful to the dowager or any other lady hereabouts! She knew the truth, by the Cross, but she planned on keeping it to herself!

As Catherine reached the stairwell, it struck her, and she stopped dead in her tracks.

"What's the matter?" Susan asked.

"Adam's mother!" Catherine said quietly. "Auld Mab told us she'd not reveal anything that might hurt Lady Anne or any other *lady hereabouts*! 'Tis a noble woman, and she lives nearby!"

"Aye!" Susan said excitedly. "It must be! Why else would Auld Mab still be so defensive about it?"

Together, the two women turned their steps down the stairwell.

"Who else can we ask?"

"There is no one else in this keep—that I can think of—who might remember back that far."

"What do you know of the dowager's friends?" The two women stepped past the entrance to the Great Hall. "Has she ever spoken of people that she and the earl might have been friendly with years back? There must be someone whom Lady Anne has spoken of."

Susan followed Catherine toward the door to the earl's outer chamber. "Well, I've heard her speak of the earl of Bothwell and his wife."

"The parents of Patrick Hepburn, the bishop at Elgin cathedral?"

"Aye." Susan frowned then and shook her head. "I met the countess of Bothwell once, though, at my parent's holding near Linlithgow. I cannot imagine her having an *affaire d'amour* with someone else's husband. She's a tiny, timid woman with only one good eye . . . and she's very devout. A model of piety, you might say."

"Some women are not pious from the beginning. Some become devoted to religion later . . . because of what life brings them."

"Still"—Susan shook her head—"I think 'tis safe to rule her out."

Trusting Susan's judgment, Catherine nodded and took a burning wick lamp from the wall as the two of them stepped into John Stewart's chamber. An unlit fire had been set in the hearth, and Catherine now lit the dry tinder beneath the logs. In a moment, they were sitting in two chairs before the crackling fire. It was important that they sort out whatever they could before Athol returned from Huntly Castle.

"Can you think of anyone else?"

"Well, the earl of Moray and his wife are old friends of the family, but I do not think the countess is a likely paramour. I've never met her, but I know that a horse fell and rolled on her when they were out hunting. They'd only just been married, as I remember it, and she's been crippled in both legs ever since. She's never borne children, Catherine."

Catherine got up and moved to one of the narrow windows. Opening the shutters, she looked out into the gray mist that was now falling. "I guess there is not much chance of her being Adam's mother."

"The Earl of Huntly has been another close friend. But he never wed." Susan turned in her chair and looked at Catherine. "And then there are others more distant. The Macpherson clan has a great holding down the River Spey, and the Ross clan has a number of castles farther to the east. And the MacI—"

"What about the MacInnes clan?" Catherine asked, facing Susan. Even as she said the name, she knew she must push aside her uncertainties about the past that her husband and Joanna MacInnes shared. Nay, she chided herself as she returned to her chair, focus on the answers that they were seeking regarding Adam's origins. "The two families had arrangements of marriage for their children, I understand. There must have been a connection of some sort."

Susan brightened. "You are correct. I forgot the most obvious. From what I've heard from Auld Mab and the dowager, the two families have been allied since the time Duncan MacInnes first brought his family to Ironcross Castle."

"With their lands adjoining," Catherine couldn't help from saying, "of course, it only made sense for the future earl of Athol and Joanna MacInnes to . . ."

Her voice trailed off, and Catherine felt her face redden.

There was a long pause, and when Susan spoke, her voice had taken on a reassuring tone.

"I do not think that you need to fear anything from that quarter, Catherine. I believe there was a great deal more speculation about that union than there was truth to it. I've only been at Balvenie castle for little more than half a year, but I have had the opportunity to get to know Joanna MacInnes Kerr fairly well. And I speak honestly when I say that she is a woman who is in love with her husband. And I have never seen any intimation by either Joanna or Athol that they were anything but good friends before her marriage to Gavin Kerr."

In an instant, Susan's words washed away a doubt that had been nagging at Catherine from the time she first heard the name "Joanna MacInnes."

"As far as the family, though," Susan continued, "I would be hard pressed to say much about them . . . well, aside from the . . ." She paused. "Well, other than what I know of Joanna and her grandmother, Lady MacInnes, the history of the women in the family is a wee bit of a jumble."

Catherine noticed Susan visibly shiver, and she started up to close the shutters again.

"Nay, do not close them. 'Tis not the weather, Catherine."

"What is it, Susan?"

"I see no one has told you the tales of Ironcross Castle."

Catherine shook her head.

"Well"—the young woman paused and gazed into the fire—" 'twas known for a long while, centuries maybe, that Ironcross Castle and those who lived there were cursed."

"Oh, Susan! You do not believe in—"

"Not a laird—for as long as anyone remembers— died but violently there. And many of their families, too. There are horrible stories, Catherine, of a thousand women buried in a crypt deep beneath the castle."

Catherine gaped as her friend paused. Clearly, Susan believed the stories. "Did the dowager tell you all this?"

"Nay, she never speaks of Ironcross Castle or the MacInnes family. Auld Mab told me these things when I went to visit the place for the first time."

"And this . . . this curse has never been lifted?"

"Aye, it has. Auld Mab says that Joanna and Gavin Kerr managed to put an end to it somehow." Susan's face brightened into a gentle smile. "I do not know what the place was like before, but Ironcross Castle is now the most peaceful place you could care to visit. Of course, that is, when their wild band of urchins are not whooping after the dogs in the Great Hall or getting themselves stuck climbing in the chimneys. In fact, with the new twin bairns in the keep, I'm certain Ironcross must be in even more of an uproar. Never mind what I said about peaceful."

Catherine smiled, as well, at the image. She hadn't yet told Susan about her own good news. The thought of young children taking charge of the somber passages of Balvenie Castle was a most enchanting notion. But also, the prospect of taking a trip to Ironcross Castle and meeting this family held a new charm for her.

"I believe that Lady MacInnes, Joanna's grandmother, has lived in Stirling for many years, though Mab hinted to me that in her time, she suffered greatly at the hands of—"

"Her husband?" Catherine asked excitedly.

"Aye. 'Tis only recently that she has moved back to the Highlands. She's living now with—"

An abrupt knock at the door interrupted Susan's words. Calling for whoever it was to come in, Catherine watched Tosh enter, carrying a sealed letter in his hand.

"From the earl?" she asked, anxiety suddenly evident in her voice.

"Nay, m'lady. A message from Ironcross Castle. 'Twas sent to the earl, but the messenger had word that he was to give it to you or to Mistress Susan if the earl was not in the castle."

"Not to the dowager?" Catherine asked with surprise.

"Nay, m'lady," Tosh replied, a frown creasing his battle-scarred face. "To you or to Mistress Susan, he said."

The two women turned and looked at each other. Catherine took the packet from Tosh, and with Susan looking over her shoulder, she broke open the seal.

The two of them read it silently and knew immediately what needed to be done.

"Tosh, I want someone to take a message to Huntly Castle," Catherine said decisively. "And we'll be needing an escort for a short journey of our own."

Huntly Castle's gates were no more than an hour behind them when Athol and his men surprised the two outlaws coming over a boulder-studded hill.

The two put up very little struggle, overwhelmed as they were by the earl's warriors. Under Athol's steady gaze, the blood drained rapidly out of Roy Sykes's normally ruddy face, and the other goodly-sized Highlander—whom Sykes had called by the name of Ren—grew sullen and surly in captivity.

Moving quickly, Athol and his men checked to see if any more of the outlaw band were in the vicinity—they were not about to be surprised themselves. There were, however, no signs of any other brigands.

Saying nothing to them directly, Athol ordered that their hands be bound and that the prisoners be tethered behind the horses of two of his men. As they worked their way up and down the rugged hills toward Balvenie Castle, he could hear his men talking with grim humor about how far methods of torture had advanced since the days when the Spaniards had raised the practice nearly to an art form.

After learning what Huntly had deemed appropriate to tell him, John's initial reaction had been simply to let the two go, forgiving even Roy Sykes's disloyalty. With good reason, John Stewart had lost what zeal he had for bringing to justice those outlaws who had been plaguing him for the past six months.

But as he considered freeing them, he realized that somehow he must find a way of contacting Adam of the Glen—and these men might just provide the means. He would take them to Balvenie Castle, but he would not punish them. Perhaps through questioning them—not by means of torture, though—the Highlander might learn of Adam's whereabouts.

The last thing he wanted now was for his half-brother to disappear for another lengthy span of time before they had a chance to resolve their differences.

They were nearly halfway back to Balvenie Castle when, passing a particularly suitable tree for hanging, the ugly outlaw named Ren planted his feet and nearly jerked the warrior leading him off his steed.

"M'lord," the burly Highlander croaked, dropping to his knees while Roy Sykes looked on, his mouth hanging open. "Hang us here and be done wi' us. Have mercy on us two, poor, beggarly creatures. We ne'er hurt none o' yourn. On 'is Bones, I swear!"

Athol stared at the two for a moment and then glanced at the tree, before looking back again.

"Very well," the earl said with as fierce a look as he could muster. "Say what you have to tell me, and I'll consider hanging you here."

In a few moments, the two men had conveyed a fairly concise tale of Adam's activities—always swearing that no one was ever hurt. This much Athol had already known, and he did not hesitate to tell them as much with a menacing growl. The next information the two revealed, however, drew his interest immediately. When asked why they were separated from the rest of their band of blackguards, Roy Sykes had blurted out in tones that were probably heard in Elgin.

"He has dispersed all his men, m'lord," the red-haired stable hand cried out. "After returning from Huntly, the master gathered us together, divided what we had between us, and directed us to go our separate ways. Adam told us the days of raiding your lands were over, and that he'd skin us himself if he ever heard of any of us stealing from your crofters or your flocks."

Athol frowned at the two men. "Did he say where he himself was going?"

"Nay!" Ren croaked. "Swear, 'e said nothing!"

Roy Sykes crossed himself and looked steadily into the earl's piercing gray eyes.

"Nay, m'lord! Many of us offered to stay by him— to do whatever he asked of us. But he said nay to that. He said, what he had to do and where he was going, he didn't know himself. He told us to go south and try to find a respectable living."

Athol looked away and breathed a deep sigh of relief. At least his brother was done raiding his lands. But he still had to find Adam and offer him the life that he should have had for all these years.

"Cut them loose," he said to his men before looking into the two stunned faces of the former outlaws. "You are free to go, but if I see either of you . . . or any of your band . . . again, I'll string you up and make you food for the crows. Now, do as your master commanded, Roy Sykes. Go and find a respectable living."

Chapter 22

Adam didn't know what to say or what to ask when they met. He didn't even know if he would be angry or joyous when they finally came face to face.

But more important, he didn't have any idea how to get through the legion of Kerr warriors sure to be guarding the gates of Ironcross Castle once he got there. Wiping the mist from his face, Adam spurred his horse on and tried to imagine how would he ever get to the woman.

The earl of Huntly had mentioned her name only briefly. A mention, in passing, of her interest a year or so earlier in knowing what had happened to Adam, about his situation in prison, about what had been done to free him. Her anger that Huntly's own efforts to have him freed from the English prison had not borne fruit.

The earl had not once, though, named her as Adam's mother. But what else could he have meant?

When he had been freed from the Tower of London, spirited onto the sleek sailing vessel waiting in the Thames, he had been fully aware that there were still other Scots languishing in the English prison. For the past six months, Adam had puzzled over the identity of his benefactor. Now he knew.

Now it was time to meet Lady Agnes MacInnes.

When Huntly had told him about John Stewart's complete lack of knowledge of everything that had

befallen Adam over the years, his ignorance even of
having a half-brother, Adam had felt the breath
knocked out of his chest. It had always been so much
easier for him to focus on Athol as the object of his
hate—so much simpler to plan his revenge against
someone that he knew would feel the cutting edge of
his rage.

But now, learning that his half-brother was innocent, that he himself had been unjustly tormenting
Athol and his people without cause—without Athol
even knowing what lay at the bottom of it all—Adam
felt more like a petty thief than an avenging crusader.

So he had sent his men on their way.

What he needed now was to find and speak to Lady
MacInnes. Deep in his heart, he could feel that hope
that had never died, pinching and clawing and gnawing
at him. Perhaps she was indeed his mother. He would
never know until he could see her, speak to her, look
into her eyes.

Beyond that, he could not think. Perhaps once inside Ironcross Castle, his days would be numbered. He
didn't care. Perhaps spending so many years in
prison had preserved the sentimental child in him,
rather than crushing it out of him. Whatever it was,
he would have his answers. Whatever it was, he would
know why both his parents had rejected him.

He was no fool, though. Adam knew that if and
when he received the answers he sought, they would
probably be more condemning than any he might have
imagined himself. But he still needed to see some purpose, some end to the searching of these past six
months.

And then, guiding his steed through a grove of pines
lining the steep hillside, Adam realized what his next
move had to be. That is, after he was done speaking
to Lady MacInnes.

He had no future in the Highlands. He had no kin

and no interests in the Lowlands. But Ambrose Macpherson, the diplomat who had negotiated his freedom, had ships. If Adam wanted to try his hand at that, he'd said . . .

He had no training as a sailor on a ship, but there was no task that he could not learn. Aye, that was it. He'd sail the seas—perhaps even fight his old jailers.

As his mount worked his way along the hill, Adam cast a glance far down the steep hillside to the loch lying wreathed in mist. At the mere thought of leaving the Highlands again, he felt the tightness in his chest.

But it was not the land that pulled at him. It was the love he felt for Susan.

He had warned her to stay away. He knew from the first day that they would never have a chance together. But then, his own untrustworthy heart and her stubborn persistence had won out. There had been no turning back for either of them from that first day in the stand of trees beneath the village.

When he'd gathered his men together and ordered them to go their own way, there had been only one thing he'd asked of them to keep silent on if they were ever caught. And that had been Susan.

They both had been cheated that last night when he'd allowed his brother's wife to return to the castle. He had not known then that his parting with Susan would be their last. Adam slowed his horse and looked up into the iron-gray sky. Suddenly, he wanted to cry out!

The thought flickered through his brain that so much had changed since that night when he'd been rowed out through the river gate of the Tower of London. How much had changed!

Having to leave Susan and never see her again was by far the greatest loss of his life. He would mourn that more than the twelve years he'd lost in prison.

More than the parents that he'd never known. More, perhaps, than life itself.

Suddenly, reining his horse to a halt, Adam saw everything in a different light. Suddenly, his past no longer seemed as important as his future.

Suddenly, he knew—above all else—that Susan must be by his side.

The rain was falling hard by the time Adam descended out of the Ladder Hills, and he could barely see the rounded peaks of Carn Mor to the south with the weather rolling in from the west. Reaching the crest of a heather-covered hill, the warrior stopped abruptly, peering curiously through the downpour into the glen where the Crombie Water flowed.

Yanking the steed's head around, Adam quickly withdrew behind the hill, and tied the animal to a small, twisted pine. Yanking his sword from the scabbard tied to his back, he trotted back to the crest of the hill and, dropping to the ground, crawled up until he could see the activity below.

Twenty to thirty men, some obviously Highlanders by their gear and some not, were gathered by the rushing waters of the Crombie. The river, usually an easy thing to ford, had turned into a wild torrent, and the men were clearly in some disagreement about their next move.

Adam stared. What kind of renegade band was this? he wondered. Aside from his own, he'd heard of no other group of outlaws in this region. He tried to pick out any familiar faces. None of his own men were visible, and the two Highlanders who seemed to be arguing the most heatedly, seemed to be in command. The rest, for the most part, were just looking on. From the gesturing and pointing, Adam decided it was an argument about whether to try to camp for the night, or to continue to the south along the river.

He was thinking that there were several hours of

daylight left when he saw that, beyond the assembly of warriors, beside the raging river, a handful of men lay either dead, injured, or bound on the ground. There had been a fight here, no doubt, and Adam was wondering what could have been the cause.

Then he spotted them and froze.

The two women appeared to be unhurt. Susan and his brother's wife sat in the midst of the throng, two warriors holding the reins of their steeds. His anger flared and he half rose.

What could he do against twenty armed warriors? Panic gnawed at the edge of his brain, and the sickly heat of helplessness washed down his back.

He needed to get help. Adam looked around at the mountains and wracked his brain. There was a chance, of course, that he might find a few of his men to the north, but only a chance. Why the devil had he released them? he cursed. Those who'd followed his directions were by now, no doubt, spread far and wide. It would take too long to go back to Huntly Castle. But he could not let these blackguards simply take the woman he loved.

Athol.

What choice did he have? His brother would hang him, to be sure, but if Athol would at least act and send his forces after these brigands—after Susan and his own wife—it would be worth it.

Seeing that the decision had been made to camp, Adam watched as the band of men rode to a stand of trees by a bluff on some higher ground a bit to the east of the river. They obviously thought they would have some protection there.

Running back to his horse, Adam leaped into the saddle and spurred the animal to the north, toward Balvenie Castle.

The warriors had kept up their brisk pace without regard to the driving rain. They had just passed the village of Bakebare, an hour or so from Balvenie Castle, when the two messengers galloped up with the news.

Athol, trying to preserve his calm as the rain streamed down through his long red hair, listened to the men's account of an urgent letter arriving from Ironcross Castle. Of how the countess and Mistress Susan had ordered that Tosh and a group of the laird's men accompany them immediately to Ironcross. Hesitantly, one of them conveyed the message that the countess insisted on the earl following them there as soon as he could.

"Oh, the countess insisted, did she?"

"Aye, m'lord," the man said, handing him a leather pouch containing a letter.

Well, this was an improvement, Athol thought wryly. To have Catherine actually tell him where she was going and want him to join her there!

Although he didn't have to read the letter to guess at its contents, he pulled the message from the pouch while one of his warriors held up a shield to ward off the rain. As he thought, the message from Ironcross Castle had indicated that Lady MacInnes was dying. The old woman had been in poor health for some time now. It was curious, though, that Catherine and Susan had felt compelled to head south in such terrible weather and not wait for him.

He wondered what else the message from Ironcross had contained.

Even if she were, once again, withholding information from him, at least this time she had taken Tosh and an escort. At least, with Susan and Tosh and the rest accompanying her, Catherine should be able to stay out of trouble during the short trip.

Turning his men to the south in order to follow the well-traveled paths of Glen Fiddich, John Stewart again allowed his thoughts to return to his brother and the possible ways he could at least arrange a meeting between the two of them. Considering the absolute happiness he'd found in marrying Catherine, and knowing now that she was with child, he would not rest until he had found a way to mend the rift between himself and Adam.

It was true. If there were one thing that would make his life complete now, it would be the chance to find a way to recompense Adam of the Glen for even half of all he had been deprived of.

At this stage of his life, resolving their differences would be worth any price.

The small overhang of rock over the patch of wet, sandy ground did little to hold back the stinging lash of the icy rain.

With their backs against the cold, wet rock of the bluff, Catherine quietly shifted her position a bit closer to Susan's side and motioned toward the unconscious Tosh.

"Can you tell how badly he is hurt?"

Dragged through the mud to the hillside, the Highlander had been knocked cold during the attack when one of the brutes had given him a blow to the head from behind. As far as the condition of the rest of the men who had accompanied them, Catherine knew that they all had been wounded, if not killed. There had been considerable discussion among the attackers whether the warriors had any ransom value or not. The two leaders, seemingly unable to agree on almost anything, had argued about that, as well. One of them, a fierce-looking man missing most of the fingers on his left hand, wanted to go south as quickly as possible, but the other's apparent greed seemed to have met with the approval of many in the outlaw band.

"I cannot say for certain. But I think he is breathing." Susan's voice was a hushed whisper. "I believe they knew that he was in charge of our warriors."

"And so, all the more valuable to them!"

Catherine wearily looked at Tosh's unmoving body sprawled on the ground. The attack had been unexpected. It had come all too suddenly. The outlaws had been many and had seemed to descend on them from all directions. It had almost seemed as if they were waiting in ambush. And unfortunately, having Susan and herself in the party had proved to be the great disadvantage to Tosh and his warriors. Rather than taking the fight to the renegades, her escort had been forced to fall back and try to defend the two women. And for that, Catherine blamed herself bitterly.

She had promised her husband that she'd never do anything to bring harm to his people. And here, warriors from Balvenie Castle lay wounded—perhaps even dead or dying—and all of it because these roughs had come in search of her.

"You called me by the name of Laura and told them I was your sister," Susan whispered, keeping an eye on the warrior standing guard nearby. "What reason did you have for doing that?"

Catherine leaned her face closer to Susan's ear. "When the attack came, I heard the fingerless one shout my name and point at me with his sword. They've been sent to bring me back to England."

"But they're Highlanders, mostly!"

"Aye, but the leaders referred to the name Percy."

"That's true, I heard that."

"They wouldn't come all this way just to kill me. They want . . . they want something. I know that these brutes had to have orders not to allow any harm to come to me or to my sisters for the fear of us taking a secret we keep—a secret they want—to our graves."

"So you saved my life."

"I think all I did was to confuse them enough so

they wouldn't bring—" Catherine quieted down as one of their captors carried a horse blanket up the slight rise to the base of the bluff and dumped it on the ground at their feet. She returned the man's leer with a frown, but he moved off to their guard.

Silently, the two women watched the two outlaws mumble complaints to one another about spending "another night in the cursed wet." After a while, though, the man headed back down the hill in the same direction where he'd come from. It was nearly dark now, and men were scrounging around for dry tinder to start the night's fires. She eyed a ragged, filthy young fellow who was wandering their way.

"So you think their plan is to drag us all the way to England?" Susan asked hurriedly.

"Aye. So, 'tis up to us—" Catherine stopped abruptly as the young man bent down a few paces from her feet and yanked a yellowed shrub out of the ground. As he turned away, a ribbon of gray, an adder half again as long as her arm, slithered with incredible speed out of the disturbed ground and up the sandy heath bed toward the bluff. She stared at the dark V-shaped mark behind the head and the dark zigzagging line down the back.

Vaguely aware of Susan's sharp gasp of fear, Catherine casually reached for the horse blanket and with a sure movement, trapped the head of the snake beneath the cloth with her hand. In an instant, she had quickly covered the rest of the wriggling creature with the edge of her cloak.

When she looked up, their guard was scratching himself and staring longingly at the fires that were just beginning to crackle by the stand of trees. Susan's face was the picture of shock and revulsion, and Catherine almost laughed in spite of their situation.

"Aye," she whispered with a wink. "A viper . . .

come to call. And you know, I never expected help
to arrive so soon!''

The rain had turned almost entirely to sleet, and
the wind was continuing to lash at the warrior's faces.
Athol was determined, though, to reach Ironcross Castle this night, so he relentlessly pushed his weary horse
and his warriors ahead.

At first, when they'd turned their steps southward,
he had not thought much about the urgency of this
trip. He knew that Catherine, for the first time, had
proceeded appropriately. With Tosh to accompany her
on the journey—and Adam's band dispersed—there
was little to fear. Everything would be well, and she
would be waiting for him when he arrived at his
friends' holding.

But the farther south they traveled, for some reason, the less comfortable he felt.

He didn't know why. But a tiny prickpoint of worry
that had begun in his belly, had lengthened into a
sharp, thin line extending up his spine and burning
the skin of his neck. Now, the taste of iron was there
in his mouth. It was the taste of fear.

He spurred his horse on as quickly as the darkening
trail would permit.

And then, she was there in his head. Her thoughts,
her voice—the same way that, so many times in the
past, she had been present in his mind. And something
was wrong.

Wiping the rain off his face and pushing ahead even
faster, he knew she was in danger. She needed him.
Visions of dragons and giants with stumps for arms
flooded his brain, clouding his thinking.

John!

He could hear her. This time, she was calling to him.

Coming over the crest of a hill, he was the first one
to spot the lone horseman coming across the meadow.

Like himself, the other man appeared to have a devil in pursuit of him. Moving down the hill, Athol slowed his pace. His small company of warriors followed his lead and slowed, as well.

Almost immediately, the traveler saw them, for he reined in his horse for a moment, and then came on, approaching at a near gallop. The horseman did not appear to have a sword or lance in his hand, but he was riding toward them at a gait that made the men behind Athol begin to murmur among themselves.

Through the rain and wind and descending darkness, there was no way Athol could identify him. He could have been one of Gavin Kerr's men, or even one of his own men, though the horse was not—

Suddenly, the truth descended on him like a sharp cuff to the ear. Feeling the sudden tightening of his chest, the blood flooding into his face, Athol jerked his horse to a full stop. His men gathered behind him and watched the oncoming rider with narrowed eyes.

John Stewart, as well, assessed the man. His large build. The hilt of the weapon that he could now see strapped to the man's back. The determination and skill with which he pushed his horse ahead. Athol motioned for his men to stay and spurred his own steed forward.

The two reached each other by the rushing creek at the bottom of the meadow. Bringing their snorting horses to a stop, each man studied the other. Two pairs of piercing gray eyes exchanged looks of amazement as they took in their likeness.

With the Highland wind whipping about them, Adam broke the silence.

"I was coming for you."

"I've been looking for you, as well."

Adam gave a curt, comprehending nod. "I ask you to put your anger aside for the moment. There is a matter of much more grave importance that we need to see to."

"My anger? Have no fear on that score. But whatever you are about to ask, I only ask that you give your word not to disappear afterward. I need to—"

"My word?" The corner of Adam's mouth curved in a look of long-accustomed scorn. "You are asking for the word of a thief—of one who has been robbing you and your people of their peace for half a year?"

"I am asking the word of my brother."

The two horses tossed their heads and circled one another. Adam's voice dropped to a husky growl. "I was told that you didn't know you even had a brother."

"What you were told was true. But I know now." Athol tried to calm his own agitated horse. "I believe we have both lost a great deal—you far more than I— by our ignorance of the truth."

Their faces glistened in the pouring rain.

"I cannot change the past," Athol continued. "I cannot undo what was done to you. But I can ask for a chance at a better future. A chance to know the man who is my brother."

Adam stared at him, and Athol could see the uncertainty in the man's eyes.

"I . . . I didn't expect this," Adam said finally. "I was coming after you, certain that you'd slay me before giving me even a chance to speak of the danger that lies ahead."

"I've just been to see the earl of Huntly. He told me that you had left there before I arri—" Athol's frown suddenly deepened as Adam's words sank in. "What danger?"

Chapter 23

As the rain and wind continued to whip about them, the band of renegades huddled beneath an assortment of cloaks, tartans, and horse blankets around the smoky, sizzling fire. No attempt had been made to cook anything, and Catherine had a sense that they would be moving on as soon as the weather allowed. The bickering had subsided, and a surly silence had settled over the troop.

This was not what Catherine had in mind.

The viper beneath the blanket had also settled down, only occasionally thrashing its long body as she held it tightly just behind the head. Catherine knew the adder was poisonous, but she was not afraid of it. Thanks to Brother Egbert and his interest in the natural world, she and her sisters had handled snakes and other small creatures their entire lives.

Catherine and Susan sat close together, pretending to be sleeping. Both of them were keeping their eyes trained on the darkness beyond the renegades' camp.

She couldn't explain it, but there was no doubt in her mind that he was coming. In fact, she knew that he was very close at this very moment. She knew that, just like her knight of a thousand dreams, John Stewart would be stepping through the smoky light of this fire, sword in hand, eyes flashing.

And until he appeared, she would keep up her silent vigil and her quiet struggle with her venomous friend.

Now, peering into the darkness again, she considered her role in battling these blackguards.

From what she'd been able to glean from the arguments of the two leaders, they were clearly in the pay of Sir Arthur Courtenay, the king's Deputy Lieutenant in Yorkshire. Hearing his name on their lips had by no means surprised her. Sir Arthur was a pox-faced weasel who had been a vicious enemy to her family since her father's original capture and imprisonment. He'd seemed to enjoy persecuting her family, but she'd had no idea he was one of those searching for the Treasure of Tiberius.

Foolishly, Catherine had thought that when they'd left England, Courtenay and his vile threats would have been left behind, as well. Certainly, he could have had no power to touch them in Scotland. She— and her mother, too—had obviously underestimated the reach of the brute's tentacles. Gold is a powerful tool, and greed a great motivator of men.

Catherine felt the other woman stiffen and then nudge her with her elbow. Fully alert now, she followed with her eyes the line of Susan's gaze. First she saw nothing in the darkness. Then she saw the flash of the sputtering firelight on metal. There were men between them and the river.

John.

Looking about her, though, she could see that her husband's warriors would be forced to fight their way up a rain-soaked hillside. By taking shelter against the jagged rocks of the bluff, her captors had strategically eliminated any chance of anyone approaching them from behind. It would certainly only be a moment before one of the brigands spotted the advancing rescuers. To her left, by the line of trees, the outlaws' horses were becoming restless, and she saw some of the huddled blankets stir.

Catherine's mind raced. She had to think more like

her youngest sister, Adrianne. In all their years of growing up, Adrianne had been the most courageous of the three. The one who from a young age had insisted on arming herself and learning the strategies and techniques of battle by hiding in the hayloft and watching their father in the courtyard, training his men for the possibility of war. Laura and Catherine had always teased her that, as a woman, she would never need protection—but would instead provide it for some lucky man.

Always be prepared. Examine your opponent carefully for possible strengths and weaknesses. Try to think like him. See his advantage. Take steps to diminish his power if you can—before the first blow is delivered.

Catherine turned her head and whispered directions to Susan.

Quickly, she scanned the group of outlaws once more. The two leaders had positioned themselves closest to the two women. There was no doubt in Catherine's mind that, in the event of an open attack, these brutes would not hesitate to use her and Susan as human shields or as a means of forcing her husband to lay down his weapon. Well, that would not happen if she had anything to say about it.

Taking a deep breath, she nodded to Susan.

" 'Tis time!" she whispered.

Elgin Cathedral's ancient crypt must have been a lively place that night, for the two women's piercing screams were surely loud enough to wake the dead, and Athol was certain the two could be heard at least that far.

His men were ready, waiting only for his signal to rush the renegades. The brigands outnumbered his men, and he knew they would never reach them before the alarm was raised, but John Stewart would die before he let these pestilent dogs take his wife another step.

He felt Adam's firm hand on his shoulder.

" 'Tis a distraction," the earl said with certainty, watching the renegades leap up from their places around the fire and race toward the bluff.

By St. Andrew, at least he hoped it was. Even from this distance, Athol could see the snake dangling by its tail from Catherine's hand, writhing and hissing menacingly at her.

"I know," Adam replied. "I saw her pull the snake from beneath the blanket."

In a moment, the entire band had formed a half-circle around the screaming women. Athol paused not an instant longer.

"Now!"

Running close to the ground, Athol, Adam, and the rest quickly closed the distance between themselves and the noisy group of outlaws.

Catherine and Susan's diversion was indeed more valuable than he could ever have imagined. With the two women's incessant caterwauling and with the viper's unsuccessful attempts at striking anyone toward whom Catherine swung the creature, Athol and his men were on the brigands before they even knew they were under attack.

With the fury of two avenging angels, the brothers fell on the necks of their adversaries, swords arcing through the night rain and carving a bloody path toward the two women.

Though they were outnumbered at least two to one, the element of surprise quickly evened the odds. Fighting side by side, the two brothers hacked their way toward their women, who had at the onset of their attack moved swiftly toward a wounded Tosh and were now standing over him. Catherine still waved the snake around them, and Athol and Adam showed no mercy on the band of thugs.

The wind howled as the battle continued. The blood spilled on both sides, mixing with the falling rain and churning the earth into a blackened mud. Then, one of the leaders broke away from the bloody fray and rushed toward the women, his fingerless hand outstretched. As Catherine held the creature up, the snake struck out at his hand, stopping him in his tracks. He stood there for a moment, but then the stunned look suddenly gave way to one of intense pain. Clutching his hand, the man turned and ran screaming into the night.

Almost as if by magic, that signaled an end to the outlaws' resistance, and in a few moments, it was over.

With the surviving renegades subdued, John moved to see to Tosh. In a moment, he realized that Catherine was no longer near him. Looking about in a flash of panic, he quickly calmed down as he saw her standing a bit farther along the bluff, gently tossing the viper to the ground by a pile of rocks. As he watched her, the rain stopped.

She turned and he let his loving gaze wash over her. He knew that he would never satisfy the unquenchable thirst he had for the sight of her. He knew that in a millennium, he could never tell her how much he loved her.

But he would try.

He couldn't help but laugh at the way she ran back to him. Her hug was fierce—her voice joyful—her tears the sweetest nectar he'd ever tasted. And John Stewart, for the first time in his life, tore down the barriers around his heart and whispered softly in her ear.

"I love you, Catherine Percy Stewart. And I swear for as long as I live, I will strive to save you from yourself."

She drew back and gave him her prettiest scowl. "And what do you mean by that? Nothing that happened here was—"

"I said, I love you, Cat!"

He watched the way her magical eyes rounded—her full lips parting to say something but then saying nothing. The way her perfect face shone with the warmest glow he could ever imagine existing this side of heaven.

He leaned down to kiss her lips, but she pulled back slightly. "What did you say?"

"I love you, Cat. I have for a long time. 'Tis just that I've been so ignorant . . . about so many things. Why, I—"

She kissed him with all the passion in her soul, and John Stewart was the one left breathless a moment later, standing and staring vacantly at his wife.

"You were saying?" she cooed mischievously.

"I was saying?" he replied vaguely.

"So, now 'tis you who are forgetting your words."

Rather than denying it, he lifted her off the ground and hugged her slender body tightly against his.

"And I suppose this kind of persuasion is something else that you plan to steal from me."

He quieted her words with another kiss. "Aye, I can steal . . . nay, I will learn whatever I can from my perfect wife."

She nestled against him contentedly, but only for a moment, before her gaze darted to Tosh, who was sitting up, woozy but clearly conscious, against the wall of the bluff.

"Oh!" she blurted out, trying to break away. "Tosh! Did you see him?"

"Aye, I checked on him while you were sending your slithery friend on his way." He held onto her hand and they made their way past the bound prisoners huddled together on the ground. "He has a good lump on the side of his head, but as far as his wound, the bleeding has stopped. He's had worse. You do not get a face like his tending sheep. He'll be back to his old self in a few days, though I do not know that he'll survive the knowledge that he spent the entire battle under the protection of the lasses *he* was supposed to be protecting!"

"I saw Adam of the Glen."

"Aye, 'twas my brother, indeed, fighting beside me." Athol's smile disappeared as he turned a sharp glance on Catherine. "But how is it, wife, that you recognized him?"

She patted his arm soothingly. " 'Tis a long story, my love. And one that I'll be happy to give you in elaborate detail, once we are in dry clothes and sheltered somewhere."

Just then, Athol saw Adam come up from the horses with a very bright-faced Susan on his arm. Looking at the protective way that Adam had wrapped his arm around Susan, Athol frowned and then shrugged. "I can see that there is something else, as well, about which you'll need to be enlightening me."

"In good time, husband. I promise you, there will not be a secret left between us when I'm done telling you all I know, including the reason why these gentlemen wanted to kidnap me and take me back to England." Catherine again patted him gently on his arm and whispered. "But if you'd like to keep my company, I'm going to go and fuss over some of your wounded men."

Together, they moved to a group of warriors by the fire. Thankfully, none of his men had been seriously injured, and in a moment, she was busy wrapping slashed arms and shoulders as Athol looked on.

" 'Twas the most amazing thing, John," she said.

"You were not here, but I swear I could sense you coming through the night . . ."

She continued to talk, but John Stewart, the fourth earl of Athol, found himself drifting off into a land of dreams. To a place where the sky was blue, and the bounty of the Scottish earth reflected the happiness in his life. He saw himself walking through a glen with Catherine on his arm. She shone with the brightness of the sun. She was holding his hand against her swelling belly, acquainting him with their bairn.

He then saw himself holding her high in the air, her beautiful face and silky hair cascading around them, the sun gleaming through the ebony locks. And then, tumbling into the soft grasses and heather, they held one another—their tender lovemaking a sign of the longing, the affection, the love that would last as long as the Highlands itself.

Her voice came softly through the vision.

"You're daydreaming!"

He smiled into Catherine's midnight-blue eyes.

"Aye."

The oak door of the cell swung open heavily, and the man hurriedly stepped into the dark chamber.

"Get up, monk! Get up!" The Deputy Lieutenant moved toward the huddled body of his prisoner. The man was clearly broken. "I've decided to have mercy on you and give you another chance to serve the king."

A low, hoarse chuckle escaped the monk's throat, quickly becoming a rumbling cough.

Sir Arthur gave a hard kick to the man's lanky body, doubling the monk over in pain and eliciting more hacking coughs. Removing the man's shackles, he cuffed the cleric behind the ear and backed away, tossing them to the side.

"Get up!"

"You had the abbot killed." The monk pushed himself up and looked toward the Deputy Lieutenant. "You were a fool not to believe him when he said he knew nothing about the Treasure of Tiberius."

"I still say he lied. You are all in this together—all you monks! You're all liars. You're all filthy buggers and liars."

"And you are as good as dead." The monk announced, slowly pulling himself onto his knees, moving even more slowly to his feet. "I heard the jailers talking. I've even spoken with them. They said that word went immediately to the king. They said that men from the king have arrived this very day."

"I know nothing of this nonsense." At the sound of some commotion down the hall, the Deputy Lieutenant glanced nervously in the direction of the open door. "Those men were impostors! Court idlers. I take my orders only from King Henry himself. We're going. Move."

"But you know, now, that the abbot was an uncle to Anne Boleyn—the king's new wife. Did he neglect to tell you that? Did these 'idlers' tell you, before you killed them, that the king has ordered your head on a pike for killing a member of his wife's own family?"

"The fool could have talked!" Courtenay blurted out. "He simply refused to say anything of the treasure."

"What treasure is that? the king might ask," the monk taunted. His eyes were burning black slits. "I can hear him now. 'Whom have you been serving, Sir Arthur, since we have not heard so much as a whisper about any treasure? Tell us, lackey, what you've been up to and what is this fortune you kill our uncle for.' "

The sound of shouts could be heard in the manor yard.

"Move your lying carcass, monk! We are leaving *now*!"

The monk raised himself to his full height and turned fully toward the king's deputy. In the darkness of the cell, all Sir Arthur could see for a moment was a light burning in the depths of the man's eyes, like a light shining at the bottom of a grave. Courtenay's mouth fell open. •

"You are finished, Sir Arthur. This is the end. The last map, the one you tried to keep from me, pointed you to your final resting place. You were just too stupid to understand the power—the force of Tiberius."

The king's deputy shoved hard at the man to move him along. But surprisingly, despite the days of torture he had undergone, the monk didn't move an inch.

"Get moving!" he snarled. "My men will be bringing Catherine Percy back to England any day now, and between you and me and what we force her to tell us, we will need no king—no country. We'll be rich enough to buy our own kingdom. We—"

As the dagger pierced the wall of his chest, the Deputy Lieutenant dropped his head and stared with a look of sick surprise at the hilt of the dagger protruding from his doublet. As he looked, a dark-colored stain, almost black on the deep green velvet, began to spread out in a widening circle down over his belly. Sir Arthur choked, sputtered, and looked up into the face of death.

"How . . . why?"

"I told you this was the end!" the monk whispered. "They have always been with me. 'Twas easier still to gain my freedom once your treachery to the king became known. Your own men gave me the dagger, Sir Arthur. They'll plead that they killed you in an attempt to save the king's messengers."

"The treasure . . . treasu . . ." Arthur clung to the man's arm as he sagged to the floor.

"There was never a treasure for you, Courtenay. I used you as I will use anyone to gain back what was meant to be mine. I have touched Tiberius. I have felt its power. I alone have been blessed with its glory. And you were a fool to think it could ever have been yours." The monk pushed the king's deputy to the floor and drew out the bloody dagger. He looked directly into the man's grimacing face. "You have little time left. Prepare your answers, sinner. The lies that you use on your king in this world will not fool the King of the next."

Stepping around the twitching body of the dying man, the monk moved to the open door where he saw a tall soldier approaching the cell.

" 'Tis done." Handing him the dagger, the cleric grasped the soldier's arm and spoke in a low voice to him as they moved off down the corridor.

With Sir Arthur Courtenay, the king's Deputy Lieutenant dead, and with the treasure still out of their reach, the monk knew he would need another like him to aid in the search. Perhaps, though, not someone quite so greedy.

He sensed already that his efforts in the Highlands would prove fruitless. Though his fellow monks had followed Catherine Percy into hiding, he knew that their emotional ties to her were great. No doubt, their loyalty toward the young woman and their devotion to the pursuit of the Treasure of Tiberius were in conflict. Otherwise, they would have returned by now.

But he had no doubt that Courtenay was mad, thinking that his own men could steal Catherine Percy from a castle and a powerful husband in the Highlands. Nay, capturing or even questioning Catherine Percy was probably no longer a viable option.

But there were still Laura and Adrianne, still unmarried and still quite vulnerable. Aye! There were still many opportunities left.

He would simply need to be more vigilant!

Chapter 24

Joanna McInnes Kerr knew that her grandmother's death was near. The old woman had awakened one night and told her that the angel of death was standing by the window. After suffering through the deaths of a husband and her three sons, Lady Agnes MacInnes was ready, at last, to join them in the next world.

Her grandmother had also told Joanna that she had a single dying wish. Almost a year ago, she'd asked a favor of their friend, the diplomat Ambrose Macpherson. She'd asked the Highlander to go to the king, and then to England. She'd asked him to use whatever method he must to negotiate the freedom of a man in prison there. A man named Adam Stewart.

Her dying wish was to see Adam Stewart once before she died.

When Joanna had sent a letter to her friend John Stewart, the earl of Athol, asking for his assistance in locating the man, she had not even wanted to guess what lay behind her grandmother's wish. The dying woman had asked, and that was enough for Joanna.

Now, leading the giant, grim-visaged Highlander in the bloodstained clothes through the winding halls of Ironcross Castle, Joanna felt a bit hesitant about her decision.

He'd arrived here with Athol and the earl's new wife, Catherine, and with Susan MacIntyre. He'd been introduced as Athol's half-brother. That alone had been enough to astound the master and mistress of Ironcross Castle, since—for as long as Joanna had known the family—she'd never heard even a whisper of another brother.

But there had been no opportunity for pursuing the matter. Athol, also bloody from their skirmish with outlaws on their way to Ironcross, had begun to show her husband Gavin a wound on his forearm that was sure to form a handsome scar. But as her husband had gravely started with his questions about the brigands, and about the well-being of the two women, Joanna had simply led Adam Stewart from the Great Hall. Her grandmother would not wait much longer.

Although Joanna would have liked to pretend that her grandmother's illness was the same as those imagined ailments of the past few years, she knew that the old woman's time in this world was running short. Stepping into the newer south wing of the castle, into the area where, through her husband's efforts, a massive renovation had taken place nearly eight years earlier, Joanna shot a glance to the side, covertly studying Adam Stewart.

He was tall and handsome, with many features that called for comparison to the earl of Athol's looks. But beyond his appearance, Joanna could sense a distinct agitation, a tension that seemed to have grown since they left the Great Hall.

Taking him up the spiral of steps to the next level, where Lady MacInnes's chambers lay, Joanna couldn't stop herself from asking the question that had been plaguing her mind for this past year. "I hope you do not mind my asking, but how long has it been since you last met my grandmother?"

The tall man's piercing gray eyes narrowed, focusing on her. His voice was cold, emotionless. "We've never met. I mean, not . . . not that I remember."

Joanna nodded as she continued the ascent. "I'm

glad! Then you won't be too disappointed, for lately her health has taken a turn for the worse. But I . . . I try to make visitors aware, beforehand."

They reached the second level and moved quietly to a closed oak door. A flickering wick lamp hung on the stone wall. Turning and facing the Highlander, Joanna fought back the sudden wave of protectiveness that made her want to bar the door against this man. The coldness in his voice just now—the look of careless disdain on his face—all of this made her extremely suspicious, extremely cautious. More than anything else now, she wanted to ask him who he was and why was it so crucial for her grandmother to see him.

He spoke first. "Who is she and why is it so urgent for her to see me?"

Joanna blinked once at Adam's question. "I was about to ask the same of you!"

"What there is to know about me . . . that I am willing to share with you . . . is what you heard from my brother. Why she has asked for me, I can only guess, m'lady."

"I take no issue with your wish for privacy." She felt the edginess creep into her own voice. "But there is justification for my question. Certainly you can understand my concern over the possibility of any unpleasantness being directed at her right now."

"She called for me, Lady Joanna. But why should you think I would be anything other than civil to her?"

Joanna shrugged her shoulders. "I do not know! But I see no reason why I should risk it, either. If keeping you away from her means not granting her dying wish, I am prepared to do so, if I think she'll suffer more in meeting you."

She watched his jaw tense. His gaze drifted toward the door and then back to her face. Something around his eyes softened. "I can see she is well cared for."

"Aside from my husband and my children, I am the only family she has left."

"What happened to the rest?"

"They are all dead!" She didn't even pause in her answer. He wanted the truth; she gave it. And she was willing to keep giving it as long as he continued to become more human through their conversation.

"Your parents—both dead?"

She nodded. "Both parents, my two uncles, my grandfather. Aside from me, my grandmother has seen them all die. Hers has been a life filled with horrors . . . some real and some imagined."

She saw the passing wave of sorrow that flickered across his features. His gaze had once again turned to the door. Joanna softened her own voice as she reached over and placed a gentle hand on his arm.

"It has only been since my marriage to Gavin Kerr that she has had a chance to live again. She moved to the Highlands to stay with us, to have her grandchildren around her, and to try to forget the memories of all those deaths."

"May I ask you something about her past?"

He sounded almost gentle, and she nodded. "I'll tell you what I can, but I want you to know I'm still confused about her interest in you and your interest in her!"

"That's why I'm here." He let out a long, weary breath. For the first time, he was letting down his guard. "I am searching for answers. For the answers to questions I have been carrying about all my life."

She now caught a glimpse of an unexpected vulnerability, a mix of emotions hidden just beneath the surface. And there was pain, as well, reflected in the depths of his eyes.

Leading him to a window seat across the wide corridor, Joanna told him all she knew. She told him about her grandmother's marriage to Duncan, a man who abused his wife and other women horribly. She told him about the curse of Ironcross Castle, and how it was thought to have been the cause of her grandfather's death, her two uncles' deaths . . . and even the deaths of her own father and mother.

Seeing the questions in his eyes, Joanna told him about her own parents' death in the fire in this wing, and how she and Gavin finally found the secret that unlocked the "curse."

"My grandmother believed in the power of that curse. She had seen it destroy her family. 'Twas only after Gavin and I married that she was finally able to believe that those days were finished."

"So you think she has made peace with the past?"

Joanna thought about his question for a moment and then shook her head. "I thought she had. But I was wrong. From hearing her it appears that only meeting you will let her . . . let her die in peace."

His eyes darkened as he looked at the closed door. "Is she truly ill?"

Joanna nodded. "I've been trying to fool myself by not facing the truth. But I believe now she really is dying."

Joanna paused as she stared at his profile. Adam Stewart's features were strong and weathered. His long hair, auburn and wild, was loosely tied in back. His eyes were gray and piercing. He was a Stewart—there could be no doubt of that. But there was something else in his look. Something in the shape of the mouth, in the line of his jaw that reminded her of someone else.

And then she knew. There was something of her own father there in this man's face.

"Will you allow me to see her?"

There was no hesitation this time, and she nodded her consent. She had done the right thing in telling him the truth. And in his manner, now surprisingly gentle, she could see that there was a compassionate heart beneath the rough and defensive exterior.

Seeing Adam Stewart was a dying woman's wish. And whatever sin Lady MacInnes thought herself guilty of, Joanna now knew that this was a man with the power to forgive.

Adam stood with his back to the door and studied the old woman, propped up on pillows but asleep in the huge oak bed.

Joanna Kerr had not only given her consent to his meeting with her grandmother, but she also had motioned for Lady MacInnes's attending women to leave the chamber and wait outside, should they be needed.

Now alone with her, Adam hesitated before taking a step toward the bed. The elaborate, French damask bed curtains had been drawn back, and he could see the bony white fingers scratching fitfully at the fine lace bedclothes. The small, white-haired woman was dreaming, but it was clear her dreams were restless and troubled. Even across the room, he could hear each breath she labored to take.

By 'is Blood, he prayed fervently, let me die with a sword in my hand and an enemy before me!

Lady MacInnes's eyes opened with a start and tried to focus on her surroundings. In a moment, she looked around and, seeing none of her usual attendants, noticed him by the door.

"Gavin! Is that you?"

Adam stepped closer. She appeared so frail—her voice nothing more than a painful whisper. "Nay, m'lady. 'Tis not Gavin."

"John! John Stewart!" She lifted a fragile hand and waved it weakly in his direction. "Joanna . . . she told me you'd come. She said you've taken a bride. What good news!"

Adam moved closer and almost reached for the outstretched hand, but then decided against it, instead clasping his hands behind his back.

"Nay, m'lady. 'Tis not John, either." He hesitated, cursing himself for his cowardice. " 'Tis I . . . Adam . . . his brother!"

The old woman stared at him, her breathing no longer audible. Adam held his own breath and watched with growing concern. Finally, she took another breath. A look of pain etched itself in Lady MacInnes's features, and as he gazed at her, he could feel that pain carving itself upon his own heart. A tear formed in the corner of each of her tired eyes and ran silently down her cheeks. Adam fought back his own.

"You!" Her voice was no more than a ragged breath of air. "Adam!"

He stood still as her eyes studied his face.

"My . . . Adam!"

He had to look away and close his eyes to stop the tears from spilling down his face. He had to clench his jaw to tame the emotions which were wreaking havoc on his heart. How long he had waited to hear those words! How many long years!

"Adam!"

Her quiet whisper drew his gaze back to her. He stared through a curtain of tears at the woman who had brought him into this world. He watched the feeble, trembling hands attempting to wipe away the tears, the quivering of a chin lined with age. This time he didn't hesitate to reach out and take her frail hand in his own huge hands.

"I am here!"

"My . . . own . . . son. My Adam!" She pulled his hands to her face, kissing them, pressing them to her wrinkled cheeks. They must have felt warm against the cold of her own skin. "I never . . . I never thought God would forgive me for . . . what I've done. I never thought . . . you would come."

He sat down on the edge of the bed. The knot in his throat was the size of his fist, and he could not utter a word. He just listened to the prayers of thanks pour out of her, prayers that hung in the air for a moment—almost palpable in their presence—before floating heavenward.

Whatever bitterness he might have harbored in the past about his mother—whatever ill thoughts he might have borne about her motives—all these things meant nothing now.

Lady Agnes MacInnes, his own mother, was a woman broken by time and life's hardships. She was a woman at the end of a life that had brought her little joy and much pain. She was a woman, as Joanna had explained, who had suffered enough.

"I have so much to tell you," she whispered.

Adam had no intention of asking her any questions. As far as he was concerned, just to have her want to see him—just to have a chance to meet her, to see her, to touch her hands, her face—that was far more than he'd ever hoped for. Infinitely more.

But the older woman was determined to have her own way—to make her peace in the only way that she knew. By telling the truth. As she spoke, she paused often for breath, to wipe away her tears, to kiss his hands.

" 'Twas I who went after John Stewart, the third earl of Athol. I was a widow then. My husband Duncan was a filthy brute who had more regard for his horse than for his wife. No one missed him when he died—certainly not I. But our three sons were already old enough to see to their own lives, and I had nothing. So I let the devil sway me. I tried to rob a decent man of his honor.

"Your father was a handsome man. A good man. He was a devoted husband to Anne. He was a loving father to his son John. But never having had a husband who valued me or ever praised me for anything, I coveted that man. Aye, Adam, I cheated my own friend Anne and set my traps to charm another woman's husband.

"He resisted me at first. He tried to believe that he was mistaken about my encouragement. But I pursued him. I became more open in my advances. Never would I miss an opportunity to remind him, when our families would gather, of his foolishness in passing up the satisfaction I had to offer him. I promised him that Anne would never know. I reminded him with a whisper, a touch, a look, that I was there for him.

"He continued to resist, but I knew that I had him. As old as we were, I knew he found me desirable. I had never before used wiles in bringing a man to my bed. But with John Stewart, desire became a madness. I had a thirst to feel a real man lying with me.

"My chance came when one summer Anne took young John and sailed for France. The lad was to be schooled there. Knowing that John was left alone—understanding that this was probably the best opportunity I would ever have—I went after him.

"Even a saint could not have resisted such temptation! He surrendered to me, and I spent those first days and nights in total bliss, for he *was* the man I knew he would be. But as the days passed, a thought kept tormenting me. 'Twas the thought of how empty my life had been before him. Of how empty it would be when he was gone.

"I was tempted to forget that I had promised not to ruin his life with Anne. I considered it very carefully. But then, we had made a bargain—a pact that I would let him go when the time came. That when our allotted time together was finished, I would leave him alone forever and ever.

"We went our separate ways, and I held to my part of the bargain. I stayed away. But all along, I dreamed of him missing me—of wanting to taste once again what we'd shared. I dreamed of him coming after me.

"But he never did. He was once again true to the woman with whom he'd shared most of his life. His only true love was Anne.

"Oh, I had been persistent. I had played the wench and stolen my best friend's husband—for a time. But the reality of all I'd done—of the sin that I had committed—didn't really come home to me until my oldest son Alexander drowned in the loch you can see out that window. My Alexander died only a few weeks after my affair with Athol had ended.

"I was distraught. I recalled the curse that a simple woman named Mater had cast on me and my family years earlier. I held her responsible for deaths of both Duncan and Alexander. Then, to further confirm my fears, Thomas, my second son, nearly died. People tried to tell me 'twas an accident. I knew the truth. I knew Mater was responsible.

"And then, my life fell apart. I discovered that I was with child. That in my advanced age, I had conceived a bairn. That I was carrying the fruit of John's and my passion. I was carrying you.

"I was so distracted by grief and shock that the shame of being a widow with child did not even occur to me. Now, I thought, Mater would have another victim for her curse. So I kept my secret to myself. I went to the Western Isles, to a priory I know there. I remained there the entire winter. I gave birth to you there.

"I held my little babe in my arms. I named you Adam, and all I could think of were the horrible things that would be awaiting you in your life. Thomas and John, my other surviving sons, did not even know that you existed. But I was blinded with fear of this monster I had conjured up in Mater.

" 'Twas not shame of revealing the truth to my sons

or the world that made me send for Athol, your father. I simply knew of no one else who could protect you from Mater.

"He came as I knew he would. And he acted as honorably, for Athol was a man of principle. He took you away as I asked him to. To a place where no one would know or ever guess your kinship with me. To a place where you would be safe.

"Years passed, Adam. 'Twas not long before Thomas died, black in the face from poison. His death reaffirmed my decision to send you away. I could not stay in the Highlands any longer; I fled to Stirling. I assumed that your father had placed you with someone in the Highlands, and I feared being too close. I feared discovering where you were and . . . wanting you back!

"When Athol died, and your brother became earl, I knew you were nearly sixteen years old. I forced myself to stop fretting over your future. Knowing your father, I was certain that you had been educated well. I prayed that you were making your way in the world.

"Then a few short years later, John—my youngest by Duncan—and his wife died in a horrible fire in this same wing. For a few months, I even thought Joanna dead, as well. The curse was unending, it seemed. But secretly, I thought that perhaps I had been able to save one of my children's lives.

"About six months after that fire, Gavin Kerr was given Ironcross Castle. Somehow, he found Joanna hiding, waiting for the chance to avenge her parents' deaths. Between them, they were able to unearth the secrets of Ironcross Castle, and put an end to the curse.

"I have been so wrong about so many things in my life, Adam. But still thinking that you were safe and now assuredly well on in your own life, I chose not to doubt my original decision. For the days and the years that followed, I enjoyed the love of a grand-daughter who wanted to include me in her life. Gavin's and Joanna's love for one another, their abundant affection for all, and their lovely children showed me—for the first time in my life—a glimpse of what happiness could be."

Lady MacInnes closed her eyes and continued.

"But 'twas all a sham. Two years ago I learned of the Treaty of Bruges from Ambrose Macpherson, who was visiting Ironcross with his wife Elizabeth. Everything changed then.

"Again, I became like a madwoman," she whispered, gazing at his grim face. "I used my connections at court to find out who had been sent to London so many years earlier. And what poor souls were still there. My own child had been languishing in a miserable English prison for so long, while I was growing old with laughing bairns around my knees.

"I sent for Ambrose Macpherson. Of all the diplomats in Scotland, I knew he was the only one who had a chance to negotiate anything with the English king.

"For once, God smiled on me, for Ambrose succeeded. He sent me word that you were free."

Adam kissed his mother's hand. "Did he know of our kinship?"

"In my haste, in my madness and worry, I do not know what I told him of that. But he knew . . . I am certain of it. Ambrose Macpherson, though, is not one to divulge a confidence. I knew he would not tell even you." Lady MacInnes closed her eyes for a moment and let out a weary breath. "That was why it was so urgent for me to see you—to tell you the odious truth of your mother."

"I see nothing, in all you have done, that deserves anything less than my love and gratitude." Adam wrapped both of his hands around hers and held them, warming them. "I have already stopped mourning the past. 'Tis time to think of the future . . . Mother."

A weak smile broke over her lined face. "You are your father's son. He never blamed me for what I did." She slowly brought his hands to her lips and placed a gentle kiss on his fingers. "You are as honorable as he, Adam . . . and as true!"

Chapter 25

Lady Agnes McInnes died a fortnight after Adam's first visit with her.

Surrounded by her loved ones, she took her son's and her granddaughter's hands in each of her own, and breathed her last.

Catherine was pleased that the truth of Adam's parentage had immediately been made known by Lady Agnes to the rest of the household.

From the first, Catherine and Athol had considered sparing John's own mother of any discussion of the old earl's infidelity. But amazingly enough, after Catherine and John returned to Balvenie Castle with Adam and Susan, Lady Anne immediately requested an audience with Adam. From the relationship that soon developed, the meeting between the two was clearly one of both healing and forgiveness.

Putting the lit taper to the tinder in the hearth of her small chamber, Catherine sat back on her heels and watched the flames begin to lick at the logs, dispelling the early-morning chill. Her husband had still been sleeping when Catherine, unable to break her predawn ritual, had left his bed and come back to this chamber to gather her thoughts and begin writing to her sisters.

Adam had refused offers of land from both John Stewart and Gavin Kerr. Instead, he'd decided to take over Huntly's demesne as the older nobleman had insisted. He and Susan were to be married in the spring—as soon as arrangements were finalized with her family. More than likely, the celebration would take place shortly before Catherine gave birth to the bairn that she was carrying right now. Imagining herself, full-bellied and wobbly, standing at the door of the church with the happy couple, only made her smile. Knowing her own doting husband, she could picture Athol carrying her up the steps in his arms.

Rising from the hearth and sitting on the chair by the small work table which she'd had brought in, Catherine considered the letters she intended to write. For the safety's sake, the Percy sisters had all agreed before their departure from England that they should not attempt to communicate with one another unless there was something of grave importance to share. Although each knew the whereabouts of the other two, none wanted to put her sisters at risk.

But there *was* a matter of importance that her sisters needed to know.

When Catherine had returned to Balvenie Castle with her husband, the small wooden chest in her chamber had been broken open, and two of the monks, Brother Paul and Brother Egbert, had long since disappeared. After revealing the truth of it all to her husband and explaining how she had left the true map with the dowager—placing an imitation of her own devising in the chest—she had needed to restrain Athol from going after the thieves.

Unlike the brigands who had kidnapped her and Susan, the two monks—she was convinced—threatened no one. In fact, thinking back to the night when Catherine had followed Susan to Adam's encampment, Tosh reminded them that Brother Paul had been the one to put out the fire by Catherine's room. Catherine suggested that perhaps the monk himself had started the blaze to bring attention to her absence and to the danger he thought she might be facing.

Questioning brother Bartholomew, they quickly learned that the portly monk had been too trusting of his brethren. They even learned that the journey to the Scottish Highlands and Balvenie Castle had not been completed as a group. The other two monks had caught up to Bartholomew just north of Athol's hunting lodge at Corgarff.

In the light of all this, Catherine knew she should warn her sisters of all that had occurred and alert them, should any of their old acquaintances suddenly appear from the abbey in Yorkshire.

She had other news, of course, to tell them. Of the school that was about to open with the assistance of Brother Bartholomew and the tutors from Elgin. And of the small matter of a marriage and a bairn.

Dipping her pen into the inkhorn, she smiled. But before she could write a word, she was interrupted by a knock at her door.

'Twas still too soon for the household to be up and about, Catherine thought. Getting up and crossing the chamber, she pulled open the door. To her surprise, outside of her door, two grooms stood silently with the large cloth-covered chair from the laird's outer chamber in their hands.

She looked questioningly from one man to the next, and then noticed Jean standing directly behind the two with an odd look on her face. Her hands were piled high with clean linens.

"What is all this . . ." Catherine began, stepping out of her chamber to help her serving woman with the linens.

Her mouth dropped open as she looked down the corridor.

Behind Jean, there were two other men, holding in between them a section of the wooden frame of a large bed. And behind them, two burly stable lads were carrying a feather mattress.

Catherine squeezed past the workers. To her shock, what she had already seen proved to be only the beginning.

Working her way along the corridor, she passed a seemingly unending line of serving folk. There were men and women carrying benches, chests, chairs, coffers, tapestries, stools, trunks—even an assortment of swords, shields, and lances. Catherine lost count of the number of people and the pieces as she wound her way down the circular stairwell and past the entrance to the Great Hall. At the end of the line, she found two kitchen lasses, each carrying a pile of blankets.

In a moment, she was at the door of her husband's outer chamber. A grinning Tosh and another warrior were just carrying out the laird's huge work table, under the gloomy but watchful eye of the old steward.

Baffled, Catherine stared past them at the empty chamber, and finally stepped in. Everything was gone. Everything—including the wooden shutters from the windows!

Shaking her head at the madness, she walked to her husband's bedchamber and peeked in. That room, as well, was devoid of all furnishings.

"It took you longer than I thought."

John Stewart stood by the hearth, his broad back to the small fire. Catherine stepped in and pushed the door closed behind her.

"You forgot the fire."

He smiled in that same devilish way that made her heart melt. And then she watched him as he slowly straightened and walked toward her.

"I warned you, my love."

"Warned me?" she said half innocently, cherishing the way he gathered her into his arms.

"I warned you about continuing to leave my bed."

He started nuzzling her neck, her ear, brushing his lips along the line of her cheekbone. "I said I would come after you."

Suddenly, everything registered, and Catherine placed both hands on his broad chest and stood on tiptoe, trying to look directly into his sparkling, gray eyes.

"You are not moving all of those things into my chamber. By the Virgin, there is at least three or four rooms full of furniture waiting in those corridors. And . . . all those blankets?"

"That chamber of yours is a drafty room."

"But—but all that furniture! It will never fit!"

He shrugged indifferently, and then took possession of her lips in a deep and passionate kiss. When he broke off the kiss, she didn't care a whit about what would fit and what wouldn't.

"I told you before, lass. I want to wake up in the morning and have my wife in my arms. But at the same time, I've learned to respect your need for a work room of your own. A work room," he repeated meaningfully. "Not a bed chamber."

"So your solution is to move everything in with me?"

"Aye, and in the other chambers of that old section of the castle. Until we are done renovating this section."

Catherine looked about the large, bright chamber. "But there is nothing wrong with this part of the keep!"

"But there is, my love, and you made me see it." He drew her closer against his chest. "When we are done here, there will be a bed chamber—here in this room. But instead of one work room, I'll have a section of the corridor added to these chambers, so that we'll end up with two."

"Two work rooms?" She couldn't hold back her smile.

"Aye! And I'm thinking we should add a nursery, as well." He pulled at the laces on the back of her dress. "But, when our bairns happen to be in Jean's care . . ."

"Or visiting their grandmother . . ."

"Aye. We'll both be working quite hard. And yet, having you so near . . ."

She shivered with excitement as he slipped her dress down over her shoulders.

"We'll need . . . a place to . . . talk?"

He nodded and stepped back, spreading his tartan on the bare floor. "But before any of that—"

"We should check the draftiness of *this* room."

"Aye, my love."

Catherine sighed contentedly and followed him to the floor. He was her husband, her lover, and the father of her unborn bairn.

Here in the Highlands, she had found at last her knight of a thousand dreams.

Author's Note

As most of you have probably guessed, Catherine's story is the first in a trilogy about the three Percy sisters. In the two books that will follow, you'll be introduced to Laura and Adrianne and have a chance to meet the mysterious Nichola Erskine Percy as we move closer to learning the truth behind the Treasure of Tiberius.

In *Flame,* the novel in which the secrets of Ironcross Castle are uncovered and in which Gavin Kerr meets his match, Joanna MacInnes, we were delighted to introduce John Stewart, the 4th earl of Athol. Unfortunately, we found that we simply could not rest until we had found a suitably headstrong heroine for such a hero. And for those of you who enjoy "catching up" on the heroes and heroines of our past novels, we could not resist including Ambrose Macpherson from *Heart of Gold.* It is through his wife, Elizabeth, and her relationship with Anne Boleyn, that Ambrose is able to negotiate Adam's freedom. And to those who have read their story, *you* know why!

Balvenie Castle and Elgin Cathedral, two treasures of Scottish history, will certainly be identifiable to many of our wonderful readers, as will many of the place names in the book. We have tried to portray those places accurately, and to people them appropriately—right down to the lairds, bishops, and millers who inhabit them in our fiction.

Lastly, we'll like to give our sincere thanks to G. Leonard Knapp of the Eastern Herpetological Expo for his help with our research regarding the snakes of Scotland and England.

We love to hear from our readers. You can contact us at:

May McGoldrick
P.O. Box 511
Sellersville, PA 18960
e-mail: mcgoldmay@aol.com

Fearnoch, the Northern Highlands
December, 1535

The gold coin tumbled slowly across the knuckles of the silent Highlander standing against the sandstone wall. When the group across the open square stopped at a stall containing bundled wool, the coin paused as well, its Tudor rose gleaming even in the shadow.

"The one with a face like a pig's arse called her Laura, master." The toothless farmer talking to him spat into the half-frozen mud and glared across the market square. "The lass might be dressed only in the rags they've given her, but she's of quality . . . there's no doubtin'."

Across the cold, windswept square, the two watched the Sinclair men herding the women along. The gold coin resumed its journey along the deft knuckles of the tall Highlander.

"Though she's a young thing, from the way she talks,

there's no doubt she's English. If 'tweren't for that, I'd wager more 'n one of yer crofters would have stolen her already from these swine." He spat again. "Aye, 'tis a fearful shame, master. Why, if I were twenty years younger, I'd . . ."

William Ross of Blackfearn left the farmer without a word and, tucking the gold sovereign into his wide leather belt, stepped out of the shadows of Fearnoch Cathedral and into the midday sun. As he strode through the scattered crowds of townsfolk and farmers to a cart by the ancient stone cross at the center of the square, he was immediately joined by two of his men.

" 'Tis *her,* master! 'Tis the same one you've been looking for!"

William absently dug the fingers of one hand into the coarse wool bundled in the wagon.

"And all of them don't go together. The two other women are nuns from that tumble-down convent near Little Ferry."

Watching the group stop by another stall, William stared at the hooded Englishwoman's back. Encircled by the Sinclair brutes, she appeared to be a wee, fragile thing. At this point, though, he didn't want to even think about the hardship she must have gone through over these past three months, living as a captive among those blackguards. He reminded himself that there couldn't be any bloodshed. Not while he was trying to rescue her, at any rate. He'd promised his brother that much.

"Should we take her now?" his man continued, glancing at the scar-faced farmer standing with them. The other man's hand moved to the hilt of a dirk, half hidden beneath the red-and-black plaid of the Ross tartan. His face showed his eagerness for a fight. "They've been plenty rough with her. The ugly one shoved her—without so much as a 'by yer leave'—right out of the wool seller's tent up by the north road."

"There was talk of the dungeons at Rumster Castle."

"They've been locking her up for months, master."

"The lass had her hood pulled low over her face to hide the tears."

"Aye, and her shame, the poor woman."

"There's only a half dozen Sinclair men with her. We

can take them, master!" the first man growled. " 'Twould be a good deed to help the wee lass and set the bastards back a—"

"Wait here." William turned his back, leaving the two looking helplessly after him as he strode unhurriedly around the stone cross toward the wool merchant's stall.

As William approached, the Sinclair men visibly stiffened. They knew who he was. He ignored them.

The two nuns, gathered right outside the wool merchant's stall, were whispering in French, and William heard snatches of their conversation. They, too, seemed to know him, though he couldn't for the life of him imagine why. He'd never had any dealings with the little group of French nuns living at the convent on Loch Fleet.

Brushing past the Sinclair men, William sauntered into the stall, casually picking up a piece of fleece and setting it down. The Englishwoman, reaching over, immediately picked up the fleece and set it in another pile. Though she was speaking quietly and continuously to the merchant, she appeared resolute about bringing some organization to the jumbled piles of wool the man had carted to market.

Suddenly, William found himself listening intently. There was something captivating about the soft lilt in her voice. Although her timid attempt at mimicking the Highland tongue was charming, her English accent—as Ren the old farmer had said—gave her away immediately. Peering covertly at her, he could just see a lock of black hair that had fallen free of her worn hood. Looking back down at her small hands, chafed by hard work and cold weather, he realized that she was sorting the fleece by color and quality.

An amused smile tugged at his mouth.

Out of the corner of his eye, he could see that the leader of the Sinclairs was watching him intently. William picked up another fleece, one that still retained marks of black tar in the thick wool. He intentionally dropped the fleece on the ground and moved over a step.

The Englishwoman immediately picked it up, but as she did, raised voices could be heard from the square.

Glancing around, the Highlander realized that a shouting match between a haughty townswoman and a crofter driving a dozen, red, shaggy-haired steers through the market square had drawn the Sinclairs' attention momentarily.

William looked at the Englishwoman. She was standing with the fleece in her hand, ignoring the commotion in the square. She was clearly undecided about which pile the fleece belonged in. Without a word, he took it out of her hands and placed it in the pile of fleece that she'd deemed of the poorest quality.

She turned in shock at his forwardness, a scowl darkening her face. But then, for William Ross of Blackfearn, something stopped, and the world stopped with it. Perhaps it was her eyes that halted him in his tracks. Their deep, violet-blue color was not like any he'd ever seen. Except, perhaps, for Molly, the wench he visited occasionally at the Three Cups on the Inverness road. Nay, these eyes were even deeper, more violet than Molly's.

An eon may have passed—William couldn't be sure—and still he found himself staring. It occurred to him that perhaps it was the surprise in her pale face that made his heart pause for that lingering moment. It was a face of an enchantress, English or no.

William thought she was about to speak, but the woman hesitated as one of her captors eyed her menacingly. She said nothing and looked away.

When he glanced back at the Sinclair men, he saw the nuns had separated themselves from the party, each moving toward a different part of the market place. Turning away, William ambled as casually as he could out of the stall, stopping a young lad who was walking about hawking apples. The uproar had died down, and the cattle were disappearing down the dirt street.

"Hurry on, lass!"

Shooting a quick look back at them, William could see that the Englishwoman was still standing in the stall. The Sinclair men had no patience with her as the leader tugged at her elbow.

"If you're not back by vespers," the leader growled, "it'll mean a dozen lashes . . . if you understand my meaning."

With a hasty nod, she left the fleece behind and immediately the company was moving through the crowd toward a group of tented stalls belonging to traveling merchants from Inverness.

At the next stall, the woman paused again, but this time only for a moment as she straightened out a display of women's shoes. The disgusted curses of one of the Sinclair warriors lifted above the sounds of the market throng.

Flipping his uneaten apple to a street urchin running by, William crossed the way and slipped into the alley between the merchants' tents and a low wall behind them. Beyond the wall was a ditch and stand of trees was visible beyond that.

Working his way past serving lads sitting idly on half-empty carts of merchandise, he moved silently into the alleyway between the third and fourth tents. The merchant selling brightly colored Flemish cloth was calling out to the guarded woman. The cloaked and hooded Englishwoman drew near the tented stall, and William stepped back into the shadows.

As he did, a gypsy band came to life across the way, their tambourines and bells and flashing-eyed women immediately drawing the gazes of the Sinclair warriors.

The Highlander seized his chance. With a silencing look at the merchant, William reached out, grabbed the startled woman by the wrist, and dragged her in one quick motion into the alleyway.

"I am a friend!" he whispered against her ear.

Covering her mouth with his hand, nonetheless, William took her around the waist with his other and speedily backed along the alley. As they reached the low wall at the end, the Ross turned and released the squirming woman, setting her back on her feet and turning her to face him. Her hood was pulled forward and a lock of thick, black hair had tumbled out across her eyes.

"We've only a moment before they discover you're missing. But I've horses waiting beyond that stand of trees. You're safe now." The Englishwoman was clearly stunned. The corner of his mouth turned up in a half-smile. "You've nothing to fear. You've been rescued."

The woman's eyes swept questioningly over him, focusing on the coin that he suddenly pulled from his leather belt. The Tudor rose flashed in the sunlight.

"I've no time now to explain. If we're to get you out of Fearnoch, we'll have to . . ."

William Ross's words died on his tongue as the woman's full-throated scream—loud enough to be heard in Edinburgh—cut like a sword through the crisp, winter air.

Gilbert Ross knelt onto the hearth and tried to peer up the chimney. Seeing nothing, the young priest got up from his knees and straightened the iron pokers leaning neatly against the wall. The smoke continued to back up in the fireplace, drifting into the room and hanging like a pall just above his blond, tonsured head.

The sound of the door opening behind him drew his gaze. Two clerics hesitantly peered inside the chamber.

He gestured to them. "Father John, 'tis time we sent for the mason."

The younger of the two men nodded vigorously and withdrew, immediately disappearing down the corridor.

"And Father Francis, if you find this chamber too suffocating for our work—"

"I am used to this, Provost." The older priest stepped into the room and closed the door. "For as long as I can remember, this chimney has smoked. Father Jerome gave up on it long ago, I think." He shook his head. " 'Tis a nuisance during the winter months."

Giving up on things had been his late predecessor's guiding rule, Gilbert Ross had quickly realized after taking over the position as provost of the Church of St. Duthac. Gilbert stepped over Willie, his barrel-chested dog, who continued to snore unconcernedly while his master pulled open a shuttered window. Gilbert filled his lungs with the cold, winter air that swept in beneath the escaping smoke.

"One of the fishermen from the village has just returned from the market at Fearnoch, Provost. She is there."

Gilbert turned and found the priest already seated in his customary position at the trestle table—his gnarled hands untying the black ribbon around an oversized account book.

"And my brother?"

"He is there, as well. In the company of Ross farmers already at market, but with *none* of his warriors."

The hint of criticism was obvious in the old priest's tone and Gilbert stiffened a bit, defensively. He and his older brother, William, had been pupils of Father Francis from the time they were lads, packed off by their mother—over their father's and their eldest brother, Thomas's, objections—to the ancient church school. Even though William was now laird of the Ross clan—and Gilbert himself was now the new provost of the Church of St. Duthac—he knew that Father Francis would always view them as lads to be scolded.

Aye, he knew what was coming.

"Gilbert . . . er, Provost . . . for a man of William's position to act—"

"Father Francis, I thought William showed great wisdom when he assured me—and you were sitting right where you are now—when he assured me that he would take care of this problem without bloodshed." Gilbert moved, as well, to the table and took his place across from his old mentor. "Considering the fact that, since Thomas's death two years ago, Ross and Sinclair men have not clashed seriously, don't you think it a responsible step for William to avoid starting up the fighting again?"

Francis grumbled under his breath, his fingers traveling across the pages.

The old priest was still scowling darkly as he carried on with the pretense of looking for the last ledger entry. Gilbert braced himself. He knew Father Francis was not finished. Provost or not, he knew he would hear the frequently repeated reprimand once again.

"There was something else, Father?" Gilbert said gently.

The old man exploded. "Aye, there's something else . . . as you well know! William can no longer hold to the reckless, ne'er-do-well days of his youth. By Duthac's Shirt, William is laird now! The leader of the Clann Gille Aindrias, the ruler of all this land from Fearnoch Firth to The Minch. He carries in his veins the blood of his namesake, the great William, earl of Ross, who led our own kinsmen under the Bruce at Bannockburn. 'Twas his hand that put the Ross seal on the Declaration of Arbroath!''

"I know, Father Francis," Gilbert interrupted softly, stopping the older priest's ardent sermon. "I am William's brother. I, better than anyone, know of our name, our blood . . . and William's responsibilities."

The priest nodded sternly. "Aye. You are a fine man, Gilbert, and I am as proud of you as if you were my own son, but 'tis time you used your power as provost of St. Duthac's to benefit not only those who make the pilgrimage here, but for the people of Ross, as well."

"Father Francis, I've been provost of this church and its lands for a wee bit more than a month now, and if you are saying that my desire to bring some semblance of order to this place . . . that my plans to stop the deteriorating condition of St. Duthac's is somehow compromising my responsibilities to the people. . . ."

"I am saying no such thing." The old priest placed both elbows on the table and stared evenly into Gilbert's eyes. "What I am saying is that for the first time in your life you can wield some authority over your older brother. You can influence William. Direct him in the affairs of—"

"William is the laird of Ross, Father. I am a priest."

"Aye. You have spiritual authority." Father Francis pointed a long, bony finger at Gilbert. "I have seen how he treats you—now that you are provost. He does not deal with you as he did when you two were growing up—when you were just the younger brother to banter with and to battle constantly. There is a new respect that he is giving you now."

Only in the presence of others, Gilbert thought. "So what is it, exactly, that you recommend I do with this new power over my brother?"

The semblance of a smile increased the deep wrinkles of the old priest's face.

"You must order him to change."

"To change?" Gilbert repeated, not comprehending. "William?"

"Aye! 'Tis time William Ross of Blackfearn grew up. 'Tis time that he began putting more value on his own life. By the saint, Gilbert, he thinks more of the lowliest shepherd lass's well-being than he does his own! You know as well as I that he'd sleep in his stable if he thought some old beggar woman would be more comfortable in the laird's chamber." The old priest leaned over and lowered his voice. " 'Tis time that he learned to act the part of laird. 'Tis what I *tried* to prepare him for. He should pick up where Thomas left off by renovating that holding of his—bringing back some of the grandeur of Blackfearn Castle. Blackfearn is the largest castle this side of Inverness. He must stop ignoring his position in life. Stop acting like a common crofter— eating and sleeping in the fields and in the stables. He must take his place as the leader of his warriors and his people."

Gilbert opened his mouth to speak, but the priest rolled on.

" 'Tis true that the title of earl was stripped from your great-grandsire all those years ago. But in the eyes of these people and every nobleman in the Highlands, William is now the true earl of Ross. He is their chieftain. He is the laird." Father Francis laid a gnarled hand on Gilbert's wrist. "And as such, he is responsible for marrying properly and begetting a bairn to keep your great lineage alive."

. Gilbert again began to speak, but Father Francis raised a hand to him and gestured toward the mantle above the fireplace and the simple sketch there on a wooden board. A sketch of a little girl's face.

"And I'm not even mentioning William's failure to bring Thomas's wee daughter, Miriam, back to her own clan folk."

Gilbert sat back in his chair and nodded thoughtfully at the elderly priest. There was no purpose in arguing. Half of what the chaplain said was true. More than half. Still, though, there was no way that Gilbert could see his brother marrying.

Much to Gilbert's chagrin, William openly preferred the company of the fallen women at the Three Cups Tavern to any lass who had been properly brought up.

In fact, this past fall when he'd finally allowed Gilbert to drag him along to visit with the earl of Caithness's daughter—under the pretense of a hunting party—William had said as much to the poor lass herself. Gilbert cringed at the memory of the young woman running, horrified, across the heather-covered meadow back to the arms of an indignant mother.

Gilbert and William were only two years apart in age, while Thomas had been more than twelve years their senior. As the result of this age difference, the younger brothers had been inseparable as lads. And later on, when Gilbert had pursued a life in the church and William had been sent away to St. Andrew's—and later to the household of Lord Herries—the two had still managed to remain close. They were not just brothers, but friends as well. And it was as a friend and not as kin that Gilbert Ross had determined that his older brother was perfectly content with whom he'd become—despite the fact that he had been called upon to be laird. Changing him at this stage in his life would be as difficult as chiseling stone with a willow branch.

" 'Tis up to you, Gilbert! You have the power and the influence to do a great deal more good than repairing an ancient chimney. St. Duthac's will survive. You, however, have the ability to preserve the Ross name and, in so doing, save the undisciplined rogue you call 'brother' at the same time." Father Francis lowered his eyes to the open page of the ledger. "You have the insight to force him to settle into a calmer and more respectable life. To find the right lass. That's what he needs, Gilbert. Just the right lass to calm his wild ways."

Perhaps, Gilbert thought with a resigned smile. But pity the woman.